Also ava

Lo

Two Houses

TWO CHRISTMASES

—

Suleena Bibra

carina
press

Recycling programs
for this product may
not exist in your area.

carina
press®

ISBN-13: 978-1-335-62198-6

Two Christmases

Copyright © 2022 by Suleena Bibra

For questions and comments about the quality of this book,
please contact us at CustomerService@Harlequin.com.

Carina Press
22 Adelaide St. West, 41st Floor
Toronto, Ontario M5H 4E3, Canada
www.CarinaPress.com

Printed in U.S.A.

To romance authors.
You'll never know the joy, hope and comfort
you gave me growing up (and now).
I hope I can make at least one person feel
what you made me feel.

And to Rod,
for proving that those romance heroes
I read growing up were real.

TWO CHRISTMASES

Chapter One

"How about a pool full of otters?"

My best friend and boss Priya Gupta pauses hanging an airplane ornament on to my Christmas tree to stare at me in confusion.

"Well, you wanted a spectacular present idea. I saw a video on social media of someone swimming with otters and that sounds like heaven."

Priya immediately stops being productive and gets on her phone. She stayed over after Thanksgiving dinner last night so we could start our Black Friday traditions: online shopping, decorating, and eating a week's worth of leftovers in just one day.

Christmas is by far my favorite holiday. Not to shame birthdays or Halloween or even America's birthday, the Fourth of July. They're all perfectly respectable.

But all year I look forward to the day it's socially acceptable to free my decorations from their plastic box prisons and publicly show my enthusiasm.

Which starts at twelve a.m. on the day after Thanksgiving. If one is being precise about it. Which I am when it comes to Christmas. One year I was traveling for work, so I put up my decorations the weekend before. Better a week early than a day late, when it comes to Christmas decorations.

This year we've already hung lights, started the gingerbread-scented candles, and inspected Christmas trees at three different lots to find *The One*.

Priya deflates on my couch. "Ugh, the otter swimming is booked for the foreseeable future. Gavin got me a Fabergé necklace for my birthday! I need to get him something better for Christmas so I can win." She absently scratches her bulldog, Leo, behind the ear and he comes to offer comfort.

I frown. "Christmas is not a competition." I don't add that if it was, Gavin already won with that gift; it's the perfect mix of pretty object and fascinating history that would appeal to Priya.

Priya rolls her eyes. "Everything's a competition with Gavin Carlyle."

I mentally roll my eyes right back. Everything is a competition with Priya Gupta, and she found the perfect man to match her competitive spirit.

They make it work, even if I can't imagine being that vulnerable with anyone. Just because it worked for her, doesn't mean lightning would strike twice.

I'm not taking a risk on something that might end badly.

Monday morning, belly still full of turkey, mashed potatoes, and pumpkin pie, I make my way to the exhibition space in our offices, checking in with how the public is reacting to the pieces that will go on sale during Loot's Christmas auction.

A respectable amount of people are already milling

around and I see smiles and approving murmurs. An answering smile takes over my own face.

This is my favorite part of the job. Priya loves every part of auctioneering, from getting pieces to displaying them, to the auction itself. I can do any of those things with a smile that passes for enthusiastic, but the activity I enjoy the most is setting up the exhibitions. Placing all the art objects in interesting ways that enhance each one's beauty, while also making a cohesive and intriguing whole.

Or maybe I just love decorating spaces.

Walking into the last room, I stop in front of a Jean-Honoré Fragonard painting of a man and a woman sneaking a kiss behind a partially open door, one of his arms pushing the door closed and the other holding the woman close, with a crowd on the other side of that door.

There's a palpable sense of danger in the scene, like the couple shouldn't be together, and they could be caught any second by anyone in the crowd.

They don't care; or at least not enough to stop the kiss.

I can't imagine what it's like to want someone that badly, to be willing to sacrifice anything for the possibility of being with that person.

But the atmosphere of the painting captures my attention and makes me linger when I should be getting back to work.

"These estimates are wild. This is all too expensive. Why can't I just get prints from Amazon?"

I recoil in horror and then jerk around to confront the unwelcome opinion. This is my passion. And my livelihood.

"Let me tell you why…" I open my mouth to let the stranger know why he's so very wrong, only to come face to pectoral muscle with a solid wall wrapped in white cotton.

My eyes walk up his body and I can see the line between a pale white chest and where his tan starts at the unbuttoned collar of his dress shirt. A light dusting of blond hair peeks through that same opening.

I forget what I was about to say and drag my eyes further up a thick neck covered in a five-o'clock shadow (at ten a.m. no less) that wraps around his mouth.

Above that is a Roman nose and a set of arresting hazel eyes. Topping him off is dirty-blond hair cut close to his head. Every feature looks inviting, making me want to take my time stroking, comparing the rough-looking stubble to his soft-looking lips, and every texture in between.

What was I mad about again?

Chapter Two

"Yes? Can I help you?" the man asks in a gravelly voice. He's got a hint of Southern accent, like he just stepped off a farm. Horses were probably involved, if I had to put down money. Chickens, maybe. Cows, definitely.

He mumbles something into the phone he was talking into and ends the call, looking at me in question. Ah. So he wasn't insulting me directly as an employee of this auction house.

"Um." I remember being mad for a good reason. I don't necessarily remember what that reason was, but it felt very right in the moment. In the past. When I thought he was talking to me.

I look around, hoping the answer will be hiding behind one of the works of art.

Wait, it's the art I was mad on behalf of. Phew, because the silence has dragged on for an uncomfortable amount of time.

"This art does cost a lot, sure, but it's worth it. It's a venue to explore, refine, or criticize the world around us, bringing joy or wisdom to anyone lucky enough to experience it." I purse my lips at him to let him know he's not appreciating the honor he's being bestowed.

"All due respect, ma'am, art can't feed you, house you, or keep you warm on a cold night. Unless you burn it."

I reel back, barely suppress a gasp, and clutch my metaphorical pearls at the thought of burning any of this. His unsmiling mouth quirks up a bit, and I think that was more to poke at me than any real art critique. I hope.

I'll respond like it was real. Just in case. "Art *can* be food, or a unique architectural design, or a blanket. And it can still bring entertainment and happiness and intellectual growth. Are those things not necessary in your sad little determination of what a person needs in life?"

"None of *this* is necessary." He crosses his arms and raises an eyebrow, getting comfortable in how right he thinks he is.

I get a flash from his wrist and look down to see what caused it. I frown at the hypocrisy. "Neither is that Rolex, yet here we are." I indicate the watch, crowing. Inside, like a classy lady.

He uncrosses his arms immediately, tucking the hand into the pocket of his winter coat. "It was a gift from my mother," he mumbles, red staining his cheekbones.

"Hmm. That's a really pretty, really expensive glass house you're throwing stones from."

"I still think spending this much on art is a waste of money, when that same money could be used to buy new orchard ladders." He looks frighteningly earnest now.

"Are you comparing the sum of humanity's artistic accomplishments to *orchard ladders*?" The man is attractive, but he's clearly lacking in taste. What a shame.

"Yes," he says, but sounds less sure about it.

I point to the badge hanging off the bottom of my blazer. "Well, I'm Sonia Gupta. And I worked on this 'useless' show, so do let me know if you have any questions I can answer." My voice dips lower than the winter temperatures outside the building as I bare my teeth in a sharp smile.

Silence fills up the space between us at the awkward (for him) turn of events.

"I'm Beau Abbot." He tries a smile that's more a grimace and reaches his hand out abruptly. I take it. It's a warm hand. Calloused. A strong grip that engulfs my admittedly small hand. A not unpleasant experience.

Oh man, do I not have time for this. Just like I don't have time for the way I react to Beau's body. But a Rolex is a Rolex. And expensive.

The mercenary Gupta genes aren't going to let me pass that up.

"If you don't like art, why are you here? At an *art* auction house?"

He rubs the back of his neck with the hand I was just shaking. "It's not that I don't *like* art. It's fine. In museums or whatever. I just didn't think it would be so expensive."

"They're pieces of history. How much do you think history should cost?"

"Sure, history. But I need to decorate some new offices and don't really have a budget to buy Napoleon's chair."

"There's a lot of options between plastic folding chairs and an emperor's furniture."

"I'm an engineer and a farmer. I wouldn't be able to tell the difference."

An idea forms. I do love decorating. And Priya hasn't let me take on projects that focus on one client, to decorate whatever space they need, because she always has her plate full of auctions that she's excited about. Even more on her plate now that the Dads of Loot and Carlyle's are drawing out the merger of the two auction houses and dragging her into every argument. And Cha-cha just hates change.

But even they can't argue with a Rolex.

"Why don't you let me help? I can point out pieces here that aren't going to be that expensive at auction. I can also take you to furniture shops and other dealers who sell great pieces for reasonable prices. No stuff from rulers of any kind, promise."

I get more excited as I talk. I already have contacts with sellers around the city because of work and my love of decorating and redecorating my own space. I can convince them to run this trial with me, where Loot gets part of any resulting sale. And Beau gets help with his offices. Everyone would win.

Especially me, if everyone sees how profitable this can be and lets me do more of it.

"I don't know anything about art." He says it as a warning.

"Not a problem. I'll make sure you get the best help that Loot can provide. So good you'll be able to pass a college-level survey course on art history when we're done."

"If you want to take on an art newbie, then I won't say no to your help. But please don't actually test me after this."

"Great!" I yell just a little too loud, drawing attention from the patrons around me. "Why don't we start by checking out your office space?" A much softer volume now.

"Do you have time for that?"

"Of course; this is my job. I can call us a company car and then get started on plans tomorrow." I already have my phone out to make the arrangements before Beau fully agrees.

"I can call the car."

I smile. "No worries. This is what the company cars are for. You don't want my uncle to pay for them for nothing, do you? Plus, it's already done."

"Well, all right."

I finish making the arrangements, go to my office for my purse, and lead Beau out to the curb.

"I hope you've been enjoying the best city in the world." I give him a practiced smile. The one to lure rich people into my web of art sales, so I can get commission off them.

Hazel Eyes quirks an eyebrow. "I didn't know I was in Monetta."

"What is a Monetta?" I roll the word around in my mouth like it's a language I've never heard before.

"A small town in Aiken County. In South Carolina. We have a drive-in."

Okay. No small talk I can relate to with this one. Luckily the car gets here, and settling in makes the silence less awkward.

Then I remember I have to get to work, because I'm going to be in so much trouble if this doesn't work. Since I never actually asked for permission to offer an entirely new service to clients. "Why don't you take me through what you want out of this to get me started?"

I take a spare notebook out of my purse, one of a lot I buy because they're cute even though I haven't finished, or even started, any of the notebooks piled haphazardly on the corner of my desk.

I look expectantly at Beau in the seat next to me, fresh notebook ready to be defiled.

"My family co-owns a peach farm around Aiken, called Dolly Belle Orchard, with the family of the man

I was talking to on the phone earlier, Daniel." He clears his throat, probably remembering how I reacted to that conversation, but then he soldiers on. "But Daniel and I have recently decided to diversify the business into renewable energy. We got advice that some nice pieces around the new offices will make us look serious."

I nod. "Legitimacy is a pretty common reason for purchasing art, so you're in good company." I raise my pen and start jotting down notes as I talk. "There's a few ways we could go with this. We could search for some agrarian pieces, paintings of wheat, people harvesting, pretty fruit baskets, to reference the original company and remind clients you've already got one successful business. Or we could focus more on the renewable energy. It's modern and cutting-edge, so we can get some contemporary pieces and give clients the feeling they're in on a trend before everyone else when they come to your offices."

I take a deep breath. "Or we could do neither. You can always put up some military scenes. Or the old standby... naked gods, athletes, something Biblical. The staples. That'll give a general feeling of class that can make Western clients feel comfortable even without knowing why, because they associate those paintings with wealth."

I look at him when I finish, expecting him to decide now even though he's just been inundated with options.

"Well... What do you think?"

"It really depends on personal preference...and what you want your brand to be. I don't think there are any wrong answers, although there may be better ones based on what you want."

More silence.

"Sometimes it's easier to start with furniture, if you have an idea about that. Again, you could do antique—leather couches and wood everywhere to make people think you're more established, or metal and glass modern to show you're trailblazers. Then I can pick art pieces around that theme for you to look at."

"That's a lot."

"I mean, no need to decide *right* now." But please drop some money through us; I have to eat. "After seeing your offices, I can walk you through the show again back at the offices, this time pointing out what pieces will go with the themes I mentioned."

Soon we're pulling up to one of Manhattan's many office buildings. Beau takes me up the elevator to an office suite that is completely devoid of furniture. No, that's not true. There's some folding furniture set up in one room.

"Wow. We really are starting from scratch." I should have brought a bigger notebook.

"We've been focusing on hiring employees. We haven't spent too much time on…anything else."

"I see that."

"Are the money signs flashing across your head right now?"

"Oh yeah," I say before I think it through. "But I'll find you some good deals in the process too. But. Well. It's going to be five rooms of furnishings?"

"Yeah. The research, product development, and manufacture are all going to be done in New Jersey, but we're keeping these offices to impress investors and clients, and for our sales team."

"Right. What are you guys doing exactly, again?"

"Selling equipment for alternative energy, specifically solar panels. We'll also be researching making better panels and more efficient batteries to store energy."

"Okay." I take notes as we walk the space. "The building lends itself to a more traditional approach because it's a historic building. But that wouldn't stop us if you wanted to go contemporary."

After a few walk-throughs, done mostly in silence while I let my mind wander into decorating magic, I call it a day. "I've got a good sense of the space now. I can prepare some ideas for you tomorrow."

"Great."

"Cool."

Beau clears his throat as we wait for the elevator. "Can I take you to dinner? As a thank-you for the giant job you've taken on?"

I pause, not sure I should be around this attractive man outside of work. My reaction to him is already too strong and if I didn't see this as a work opportunity, I would be running so fast in the opposite direction I would be a speck in his vision on the horizon. Because he's too distracting.

When the silence goes on too long, Beau says, "Maybe we can talk more about this decision I've got to make. So you don't waste time researching in the wrong direction."

Oh. This guy is as ruthless as Priya. Finding my weak spot and ruthlessly exploiting it like a Southern Niccolò Machiavelli. And instead of reacting to that like a normal human, I'm intrigued.

I blame the Gupta genes: we're a contrary family.

Why not? It won't be the first time I've had to take clients to dinner.

"We're doing an informal cousin/coworker holiday party at Rolf's, before work gets too busy. It's a German restaurant that does the best Christmas meals in the city. We usually go before the holiday auction prep gets too hectic. You can come, if you'd like."

"Oh, I can't impose."

"No, please. It's my responsibility as a New Yorker to show you the city and my responsibility as an auctioneer to help you with art."

"Daniel always says I love responsibility so I can't turn that down. I'd love to come. I can call a car, as thanks for letting me intrude on your plans." Beau gets out his phone and I let it happen. I have to keep the client happy, and my phone is somewhere in the bottom of my purse.

I shiver in place as we wait, wrapping my arms around myself to keep in what little warmth I make. The closer we get to the holiday, the colder it gets, but the closer the city comes to giving me a white Christmas.

It's rare, since our snow doesn't get heavier until January, but it can happen. Especially with some Christmas magic.

Or you know, a convenient mass of moist air rising after meeting a mass of cold air and releasing its moisture. But science is basically magic anyway.

"Here," Beau says as a soft coat still warm from his body envelops me and my nose is inundated with the faint smell of cinnamon.

"Oh." I savor it for a second before trying to shrug out of it. "It's not necessary…"

Beau hunches his shoulders by his ears to ward off the cold and refuses to take the garment. "Mee-maw Patsy would appear out of nowhere and beat me if I let a lady freeze." He moves away from me as I try to hand the coat back to him.

"Sure. Right. Mee-maw Patsy." I nod like that's a reasonable thing to say. "But I'm from this city, and you're from a subtropical humid climate, so I think you might need this more than me." I chase him (at a walk), trying to give him back the coat.

Shoulders still around his ears, he ignores me. "Mee-maw Patsy is a spitfire with a big wooden spoon."

"Okay then. Wouldn't want to piss off Mee-maw." Even if I'm not 100 percent sure about who a Mee-maw is. I think it's a grandma, but I'm not willing to bet any money on it.

I settle the coat back on my shoulders, happy to be back in the comfort of the garment even though I don't need it.

The car comes before shivering, noble, stubborn Beau can freeze to death, and a short thirty-minute, two-and-a-half-mile ride later, we're at the restaurant.

"Oh god," Beau says as he walks in, and I smile as I remember what it felt like to see Rolf's for the first time. It's a German restaurant with a solid menu year-round, but it really shines at Christmas. Brightly colored Christmas ornaments, dripping garlands, and twinkling lights hang from the ceiling and wrap around every column, with Santas displayed at strategic locations.

Christmas covers every available space, like Santa went too hard on the 'nog and cookies and threw up Christmas in the restaurant.

It's heaven.

"Isn't it great?" I ask.

"It's…something. Do you know where your friends are?" Beau uses his superior height to look over the crowd. I don't know how he would recognize them, but I appreciate the effort.

"Just follow the loudest group and you should be good." I hear some raucous laughter. "Never mind, just follow me."

I lead the man through the festive restaurant, dodging happy-hour enthusiasts and long light icicles on my way to a wooden booth in the back.

"When did you start shopping in the men's department? Are you just tried of not having pockets?" a voice booms at me when I get into yelling distance of the source of the noise.

Well, yelling distance if you're Indian.

Chapter Three

"Hey, Priya. Good to know you didn't wait for me to order the mulled wine." I take the coat off and steal her glass to take a sip. She's had enough; she's far too happy.

She sticks her tongue out at me and looks around to catch our waiter's attention. More mulled wine ordered, she turns back to me. "I think the man you stole the coat from is right behind you," she stage-whispers at me.

"This kind man who *lent* me the coat is a client, Beau." I indicate the man. "He's a business-farmer who needs some art to redecorate his new offices." I don't mention that I've offered him a much more involved level of help in that endeavor.

Priya perks up, a sharp look chasing the wine-induced looseness away. "Priya. Nice to meet you." She shakes his hand.

And then the process repeats with her twin, Ajay. We slide into the side of the booth not occupied by my cousins and they restart the argument they were apparently having before we got there. Usual.

"So what would you do if you were decorating our space?" Beau leans in a little to ask me the question while the twins bicker among themselves.

"Well, we usually like the buyer to have more of a

say, so their personality can come through, but…" I have a feeling he doesn't care enough to make up his mind. "I'd go classical for you. Traditional furniture with a mix of paintings about agriculture and antiquity. Maybe some fancy people from yesteryear looking out over their estates."

"You don't see us as cuttin'-edge contemporary?" He drops the *g* for extra emphasis.

"Cuttin'-edge tractor technology maybe," I mumble, drinking my stolen mulled wine. The warm liquid goes a long way to battling the winter chill. And to making me a lot sassier with a client than I usually would be.

"You been sittin' on that one long?" he drawls.

"I've been *sitting* on it since you said you hail from a farm… Old MacDonald."

He stares at me, unamused. Mouth not even twitching to hide a smile. Okay, he doesn't love that nickname.

"Traditional." I change the subject back to what we were discussing. "There's a reason it's so well-liked. And it seems like it would suit you, and the building you're in, best."

Because Old MacDonald and his farm cannot pull off contemporary. His clothes are business casual but now that I've spent the afternoon with him, I can see him fidgeting in the tight slacks, tugging at the shirtsleeves, and flinching every time someone honks a horn. He's not entirely comfortable in the concrete jungle.

Definitely wood-paneled rooms with worn brown leather couches for this guy, instead of glass and metal.

"Then we'll go traditional," Beau declares.

"Excellent. That's the hardest part decided." This is the part where I would usually see those dancing money signs coming closer to me, but today the fantasy is filled with a shirtless Beau. With a cowboy hat. "Now we can enjoy the best Christmas in the best city in the world."

"Whoa. *Nothin'* beats a Southern Christmas."

The Gupta family boos Beau. I cut through them. "The customer is always right…" I wait for the groans to settle down. "Except about this. A New York Christmas is magic."

"And it's more likely to be a white Christmas," Ajay says.

"And there's twelve thousand fun Christmas things to do," I say.

"But mostly, the best people in the world are here to celebrate it with you," my drunk boss/cousin/best friend says, throwing an arm over an amused Ajay.

"But can you guys decorate a real tree, growing in your backyard? Or see a decorated racetrack that you can drive on?" Beau asks.

"No. Can't say we have any of that." Priya's tone suggests she doesn't want any of that.

"You can't celebrate a Christmas in short sleeves," I say.

"The West Coast does it all the time," Beau says.

"They don't count. They think an outdoor movie in a cemetery is a good idea," Priya says.

"If you had experienced a New York Christmas, you would understand why you sound absurd right now," I say.

"Why don't you show me a New York Christmas?" Beau challenges.

"Oh." More time with Old MacDonald? With him looking like a hero in a seasonal Hallmark movie? That sounds dangerous and distracting.

"If it wouldn't be imposing more than I'm already

doing, of course." Beau gives me puppy dog eyes. "Might be a good time to talk about more art."

"You should be careful what you wish for." Priya interrupts our staring contest. "Sonia is unnaturally obsessed with Christmas."

What the hell? Priya once made me take clients to a regatta for work. Like, we get it, sailboats can move fast along a designated path. But do I have to watch them? It's like NASCAR for people with too much money. So taking Old MacDonald around the city won't be too hard. I'll already be doing the Christmas stuff anyway, and Beau can tag along. Plus, spending time with an attractive man who has to leave at a set time won't be a bad thing.

"First, everyone should love Christmas this much. And I would love to. Anything for a sale," I say, in case anyone thinks I'm getting soft with emotions.

"Thank you. I'm looking forward to it."

Beau survives dinner with the cousins, even though he looks a little dazed at the end. I get it; they're a lot to take. They disagree on practically everything, and the only thing they have in common is the intensity they bring to their beliefs. Which makes their disagreements loud and long.

"I can meet you at the front desk at around five p.m. tomorrow, if you want to continue the Great New York Art Christmas tour?" I ask as we walk out of the restaurant.

"I'll see you then." Beau inclines his head. "Nice to meet everyone."

Priya waits until he's a very non-circumspect fifteen feet away before she starts hitting me on the arm. "What's with Wyatt Earp? Bringing him to cousin Christmas dinner?"

I ignore Priya's intense stare. She's not usually *this* obnoxious about my personal life, because she's more focused on work. But that changes when she's had an entire carafe of mulled wine.

"Can you not talk about the clients until they get at least a block away, my most exalted lord and master?"

"It's the city. These streets are loud."

"*You're* loud. I'm just being a friendly, helpful peon of Loot. You said I should work more."

"How come you never assign me attractive women to take out, Priya? You know how much I love Loot," Ajay says.

"Ha! Even if you spent more time at work, single, attractive, intelligent, kind millionaires are rarer than Renaissance Old Masters."

"I'll take a Newer Renaissance Master at this point. I'm not picky."

"We know," Priya and I say in unison.

"But Sonia isn't even going to appreciate her good luck in meeting a hot man at work, because that would be too many *feelings*," Priya says.

"Why go through all the unnecessary hassle of liking someone and then having to face the inevitable disappointment that will follow?" I ask.

My cousins look at each other, communicating in their secret twin language, before looking at me with looks of judgement so similar it's scary. I ignore them and keep walking to the station to get the train.

It's not that I don't think fairy-tale love exists, per se. It's just that people leave more often than they stay, so why bother getting invested in relationships when the odds are…not in my favor?

Better to have fun and not worry about having a perfect forever. Which is a long time to think about anyway.

The door to my office opens and I frantically start typing. I glance at the screen before raising my eyes to see who caught me daydreaming. About Beau.

From what I saw before looking away, I hope Priya can make sense of "ajhfasldhf iuh asdhf isaufh ;sdhj a;ksfh" because that's what's going in the catalog if I forget to fix it before sending it in.

Just another sign that Beau is too distracting to be around for too long. He needs to go back where he's from quickly so I can go back to my happy, not emotionally demanding life of selling beautiful things to people who have bank balances higher than I can count (math was never my strong suit).

"Dad wants to see you," Priya says as she sticks her head into my office.

"Me? Why?" No other words could cause quite this much fear into my heart. Being around super-focused Priya is one thing, but I grew up with her. Which means I've seen her throw a tantrum because Chachi wouldn't let her live at the office. At eight years old.

But my uncle has always been an untouchable, mythic figure. A conquering hero making deals and selling art that no one could touch. And with a dedication that is terrifying to someone who still doesn't know what she wants to be when she grows up.

"I don't know. But I want you to report back because I'm dying of curiosity."

Yeah, because Chacha almost never asks to talk to me

alone. "Well, I better get going." I pick up a notebook and my phone, wanting to get this over with.

Heart pounding the entire walk over, I pause at his door to take a breath. Then I knock.

"Come in." A lightly accented voice drifts to the closed door.

"Hi, Chacha. You wanted to see me?" I come in and sit in front of his desk.

"Yes, Sonia." He smiles warmly, and I relax a little. However imposing he is, he's also my substitute father figure. A bit absent since most of his time was spent at the office, but always ready with firm opinions and a dedication to solve any problem when I needed him. And even when I didn't think I needed him.

"I want to talk to you about a promotion."

My relaxed posture straightens again. I don't like where this is going. "I don't need a promotion."

Kabir scoffs. "You're a Gupta. And you work just as hard as Priya and Ajay. You deserve to have your own department too."

I don't know how to tell Kabir, or anyone else in this overachieving family, that I don't want it. I don't want how much work that would bring, meaning it would take too much time from the things I like to do, or the responsibility. So many people relying on me, so many people I could disappoint. That's too much commitment for me.

Kabir continues, "There's an opening coming up, in furniture. The head of that department is retiring. You're my first choice."

"I don't know..." I can't articulate my thoughts to Chacha. "Can I think about it?"

"Of course. Let me know by the Christmas sale when you want to start."

I refrain from rolling my eyes at him. No one in this family hears what they don't want to hear.

But at least I have till Christmas to figure out how to disappoint him.

At four fifty-five p.m., I shut down my computer, stand up from my desk and smooth my dress down. Even I have to admit that the dress is about 50 percent tighter and 25 percent lower cut than my usual work wear. Which everyone has noticed.

Despite the ribbing I'm getting, whenever I think about the farmer my heart starts beating a little faster and my mind starts daydreaming about Christmas outings.

But nothing beyond Christmas.

A voice interrupts those daydreams. "I'm ready to be shown this New York Christmas you've talked about. I'm sure it'll be nice, even if it won't compare to a Southern Christmas."

Chapter Four

"Those are bold words for someone from a town Santa can't find with a map, Rudolph's nose, and the smell of some freshly baked cookies to guide him." I get up and tuck my hand behind his elbow, even though his arm is still straight.

Beau bends it obligingly and we start walking. He must do actual work on the farm beyond signing checks, because his arm is firm under my hand. A fact I can enjoy despite my even firmer stance against romantic entanglements. No harm in pawing at the Old MacDonald with all our clothes on.

Winter clothes, for even more safety.

"Our first stop is the homework part, and then we'll have fun," I say.

"I'm in your hands."

Hmm. Yes, please.

I lead him down to the auction room in our offices and take some seats in the back. "You don't have to bid on anything, but I do want you to comment on the pieces we see. I'm trying to get a sense of your taste and show you pieces that will work in your theme. And Priya is leading it, so be nice about the auctioneer." Priya walks up to the rostrum and gets our attention.

I remind myself this is the business part of the night. If I have to lean in closer to hear him when the auction starts, that's the nature of physics in a loud room. If his body is a distraction when I get closer, that's less business.

Employees bring and take away art piece after art piece while Priya riles the crowd up so they bid higher and higher. She's a natural at this, exuding charm and wit and genuine love of art. She shines.

And her stellar performance proves how much I won't want her job, or anything like it. I don't want to be in front of a crowd, pushing through a list of art. I want to focus on creating cohesive spaces. Another reason to focus on Beau so I can bring a giant commission check when I propose this new venture to Chacha and Priya.

"This piece is perfect for you," I say when a painting comes up of people harvesting.

Beau whistles. "At that price? Are those kind gentlemen in the painting going to come to life and actually harvest my peaches for me?" He winks at me, probably only half kidding. He is trying to start a business, and I get he needs money for like employees and materials or whatever.

"Unlikely. But it doesn't matter, because this is just to get a sense of your style."

We watch pieces find their new homes.

"What about something like this? The lamp has Athena Nike on it and will project victory to potential clients."

As the price rises, his eyes get wide. "Is the lamp going to *guarantee* me victory? And is it even compatible with energy-efficient lightbulbs?"

"I don't think anyone has ever asked that. So I don't know."

Surprisingly, he does bid on and win a Neoclassical painting depicting Mars getting ready for war. He said he liked the confidence it exuded. I think he just likes swords. Either way, I'll take the baby steps on what is turning out to be a tough job.

After the auction, I lead us out of the Loot building. "Now this Christmas fun can be a celebration of our first piece acquired for your office! I've got a car coming for us."

He puts the brakes on. "Whoa. I can't let you do that."

I raise my eyebrows and turn my head. "Excuse me? I got the car yesterday."

"That was different. It was for work."

Isn't this too? The lines are getting blurred with this man. "Well, it's already done, so I don't think my ability is limited by your permission." This is what happens when you let a man give you his coat—you get branded incapable of standing in the cold once and suddenly you're incapable of every simple task.

Hmm. Maybe this is better off staying a purely business night. I subtly pet his arm regretfully.

"But I don't feel right letting you call the car..."

"Is this a Southern thing?" I wave his concern away with my free hand. "Calm down, Old MacDonald. The genderless company is paying for the car, if that makes your delicate sensibilities feel better."

The company car smoothly stops in front of us, making the debate moot. We both go to open the door at the same time. Beau, of the freakishly long arms, grabs the handle first.

You win this time, you attractive relic.

"Hi, Tom. Can we please have Christmas music? I

have to get this one in the mood before we get to our stop."

"Of course." He turns the radio to a station that already has a steady stream of Christmas music playing.

"I Saw Mommy Kissing Santa Claus" comes on. "Perfect."

Beau gets into the car and leans in to me. "For the record, I never need to be put in the mood." His voice takes on a new tone. One that sounds like a smooth glass of bourbon with a bit of a bite, on a porch swing, looking at a sunset with no buildings in sight. And fireflies floating around, probably.

And that damned image of him, shirtless and in a cowboy hat, pops up again.

After a pause for me to take in the words and clear my throat, he follows up with, "For Christmas, of course. I'm always in the mood for Christmas."

Old MacDonald has jokes. I smile, not verbally admitting that I was thinking exactly what he thinks I was thinking.

"Are you going to tell me where you're taking me?" Beau asks.

"Nah. There's no fun in that. Surprises and all that."

"Is the surprise murder?"

"If it is, I promise it'll be Christmas themed."

"Ah. Mrs. Claus in the sleigh with a sharpened candy cane?"

"More like unappreciated elf in the workshop with the hammer."

Tom pulls up in front of the New York Hall of Science before we can think of any more Christmas murders.

I get my phone out as we walk to the front of the concrete-and-glass building. The exterior doesn't give away any of the Christmas cheer that can be found inside this particular building around the holidays.

"This building is closed. *Are* we going to commit a crime?" He doesn't sound as jovial now.

"Not tonight. I have to test how good your general physical fitness and quick thinking under pressure are before I let you in on one of our famous Gupta capers." I send a text and a few minutes later a side door opens. "Merry almost Christmas, Sam." I give the Black man a hug.

"Merry almost Christmas, Sonia." He breaks away from the hug and beckons us into the building. "I've got you all set up."

"Perfect. Here's a little token of Loot's appreciation." I pull a gift out of my tote.

Sam takes the bag. "You never have to, but I'm not turning down one of your thoughtful gifts. Take as much time as you need. I've got some work to finish in my office, so just call when you're done and I'll close up." Sam leaves us just inside the building and I tuck my hand in Beau's arm again.

"Are you ready for *the* most exciting event in the city?" I bounce up and down on my toes as we stop right in front of a double door.

"Sure." But he doesn't sound as confident as that word would suggest.

"Then let's go." We each open one of the double doors and sweep into the room.

Beau freezes just inside and starts laughing. "What in the world?"

I laugh with him. I've seen every year's exhibit since I was five. I still get excited every time I walk through these doors. I don't remember much from the earlier exhibits, except being amazed and hungry. Exactly how Christmas should feel and look.

"It's the biggest gingerbread village in the world!" I twirl around the space next to the display. The bright colors of the candy and the blinking lights swirl in my vision, and the smell of gingerbread fills my nose, bringing comfort and more than a little hunger. "A chef makes it over the year and then assembles it here for the holidays. Sam is the best. He lets me see the village during off hours and sets me up to design my own for Loot's lobby."

"This is pretty cool," he admits, kneeling to look at the individual buildings. "An eggnog distillery...a candy cane factory...a Christmas bookstore. Many, many toy stores."

I take my own look at the buildings, admiring the design for this year. I keep thinking that it'll get boring and I'll get over it, but I haven't. Instead, there's something comforting about the fact that I can return to it every year and it stays constant. Dependable.

We wander around the perimeter for a bit, taking in the fluffy frosting acting as glue and decoration, the gingerbread, and more candy than I've seen all year. The smell finally gets to me and I can't wait any longer, so I go to the table on the far side where Sam set up the ingredients for us. Per tradition, I start by taste-testing all the items he laid out.

"Is the activity eating candy? Because that is a good Christmas activity. Even if it is in the big city." Beau filches a few gumdrops off the side of the pile.

"*Taste testing*," I correct him. "Then we're making a gingerbread auction house to put in the lobby at Loot." I ruin the grand order by eating more candy.

This is why Sam gives me triple the amount I need.
And why he always gets a grateful present for his trouble.

"All right. What should we do first?"

"Suit up." I toss an apron at him and it lands on his
head, where he lets it stay for a second while I laugh.

"Is it going to get that messy?" He finally takes the
apron off his head and puts it on.

"Not really. I make sure most of it gets in my mouth."
I start to sort out the gingerbread pieces before I realize
what I just said. My eyes are wide. "Oh, no. Um, shit."
We are a sexual innuendo a minute tonight. "Because
I like to eat. Food."

Beau is still laughing softly through my explanation.

I charge through the awkward phrasing. "Anyway,
I usually make Loot with a building front and then an
auction scene behind it."

"That sure does sound ambitious."

"I do this every year. I'm practically a professional."
I thrust some pieces of gingerbread at him to get him
started. Anything to get him to forget what I said.

"What made you guys want to expand the business
from agriculture to renewable energy?" I ask to better
know my client. Only so I can better guide him on which
pieces to buy.

"My grandfather and Daniel's grandfather started the
farming business on a plot of land they bought together.
Then our dads expanded it to multiple farm sites. Daniel
and I both wanted to do something to make the company bigger in our own way, but we weren't sure how."

Beau takes over, holding up two gingerbread pieces I
was trying to glue together with frosting and I give him
a quick smile in thanks. This is much easier with help.

As we work, he keeps talking. "We started by putting some solar panels on our farms to make us more efficient, but we both wanted to do more and expand into research. Like batteries and the equipment itself for solar power and how to make it better. I got my degree in engineering, before I ended up back at the family business. It's always interested me."

"That's very noble and environmentally friendly."

"It is. But it's also selfish, considering that our entire orchard, and therefore livelihood, could be wiped out by any extreme fluctuations in temperature and rain. It's in our best interests to stop those from happening by getting more people to use alternative energy. And it's going to be lucrative even beyond our farm, if we develop more efficient equipment."

"It's always nice when you can be both noble and selfish." I steal some more candy. "Where'd you go to school?"

"The University of South Carolina. It's in the big city—Columbia."

"Hmm. Is that a big city, though?" I mix sprinkles into the frosting.

"Big enough."

I mentally sigh. That drawl. I never want to move away from New York, but damn if that voice doesn't make me want to go to the nearest Boot Barn and get a belt buckle with a cow on it. Or some boots with a cow on them.

Cows would be involved, whatever happens.

"Did you ever want to move away from the farm? I imagine it must be easier to start a business like that in a city."

"No." He answers confidently and immediately. "I

love home. My family, my memories, everything I know is there. It's a good place to live. I want this business to succeed and that means coming to the city and setting up offices here. And probably some work trips out here once it is, but video chat should help with that. But I will be living at home while I do it. We originally tried to start this up in Atlanta, closer to home, but it just didn't work. So we're trying again here."

My suspicions are confirmed. He isn't moving away from his home anytime soon. So I don't have to worry about this turning into a thing with feelings. That is a good thing.

"How about you? What made you choose this line of work?" He connects the gingerbread base to a gingerbread wall with all the concentration he would give setting the foundation for an actual building.

"It's a family business, so choice didn't really factor into the equation too much."

"Do you not like it?"

"No, I love it. I studied art history at NYU and I get to use it every day. Parts of it are more work than others, but I'm lucky to enjoy it overall. I get to travel and every show is something different. I especially enjoy it when I get to design the exhibition, to show our pieces in our offices before the auction itself. And the view's always amazing."

Just like the view now with Beau leaning over a table, dress shirt pulled tight against his shoulders. His Christmas apron says Bite me, over a picture of a gingerbread man, and I've never wanted to follow directions more.

I look at him out of the corner of my eye, so he doesn't get too scared over the admiration. But it's there, with me wanting to smear some of this frosting on those muscles and lick them off.

Fuck it, he's gonna be my present to myself this year.

I know he's leaving, so I can enjoy him and not worry that he'll make me want to break my rule against commitment. And no awkward run-ins with this one. I'll never see him at the bodega or ride the same subway car with him. No awkward meetings at museum exhibit openings…not that the last one was a real danger with a man who doesn't appreciate art.

And his incorrect opinion can be ignored for a holiday fling.

"Plus a big part of my job is saying 'Paddles at the ready' to a room full of people in formal wear, and I'm not mad about it." A naughty pun on purpose this time. Now that I gave myself permission.

Beau gives me a small smile at the comment, one side of his mouth quirking up. We work in silence for a while, making tiny gingerbread chairs, a tiny gingerbread rostrum for the auction to be led from, and tiny gingerbread painting easels.

"But what are we going to use for the people?" Beau asks.

"Oh, I've got this covered." I search in the box of supplies and triumphantly pull out a bag. "Sam gets custom-sized gummy bears for us to put in the scene."

I bite the head off one…delicious, as always. I extend the bag to Beau. "And now, for the finishing touch."

Chapter Five

"We get to hand paint the little gingerbread canvases, based on real paintings!" I wiggle in excitement while I hold up the aforementioned canvases.

"Oh no. I will do any other job. I will build you an actual building if you want, to get out of this."

"High-maintenance MacDonald."

"Ah, yes. That's what farmers are known for—their high-maintenance lifestyles."

"Okay, *Sassy* MacDonald. You can make frosting windows and strings of lights made of jellybeans. Don't forget to paint trees and presents in the windows like a Christmas window display." I shove materials at him.

I start recreating *Starry Night*, one of the easiest to make on a small canvas.

"You're really good at this." Beau sneaks a few glances at my work while he does his Christmas tree.

"Thanks. Painting is a hobby of mine. Something creative and fun to do after work."

"You don't sell your own work?"

"No. It's not good enough. And I sell art for a living, so I'm an authority on sellable art."

I'm like a mix of my cousins, but less intense than either of them. Priya is obsessed with auctioneering, and

Ajay is obsessed with painting. I like the business and creativity and want to do them both. But I'm not trying to run the company like Priya and I don't want to sell my own paintings like Ajay is trying to do, even though I do want something creative. I just haven't necessarily found where I fit in best, yet.

I hope this decorating side project turns into something more permanent. It could be the thing I love. It's already on its way to perfect; I spent all day making plans for Beau's offices and calling art dealers and furniture stores around the city to see who would be interested in partnering with us. All from places Beau would like. It was exciting.

"Besides, I like the creativity of putting together art other people make more than doing my own. It's like making a new art piece that you live in. Art that you sit in, work on, *and* look at. Immersive art."

"That's great."

That's enthusiastic for someone who wanted to buy prints off the internet. "I didn't think you even liked art?"

He looks charmingly chagrined. "I don't really understand most art," he says, probably as tactfully as possible. "But I can understand that you are passionate about it. Why do you like it so much?"

"It's expressive. From regular materials comes a beautiful or thought-provoking piece that can be an escape or a balm or an education…or all three. You can be transported to another time, or another place. It can make you forget for a minute about the bad day you had or whatever's weighing on you. Or it can remind you that you aren't alone in feeling bad, by connecting you with another human who felt similar things."

Honesty compels me to add, "*Some* people do just

want to have expensive things because they're status symbols, but others feel genuine emotions when they look at the art or learn new things from it, about the world or themselves."

We put the finishing touches on the storefront and then I get off the stool. "Perfect."

"I don't think I've ever seen a gingerbread house quite like this." He stands next to me to admire our work.

"That's because it's not just a gingerbread house… it's a marketing tool."

"Efficient." Beau nods his head in approval. Of course he respects efficiency.

We clean up as best we can and Beau takes responsibility for carrying the gingerbread Loot after we box it up. I text Sam to let him know we're all done and call Tom for a ride back to the city.

After a quick drive back, Tom stops the car in front of Beau's hotel. "I hope you enjoyed a bit of city magic this Christmas," I say as he gets out.

"Is that all the magic the city has?" He puts his hands up when he sees my offended face. "It was nice and all. But that's it?"

"The city has *a lot* more to offer—"

"Great. So I'll see you tomorrow at your office and you can show me more of that magic. Good night, Sonia." Hazel eyes look at me expectantly. Funny, they don't look devious. And yet here we are.

"Yeah, Tricky MacDonald. Shake that dirt off your nicest pair of chaps and I'll show you more city Christmas. But come early because we have more decorating to do."

"Yes, ma'am." He tips an imaginary hat and walks into the hotel lobby.

"I can tell you deepened your accent that time," I yell after him. "Faker."

He throws a wink over those broad, hold-on-to-during-sex shoulders and saunters the rest of the way to the lobby.

The next morning, I sail into Priya's office for our daily meeting, toe off my shoes, flip my notebook open and make myself comfortable on her worn leather couch. As the boss, she has the best couch out of all of us. Because as the boss, she's had nights when she sleeps on this comfortable couch.

Not as much since she started dating Gavin, thankfully. As wary as I am of relationship malarkey, it does seem to have gone well for Priya.

"Did you hear from the owner of the Stanhope collection?" Priya asks me without looking up from her computer.

"Yes, my liege." That does get her to look at me. And roll her eyes. Success. "But they keep asking me questions I've already answered in writing. I've even had to resort to 'Per my last email,' so they know I'm salty about their lack of basic reading comprehension."

"Ooo. Bitchy. You gonna throw in a 'I'll kick you in the balls if you don't give me what I want?' It's less hostile than what you went with."

"But less professional."

"I'm sending you some emails I want you to handle as well, but please don't threaten to kick anyone."

"No promises." My phone vibrates in my pocket, signaling the work she's sending to me.

"And we have a slight problem with a piece," Priya says.

"Lay it on me. So that I may pick up my sword and

vanquish the dragon for you." I flip to a new page in my notebook. Can't let Priya take herself too seriously.

"Drama," Priya mumbles. Then gets on with it. "The Art Crime Team is convinced that Gupta Dynasty piece with the big boobies is stolen."

Calls from the FBI. I guess it is serious. "Do we still have it?"

"No. The seller didn't leave it with us when he let us examine it for sale."

"That one's going to hurt when it goes." Rude smugglers, stealing history.

"Yes." Priya does stop typing and looks up at that, letting me know it's a loss for her as well. "One more thing. I hear you've been spending some more time with the attractive cowperson." She puts her elbows on the table and her head on her hands, settling in for the gossip.

I should be honored that she thinks it's worth stopping work for this, but instead I'm terrified.

It's also déjà vu. Over a year ago I was in this office harassing Priya about her attraction to Gavin, and now I'm in the hot seat.

The tables, they have turned. For the worse. "I am wooing *a client*. So he will buy art from us. How is that different from you taking Harrison to lunch last week?"

"Harrison's older than Dad and he doesn't look like the Marlboro man if he had decided to give up smoking in his prime and live right."

Oh, Beau could look like a kale-eating Marlboro man. Especially in what I'm sure is his usual jeans-and-a-plaid-shirt uniform. "I'm not answering this question, and according to that harassment video you made us watch, frequently asking about my personal life after I ask you to stop talking about my personal life can be grounds for a lawsuit."

"Fine. I'll make Mom ask you." That decision makes Priya pick up her cell phone.

"No!" I jerk forward and yell. Or say loudly enough to get my point across without making the entire team barge in. "Okay, okay," I say at a more reasonable volume. "I *am* giving him advice on art, but I'm also enjoying showing him the city. He's nice to look at. He's fun. And he's just *nice*. Considerate. And maybe doesn't think I know how doors work."

I'm choosing to be charmed by the fact that he wants to do things for me and not mad he might think I'm incompetent.

Priya looks appropriately impressed at the nice fact. After years of dating in the city, we're literally to the point where if a guy asks us to a dinner and not just "drinks and whatever," or "just whatever," it's better than getting a five-karat diamond ring.

"Are you guys making like Zeus and a goddess? Or Zeus and a human? Or Zeus and a frisky-looking house plant?" Priya asks me, in the nerdiest way possible.

"Well, he hasn't dressed up like someone or something else to trick me into boning, so no. No making like Zeus."

"You're being unnecessarily pedantic right now. You know I just meant sex."

That's rich coming from her. "Shouldn't you be telling me not to sleep with a client? Because professionalism?"

"I slept with the enemy. A client is way better than that. Plus, I'm with the American Bar Association guidelines on this: so long as the professional exchange isn't based on agreeing to the personal one, it's fine."

"Fiiiiiiiiiine. He's really attractive and since he's country themed I want to ride him like a wild mustang."

"Yeehaw." Priya tugs at her collar.

"And maybe we will. We're both adults. Unmarried." Well, I think he is. No ring. "Why not have fun?"

"Oil him up and wrangle him." Priya pumps her fist in the air.

I look at Priya askance. There's an image. That I can so get behind. Or better yet, under.

Priya continues, "But he is leaving, I assume. To get back to the cows?"

"No cows. Peaches. But that's a good thing. I don't want a relationship anyway, so it's actually ideal."

"So he's a...peachboy? Peachperson?"

"Let's not call him a peachboy ever again."

"Well, enjoy. I haven't seen you this interested in a guy for a while."

"I don't know what you're talking about." I get up.

"Denial!"

"Yes, I'm sure *the Nile* is lovely this time of year." I purposely mishear Priya as I walk out of the office, fingers still lodged firmly in my ears.

"At least I know what I'm getting you for Christmas," she yells after me. "Therapy!"

I smooth my hands down my dark green coat in front of the Loot building.

I didn't want Priya to harass me on the way to this work event or mixed-purpose event, so I belly crawled past her office to leave.

Okay, *fine.* So I slumped down and averted my face while I speed walked past her office. But I think the point is that I would have belly crawled to avoid Priya if it had been called for.

When I don't see Beau immediately, I get out my phone so it doesn't look like I'm getting stood up. The phone in front of me means I have purpose. There could be a whole attractive rugby team's worth of men on the other end of the internet that I'm talking to, so I'm not just a creepy loiterer.

Or someone waiting to serve a subpoena.

I feel someone grab my elbow and I turn around, arm cocked back with the training of my kickboxing class and an angry look on my face, getting ready to punch whoever thinks it's okay to grab a woman in the street.

Chapter Six

I subtly (I hope) slide my arm down from a ready-to-punch position when I see who it is. "Heeeey."

"Hi." Beau looks at my fist, which at this point is awkwardly floating off to my side. I quickly pull it the rest of the way down to my side and unclench. "I hope you weren't waiting too long."

"Just finishing up some last-minute work." I hit the button to turn the phone off so he can't see that the "last-minute work" is really checking Twitter.

Wait. I do follow art world professionals. And I was just reading tweets about a money-laundering scandal in one of the newer galleries.

Damn it. I actually *was* working after work. Not cool.

I tuck my hand back in his arm and lead him to our destination. "You don't have to worry about me breaking you by calling a car today."

"I'm not that bad." He invalidates his own point by gently guiding me out of the way of oncoming pedestrian traffic.

Amateur. I live here; tourists can go around *me*. "Will you let me pay for dinner then?"

Beau looks at me, looking a little broken at the question and proving he *is* that bad. His brow is furrowed and his mouth is hanging open slightly. I try to contain my laugh so he doesn't think I'm mocking him. I mean, I am. But I do have the veneer of politeness.

"We'll just figure it out later." I pat him on the arm. "How have your work meetings been?"

Beau's face immediately relaxes after the apparently disturbing suggestion that I could pay for his food. Am I supposed to sit in a room, because I can't open doors to get out of it, and starve until a man comes to feed me?

Absurd.

"Good. I met with some potential investors and some research engineers. But I won't know how everything went until I make offers."

"Waiting, the best part of any business."

"Yeah." Beau sounds distracted.

"Are you okay?"

"Mmm-hmm. I just don't understand how this many people can live in one area. There's so much land in America. Why confine themselves to such a small area?" He keeps weaving in and out of people on the sidewalk. Again, like an amateur.

"Yeah, but is there twenty-four-hour gyro delivery in the boonies? Because that's very important to me."

"No. But there's peace and quiet."

"*Too* quiet. I need people. Even if you're doing something alone, you're doing it with hundreds of other people. Getting dinner, seeing a movie, going to a museum. People are always around. So you're never *really* alone."

Beau shivers, I assume in revulsion. "Can't think around that much noise."

I pat his arm with the hand already resting on his elbow. "Don't worry, you'll be out of the evil city soon." I say it as a reminder to him and myself. A reminder I can enjoy whatever this is, wherever this goes, without worrying about this lasting longer and always fearing he'll leave one day. Instead I know he's leaving.

It's freeing.

Now that I've got some extra brain space since I'm not worrying, I can start wondering if all those muscles he got on the farm are any good in bed.

"Not that there aren't great people in this terrible place. They're wrong about their life choices, but still, they've got spunk and they look nice in their uncomfortable city clothes." He looks directly at me with the statement.

I laugh. "That is the most backhanded compliment I have ever gotten."

Red stains his cheeks. "Yeah. So where are we goin'?" he asks, apparently not aware that I'm imaging doing dirty, devious things to his poor farm body, despite the things that come out of his mouth.

I clear my throat. "First, a furniture store."

"Oh joy."

"I've already vetted them for your aesthetic and narrowed it down to a few pieces I think you'll like. It should be quick, so we can get to the important part of the night: Christmas." This is why I'm not management material.

Beau sighs. "Would it be easier to give you the card and let you buy everything?"

"Oh, undoubtedly. But maybe unethical. You have to at least give things a cursory glance before we commit to them."

In the store, I nod to the salesman and he leads us to the section we discussed earlier in the day.

"This is exciting for Loot," he whispers to me as Beau looks over the selection.

"If it works." I cross my fingers on both hands. "Could

set us apart if we can offer something no one else does."
And I'm really enjoying it. Today I drew out some plans
for Beau's office, trying to see where everything should
go and how much he would need, while making calls to
get businesses to work with us. Like I thought, it combined creativity with business in a way that no other
part of my job has.

I need this to work, because knowing how much I
enjoy this work and then giving it up is going to be *hard*.

"I'm rooting for you, because this could be great for
us too."

"Sonia, what do you think about this piece? Between
these two?" Beau asks.

I move to stand next to him. He's looking at two leather
couches that are almost indistinguishable, except for one
detail.

"Pick the one with the scroll arms. Classier."

"You don't think it's too flashy?"

"Do I think the brown leather couch is too flashy? No.
I think you're good."

"I'll take your word for it."

After fifteen minutes of intense negotiation with the
seller, with promises of sending more business his way,
I get a modest price reduction. Looking out for Beau's
start-up costs like a good interior decorator.

"Excellent," Beau says when I tell him. "And we'll take
these desks too."

"Great," I say in surprise. This job might be over faster
than I think now that Beau's warming up to the decorating idea.

Hmm. Mixed feelings about that. I want him to leave,
but this might be *too* fast.

"Where are we going now?" Beau says as we walk out of the store.

"Only one of the hotbeds of Christmas in the city. You won't like the number of tourists there, but if you learn to lean into people watching, it might grow on you."

Beau compresses his lips and looks at me without saying a word. And yet, so many words are communicated.

"Okay, maybe not," I concede. "But you might not hate it as much as you think you will. Just trust me."

We walk another six blocks before we get to our plans for the evening.

I break away from the man and rush in front of him to present the scene to him like Vanna White. "Ta-da! Rockefeller Center at Christmas! Soak it in." I take a deep breath, turning in a circle with my arms out to soak a bit of it in myself.

"It smells like week-old trash and urine."

Well, he's not wrong. "Maybe soak it in with your eyes. The tree is almost a hundred feet tall. It had to have scaffolding." I jazz hands toward the tree.

We stand at the ledge and take in the tree, decorations, and the open-air ice-skating rink on the level below.

Rockefeller Center is all decked out in its best festive finery, with its grand Norway spruce at the head, lights twinkling on its branches. The smaller trees that surround the plaza year-round also get their own decoration, their branches trying to outshine their seasonal cousin. Angels blowing trumpets compete for the crowd's attention with snowflakes projected on the buildings.

People mill around the spectacle, taking in the best city in the world dressed up for their enjoyment.

"It is impressive." Beau bumps into my shoulder lightly. "It's no sunrise over the orchard on a fall morning, but it's nice. For a little bit."

"Wait, shit. How early do you have to get up to see a sun*rise*?"

Beau flashes that charming smile and opens his mouth.

"You know what, never mind. Whatever you answer is not going to make it okay." I wave the answer away.

"What's the plan?" He changes the subject obligingly.

"That." I tilt my head to the skaters below us. Another Christmas season first I'm having with him: ridiculously overpriced, crowded skating at Rockefeller Center. Where the people watching is amazing.

"That there? You want me to get on frozen water that, if someone miscalculated and it gets a few degrees warmer, could go back to its liquid form? While I'm on it?"

"You just described ice-skating, yes. Have you not skated before?"

He looks so nervous. And his accent is getting deeper. Does this happen with other emotions beside fear? He did deepen it at least once on purpose, for effect. "It doesn't get very cold in South Carolina…"

"They make outdoor rinks in Southern California now."

"It just doesn't seem prudent…"

"Of course not. When is fun *prudent*?"

"Running a 5k is prudent fun."

I recoil in disgust. "Oh no. Is there like wine or a doughnut cake at the end?"

I mean, I like kickboxing as exercise. I get to punch things, and people say it's healthy. But running? Pass.

I turn to our planned activity for the evening and feel

his hand rest on the small of my back as we walk. This is nice. "I could only get a later reservation, so we have to wander for a bit."

"Maybe they won't even have time for us. They'll probably get a bus full of schoolchildren who want to celebrate Christmas. We can't stand in their way. They're the kids."

I laugh. "You're afraid of this but you'll let poor innocent children take the risk?"

He looks chagrined. If he says, "Aww shucks," I'll melt into a pile of seduced lady.

He doesn't oblige. "It's really safe. I hear they're even doing it in California."

I laugh and lead him to a building on the outer edge of the rink. This should make up for the unintended terror of the activity.

"I don't think I need to go shop—holy shit, are we going to the LEGO store?" His hand leaves the small of my back, and Beau looks at the storefront with a bemused expression on his face.

"We definitely are." Their window is already decked out in the Christmas spirit, with a giant LEGO tree and LEGO people, holding, well, LEGO presents made of LEGOs. Very meta.

"Sorry about the language," he says.

"I truly do not give one fuck. Now get in there, tiger." I pop him on the butt. His firm butt.

The store is packed with families, meaning small children are running amok among the multiple LEGO scenes in the store, especially the giant reconstruction of the Rockefeller Center, complete with LEGO Spider-Man.

"I'm going to win uncle of the year this Christmas." Beau grabs a set.

"Are you going to get any for your kids? Or maybe for your wife? Or girlfriend? Or husband? Nonbinary partner? For your vow of celibacy?" Yup. That's out there now.

"Wow. Do wives like LEGO sets?"

I scoff. "Everyone likes LEGOs. Sexist."

"Well no, I won't be getting LEGOs for any of those things you said, because I don't have any of those things. Just an adorable niece and nephew at the moment."

"Cool. I mean, whatever." I physically shrug to show him I wasn't waiting for his answer. Even if I was. "Here, you should get them a New York Skyline. Maybe they'll develop healthier attitudes about the city." I shove a box at him.

"Are you going to get any for your child, or any of those things you said?"

"No. I don't have any of those. Especially that vow of celibacy." Hint, hint, Old MacDonald.

"Okay, then."

"I am going to make you a key chain though." I walk to the make-your-own-key-chain station and steeple my hands together like I'm plotting world domination, or how to leave work early on summer Fridays to beat the traffic out to the Hamptons. "You're going to love this. And by love, I mean you're going to hate it." I reach over a kid to start the present.

"I should reciprocate all this goodwill and cheer." Beau puts down his boxes and reaches over the two children in front of him.

I cackle as I see a chest piece I know he'll hate, snatching it up like it was the last cronut in a bakery when they first came out.

"How come you like coming to places like this? I thought all New Yorkers were supposed to be jaded and avoid tourist traps."

"Mostly I do. But I like seeing happy people, especially at Christmas." I find a head for the key chain and elaborate on my answer, the loud ambience of the LEGO store making my lips looser than they usually would be. "My parents weren't really around a lot, so I liked coming to places like this around the holidays and seeing the happy families. And even the unhappy ones. It just made me feel part of something, even if it was celebrating Christmas among strangers. The tradition kind of stuck. And I got so into the holiday that Ajay calls me the Christmas Manager because I end up coordinating all the events and keeping everyone on track during opening presents."

"That must have been rough. To not have family around."

I shrug. "It's fine. They originally came with my aunt and uncle from India before we were born to start the New York office of Loot. But then there were some issues with the headquarters, and they decided it was best for the business to move back. I was around five at the time, and they thought it would be better for me to be raised here, so we did that. And they were right; it was a great opportunity. They visited, but it wasn't really the same. And my aunt and uncle were great, obviously. They even let me plan Christmas events for Christmas Eve because I could never wait for the actual day."

It usually takes me longer to open up to people about my childhood, like never mostly, but I want him to know.

"My dad had to work a lot when we were growing up, so I got a very small slice of that. I hated it the times he left or worked long hours, so I can only imagine how you felt about it. It didn't feel like home unless everyone was there. But when everyone was back, it was perfect." He smiles in satisfaction and I get jealous of that feeling.

After my parents left, visits were awkward because they were practically strangers. And it just felt different with Chachi and Chacha since they weren't my parents, even though they gave me plenty of love and support growing up.

"Yeah." Done with the conversation, I dramatically (the only way Guptas can) shove the key chain behind my back and let out a shimmy that won't be contained. "Are you ready to be amazed? Astounded? Annoyed?"

"Afraid." Beau laughs and puts his own creation behind his back. "You should prepare yourself as well."

"On the count of three." We square off on opposite sides of the key chain area.

"One-two-three!" We both rapidly move our hands from behind our backs, revealing the pieces to each other.

I laugh at my first view of his masterpiece. He made me a little cowboy! In a plaid shirt and little boots and a little cowboy hat and a little lasso. He's adorable.

But none of that compares to the confused look on Beau's face as he's holding my gift close to his face, trying to figure out what he's looking at.

"It's a tourist with a selfie stick. And look at how

much he loves New York." He has an I heart New York shirt on and everything.

Beau good-naturedly laughs at my artwork and goes to put my genius back in the bin.

"Oh, no." I snatch it out of his hand and head to the register. "I'm getting it for you."

I scurry away before his head can explode all over the happy holiday shoppers. I make the purchase and step outside to watch the circus of people in the plaza, waiting for Beau to get the gifts for his family.

The evening air got a lot chillier while we were in the store and I zip up my coat to get ready for the rest of the date. I mean, for the work thing/maybe more.

I feel that touch on my lower back and this time my first thought isn't violence. I turn, ready with a smile for the man.

He looks back at me, suspiciously happy after I up-ended his worldview by paying for a thing. Speaking of that thing…

"Here's your present." I hold up a yellow LEGO store bag under my chin. "Sorry about the poor wrapping job." I extend it out to him, hitting him in the large pectoral muscles that are at my eye height.

I'm not complaining about my lack of ability to reach high cabinets when I get this view.

He takes the offering. "I don't know what you're talking about—this is my wrapping paper of choice."

I shudder. "Blasphemer."

"Well then you won't be happy about the wrapping on your gift." He lifts a small bag out of his larger one and I eagerly grab it. I equally love giving *and* getting presents.

I peek inside and see the cowboy key chain from be-fore. "Thank you. He's great." I slide him into my pocket.

"It's time," I say with my most serious facial ex-pression.

Chapter Seven

"Are you sure? Wanna shop more? Get food? We can fly to Paris, if you want?"

I pause. "I mean, yes. I would go to Paris right now if that's on the table."

Beau sighs. "I have a meeting in the morning. And last-minute flights probably only have middle seats available."

"Paris will have to wait then. And that means we can do this thing, right here." I hustle us down to the rink.

"Fine." He has all the enthusiasm of me finding out I have to work on a Saturday.

"If you don't want to do this, we can just leave." I don't want to make him hate me when I want him to stick around. For a little bit, at any rate.

"No. I can do this."

"If it helps, I think there's a group of kids on the ice right now. And they look mean and ready to mock."

"How is that supposed to make me feel better, exactly?"

"Oh, yeah. I guess that's more for me."

"That is not very hospitable of you."

"Hospitality is your thing, Southerner. Honesty is ours. And sometimes that honesty is so honest it borders on cruelty. You need a thick skin in this city."

"Charming."

We walk to the ice-skating area, where he drops off his purchases and we pick up the skates. Standing outside the rink, the cold plastic of the side wall under my hands, I try to stop this one more time. Because Beau's grip on the wall of the rink is so tight it's going to crack it, if those white knuckles are any indication.

"We can get some food in a nice warm restaurant, sitting down, on a non-slippery surface."

"Nope. We're doing this."

"You're stubborn for a nice guy." With sticky kids' hands pushing at our backs as we stand near the entrance, I glide onto the ice. I skate a tight turn and meet him on the other side of the rink while kids flood in.

"I am not a nice guy."

"That's a compliment."

"Not when *nice* means *boring*." His eyes are locked on the smooth ice in front of him, telling me where his attention really is.

"Nice is not boring. It's refreshing and…well, nice. And you have to leave or get on this ice, because the kid behind you is going to douse you in hot chocolate and maybe stab you with a candy cane shiv if you don't move."

Beau turns his upper body to protect himself from the candy cane bandit only to see there's no one behind him but a few parents getting their kids ready for the ice. He turns his upper body back around to face me, giving me just about as much enthusiasm as TV's Daria had for… anything.

Funny how much can be conveyed with a look.

But he does get moving, right into the middle of the entryway. He slowly puts one skate on the ice, refusing to let go of the sides of the entrance. Respectable. Except he's taking a while to get the second foot on the ice and a small crowd is forming behind him.

"I was kidding about the shiv, but it's getting more likely with every second." I skate to him and grab his arm.

After some tugging, he puts his second foot on the ice, still holding on to both sides of the entry doorway.

"Half of the battle won. But now you have to choose a side and go that way. Or you're going to be playing a very lonely game of Red Rover."

He ignores my solid childhood reference. Instead he awkwardly and very slowly, to the chagrin of the people behind him, moves his left arm to the wall on his right. He has an intense look of concentration on his face, brow furrowed.

"First step accomplished. Now let's move on to step two. It's a literal step...well, more a glide. Just move either foot back."

He looks down at said feet without moving anything.

"Anytime is good, but sooner is better."

The judgement spurs him to action, and he makes small, choppy steps with each foot in turn.

"You're getting it, just trust the skates."

"They're instruments of death. I'm not trusting anything they do."

"But you're the one wielding them. So trust yourself." I skate around in a circle to emphasize the great advice I'm giving here.

He snorts. "That's not a real convincin' argument."

"Oh, this got very deep for ice-skating. Where do you think your self-distrust stems from?"

"Probably because I didn't get that second puppy when I was growing up."

"I cry you a river. I didn't even get one dog."

"I sense the sarcasm. But the one dog was a working dog and didn't have time to play moonshiners-and-the-sheriff."

The conversation distracts Beau enough that his strides have gotten a little longer, but he's still clutching the wall with one hand and moving slowly.

"Wanna go off wall now?"

"Sure. I can do this." A group of elementary school students whiz past him, taunting him with their speed and skill.

He slowly lets go of the wall, jutting his butt out and his hands in the opposite direction for balance.

"Here, grab my hand." I turn around and skate backwards, hands extended out toward him.

"Now you're just showing off," he grumbles, but grabs my hands.

Note to self: he does not like being vulnerable. I mean, I don't either, but he's whining harder than Ajay when he has to do actual work.

"Do you need one of those little helper plastic penguins the kids use?"

"No, this is embarrassing enough." Despite his words, he's getting a little better at this, moving smoother as we go.

To be fair, it would have been difficult for him to get worse at this.

We're still being lapped by children, but Beau gets enough confidence that I let go of one hand and skate next to him instead of in front of him.

He still has a death grip on my hand, but his shoulders aren't around his ears anymore.

An hour later, I call it quits. "Thank you for being such

a good sport and for having the first skate of the season with me." We take off the skates and walk to the rental tent to return them.

Beau, relief making every muscle in his body loose now that he's on solid ground, says, "No problem. Now that it's over."

I let that go since he was such a good sport in trying something new. Speaking of...

"I have some dinner planned if you're hungry." I'll be eating either way since I haven't eaten anything since breakfast. It's been a hectic day with the Christmas auction looming, plus all the other work for upcoming auctions. And taking on Beau's decorating job, which still hasn't been approved by anyone, so I have to do it in secret on top of my other work.

I could eat.

"I'm ready for what I'm sure will be the fanciest restaurant in the hottest new neighborhood that New York has to offer." Beau turns in the skates and collects his purchases.

"Oh. Then you're going to be disappointed because I thought you'd want to go low-key. Maybe some street meat."

"Street meat?"

"Meat, from a street vendor. A venerable New York tradition that everyone should experience when they're in this great city."

"That's not just a TV thing?"

"Well, for health reasons I try not to eat *too* much street meat, but yes, I do partake."

I tuck my hand in the crook of his arm again, a place that it's gotten too comfortable in over the last few days. It started out as a way to direct the tourist where we were heading, but now my damn hand reaches for him before my damn brain can approve of the move.

Not that my brain would stop my hand. It wants Beau just as much as my hand does.

I direct him to the nearest food cart around the corner. Which, to be fair, serves artisanal hot dogs from Brooklyn, if he's worried about it not being fancy.

Hot dogs and fancy sauces consumed, we stroll along Fifth Avenue, taking in the Christmas window displays, all vying for attention and money.

"These are just obvious attempts to get you to spend money."

"Sure. But that doesn't mean it can't be entertaining and even beautiful. Most of the highbrow art in museums was made to glorify a patron, to advertise how rich and tasteful they were. But it can still be beautiful."

"Another art lesson for free?"

"Possibly the most important art lesson." I point to a window of two elves playing video games while a conveyor belt dumps toys on the ground in the background. "And window displays have gotten a lot cheekier over time, which is fun."

"That is good."

I shamelessly move closer to him on the walk. For his sake, because a New York winter is nothing to scoff at, especially for a Southern boy. And if I enjoy getting closer to his solid mass of warmth, that's just the joy of doing a good deed, I'm sure.

"This is me." Beau looks up at his hotel.

"Of course the man who lectured me on excess is staying at The Fucking Plaza."

A light dusting of red blooms in his cheeks. "I think

this is still *functional* excess. Different from a painting,, which was my original argument."

"It's a very nice hotel." I try to comfort him, adorable little hypocrite that he is.

"I know it's a work night for you, but do you want to come in for a drink?"

I'm surprised to find that I don't want the night to end. "Sure. But only something Christmas themed. So this still counts as me showing you a good city time."

Beau opens the door for me, letting me into the famous decadent white-and-gold paneled lobby. And then puts his hand on my lower back again. I should be irritated at the cheek it takes to lead me around my own city, but since I melt inside whenever his strong hands are on me, I choose to find it charming.

To distract myself from that unsettling thought, I take in the surroundings. Like the rest of the city, the hotel is decked out for Christmas. Their giant tree fills the space, decorated with bright lights, classy ornaments, and a pile of enticing (and probably fake) presents under the tree.

We walk to the Palm Court and settle in the atrium for a drink. True to its name, the room is lined with greenery amidst its white walls, golden furniture, and stained-glass skylight—a mini oasis in the chaotic city. With drinks.

"I'll have a Balvenie, please," I say to the bartender.

"I'll have a Pappy."

"Seriously?" My voice rises a few octaves in disbelief. "The watch, the hotel, and the bourbon? You have the most expensive tastes for someone who gives art shit for being fancy, Old MacDonald. I'm going to start calling you Old MacHypocrite. Or Hypocrite MacDonald."

"Us farm folk can appreciate nice things. When they're *practical*." He looks indignant for a second, then gives me a considering look. "Says the woman who knows her way around whiskey."

I shrug. "Turns out our clients *really* like whiskey tastings. After the sixteenth one, the drink grew on me, against my will. Now, back to your very expensive taste for someone who's supposed to be practical and utilitarian. Because whiskey is not practical."

"I deserve some rewards for enduring the big bad city." He mumbles the defense.

"The city is not that bad."

"No? I saw a man grooming himself on the subway."

Well, that is gross. But still—"Mind your own business. As long as he wasn't making a mess, let him live his best life."

"And there's always trash on the streets."

The bartender delivers the drinks and makes a quick getaway to avoid the increasingly passionate argument brewing in front of him.

"It's trash day. What do you want us to do? Teleport it into the dump?"

"Why is everyone always rushing?"

"Because they have things to do." With each point, we move closer and closer to each other, two boxers warily dancing toward each other in the gilded ring of the Palm Court.

"But you miss the sense of community. That's the best part of home—my family is always there when I need them. And so is an extended network of honorary aunts and uncles to look out for me." If I needed reinforcement that he isn't leaving his home, he's giving it to me every time he defends it.

"There's community here. And when they annoy you, it's very easy to find new community. Because of all the people here." We get closer so I can feel his warm breath on my lips with each complaint.

"There's no open space."

"But why have open space when you can have buildings with fun things to do in them?"

"No one is nice is the city."

"No. No one is *polite* in the city. They're plenty nice. Last time I was coming home from a big trip, I had a lot of luggage and had to go up some stairs at my subway stop, and one guy wordlessly picked them up and helped me, and then he was gone before I could even say thank you, so he also saved me a conversation with a stranger. He double helped me."

"I don't like to tell a lady she's wrong, but you are incorrect." The accent's getting deeper again. So far, we have it getting deeper for nerves, frustration, and for effect.

What about arousal?

Because I might be feeling some of that if the warming in my body can be trusted. It could just be anger on behalf of my hometown, but I doubt I'd get that lucky.

"Well, I will tell a *human* they're wrong, if they are indeed wrong. And you're wrong." Just in case he didn't catch where I was going with that.

Laughing, Beau throws his hands up in the air and leans back in his chair. I kind of miss him in my space. "If you came to Monetta, I could show you the charms of a small town."

Whoa there, Old MacDonald. None of that will ever happen. Because I don't see hometowns or meet family. But I'm not telling him that; he'd just ask questions like "Why?" that I don't want to answer. "Then you'll just be wrong in another state."

"You don't give an inch. What if I say the city has its advantages? Then can you concede that a small town could have its charms?"

I look at him, digging deep to see if I can concede. I really do make a good effort. I even take a sip of some very smooth liquid courage. And do some yoga breathing.

It doesn't help. "No. I can't do it. Sorry."

Beau, being a smart Old MacDonald, lets it go and changes the subject. "How about them Carolina Predators?"

Oh great, sports. Can we go back to the city vs. country argument?

Two drinks later, we've jumped to multiple non-sports topics. Thankfully. Despite our differences, we do find some topics we can both talk about. I even manage to talk about some pieces I think he should buy from some online sales we have going on, and he makes some bids.

Priya would be so proud.

I finally look at my phone. "Oh god. It's much later than I thought it was. I should head out."

Beau looks at his own phone and signals for the check from the bartender. "Wow. I didn't mean to keep you out late on a school night."

"No, you're fine. I was having fun."

I reach for the check, more to watch his brain explode than out of any real burning desire to pay, and I'm not disappointed. He snatches it from my outstretched hand, throwing a surprisingly dirty look over his shoulder for someone who's supposed to be all nice.

I laugh right into his face and he doesn't respond in words, signing the bill in silence. He winks at me when he's done to show there's no hard feelings. Or maybe to gloat over his win.

We get off the bar stools and for the first time I notice that we're the last ones in the room.

"Thank you for another fun city night," Beau says as he walks me to the lobby.

It was a fun night. If this wasn't technically a client-wooing with vague personal overtones, this would be one of the better dates I've had.

We had great conversation, and those hazel eyes remind me of a Christmas tree with their mix of green, brown, and gold. Mesmerizing to someone who loves the holiday as much as I do.

And he is genuinely nice, despite his severely misguided opinions on town size, geography, and my abilities.

I want him. For now.

And I'm going to have him.

"I'll call a car and come with you to drop you off." Beau gets out his phone.

I put my hand over the screen of his phone, my heart pounding with the choice I just made. "None of this is related to, or a condition of, any sales that we make."

Beau's eyebrows draw low over his eyes. He looks back to the bar we just walked from, like the visual reminder would give him clues as to what sparked that statement. "What are you talkin' about?"

"I think, as an ambassador for the great city of New York, I should come inspect your room to make sure it's up to our fine standards."

I hold my breath for his response.

Chapter Eight

Beau's eyes get wide, giving him a deer-in-headlights look. Not that I've seen one of those outside a TV or zoo. But if popular culture can be relied upon, they freeze when presented with surprising or scary stimuli. So it's not a good sign that he has the look now.

He doesn't say anything and my stomach drops, the smile freezing on my face. "No worries if not. We can keep this profesh." Someone help me, I just said *profesh*.

Oh god, this is embarrassing. Did I misread this whole situation? Without any conscious thought, my feet make baby steps toward the door and the freedom of the city night outside. At least all the people outside don't know about the rejection that occurred inside these gilded walls. One of the perks of city anonymity.

"No." He jerks to life, hand back to its favorite resting spot on my lower back. It stops my nascent attempts at escape. "These city hotel rooms can be so dangerous…" He stands there, hand not pushing me to the elevator, letting me make the decision again.

I do, starting toward the elevators. I push the button, his hand rubbing a slow circle on my lower back while we wait for the doors to open. The movement causes sparks of warm electricity under my skin through all the winter layers of my coat and dress.

I'm not expecting the sensation, so I automatically shift away but immediately regret it when he withdraws his hand. I take a small step back into Beau, a little too abruptly, crashing into him until my side is flush against his. Thankfully, he takes the hint and puts his arm back around me. Since we're closer now, he slides the hand all the way around my back and tucks it in the dip of my waist this time.

I like this new position even more than the other one, shifting my body even closer into him. From here, I can smell his woodsy cologne coming through. Liking the smell, I tuck my nose into the crook of his neck, inhaling the smell and stealing the warmth for my always chilly nose.

Though with Beau, this woodsy smell is just as likely to be the result of him rolling around in some leaves like a giant German shepherd as it is a high-end cologne. I stifle a small laugh into an awkward cough at that image. Beau leans his head away from me to check out what the commotion is about.

There's no way I'm going to tell him what I was laughing about, but I'm saved from having to make any explanations when the gold-and-mirror elevator doors glide open. I shuffle into the space with even more gold and mirrors and Beau follows me in.

I catch a glimpse of us in the mirror as the doors close. My curly black hair cascades over his arm around my waist, while the head it's on is tucked in close to his shoulder. My curves fit into his body like we're jigsaw pieces. Finally united after trying too many pieces that don't fit this well.

The doors slide shut, enclosing us in the finely decorated space. I shift a little in the circle of his arm to look up at his face directly, not just the reflection in the mirrored walls. He's got some scruff growing on his cheeks from the day, and I reach up to do what I've been wanting to do since I met him, feeling the rough beginning of a beard and the soft skin right above it.

He grabs my hand to stop the movement, his hand covering mine on his face. Before I can apologize for pawing at him, he dips his head closer to mine.

"Do you want to kiss me as much as I want to kiss you?" he asks, not getting closer until I answer the question, despite my attempts trying to move us along by getting on my toes to get closer to his lips.

"Yes." I don't even have the patience to tease him in this moment, I'm so far gone.

"Thank god," he breathes out, *finally* lowering his mouth the rest of the way to cover my lips.

The whiskers I was feeling up a second ago tickle my mouth, making my nose twitch at the sensation. They also cause a giggle to escape, my lips parting with the movement and putting us in deeper contact. The move sends some more of those sparks of electricity through me, and I decide to devote all my time to getting more of that sensation.

The move unleashes him, and he puts both hands on either side of my waist to push me firmly against the wall of the elevator, his tongue coming out to join the kiss, *aggressively*. My eyes widen in shock as lust races through me when my back makes firm contact with the wall and his hands pin me in place.

Nice guys aren't supposed to make out like that.

His hands slide under my heavy coat to grab my ass.

Encouraged by his hand, my right leg lifts, rubbing my tights-clad crotch against his dress pants, my dress riding up in the excitement. Beau's hard dick meets each thrust of mine.

His lips return to mine, devouring me in his urgency. I hear the ding of the elevator indicating we're on his floor but ignore it.

I'm perfectly happy where I am, and I won't be told what to do by an elevator ding.

The sound of a throat clearing breaks into the moment with more success than the ding had. We break apart and I see with satisfaction that Beau's breathing is jagged. I focus on that instead of the unlucky spectator as we stumble out of the elevator, because the judgement would be a real mood killer.

But as I get an eyeful of Beau's solid outline striding past me, grabbing my hand to pull me in the right direction, I don't think a little thing like judgement is going to dampen this electricity any.

Beau stops in front of a door and fumbles for his key. He's taking too long, so I cuddle against his back and reach into his pants pocket to surreptitiously stroke his erection from the side. Beau groans in response, resting his head against the door.

I immediately withdraw my hand. "Open the door, Slow MacDonald, or we're going to give everyone on the floor a show."

Beau stiffens his shoulders and gets his key out of his other pocket. He quickly presses it against the lock, *finally* opening the door. As impatient as me, he rushes through the doorway and I fall in behind him since I was leaning on that back.

Beau catches me before I can face-plant into the thick

carpet, sweeping me over his right shoulder before I can trip over anything else. I giggle at the sudden rush of blood because of the movement and because of the joy of being around him.

He shoves the door closed with his foot and hits the light switch with his elbow, his hands still firmly on my ass. The room is a blur as Beau's long legs eat up the distance to the bed.

He gently tosses me onto the bed, kissing me as his hands push up my dress. He finds the waistband of my tights despite the bouncing movement of my landing and slips his hand under. He makes a low sound in his throat when he can't get very far under the control top garment. His mouth leaves mine and he looks at my waist in confusion.

"Are you wearin' a chastity belt?"

"No, they're just tights." If I had known this was going to happen, I would have worn much easier undressing-for-sex clothes.

I move my hands to help him, but he gently brushes them away.

"I have protected peach harvests from tornados. I think I can figure out your damn underwear."

There's that accent again, getting deeper. With lust, this time. Although it could be frustration.

He starts with my shoes this time, tossing them over his shoulder. Then he slides his hands in at the top of the tights again and this time peels them down. They get stuck a few times, requiring some impressive feats of strength. The effort makes me laugh, the up and down motion on a bouncy bed not helping Beau in his task.

When he's done, he holds up my tights like he's Arthur and he just got the sword out of the stone.

I laugh harder at the image, getting up on my knees to take the offending garment out of his hands and toss it to join my shoes in the land beyond Beau's shoulders.

Hands free, I slide them around his shoulders, drawing him in for a kiss. We tear at the rest of each other's clothes while sloppily kissing, until we're naked. I don't get very long to savor the view, since Beau wraps his arms around me and lifts me up so he can readjust me.

I wrap my legs around his waist to bring the good parts together and he jerks away from me before I can rub against him fully.

"Wha—" I reach for his shoulders to pull him back to me, not liking the sudden cold I feel in his absence.

"One second, Baby Girl, one second." He gets all the way off the bed and rushes to his bag. He rummages through it, cursing the longer it takes, and then finally finds his treasure and returns to the bed.

He opens a condom package and slides it on over his dick, giving it a few extra pumps once it's on fully. The sight fries what little brainpower I had and I flop back flat onto the bed so we can get to the good part.

"Okay, I'm back."

"Thanks," I say in appreciation over his concern for safe sex. Now that's more like how a nice guy fucks.

He gets back into the position he was in before he left, but this time he rubs his wrapped dick against my clit with no hesitation. The heat in my lower stomach builds up slowly, until I'm a squirming mess under him, legs pulled up to cradle his hips.

"You're so beautiful, Baby Girl." He rains kisses down

on my face and neck, only stopping when I catch his mouth in a kiss. The endearment makes my chest warm, a confusing development when I thought all my heat was traveling south. And I'm not entirely comfortable with the fact that he can make that heat rise in so many different areas...some *emotional* areas.

"You feel amazing," I say, pushing away my discomfort and ending on a gasp when he starts thrusting shallowly into me, his fingers replacing his dick at my clit.

I want more of that.

His other hand fists in my hair causing a sting, holding my head steady while his tongue does to my mouth what his dick is doing to me further south. He keeps up the rhythm until the combined movements push me over the edge and I come around his dick. He lasts a few more thrusts before he gives in with a mini roar.

He collapses next to me, tossing the condom in what I hope is the trash can, and pulls me in close to his side, sticky bodies fusing together. Beau's breathing immediately evens out and I spare a second being impressed by his ability to fall asleep so fast before I make my great escape. It's not easy to leave this bed, but necessary. Before any more of those emotional parts get more confused. And cuddling would not help the process.

I flinch as I pull away and our skin unsticks, hoping the noise won't disturb the sleeping man next to me. Orgasms seem to be the last of my luck, because he groggily looks up at me.

"Just going to the bathroom. Go back to sleep." I escape to that room, grabbing my clothes on the way. My tights take longer to find, but it's even colder outside than it was when I came into the hotel, so it's worth the extra time.

Facilities used, I quickly dress and tiptoe to the door of the hotel room. I risk a last look at the sleeping farmer and see him waiting with the sheet lifted up in invitation.

"Hey, where are you goin'?" His eyes are half-closed and his voice is rough with sleep, making his accent deeper again.

Chapter Nine

"Um. Nowhere." I have my shoes in my hands calling me a liar, so I feel compelled to clarify. "Well, obviously somewhere. Home."

Beau sits up in the bed, covers falling to his waist. "It's the middle of the night. You don't need to rush off; you can stay over."

Oh. That's a new one. Most of my previous romantic partners were either firmly against sleepovers like I am, or the few times I bent my rule we had awkward morning afters where I wished the person had left after sex.

I was hoping to avoid any awkwardness with Beau, but now we're doing an awkward *moment* after, and it's a lot worse.

"I don't want to impose," I say, overly formal to someone who was just inside me.

"Jesus, you're knee high to a June bug. I don't think you'll take up too much space in this king-size bed."

"What is a June bug? How big is it if I'm knee high to it? Nope." I shake my head and hold out my hands with my shoes still in them. "Irrelevant. It's a busy time at work and I just want to sleep in my own bed."

Beau yawns and stretches, contracting and lengthening all the muscles in his arms and chest. And abs. The heat in my lower stomach starts building again, despite how sexually satisfied I just was.

He doesn't know how close he is to getting jumped by a lust-crazed auctioneer.

"Well, hold on a second and I'll get dressed and ride back with you." Beau starts to get out of bed.

"This is my home city. I can get back alone. In fact, I've often gone to and from my own apartment."

"But it's the middle of the night. I can't let you go out there by yourself." He gestures out his window like it's London during the Blitz.

My hands move to my hips, and I snort. "I thought we had this conversation about your permission and my ability and everything." Plus now I want to go home alone just to prove I can.

He hurries up gathering clothes from the floor and shoves his legs into his pants, sensing I could sprint out of here at any second on a wave of the most righteous indignation.

"Of course you can. I have no doubt you could leave here and travel to Buckingham Palace or the pyramids or Machu Picchu and be fine. You're incredibly skilled. But just because you can doesn't mean you should have to. Not when I'm here. I can keep you company and I'll feel better knowing you got home safe."

He sounds so reasonable.

It's really hard to argue with reasonable. It's one of the best things about working with Priya and Ajay, because they're hardly ever reasonable, with the Gupta love of drama and rash, loud proclamations with little to no logic or evidence.

It's kind of taking the wind out of my sails.

What's the harm in one night anyway? It has to be better than this conversation. Or a silent car ride in the dead of night.

"Well, maybe I can just stay."

He freezes in the process of putting on his shirt, arms stuck in the sleeves with his head buried somewhere in the rest of it.

"I don't want to pressure you into staying if you don't want. If you're really set on going without me, I can call a car from a company we use," he says as he frees his head from the shirt, the garment now half on and half off.

As a concession since he's being so reasonable, I don't roll my eyes at him. I could have just called one of Loot's drivers, providing just as much, if not more, safety as his anonymous driver.

I slip out of my clothes again, not hearing any complaints as he watches the skin that's being exposed. I take his shirt off his arms and put it on me before getting back under the covers.

"What are you waiting for, Beau? It's the middle of the night," I say with indignation, pulling the covers over my head.

"Woman, you can be aggravatin'," Beau grumbles, kicking aside his pants and following orders back into the bed.

From Baby Girl to Woman…at least I'm growing up in the world.

I dart up in bed the next morning, heart pounding because I am not in my tastefully decorated SoHo condo. But there's elaborate molding on the ceiling surrounding a chandelier dripping with gold leaf and crystals.

Wherever I am, at least it's nice.

I turn to the loudly breathing (snoring) body next to me, brain finally remembering exactly what happened last night. I take in the way the early morning light hits Beau's peaceful face. He's just as perfect today as he was the night before, so I can't blame whiskey goggles for what happened in the elevator, or in the bed.

I wait for him to wake up and tell me he has an early meeting, or his grandmother needs him in New Jersey to help fix the air-conditioning, or he has an appointment to save a bus full of puppies. And that I need to leave to make that happen.

On the few occasions that a guy doesn't leave before three a.m. like they melt in the sunlight, those are the caliber of excuses I get. I don't mind since I want them out anyway.

But I don't know how I'd feel if Beau used one of those excuses on me. I think it would be bad. Another reason I should be heading for the hills because I know where relationships go—they end.

True, Beau didn't kick me out last night. But that could have been an antiquated chivalry thing. I'm sure he'll want to make with the excuses now that the sun's out. So when Beau opens his eyes, I brace myself for the inevitable.

"Mornin', Baby Girl." He reaches for me, a genuine smile on his face.

"Morning." I'm still a little stiff and unsure about how I feel about any of this. But I don't have time to dissect it while his face gets closer to mine for a morning kiss.

I decide to go back to my fallback position: enjoy the

perks of him being here while we're in the same city. I kiss him back, relaxing next to him.

He pulls away and runs his hand down my cheek in a gesture that has me relaxing even deeper next to him.

Until I see the clock on the bedside table. "Oh, shit." I shoot up in the bed the second time in a few minutes, this time throwing him off me. "Please say you set the clock ahead an hour for fun." I get up, frantically gathering my clothes together and darting to the bathroom to get ready.

"I would love to make you happy, but I did not do that," he yells after me. "I wish I had, because I'm late too."

I hear him toss the sheets around and rummage through his suitcase.

"Do you want breakfast before you go?"

I shut off the faucet and tear through the suite. "Yes. But no time."

Beau snags my waist as I speed past on my way to the door. He plants a kiss on my lips and gives me a squeeze before asking, "Tonight? Dinner and more Christmas activities? Or I'll look at art. Whatever you want. If you're not busy."

He's not going to make this awkward. He's not playing it cool now only to text me at eleven p.m. to say, "What's up?" He wants to see me and he's making a plan to see me.

How odd.

How…nice.

"Meet you at three outside our offices? For art then Christmas?" I twist out of his arms, looking through my purse for my MetroCard. I find it, so something is going right this morning.

"I can take you to work," Beau yells at me when I open his door. I throw an unamused look over my shoulder, taking a cue from him and not answering with words. I do not have time to have this argument again.

I should probably just write up a Word document with my salient points about how I am an adult and can take care of myself and email it to him whenever this comes up.

I rush to the office, along with the rest of the world. I'm already uncomfortable in yesterday's clothes and it doesn't help that I keep getting jostled in the crowded train. It all puts me in a surprisingly grumpy mood, considering how good last night was.

I greet the receptionist at our front lobby, our ginger-bread auction sitting behind him. It reminds me of Beau and puts me in a better mood immediately.

Huh. That's interesting. And concerning.

Once I get to our floor, I move fast, not making eye contact with anyone who would realize I'm late and in yesterday's clothes. I just have to keep walking quickly and with purpose and I can fool all of these people.

I make it to my office and turn on my computer without ambush. While it wakes up, I check my work phone, but no one has called me or sent any urgent emails. Relaxing more, I go to my closet and look through the small selection of emergency clothes I keep here.

Score! There are enough separate emergency pieces in here that make one cohesive outfit. One that looks purposeful and not thrown together after a wild night out that I thought I was too old to be having. A few minutes in my private bathroom later and I've almost com-

pletely hidden the fact that I didn't go home last night.
I can breathe normally again.

Back at my computer, I get an email from Priya asking me to meet her in her office in fifteen minutes. It
has zero emojis, so I can tell this is going to be a serious meeting. At least there's enough time to get a bagel
and tea on the way to Priya.

Fifteen minutes later on the dot, I walk into the office. Since it sounded important, I don't throw off my
shoes and lounge on the couch the way I usually would,
instead taking a professional seat in one of the chairs
opposite her.

"Good morning, Priya."

She doesn't look up from her computer screen, so I
start eating the bagel. Her nonresponse when she gets
wrapped up in work is so normal I'm not prepared for
what she says next. "Hmm. It must be a nice one since
you walked in wearing yesterday's clothes and a satisfied smile."

I choke on my bite of bagel at the unexpected question. "But how did you know? I changed in my office."

"Not even going to deny it. Graceful." She nods at
me, approving of my high road path. "I wish I could say
I'm omniscient, but I was getting coffee when I saw you
slink into your office like a cat burglar."

"Not a good one, apparently."

"Were you smoothing over the urban-rural divide last
night?"

"Oh god, this is happening now." I bury my head in
my hands.

"Are you going to paint him like one of your French
men?"

I knew I shouldn't have told her one drunken night that I liked to paint. "No."

"Ooh wait, did you take a bite of his Southern peaches?"

"That is low-hanging fruit." I continue the puns, mostly because I can't help myself.

"I bet they are." Then she leers. *Lasciviously.* "One more, I promise... Did y'all do a boot-scootin' boogie or a honky-tonk together?" She tries to squash two into her "one more."

I squint at her. "I don't think you're using any of those words right." I'm not 100 percent sure, but it just doesn't sound right coming out of that New Yorker's mouth. "This is why people say coastal elites are out of touch with the common man."

"Does the common man scoot his boot?" Priya never breaks stride in her typing. And she refuses to teach me how to do that because she's rude.

"Probably both of his boots, cuz."

"Fascinating as the common man's boots are, would you like to do some work today?"

"Could go for a nap honestly." Debauchery is hard and just watching Priya is exhausting even when I've had a good night's sleep.

I just want to do my work and then enjoy my weekends without the stress of responsibility hanging over me, without the stress of potentially disappointing people relying on me. I'm getting itchy under the collar just thinking about it.

Priya mumbles something under her breath about regretting she can't fire me and/or drop me in the middle of the desert somewhere I can't make her life harder.

I blow a kiss her way. Once that's out of my system, I finally get serious.

"Okay, my liege. Let's get to work."

If my mind wanders more to Beau and what we're doing tonight than I'd like, she doesn't need to know that.

Chapter Ten

My alarm goes off at two fifty p.m., jolting me out of the catalog entry I'm writing. I seamlessly shift from focus on work to a special mix of pleasure and terror that Beau inspires in me. I pack up my purse and clean my coffee mug to distract myself from it, standing in my doorway when the tasks are done and I don't have anything else to do.

Ajay passes by my door and then doubles back when he sees me standing just inside my office, all my stuff in my arms.

"Wait, is everyone frozen and only I get to roam around the world, unsupervised?" The mischief in his tone has me putting my hand on my hip and giving him the stink eye.

"The thought of you without a keeper is terrifying."

"If the world isn't frozen, then why are you standing here like a mannequin?"

"I don't want to leave the office."

"I never have that problem." Ajay runs his hand through his thick hair, flopping some back over his forehead. "But I think I know what might be causing some of that hesitance."

"Damn twin bond." I don't know when Priya told

Ajay about me getting closer to Beau, but I bet it was in a hyper-efficient email where she also got three additional tasks done.

"It's a recognized exemption to snitching." He nods sagely. "I hear you're getting close to this peachperson." She really did tell him everything. "Maybe this one will even last longer than usual."

"Nope. You and Priya are not allowed to gang up on me."

"You never got that in writing." He slides his arm around my shoulder. "I'll walk you out."

"You just want to be nosy."

Beau is waiting for me outside our offices, his head bent over his phone. He's bundled up for the New York winter, but I can still remember exactly how he looks, and feels, under that coat. I take a deep breath at the memory, trying to remember that right now I'm in public and it's considered bad form to have sex in public.

Bunch of puritans.

But I need to remind myself that he lives where the peaches grow, and I live where there're more buildings than stars you can see at night. He's going back to his peaches, and I'm staying here with the buildings.

That's supposed to be a comfort. It *is* a comfort. But... still.

It might not be as big a comfort as it originally was.

"Hey." I walk up to him, leaving Ajay behind, bracing myself for any of that awkwardness that wasn't there this morning.

"Hi, Baby Girl," he says with a smile, wrapping his arms around me and lifting me slightly up off the ground to kiss me.

The combination of his kiss and his arms is so potent

that I immediately forget about the crowd around us, and my own cousin, to get lost in Beau. Until a loud, obnoxious, *definitely*-not-getting-any-help-from-me-with-his-work-from-now-on person clears his throat next to us.

Beau raises his head but doesn't set me down. "Oh. Hi."

"Just pretend I'm not here. This is more entertaining than my stories," Ajay says.

"Ajay's leaving now," I say from the perch of Beau's arms, kicking a leg out to symbolically kick Ajay away. Because I can't reach him from where I am.

"Oh." Beau drops me lightly to my feet and turns to the annoyance. "Well, it's nice to see you again." He moves me to one side to extend a hand to Ajay.

I glare at Ajay. I should still be a foot taller and have both arms around me right now.

Ajay boldly smiles in the face of my glare and takes Beau's hand. "I hear you've been enjoying the city. And Sonia."

My glare intensifies.

"What are your intentions with my cousin-who's-like-a-sister?" Ajay throws a paternal look my way.

Ew. "Please don't answer that. Ajay has to leave, because I don't want him to be late for the many important things he has to do." There's fake sweetness in my voice, but I hope it's not as obvious to everyone else. Well, not obvious to Beau; who cares about Ajay?

"Late for what?" Ajay sends me an even wider smile.

"You have to personally edit the catalog for the upcoming contemporary Indian art show."

"Right, I'm going to leave before she assigns me more work. See you around, peachperson." Ajay drops a quick kiss on my head, nods at Beau and strolls in the opposite direction, heading home. To not work on that catalog.

"Peachperson?" Beau looks down at me, eyebrows lifted.

"We started at cowboy and I just barely convinced them you're not a moo Old MacDonald and you're a peach Old MacDonald." I shrug. "Can't tell those city folks nothin'."

Oh man, a few days with him and I'm ready to lasso a hot dog cart.

"Hmm. Yes. *Those* city folk," he says dryly, putting his other arm back around me. Heat flares in my stomach, expanding to every extremity to keep me warm in the cold air.

"Ready to buy some more art?"

"As ready as I'll ever be." He has all the enthusiasm of a kid gearing up to eat vegetables.

"I thought you'd be that excited. So we're going to change things up. I convinced the warehouse manager to let us into storage. You can see some of the pieces on our online sales in person. And I've staged a couple of scenes so you can see the pieces together." If Loot does this long term, we might need a space for this that isn't storage. I'll have to look up those costs before I present the idea to Chacha.

I lead him back into the building, around the public spaces and into our warehouse. "Watch your step, because things are stacked precariously, and we're not supposed to have people back here for lawsuit reasons. Also, please don't sue us."

"I can promise to stay away from lawyers."

Shelves fill the entire space, all overstuffed with furniture, statues, and paintings.

"A lot of our stuff is Indian, but Priya's been pushing to sell all types of art. I've pulled the relevant pieces here. And by 'I've pulled' I mean the very kind warehouse employees did the heavy lifting."

I lead him to the largest open space in here, where I have some groupings set aside. "I know you already have desks and chairs, but I put these in for reference. See how you feel. Have a wander."

"This is all a lot of art." He moves his head around, scanning the shelves around him.

I gently direct his head back to the art in front of him. "You can look anywhere, but I thought you might want to focus on the pre-screened pieces so you don't get overwhelmed. And these pieces are all ready now, through our online auctions."

"These are nice. Everything you showed me is. And I can understand why they're helpful for what I want. Well, now I can." He flashes me a smile. "But it's still overwhelming."

"Sit down. Get acquainted with the pieces and how you'll interact with them on a daily basis. Here." I push him down on one of our more modern couches, gently, because it's expensive. "You sit there."

I back up and pantomime opening a door. "Hello. I'm here for some fancy energy."

Beau raises his eyebrow at me.

"Well?" I sit on a chair across from him and cross my legs. "Ah! Lovely eighteenth-century Zeus you've got there. I feel very comfortable with this company all of a sudden. Take my business money!" I pantomime extending money his way.

Beau's outright laughing at me now. "Don't you want to hear about our product?"

"Nope. You've got electricity, and I've got a TV. And there's something soothing about this place. Especially the Priapus." I wink at him and direct him a piece he clearly hasn't seen.

He turns his head and then jumps up in his seat when he sees it. "That erection! It doesn't feel appropriate for a workplace."

"Maybe. But Romans put statues like that in their gardens for prosperity of crops and as protection against trespassers. Maybe some of that would be helpful in a business?"

"In their gardens?"

I nod.

Beau shakes his head. "The only thing that's going to get us is a lawsuit."

"Very probably." I nod. "Look over here." I direct my attention to his other side. "I pulled some harvest slash agriculture scenes from different cultures. Can't hurt to remind people you already have oodles of money. Stay-at-The-Plaza money."

Beau looks down, bashful again. "I like that idea. It'll be nice to see the familiar scenes when I visit. Remind me of home."

"Yes. And with the different styles, locations, and time periods, they would make your company seem more international right out the gate."

"It's all so manipulative."

"It's marketing. They're the same techniques that your salesmen will use once it's time to market your product."

Beau sighs deep and stands. He walks around, considering all the pieces on display. And then walks back and forth even more. "Okay. I like these pieces." He points while he walks back and forth, and I make notes on my tablet.

"Excellent. I'll make the bids for you and keep you updated if the prices rise."

I smile contentedly while I do that on my tablet. It's unreal how much I've been enjoying this interior decorating gig. I was actually excited to come to work and arrange all this for Beau's office. I even worked through lunch because I was in such a working groove. I don't even recognize work-me anymore. But I like it.

I'm less excited to tell everyone I'm doing this.

Beau finishes looking through my ideas (avoiding the Priapus), and we leave the warehouse behind, work done for the day.

He wraps his arm around me and looks down into my eyes, an intimate smile playing on his lips, the same one I saw last night in his hotel room. He's transitioned nicely to the pleasure part of the evening.

"What's next on the Christmas agenda?"

Chapter Eleven

"You have to trust me some more." Plus, I love a good surprise reaction, love seeing the happy excitement on a person's face when I nail the perfect present. I'm definitely going to miss seeing *Beau's* responses to my surprises; they've been fantastic so far.

Beau sighs. "Baby Girl, does this mean that you're not gonna let me get us a car?"

"No. I already ordered one when we left the warehouse," I smugly say.

He pulls me in for a squeeze, and I don't know if he's resigned or mad about it. His face doesn't give me any clues, remaining neutral and keeping his real feelings a mystery.

"I saw our gingerbread auction in there." Beau changes the subject and jerks his head as we pass through the lobby. Our project sits behind the reception desk, welcoming visitors like it welcomed me this morning. "I sent a picture to my mom and sister when we were done. They couldn't believe I made something so artistic. They think you're magic for getting me to do it."

I look up at him, unsure of how to react. Talking about me to his parents is deepening the relationship past a casual fling. And I'm not sure how to deal with that.

But Loot has the best employees in the world, because Tom, with his impeccable timing, drives up to the curb before I have to think about that more.

Beau opens the door to the back seat before Tom can get out and I scoot in to make room for him.

"Hey, Tom."

"Hi, Sonia." He does some technology magic and Christmas music fills the vehicle. And it's "All I Want for Christmas is You."

"I got hot chocolate for you both in the thermos back there."

"Thank you!" I pour out the hot chocolate into some mugs and throw in some marshmallows that Tom had the foresight to include. The man knows Christmas.

"I'm getting really curious. Any chance of you telling me where we're going?"

"Live in the moment," I say. "But if this doesn't make you think the city has the best Christmas hands down, then I might have to throw my hands up in defeat."

Beau snorts. "I've only known you for a few days and even I don't buy that statement."

"Hmm." I snuggle back into Beau's side, relieved that we moved right past any awkwardness from sleeping together last night. It was touch and go when he started talking about his family but that didn't last long.

He's wearing whatever cologne he has that smells like cinnamon and it mixes with the smell of the hot chocolate to make my new favorite Christmas smell. One I'm going to pay serious money to recreate once he leaves.

"Here we are." Tom stops the car.

"Thanks. You come inside too, Tom. I'll call when we're ready."

"I'll park and take you up on that."

We get out of the car and I shuffle ahead of Beau. "Are you so excited?" I bounce and point to the sign above me. Bouncing in excitement being my default whenever Christmas is involved.

"The New York Botanical Garden? What's here for Christmas? Poinsettias?"

"No. Well, yes. There's probably some in there. Being a garden. But we're here because every year they do a Holiday Train Show and they make New York buildings out of plants. And little trains go around them."

"Trains? All right, that sounds pretty cool." Beau assumes his standard position, where he slides his hand to my lower back like we've got magnets in my lower back and his hand, and we walk to the visitor center.

"So can we just say the city wins and call it a night?" Maybe we could call it a night in that fancy hotel room, or my less fancy apartment.

"No, ma'am. I never pass up trains and other things with motors."

"Figures." Rejected for a tiny toy.

Beau pays for the tickets before I can find my wallet in my purse and I vow to clean it out when I get home so I don't lose the paying competition again. Because his face when I pay is too good to pass up.

"How was your day?" I ask as I speed up to open the door to the conservatory. I stand firm when he tries to take the door from me, making him go through it first. Which he does, with a roll of his eyes.

Take that, Old MacDonald. It's the future and the future is female…s opening their own doors. And being equal, also.

"Really good. I saw some research and manufacturing spaces. I hope we can get everything decided by the end of the week. Next week by the latest."

"Oh, that's fast." He's going to be gone soon? In a week? I mean, I knew this was coming. He never lied to me about his residence and I'm a smart enough girl.

It's the reason I was so comfortable going up to his hotel room last night.

But even though I *knew* he was leaving, I haven't really *thought* about him leaving. Not as something penned into my planner. It was more like an abstract idea. Like gravity. It's there, it's comforting, but I don't have to think about it all the time and if I really thought about it, it would just confuse me.

I mean really, how do we all not float away from this orb we're on?

"It is. I had done a lot of the groundwork before I even got to the city, so this trip was just for some face-to-face meetings to finalize plans. And for art." He winks at me.

"Congrats," I force out, still freaked out by…gravity. Sure, that's what's freaking me out.

"I can't wait to get home. Mom's sending me pictures of the peach tree that we decorate every year for Christmas, still plain, and my sister's sending me pictures of the tree decorations. Threatening to do it without me if I don't come home quick." He can't keep the fondness out of his voice when he talks about family. That seems like a nice, normal, healthy relationship.

I don't think I've ever had that type of relationship with my parents. When they left me in the States, I resented them. I didn't take their calls, didn't speak to them when they visited, and didn't respond to their gifts. And then when I got older and could understand their reasons, it was too late.

Even if the resentment wasn't coursing through me anymore, it was just habit not to be close to them. Habit to not text them when I got good news. Habit to turn to Chachi and Chacha when I needed help.

And then when their visits got less frequent, being with them was like being around strangers.

But Beau has so much fondness for his family. It's apparent in his voice and the way his entire demeanor softens when he talks to them. I doubt he'd ever want to be far from the cause of that deep contentment. Why would anyone go away from happiness?

"That's great." I focus back on the miniature landmarks in front of me. "These are the highlights of our fair city, made of plants."

"Let me get this straight. You guys concrete over the plants to build buildings and then make little versions of the buildings out of plants?"

His observation rips a laugh out of me, jolting me out of the funk I slipped into when he spoke about leaving and family. A one-two punch of things I don't want to deal with. "I never looked at it like that. But yeah, I guess that's what we do."

"That's a power move. Those trees know who's boss. Sorry, the one tree left in Central Park knows who's boss."

I bump him with my shoulder. "You know we have more trees than that. At least a baker's dozen, probably. Per park. Even more in that central one."

We walk along the pathway, seeing a little Statue of Liberty, little Empire State Building and little St. Patrick's Cathedral among the tropical lush greenery. Little trains decked out in Christmas lights and decorations zip around the buildings, which are also all lit up.

"The city just doesn't have the beauty of the country."

"Nothingness isn't beauty." Yes, this I can do. I can argue city vs. country all day if it means I don't have to confront any feelings.

Because really, what's the point of analyzing them if you can't change them?

"It's pure."

"No, it's boring. Whereas buildings are perfectly planned beauty. Human ingenuity on display."

"But nature is peaceful."

"Nature irritates allergies."

He doesn't respond to that one and I look over, watching him bend down to see a train roll past a tiny Yankee Stadium. The Christmas lights from the trees project a colorful show on his face, making him look pretty festive himself.

I lift an eyebrow even though he's not looking at me. I've always found that gloating is such a strong emotion it can be felt even if the person isn't looking directly at you.

When he doesn't respond to it, I prod him, wanting some verbal validation. "Nothing to say to that?"

"I'm sure people are allergic to city things. But the allergies on the orchard are bad," he concedes with a self-deprecating smile.

Kids with so much energy they must have injected liquid candy canes directly into their veins cut between us. The stampede of wildebeest is followed by harried parents at a much slower pace.

"I don't think I was ever that wild." Beau shakes his head at them, putting the "old" in Old MacDonald.

I laugh in his face. "I think we should ask your mom to see how she remembers that."

"Let's not do that." He puts that hand on my lower back

as we continue the walk around the conservatory. While I imagine a tiny Beau running around, creating havoc. Kind of adorable. Even from me, who isn't entirely comfortable around children.

After making a full circuit, I tug on Beau's hand, bringing him back outside to the cold. "I'll text Tom and then I have one more Christmas event for the day."

Beau absentmindedly rubs my arms to ward off the cold as we wait. "You guys are serious about your Christmas. I think there may be *too* much to do in the city."

"That's a possibility." I agree easily, tired myself from the Christmas activities and all the bedroom activities, meaning I've had very little sleep in the last few days. "But I usually don't cram so much Christmas into quite this short a time. Usually it's spread out from the entire month between Thanksgiving and the holiday."

"A Christmas sprint. I'm so lucky." His voice is thick with sarcasm.

Now I feel guilty. "I don't want you to hate the city. We can call it a night so you can get some rest."

"No. I'm enjoying myself." He pulls me in closer and I tuck my head into his shoulder and neck area. I inhale the scent of cinnamon and snuggle close to him on the exhale. The only way this would be a better moment is if it started snowing.

Tom brings the car around and we get in. "You replenished the hot chocolate? You're the best." I help myself to another glass.

"There's Baileys and peppermint schnapps in the back if you want to spike the drink. I won't tell Mr. Gupta." He winks conspiratorially as he turns to focus on the road.

"Tom, you outdid yourself," I say, shoving tumblers, thermoses, and tiny alcohol bottles at Beau. He gives me a nervous look every time I rearrange the equipment so I can make the drinks, probably thinking I'm going to spill. No faith.

But he keeps up the intricate juggling act every time I take something and shove another thing back at him. I top off the hot chocolate with marshmallows. Sugar and alcohol. The way to a perfect Christmas night.

I take in the festive lights of the city as Tom whisks us away to the next event.

Forty minutes later the car stops and I turn to Beau. "I hope your stomach is ready for what is about to occur."

Chapter Twelve

"I can't tell if you're being serious or if you're going to take me to a place that serves a seven-course meal but all the courses are only a bite each."

"You'll have more food than you could eat in one sitting." I get out of the vehicle. "Ready for the best Christmas market in the States?" I ask, pulling him toward the stalls.

"Who's making this determination?"

"Me. I am." I stride confidently into the crowd, knowing every nook and cranny of this market from the numerous visits I've made over the years.

"Have you visited every Christmas market in the States? You ought to get a decent sample size." Beau follows behind in the path I clear.

"Yup. I've visited them all." I boldly lie with a straight face. Not that he can appreciate it since he's behind me.

"Well then lead on, Christmas Market Expert."

I take him through the rows of enclosed stalls, barely glancing at the different items for sale, from paintings to apparel to ornaments, all with cute winter animals and other Christmas perfectness.

Each stall is decorated for the holiday, with lights and sparkly decorations in red, green, and gold being the most popular colors. All to separate the people from their money (me; I'm people and my money is theirs). The best decorations, though, are anything with dogs in Christmas outfits on it.

We wander around the stalls, me following my nose and memory until I get to where I want: the indoor food hall.

"Christmas pierogis!" I say when we get to my favorite savory food stall. Not to be confused with my top three favorite sweet food stalls. Because I can't pick just one and this holiday supports excess.

We get in line. "What makes it a Christmas pierogi?" Beau asks.

"Because I'm buying it in a Christmas market. Obviously. There's also Christmas fudge, Christmas hot chocolate and Christmas popcorn." I point to the different vendors as I list the foods.

Beau's eyes glaze over. "There's *too* many choices here. How do you even decide anything in a market this big? We have a Christmas market but it's about four stalls in our park. And it's all just hot chocolate and candy canes."

"There are over a hundred and seventy here."

His eyes widen in panic.

"But you just have to take it section by section." I pat him comfortingly on his arm. "And come back if you see something you want later."

"There's so much in a small area." He shakes his head. "My mom's actually from here. And she always complains about the lack of options at home. I guess I see where she's coming from now. I don't agree, but I get it."

I lightly slap his arm, and my mouth falls open in shock. "You big hypocrite! All this time you've been giving the city flak and all along you've had city blood in you." I poke the chest that holds all that blood.

"We try not to talk about the city blood. And no one is uncouth enough to bring it up to our faces." He sticks his nose in the air, I hope facetiously.

"I don't even know what to do with this new information, but it's going to involve hot chocolate."

I motion for him to stay in line so I can go get some of that. When I come back with two glasses, Beau raises an eyebrow in judgement.

"How much of that have you drank today?"

"It's Christmas, Scrooge McGrinch. I can drink some hot chocolate. And one's for you." I hand him a cup and bounce on my heels in line, taking a sip of the magical liquid from the remaining cup.

"Oh, save our place. I've gotta get my new Christmas ornament for the year." I get distracted by the ornament stall next to us. Thank god for long New York lines.

When I come back, multiple bags hanging off my arm and hot chocolate half gone, Beau starts laughing at me. "This is why parents limit their children's chocolate intake."

I sniff, my own nose firmly in the air. "I'm an adult and I can consume as much chocolate as I want. That is literally the only good thing about adulthood, which in general, kind of blows. Well, that and buying people presents." I hand him a bag with a New York themed ornament in it…complete with painted Statue of Liberty, iconic yellow taxicab, bridges, and tall buildings.

Beau takes the bag, unwillingly. "Another present? But I don't have anything for you."

I roll my eyes. "You can buy the food. Also this one you can't open till you get back home."

I not-so-subtly remind both of us where this is going, in case anyone (like me) forgets and gets too comfortable with someone to hold my place in line while I go shopping. This is why I never did couple things with partners in the past…it's too easy to get distracted by the good times sucking you in, little by little, and to forget that every time the high gets higher, you have further to fall when it all goes wrong.

Finally, we get to the front of the line and order a variety of savory pierogis. We claim an empty barrel in a row that are set up as tables and lay out the food like a feast.

"The people watching is much better here than at home. I'll give you that." Beau munches on his food and looks over the crowd in front of him.

I follow his line of sight and see a little boy steal the last bite of chimney cake from who I assume is his sister. Instead of telling the two adults in front of them, the little girl gives her brother a wedgie. The parents, oblivious to the battle unfolding in front of them, cuddle into each other, enjoying the moment of peace on their night out.

And that's just what's happening at the table next to us. I haven't even gotten to the table on the far side, where a couple is in the midst of breaking up or passionately debating the best Christmas traditions; verdict unclear without hearing the conversation. Either way, strong emotions are involved.

"I'm telling you, Christmas markets are one of the best parts of the season."

"Better than presents?"

"It's *one* of the best parts of the season."

"You know, Christmas is my favorite holiday of the year as well," Beau says.

"Hey, you do have okay taste. Sometimes."

"Hmm." He doesn't comment on the dig. "It was the one holiday that Dad made sure to be around. Birthdays and accomplishments came at an inconvenient time during harvest or planting seasons, but Christmas was always during the winter season, so Dad didn't have as much work to do."

"That sounds like it was a special day." His dad sounds like a watered-down version of my parents, except closer geographically. I chew the inside of my mouth, aware that we're getting even deeper in this fling. It's hard to keep a distance when I keep finding things we have in common. And realizing how much I like doing my favorite things with him.

Which are not things I was prepared for with this man from the South.

And there hasn't been any awkwardness all day. He hasn't changed how he treats me after we slept together. He didn't make an excuse to blow me off today, just so he could call at midnight to ask me to come over for some late-night business. He's been the same considerate, sometimes contrary, sometimes flirty Beau that he's been since I met him.

Maybe even sweeter.

A nice surprise, but a surprise that makes it even harder to keep my distance. A distance that's necessary since he's leaving, and I still don't want a relationship.

This Christmas is a lot more fraught than last year.

Pile of pierogis demolished, Beau tosses the empty plates in a trash can nearby. "I couldn't even begin to choose dessert, but I think you'll have a pretty good idea."

"Wait till you have oliebollen." I direct him to one my favorite dessert stalls of the market.

"What's that?"

"Dutch doughnuts," I answer succinctly, knowing they'll speak for themselves in a second.

Dessert eaten, we wander around the stalls, looking at all the wares. I use the excuse of the crowd and the cold to get closer to Beau's body. Very obliging, this Christmas season.

I pick up some holiday socks for the family to wear on our Christmas Eve celebration, and Beau gets his sister a shirt with Santa and Mrs. Claus in bathing suits, by the ocean. He said it best represents his Christmas, which doesn't get beach warm, but is a lot warmer than here.

"One last food item," I say.

"More? I'm stuffed fuller than our Thanksgiving turkey." He pats his stomach.

"This is worth any stomach discomfort that will follow. Trust me." I tug him in the direction I want him to go, hands intertwined like they have been all night except for when we dipped into stalls to do some shopping. I stop in front of a stall that's set up like an ice cream stall.

"Ice cream? I can get that anywhere."

"It's not ice cream." I tug him even closer to the glass counter and he settles in behind me, both arms around me as the crowd pushes against us.

"Cookie dough?" There's laughter in his voice, delight at the unexpected treat.

"Yep, cookie dough!"

"You're right. I need this is my life, just like I needed those Dutch doughnuts and the pierogis and the fourth cup of hot chocolate. And probably whatever's in that bag you gave me. You know Christmas." He kisses my head affectionately and takes in the display in front of him. "Do you want to do the sampler bites?"

"Sure." I've created a monster. Oh well, I get more food out of it.

Beau takes the box from the server and hands it to me to pick first. I stick with some classic chocolate chip and he takes out the peanut butter. After too much cookie dough, I yawn and look at my watch.

"I better call Tom." I get out my phone to do that, dreading that the night has to end.

Because no matter how laid-back Beau's been, there's no way the end of the night isn't going to be awkward. Is he going to invite me to the hotel? Should I invite him to my place? Was he only so quiet about the fact that we had sex because he hated it so much he never wants to even talk about it again, much less do it again? Was it so bad he scrubbed it from his memory??

And do I even want him to remember?

Okay, that question is ridiculous. Of course I want him to remember. And I want him to do it again. He's amazing at sex and I'm not in the habit of denying myself things that give me pleasure. Look at how many cups of hot chocolate I just drank!

The uncertainty makes me quieter than I usually am if the concerned look Tom shoots me after he picks us up means anything. I practically throw the box of oliebollen at him as a distraction, and it works. His eyes light up and I know he's going to spend the rest of the drive counting down the moments till he can tear into that box at home, just like he always does when he drives me here. I would have gone for it in the car, but Tom says his husband would kill him if he ate the pieces of heaven without sharing, so he always waits.

That *may* be an example of true love. If I believed true love actually existed.

"Where to?" Tom asks.

"Ask our guest. Are there any last-minute New York sights you want to see before the night is over?"

"Probably. But I don't know enough about the city to know what I should do." He flashes that genuine smile over at me. "And I'm so tired I doubt I could drum up the amount of appreciation that New York would demand."

I laugh. "New York does demand fervor. And she doesn't mind getting feisty with you when she doesn't get it."

"To the hotel then. Unless you're closer? I wouldn't want Tom to go back and forth."

"I'm closer. To my place then."

One anxiety-filled ride later, I almost chew a hole through the inside of my cheek and develop a nervous tic where I flinch every time the car stops because I think we're there. I really don't have a good excuse since I know this city inside out and I know exactly how far we are from my condo.

Finally, we do stop in front of my building. My heart, now knowing it's really the time to freak out, runs with the permission, beating in my chest in anticipation. There's a slight silence when the car stops, both of us searching for a way to say good-night.

Tom clears his throat slightly, probably worried about his food getting colder. The noise spurs Beau into action. "I'll walk you to the door. No need to wait, Tom, I'll get the subway from here."

"Are you sure? Tom can take you all the way." I don't want to wake up tomorrow to the headline Out-of-Towner

Starves to Death Wandering the Subway; He Got on the Express when He Should Have Been on the Local.

Beau, proving he can read my mind, throws a contrary look over his shoulder when he closes the car door. "I'll manage. I'm not a hayseed out in the city for the first time. My mom is from here."

"I believe you." I hold up my hands. "But transit maps don't usually get passed on via DNA."

His hand finds my lower back without looking and we move toward the building. "Thank you for another great Christmas night," he says in front of the building.

"You're welcome." I move back and forth on my feet, wondering if I should offer him some eggnog or yet another cup of hot chocolate.

Before I can, he interrupts my internal monologue. "Do you want to come back to the Plaza? Maybe order some more hot chocolate? I heard adults can have as much as they want."

Chapter Thirteen

I smile in genuine relief. I don't mind being the person to initiate sex, but it's nice to know that he wants me as much as I want him.

"That sounds really good. Especially the part about the hot chocolate, but my apartment is right here." I point to the building we're standing right in front of. "And it has a fully stocked hot chocolate bar. Even a hot chocolate charcuterie board, if I haven't used it all already."

"Lead the way." Beau tries to open the door, but it needs my key access, which I get out of my purse to swipe by the side of the door.

In the elevator, I swipe my key fob over the reader and push in my floor. Beau pulls me in from behind me to kiss the back of my neck and then lingers by sucking lightly in the area. I smile, looking at our reflection in the reflective metal wall and wonder what it is about Beau and elevators. Not that I mind, but it makes me want to take him to the Empire State Building.

That elevator ride still only lasts about a minute, but I'm sure Beau could do some amazing things in a minute.

This much shorter elevator ride is over too soon, and I pull him directly into my home once the doors open, since I'm the only one on the floor.

I dump my purse onto the table by the entrance and throw my coat toward the coatrack, not caring if it lands on it. I slip out of my shoes and motion for him to do the same with his. He doesn't complain, and I breathe a sigh of relief at the compliance without an argument or explanation.

Some people are adamant about traipsing around my house in their dirty shoes. Do they know what they've been walking around in all day? Dog pee, that's what. A lot of it supplied by my puppy-nephew, who loves marking the sidewalk right outside my building.

"I'll make some hot chocolate, or some eggnog, if you want?" I move through my space to get to the kitchen, looking at the familiar colors of my couch and walls along the way.

I went traditional in decoration, with dark wood paneling and damask wallpaper in deep reds, greens, and blues in the different rooms. Pieces of furniture are large and comfortable, not just showpieces. Some of my favorite art dots the area, from any period or place that struck my fancy, alongside pictures of family, friends, and travel. Like an eclectic English country house, but smaller and with a bodega next door. And currently looking like Santa Claus threw up on it.

Perfection.

I really should have suspected how much I would love interior decorating with how obsessive I became when I was decorating my own home. Pinterest boards, spreadsheets, drawn plans on my iPad. Chasing down pieces I wanted all over town (and beyond thanks to the internet) and feeling like I just won a Nobel prize once I got what I wanted, or when I saw the rooms come together. I thought it was the thrill of decorating the first place that was mine. And that was part of it. But I felt shades of the same excitement designing exhibitions at work, and much more now, doing the same work for Beau.

"Make yourself comfortable on the couch," I call out.

"Maybe let's do eggnog? To change things up? How can I help?" Beau already has his jacket off and he folds back the sleeves of his button-down up to his elbows as he follows me into the kitchen.

I almost drop the pitcher of eggnog at the skin that's exposed. The *forearm* that's exposed. I swallow a few times, reminding myself that I've already seen him naked, so there's no way I should be this affected by just his forearms. Muscular, veiny, dusted-with-the-perfect-amount-of-hair forearms.

But there's something about seeing that particular stretch of skin that makes me want to swallow my tongue. Something about it that makes me hot even though it's a cold New York winter night.

"It's already done. I make a pot from scratch every few days during Christmas time." I warm it up, then pour some into mugs and sprinkle extra cinnamon and nutmeg on top.

I hand one to Beau and lead him into the living room. "We could watch something." Or bone. That's an option too, even if I haven't verbally offered it. "Do you have any preference?"

"I have faith you'll put on an amazing Christmas movie." He gets comfortable on the couch and extends his arm over the back, inviting me to snuggle in. Or at least it looks like an invitation to me.

I put on my favorite Christmas movie and take him up on his silent invitation by getting as close to his side as I can, pulling the blanket down from the back of the couch to envelop both of us in Christmas coziness. "This is my favorite Christmas movie."

The movie starts and Beau laughs. "*Home Alone* is good, but *The Nightmare Before Christmas* is the superior movie."

"You know what? I don't agree with you, but I respect that opinion. Unlike your completely incorrect opinion that a Southern Christmas can even come close to a New York Christmas."

"Good to know one of my Christmas opinions passes your muster."

Beau snuggles me in closer and I go willingly. I yawn, the late nights catching up with me and hitting me even harder now that I'm comfortable on my couch, which has defeated my good intention to stay awake more times than I want to admit.

I put my empty glass down and think that I'll seduce Beau in a second. After I rest my eyes for just...one... second...

I shoot awake for the second time in two days. A sharp pain stabs into the right side of my neck and my hand massages it without any relief. Great, I'm just going to have to wait the pain out. The joys of getting older.

I try to turn my neck to look at the man next to me, but the sharp pain in my neck stops the move, so I move my entire torso to look at him. Beau's still asleep through my morning injury.

We never made it to the bedroom upstairs...we didn't even have sex. One of us (I have no idea who) shifted us down to lie on our sides, and I've never been happier to have bought the extra-wide couch. I'm still in pain but less than I would have been without it.

The clock on the TV says there's still an hour before I have to be at work. I force out a breath of relief. That means I get a few more minutes of freaking out over Beau. Because I am freaking out over the fact that we didn't even have sex and it was still a surprisingly intimate night, just to sleep in his arms.

From someone who isn't used to sharing the bed, or couch, it's a big step. One I didn't plan on taking with anyone. Because I don't want to deal with the emotions involved with spending the entire night with someone.

But I've done it twice with Beau now and there's no panic. No itchy feeling under my collar that signifies I'm getting too close to someone, telling me to flee at the first opportunity.

That lack of itchiness actually kind of makes me itchy under the collar. Ironically.

"Hey, Beau." I gently shake him awake, not sure when he needs to get his day started. "We fell asleep on the couch."

Beau's Christmas-tree-hazel eyes flutter open, focusing on me and lighting up when he does.

"You did," he corrects me. "I was just going to let you sleep for a bit in thanks for your tour guiding and then wake you up to let you know I was leaving. But then you were so comfortable, I feel asleep too at some point," he says sheepishly.

"Mmm." I rub his cheek. The contrast of his soft skin and his prickly morning beard is just as enticing a combination of sensations as it was last time I touched this face. Not a fluke that first time, then. "When do you have to be at work?"

"My first meeting isn't till ten, but I do have to review some stuff before it. How about you?"

"I have to be in by eight thirty."

Beau looks at his watch. "Do you want to get breakfast?"

My first instinct is to say yes and the answer is already halfway out of my mouth before I corral it back and lock it down deep. Because it would be too easy to think that we could have breakfasts together every morning. Too easy to imagine him as being the person I fall asleep next to every night, whether on the couch after a fifteen-hour Netflix marathon, or in bed after really satisfying sex.

But no matter how good it starts out, people leave. It's not their fault. They always have the best intentions and never mean to hurt you.

But they do.

And Beau doesn't live here, so it's not just my wild paranoia thinking he's going to abandon me; it's a certainty. It was a selling point to enter in this relationship.

"No, I've got to get to work. Maybe a raincheck?" Like after I've had time and distance to build back up the ramparts that are a second skin around me. They don't seem as solid against the charm offensive from this Southern farmer as I thought they would be.

"Whenever you want." Beau sits up and stretches on the couch. I allow myself the luxury of watching the show for a few seconds. But only a few seconds of the visual feast before I get up.

"Do you want me to call Tom to give you a ride back to your hotel?" I ask.

"No. Like I said last night, I can take the subway." Exasperation fills his tone.

I stare at him blankly, not wanting to be mean enough to say it out loud after the cozy night we had.

"I have a smartphone. I can handle this."

Satisfied that he's going to make it back to his hotel room in one piece, even if I mentally place bets on how long it takes him, I run to my bathroom on the second floor.

"Feel free to use the bathroom downstairs and help yourself to anything in the kitchen," I call out over my shoulder.

I strip an hour-long morning routine into the basics and I'm back downstairs in thirty minutes.

"All right. Well, time to get to work." I grab my purse and pick a pair of shoes from the closet near my front door. Favorite pair of velvet burgundy smoking slipper flats found, I slip into them and rise to look at Beau.

His suit is a wrinkled mess and he gave up on his tie, taking it off and shoving it in his pocket haphazardly so bits of it are still hanging out. The first couple of buttons of his shirt are undone and I want so bad to call in sick and get back on the couch, burying my nose in the warmth of his neck again.

But that is kind of the opposite of time and distance, so I force myself to turn to the elevator.

Beau follows me out, close enough that I get the hint of cinnamon. How is he doing that? He can't have put on any cologne since before our date, which was a solid twelve hours ago.

"I'm excited to see what city Christmas event you're going to surprise me with tonight," Beau says.

Now is the best time to implement Mission: Space. "Ah, I don't think I can make it tonight. I'd love to, but I have some work to finish off." I take the coward's way and blame work instead of coming clean about how scared I am of the feelings he inspires in me.

"Of course. I'm sorry. I didn't mean to monopolize all your time."

"No. It hasn't been a problem. It's been a lot of fun showing you around, and we are working together, too. I just have to get some other work done and I'll have to stay late to do it. We can meet tomorrow to continue the decorating fun." During business hours.

"Sure. Let me know if you get done with work early and want to meet. I'll probably be eating mediocre food at a tourist trap."

"I'll send you a list of restaurants to help you avoid that fate."

"Oh, no. I didn't mean to guilt you into doing more work for me. I'll be fine."

Ahh. Here's the awkward morning after I was dreading. And I have no one to blame but myself; he's been wonderful.

We get to the ground floor and exit the building. "Well, I'll see you later." I wish I could have avoided this by leaving him asleep in my own apartment while I snuck out like a ninja.

"Yeah. Let me know about tonight. If you want." Beau raises a few fingers in goodbye.

Fat chance of me caving in.

Chapter Fourteen

By lunch, I want to cave in.

I remind myself again that people leave, but it doesn't have as much weight when it's been four hours since I was snuggled up to Beau. And I miss it. I miss him. Despite not wanting something serious, I've gotten used to seeing him, and knowing I won't be tonight is making me uncharacteristically melancholy. And then mad at the melancholy.

I'm so wrapped up in trying to manage my emotions and edit a sale catalog at the same time, that the first I hear of Priya is her clearing her throat.

I jerk up to see where the noise came from, hitting my knee on the corner of my desk as my entire body lifts. I see Priya sitting right in front of me, legs crossed, iPad on the desk in front of her, coffee in hand.

"How long have you sitting there?" Please let the answer be something short so I don't have to feel the crushing weight of embarrassment.

"Five whole uninterrupted minutes. I cleared my throat. Thrice."

No Christmas miracle here. Just the cold misery of embarrassment.

"I've been really involved in this catalog..." The intense workaholic in front of me can't fault me for that.

"I *would* believe that. I *want* to believe that. Except you haven't touched your computer the entire five minutes I was here."

"There's a lot of text on the screen and it doesn't need fixing?" I ask, my excuse coming out more as a question. "Because of how smart I was the first time?"

"This is painful to watch. Please don't try to make excuses. Or make better excuses, if you must lie to me."

"Was there something you needed?"

"Yes. But now I'm more interested in what's happening here." She indicates me and my desk in one very judgemental finger.

I give in...because she'll only harass me until I tell her what she wants to hear and I don't have the mental fortitude to battle her in the confused, weakened state I'm in. "Beau spent the night at my place last night. It makes the second night in a row we've spent together." I bury my head in my hands, finding it easier to talk to my fingers than Priya.

"Get it, Sonia!" I can hear her dancing in victory in the seat. But I can't see it because I refuse to look up.

"No. We didn't even have sex last night." I'm still incredulous about the fact that I enjoyed it as much as the night when we did have sex. "We fell asleep on the couch watching Christmas movies and drinking eggnog."

"But that kind of sounds like your fantasy. Because you're an odd duck."

"Okay. Was this just an excuse to sass me or is there a productive reason for the visit to the common folk?" I indicate myself.

"The fact that you don't think I can do both is a personal affront and the only remedy is pistols at dawn in the park."

I love my family. I do. And I know I have my own moments of high drama. But sometimes they're too much for even me.

"You know you won't have access to the internet in prison, right? You can't run sales in prison without internet. Do you know how much this company will suffer if you get put away for cousin-cide?"

Priya purses her lips and nods. "Yup. Thought about it. I retract my gauntlet." She wakes up her iPad and opens her email. "I did come for real reasons. How is the prep for the night of the Christmas auction?"

"Slightly ahead of schedule. The show exhibiting the pieces is getting good buzz and we've got most of the details sorted for the night of the sale itself. Should be good."

"Great." Priya makes a note. I hope it's to send me a smiley face emoji. I need the positive reinforcement. Maybe we should bring back stickers as prizes. Lisa Frank stickers, hopefully.

Then she closes her tablet case.

"Was that all you came for? That could have been an email. A short one. Or a text. Even a comment on an Instagram post."

"*Fine.* I did want to harass you about your personal life. Now that you're having sleepovers with him, are you going to invite the peachperson to the Loot Christmas party tomorrow?"

We're back to Beau? "I hadn't thought about it." I've been too busy alternating between enjoying him and worrying about the future to think about the Loot event.

"Well. Think about it now." Priya goes back to her tablet, reviewing some text and letting me know she won't be going anywhere until I decide what I'm going to do. Damn technology letting her wait me out.

I do want to spend more time with him. And show off a little with our extravagant Loot holiday party; it makes an epic city event. Most importantly, the party is open to some of our clients, so it won't be too strange if I bring a non-employee.

The lengths of mental contortions and twisting myself into an approximation of a pretzel to justify inviting him is worrying, but it doesn't stop me saying "Yes."

Priya looks up, and missing nothing, starts to clap her hands.

"As a client," I say before she gets too excited.

It works, and she dims immediately. "But you love love. You watch *Love Island* and get so invested in the relationships that you get mad when you find out the couples don't stay together after the show even though your brain can't possibly think they're going to last. They only knew each other for an eight-week, alcohol-fueled competition. Maybe less if it was a person who came in late."

"They made me watch them fall in love. The least they can do is stay together or lie to us." And believing in love for other people has never been my problem. I encouraged Priya to get to know Gavin, when it was clear to everyone that they were into each other. It's just harder to believe in it for myself. Or to take that risk when it comes to me.

"You watched them fall in lust," Priya corrects me.

"He's coming as a *client*. Who is leaving soon to go home."

"That part is less than ideal. But we can work on that. I'm still telling Mom in the meantime. She worries."

"No. Wait—" But I'm too late, because scarily efficient Priya has already sent me an email on her way down the hall.

I get back to work and ignore my phone, knowing how many texts are coming.

Beta, are you dating a boy??

What does he do?

What is his birthday? And his birth time?

I scroll through Chachi's texts right before I turn my work computer off, ignoring the fact that she's trying to get his horoscope information from me to do a compatibility check.

This is the downside to inviting him to the party. People will assume, even though he is clearly just a client. With some benefits, I guess. Besides profit.

I text back that this is a work thing and leave out the rest, knowing that isn't going to deter her curiosity but trying anyway.

I close the laptop and send a quick text to Beau, telling him my schedule has freed up and offering to take him to another Christmas event, if he still wants to. I've been thinking about him all day, with the help of everyone who keeps mentioning him, and I want to see him. So what the hell? He's leaving soon either way. I either get more of him and then he leaves or less, and it'll suck either way. Might as well enjoy while I can.

He texts back after a few minutes, confirming that he'll be there.

This is the first time we're going out without first doing work stuff. I can't even try to pretend I'm being forced to spend time with him for work. This is all about what I want.

I make it to the ground floor and all the way to the subway station without getting accosted by any of my family, so the night is already off to a great start.

At the Paley Center, Beau's waiting for me at the entrance, head bowed over his phone. I take in the usual happiness that warms me from toes to head at the sight of him and pause to savor the feeling that I'm only going to get for a short time.

After a not insignificant amount of time passes, I call his name before I get caught staring with no other excuse other than I'm really into him.

Beau looks up and then lifts me completely off the ground again in his welcome hug. And this time there's no Ajay to ruin the moment. He lowers me down, not removing his arms from around me. Which is fine because mine haven't left his shoulders either.

"What do you have in store for me tonight?" he asks.

"Something very low-key." Something both of our old selves need if we're falling asleep when we could be making the beast with two backs. "The Paley Center plays Christmas movies and Christmas episodes of shows like *The Rugrats*. It's great and there's hot chocolate."

"I wouldn't expect anything else."

We get the tickets that I was quick enough to pay for, earning a hard look from the man. He's going to have to be quicker than that if he wants to beat me.

"I'm getting the hot chocolate," Beau says with authority.

"Sure. You can even buy the second *and* third rounds." It's free. But he doesn't know that yet.

I settle into the theater while he gets the drinks, sinking into the plush chairs. A short time later, Beau finds me and hands me a drink. "You knew it was free, didn't you?" he whispers as he settles into his own chair.

"Oh yeah. Remember, I live here. Well, in this city. Not this particular theater."

I snuggle into his side, armrest already up, nudging his arm. He gets the hint and puts his arm around me, drawing me even closer while I take a sip.

We watch a *Fresh Prince* Christmas episode and I wonder exactly when he's leaving. The thought puts a damper on my Christmas spirit, the way it does every time I think about it. A funk that not even Christmas shows can get rid of.

Knowing he's leaving should be enough to brace myself for the loss, should even be freeing because I know the end is coming so I don't have to anticipate it, but it isn't really working out the way I planned.

We spend the rest of the night watching Christmas videos. And snuggling.

After a few hours, Beau taps my side and leans in to whisper, "Do you want to get some food?" His whisper tickles my ear and I scrunch my shoulder up to my ear before I break out laughing in the dark theater.

"Yeah. That sounds good."

We leave the theater and wander around midtown until we find a restaurant that looks good.

"How were your work meetings?" I sip on my water while we wait for our food.

"Really good. I'm getting a good team and a good location, so I should be about done with the setup. It might almost be time to go home."

Chapter Fifteen

I choke on the water a little but try to recover. "Oh. That's…good for you. How much longer do you think you'll be here?"

I wasn't going to ask, because it makes it real, but obsessing about it also isn't really healthy, so I should get a date. Since Beau brought it up anyway. That way I'll know when to plan a work trip to somewhere overseas and beautiful to check the collection of some too-rich collector.

"Next week probably. I didn't buy the return trip since I wanted to leave my options open, but the tentative plan right now is the end of next week."

Okay. Maybe there'll be some energy-related emergency and he can stay longer. New Year's in the city is fun too.

Well, not Times Square. That's just hours of standing in the cold with no bathrooms. Sure, I've done it once because I firmly want to try everything in this city once, but there's zero need to do that again.

"How about your work?" he asks.

Yes. A subject change so I can focus on something not related to the impending end of…whatever this is. "It's good. I'm enjoying helping you decorate your office. The rest is fine." Because Beau is like an overshare serum for me, I keep talking. "But my uncle keeps trying to get me to take on more supervision."

"Promotions are usually exciting. But you don't seem very happy about it. More of an Eeyore vibe, actually."

I give a small un-Eeyore-like laugh at the comparison. It fits, to be fair. "I guess. I like the work well enough, but I also enjoy not staying up late at night worrying about being a bad manager or messing up a sale. I like leaving that to Priya and having a healthy work-life balance." Even though working this job with Beau has made me work outside of business hours. The ideas keep coming and not leaving me alone, forcing me to open my work laptop at all hours. Is this what Priya's brain is like?

Because I could imagine doing more of this. If I can just convince everyone else it's a good idea.

"Actually, talking about work." I take a deep breath. Might as well go all in since I only have him for a bit before he disappears back to the farm. "Loot is having their annual Christmas party tomorrow, if you wanted to come? We invite some of our clients too, so it won't be just employees and their families."

"That sounds fun, I'd love to go. You are showing me an amazing Christmas."

"Are you ready to admit that Christmas in the city is the best Christmas?" Yes, no more talking about heavy topics.

"Nothing can ever beat Christmas in the country, but you're giving it an admirable try. There's no shame in silver."

"I've still got some time." New York isn't going to be second place, aka first loser. No thank you.

"One day you really will have to come to South Carolina and let me return this favor."

This is not the easy, unemotional banter I was hoping for. Instead, this makes for the second time he's mentioned me coming to his home, suggesting an extension of our Christmas fling.

Does he mean it or is it just something he says in the moment? Do I even want to go see this rural utopia he goes on about?

"I don't think I'd do well there." I joke off the suggestion, at least sure I don't want to have a deeper conversation about an actual future. "I mean, what would happen if I ran out of coconut water?"

"You could order some off Amazon."

"But could I get next-day shipping?"

"Patience is a virtue. You'll get it eventually. Or you can plan ahead."

"What happens if I get a craving to eat falafel at midnight? Can I get it?"

"Most doctors don't recommend eating that late, so you should drink some water, maybe some of that coconut variety if you'd like, until the feeling passes and you go to sleep. Or we can fry anything you want and you can eat that."

"What if I want to have cell reception?"

The ensuing silence means I might be winning this.

"Doctors also say we should disconnect more and enjoy the world around us. And there is good Wi-Fi in the house. So, you can be as connected as you want… close to the house."

The words are right, but his tone lacks any real conviction. I sense victory is almost in my grasp.

"If you can say a lack of cell service is good like you

believe it, then you win this entire argument and I say the country is better right now."

Beau looks physically pained and gives up quickly. "There are other benefits that make up for that lack."

"*Nothing* can make up for that."

"I should concede that one. Just the one point," Beau says quietly.

And he can admit when he's wrong? He really is a nice guy.

Since he's being so obliging, I don't rub it in. But he can see my smile, so he sends me a mini glare. We both soon forget the debate, enjoying the food placed in front of us. After the meal, we walk out of the restaurant, and I inch closer to Beau. Because I can't not be close to him.

"Do you want me to take you back to your place?" he asks.

"Yes, please." In for a penny, in for a pound. "And then you can stay too, if you want." And we're not turning on the TV this time.

"I'd like that." Beau nods once at me.

"Cool."

Beau orders the car after I give him my address without fighting. After what is probably a very reasonable (but simultaneously what feels like an epoch) amount of time later, the car gets here, and I practically throw myself into the back of the vehicle.

Beau, as impatient as I am, puts one arm around me and with the other he entwines our fingers together to rest on my thigh. I like knowing he wants to touch me as much as I want to touch and be touched by him.

We make it to my building without tearing each other's clothes off in the back seat of a stranger's car. For which

Beau better get five stars on his damn app. It was hard missing a night after the best sex of my life and knowing that the opportunities are limited in the first place.

The elevator doors open into my condo and I head straight to my stairs. Beau falls behind me, slowing down near the kitchen.

"Do you want a snack…something to drink?" Beau asks.

I march back to where he is. "Maybe later." I grab his hand and tug him along after me. He's smarter than your average bear, so he follows behind without complaint.

I don't want to give us a chance to fall asleep in a food/alcohol/TV coma.

"This is my bedroom." I lead him through my hallway to the door at the end, pushing it further open and turning to see his reaction.

He looks around, but I don't give him a chance to take in the purple damask wallpaper or the Regency dresser. Instead, I drop my purse and launch myself in the direction of his torso. He catches me, arms under my butt, hoisting me up closer to reach his mouth. I pass his erection on the way up, silently vowing to give the appendage more attention.

In a second.

We kiss, more urgent than the first time after our one-night abstinence. Hands tear at clothes and Beau sets me down when it's clear that him holding me won't get anyone actually naked. We keep kissing, becoming fully naked in the distance it takes for us to walk from the door to the bed.

Beau deftly navigates the small piles of purses, shoes, and books on my floor. I'm glad he still has some presence of mind, because falling and cracking a skull open would be a definite mood killer. But at the same time, how dare he have more mental capacity than me right now?

Am I more affected than he is?

But then I look down and see visual evidence that the man is indeed affected. Now naked, Beau lifts me up again, our bodies sliding against each other, creating a friction that makes me wetter with each movement.

I think we're going to the bed, but instead he changes course and walks away from it. I make a sound of confusion and lift my lips from his to ask what's going on, but before I can, he sets me on the same Regency dresser I wouldn't let him appreciate earlier.

It's the perfect height and I feel his hardness pressing up against my clit, sliding against the wetness it finds there. I rock my hips faster leaning back against the mirror, loving the way he feels rubbing against me.

And take a moment to wonder how many people have fucked on this dresser, now that I know it's the perfect height for the activity. Hazard of the industry to imagine the past lives of old items.

Beau drags me back to the present by growling low, a sound that I'm going to tell him isn't very polite when I remember how to talk, and pulls away, disappearing from view. I look up in confusion but then he reappears with his head between my thighs, and I close my eyes when his tongue touches my clit.

I writhe under his mouth, putting my heels on his shoulders as I sink down lower on the dresser, pressing me firmly against his mouth. His hot tongue swirls and caresses as I lose the ability to think clearly, becoming a being of sensation that's centered around my clit. Just when I think he's going to make me come, he pulls away. For the second time tonight.

I growl back in frustration but cut myself off when I see him grab a condom from his pocket and put it on quickly. I should really trust him and his disappearances more; they always end well for me. He stands back up and pauses to look at me sprawled on the dresser. He looks at me like an artist looking at a blank canvas, full of possibilities, contemplating where to put the first stroke.

I've got some ideas.

Ideas so strong they're making certain body parts arch up to get closer to him, so he can catch onto what those good ideas are.

He's not as indecisive as some of the artists we work with, because he grabs me by the sides of my face and kisses me. His lips stay where they are, tongue caressing mine while his hands travel two parallel paths down my body.

They lightly play with my nipples, before continuing the path and resting on my hips. They dig in, pulling me close to him as he slides the tip of his erection in, and then deeper. I gasp against his lips at the sudden fullness and wiggle my hips to accommodate the new addition.

He stops and lets me adjust before going in further. To help me along, he reaches down and starts playing with my clit, each stroke making me wetter and opening me up more to let him in deeper.

Once he's all the way in, he tears his lips from mine on a groan. His eyes are closed and he rests his forehead on mine, savoring the moment. I let him have the moment but get impatient when he doesn't move fast enough for me. I undulate my hips, deciding to get what I want even if he's going to be obstinate about it.

"More."

"Getting to it," he grunts back.

On a strangled groan, he starts thrusting into me, one hand gripping my hip while the other plays with my clit. I throw my head back in abandon, hoping I don't shatter the mirror, and brace my hands behind me, back arching to drive Beau even deeper into me.

My orgasm tears through me a short amount of time later, pushing Beau into his. I slump against the furniture and Beau collapses on top of me, his feet still on the ground and his body bent at almost a ninety-degree angle at the waist.

This can't be comfortable for him. It definitely isn't for me. But it's very hard to move.

I wiggle from my position under Beau, breathing heavily, trying to get around the mass of muscle to my bed. After a minute of my sad attempts to get free, getting slowly more crushed by the weight, Beau rouses enough to get off me.

I might be glad my bones aren't in danger of being crushed, but I do miss the feel of his skin on mine, and the scent of cinnamon that's a lot stronger when he's naked on top of me.

Before I have the opportunity to miss him too much, he slides one arm behind my back and the other under my knees. He lifts me off the dresser and walks me to the bed, depositing me on it and following me down. I pull the covers over us and push him to face the opposite direction so I can big spoon him for the night.

Because he's so obliging, he goes quietly.

Settled in for the night, I take a look at my side table

with no phone and sigh in relief that I don't have to set an alarm tonight since it's finally the weekend, because I don't know where I threw my purse and my phone before we started to have sex.

I hope in my apartment, but who knows.

Chapter Sixteen

"Sonia, are you awake?" Beau whispers into my ear.

"No." I hope that'll be enough to make the voice go away and let me sleep. At some point during the night, we changed positions, so I woke up the little spoon with Beau curled around me.

This position isn't bad either. And I'd like to get back to enjoying it, but the owner of the body has other ideas. And is being real vocal about it.

"You sound awake."

I bury my head deeper into the pillow. "I'm sleep talking. Now let me go back to putting emphasis on the sleep part of that sentence." My voice is muffled by the fabric.

"Are you sure?"

I sigh. I don't think I'm getting back to sleep. "Is this a farm thing? Do you always get up with the sun? There's no land to till or cows to milk here, I promise."

"Cute. I actually have a lunch meeting and I didn't want to leave without saying bye."

"Oh. Well. Bye." I raise my neck to get a kiss, eyes still closed. I get the kiss and then I feel a rush of cold to my back when Beau gets out of the bed. I bury my head back into my pillow and Beau pulls the covers back over me, tucking me back in. They still have some of his warmth, so it's a little bit of a consolation. But only a little.

"Are you still going to be able to make it tonight?" I mumble in the direction I think he's in, my eyes still closed.

"I wouldn't miss it." He drops another kiss on my lips and gets dressed in last night's clothes. I go back to sleep—what every sane person should be doing before eight a.m. on a Saturday.

I wake up to the sound of my elevator doors opening. I sit up in bed and eye the Tiffany lamp on my bedside table, prepared to weaponize it, history be damned, before I hear my cousin's voice.

"I hope there's no horizontal shenanigans going on. It would be super awkward to see my cousin naked and getting it on. I'd have to charge her for years of therapy. With the best, and probably most expensive, therapist in Manhattan," Priya yells as she stomps up my stairs.

"Leave the woman and her sex life alone, Riya. She deserves her privacy." My cousin-in-law's voice comes after in a more appropriate inside volume. And further away.

"You've only been married to an Indian woman for a short amount of time, or you'd realize how ridiculous you sound right now." Priya lectures her husband while continuing her march to harass me.

She sails in through my bedroom door, ignoring the fact that I am indeed naked in bed, albeit not having any shenanigans, horizontal *or* vertical. Or somewhere in between like last night on the dresser.

"I tried, Sonia." Gavin is right outside the door, but he has his hands over his eyes like a family member who understands boundaries. "I'll make some chai." He goes back down the stairs.

Priya rolls her eyes. "Mom just taught him how to make proper chai and he's proud of himself. He's been making me chai all week. Even more cups than *I* can reasonably drink in one day." Priya marches into my closet and throws some clothes at me. "Get dressed. We've got last minute seating chart details to go over."

"There are labor laws that prohibit you from invading my home on a Saturday."

Priya scoffs. "Hah! You're salaried. And you have no union, which you should get, immediately. Plus you're family. But I don't think they make unions for family." She holds up the spare key I gave her...*for emergencies.*

I curse the bad decisions that led me to this point but get dressed.

"Where's the peachperson?" Priya, lacking any attempt at subtlety, snoops through the room, including spots too small to hold a human person. Like in my underwear drawer.

"He's not here." Technically the truth.

"What? Noooo." She peeks in the bathroom; in case I would lie to her. Which I would. But I'm not this time.

"Because he had to leave earlier this morning to do some business things." Okay, so I don't let her suffer long.

"Yes!" Priya does a victory dance. Awkwardly. Because that's what happens when you spend too much time studying like a nerd and not enough time cutting loose in the club.

"He's also leaving next week."

"There are planes. Trains exist. Automobile if you're desperate and you have the time. Could put on an audiobook, get road trip snacks..."

Clothes on, I abandon the intensity behind me and go down the stairs, ignoring the fact that I deserve this after how I pushed her at Gavin.

"Here you go." Gavin puts a freshly brewed cup of chai in front of me as I sit down at the island in my kitchen.

"Bless you, favorite brother-in-law." I lift the cup to me to inhale deeply. It smells great. And like home. Or like Chachi's home.

"Do you have those Indian cookies with the baby who's been on the package for like fifty years? Priya's got me hooked."

"Parle-G. You know I do." I go to the pantry and get out some of the familiar packages.

"Ooh, Parle-G." Priya finally makes her way to the kitchen. "Hey, where's my chai?" Priya gives me a dirty look while I take a deep drink of my mug, then stick my tongue out at her.

"Right here." Gavin gives his wife a mug.

I take another sip. "Mm. Gavin, this is just like Chachi makes it." I lift my mug in his direction in congratulations and take another sip.

"He knows," Priya says. I can tell by her tone that they've had this debate before, to determine which of them can make the drink better. Over-competitive couple of the year over here.

"She's jealous." Gavin confirms my suspicions. "Anyway, I was just chauffeur and chai maker. I've got to meet a client for lunch. But I'll see you guys later. Have fun with the seating chart." He drops a kiss on Priya's lips, gives me a hug and puts the pot in the sink on his way out.

"What's the emergency anyway? I thought the event coordination department handled those details."

"Yeah. And then I saw they put exes together. And rivals. And you know how much I love drama. But not at my work events."

See, I would have just let them fight it out because I'm messy. Another reason I'm not management material.

Boxes of takeout food surround us and I can't see the seating chart that Priya brought anymore. Which is fine, since we got done with that task early and turned on Bravo for a marathon of reality TV, while ordering the delivery laid out in front of us now.

"We should get ready for this party soon," I say from a burrito coma on one side of my couch.

"Yeah. But now I don't think I'm going to fit in my dress," Priya says, getting another slice of pizza and compounding the issue.

"Amateur. Empire-waisted dresses."

"I know that Empire-waisted dresses exist. But I didn't realize I'd be going so hard on an international buffet the day of the event. Where we'll have amazing food catered from Mom's favorite Indian place."

I groan. "Are you going back home to change?"

"Nope. Brought my bag for an evening out." She uses the pizza to point at a garment bag and a duffel bag by my door that I hadn't noticed before now.

My intercom chimes and I'm about to say, "Not it," but Priya beats me to it.

"Fine. I'll get it then, shall I?" I get off the couch and stretch, feeling the TV marathon.

"It's your home," Priya yells at me as I walk to the box.

It's Beau and I buzz him in. A minute later, the elevator doors open and Beau slides in, wrapping an arm around me and kissing me before I can say hi or that Priya's here.

He probably gets the hint though since there's whistling and cheering going on from behind us.

Beau lifts his head without removing his arm and looks to see who the audience is. "Hi. Priya, right?"

He lets go of me and reaches out to shake her hand. She takes the hand and pulls him in for a hug. "Good to see you again, Beau." She throws a proud look at me over his shoulder, and I know she wants praise for not calling him a peachperson to his face.

She is not going to get praise for doing the bare minimum. And I hope my glare tells her that.

"I've always been so interested in cows," Priya begins and I glare at her even more, while Beau explains he has peach trees. Which she already knows. But this is her revenge.

Family.

Beau takes off his coat as Priya leads him to the couch and I take the moment to appreciate how nice he looks in a suit. I'm still surprised I haven't seen him in flannel or jeans, but maybe he left them all back at the orchard.

I'm not complaining. He wears suits well, the quality material cut to fit his frame perfectly, giving the suggestion he could hulk out of the clothes at any moment. It's also harder to remember we're different when he looks like he blends so well into my world.

"I'm sorry to be early and intrude. I wanted to make sure I didn't get stuck in any traffic."

"Or did you want to spend some time with Sonia? It's okay; we all know how awesome she is." Priya digs for intel, nosy as a suspicious matriarch on an Indian soap opera.

I knew we should have limited her access to TV when we were kids, but no one listened to me.

"Priya. Let's get ready so we aren't late." I snag her arm and drag her upstairs, almost knocking her off the couch in the process. Anything to get her away from Beau and to stop the embarrassment.

"Don't worry, I'll be back." Priya says it in the style of the Terminator, and I roll my eyes.

Does Beau hear the threat in her voice? "Feel free to watch whatever and make yourself a drink or help yourself to any food," I yell back at him while I drag her further up the steps.

"Payback," Priya crows at me when we get into my master bedroom. I quickly shut the door so Beau can't hear.

"I was never this obnoxious. At least not to Gavin's face! Boundaries, woman!"

"If he can't take the heat, he will *not* last in this family."

That makes me anxious. Because I'm not doing forever. Unless it's a commitment to watching Hallmark Christmas movies all year long, for forever. That, I can do.

"We haven't even discussed if he wants to be in this family, or if I want him to. *I* don't particularly want to be in this family right now, if I'm being perfectly honest," I whisper to her.

"Lies." Priya starts rifling through my makcup boxes. "You know you dragged me out here without any of my stuff to get ready?"

I throw out my hands to stop her from walking to the door. "I'll get it. You stay here. Please don't think of new ways to embarrass me." I wait a second to see if she's going to comply. She starts putting on some makeup, so I'm as optimistic as I can be about my chances.

I run down the stairs, not sure how long I have before she gets bored and comes downstairs to wreak havoc.

Then I remember she doesn't have a lot of patience where makeup is concerned so I run a little faster.

Chapter Seventeen

"Hey, Baby Girl." Beau greets me from the couch, waving my own remote at me.

"Hi, Old MacDonald." I grab the duffel bags and then retrace my steps back to the couch, leaning over the back and kissing him. "Sorry about the hectic day." I really did want to spend a nice, peaceful day with him. But my family is getting in the way of that.

"It's cool. I found *Reno 911* so I'm happy."

"Sonia, where's your curler?" Priya asks from the bedroom.

"I better go, or she'll come down again and harass you."

"I don't mind. She's nothing compared to the gold medalist in annoying that is my little sister."

I nod along, letting him have his delusion since I'm abandoning him in my living room. No one is more annoying than Priya. Except Ajay. And they're twins, so they get exponentially worse when they join forces. "Still. I better go entertain her." But I don't want to leave him.

"I'll see you in a bit." Beau presses play on the show and I watch him for a second before heading back up to my cousin.

I might have gotten freaked out when Priya talked

about Beau joining the family, but I do like seeing him on my couch. The contradiction doesn't help me sort out the jumbled mess of my feelings at all. So instead, I take a detour to the kitchen and get an entire pitcher of spiked eggnog and some glasses.

This night calls for reinforcements.

The spiked eggnog does its job better than I thought it would, the liquid helping me get ready with Priya despite her teasing and also distracting her enough so I only get a fraction of her typical intensity.

Cocktail dresses on and faces done up with more effort than we both usually put in, we walk downstairs. At some point when we were getting ready, Gavin got here and made himself comfortable on the couch with Beau.

They're still watching *Reno 911*, a lot further in the season than Beau was before. Gavin made some more chai and found my liquor stash as well as more snacks and now they're both lounging while they watch, a mountain of snack wrappers and glasses forming on my coffee table. And the men look like they're getting along just fine.

Beau looks at me when I walk into view, eyes staying on me and not going back to the TV. "Wow. You look amazing." He stands when I get to the couch.

"Thank you." I do a twirl in my dark emerald tealength dress. It's fitted over my curves and has a shining floral motif on it that glitters every time the light catches it. The main thing that attracted me to it in the store, like a fish drawn to shiny objects.

Priya hits Gavin on his shoulder. He responds while rubbing the appendage. "Ow. I already told you that you look amazing in that dress when you tried it on last night. And the four others you tried. And when you finally got out of them, I told you that you looked even better." Gavin finally turns away from the TV to wag his eyebrows at my cousin, making me feel like a voyeur.

"Let's go, guys. We can't be late for our own party." I move them along before they fornicate on my couch. I know what they got up to in other people's homes when they were dating, and well, I'm not leaving them alone in my castle anytime soon.

Beau helps me with my coat and rushes to get my elevator door. He does the same with the door to exit the building, and then the door to the car.

"First I thought he was being polite, but does he legitimately not think you can open a door by yourself?" Priya whispers to me from the back of the Loot SUV she called for the night.

"I don't know. I think he's just being nice. Like a gentleman thing, maybe?" I respond, at an even lower volume. I hope he thinks I can open the door by myself. I've also been known to own my own property and even vote.

No. I'm going to think positive—this is politeness.

We catch the omnipresent city traffic, giving all us couples longer to make eyes at each other during the stop-and-start ride. I never thought I would be in a similar position as my besotted cousin, but I catch myself smiling at Beau in the reflection of the car window behind him and I can't deny that I look exactly like Priya.

Except we aren't some old married couple. There's an expiration date on this…relationship-lite thing we have going.

The car stops in front of the venue, the Angel Orensanz Center in the Lower East Side, before anyone jumps their partner.

But just barely.

Instead of thinking of Beau, I focus on our breathtaking venue. The building was originally built as a synagogue, but now it's an event space. Inside, the beautiful, blue-lit ceiling soars above our party decorations, with intricate Gothic arches carved into the far wall. A row of thick columns supports a balcony running on each side, and minimalist chandeliers light the space. It's one of my favorite event rentals in a city filled with an embarrassment of riches when it comes to beautiful architecture, and we've held some of our most popular parties and sales here.

Tonight, it's dressed in an anonymous "classy winter evening" theme, but if anyone had asked me, I would have told them it could have used some actual Christmas decorations. Christmas trees dressed in colorful ornaments. Santas. Rudolph and the others. Frosty and his snowman family.

But alas, no one asked me.

We're the first ones to arrive, Priya making us get here early in case of emergencies. I find our table and set our jackets on the chairs, the warm room making them unnecessary. And then we leave the guys at the table.

"If you steal *any* of my clients tonight, you can't come to any more company events and I get to choose what we watch for the next month. And the first thing I'm going to choose is that British television show that you can barely understand, where clergy members solve crime in a quaint English village with an improbably high murder rate," Priya warns the love of her life.

Really, they're a couple we can all aspire to be.

For the next half hour I run around after Priya, not so much to help her, but mostly to talk her down from her annoying perfectionism and give out extra tips when she leaves people in a daze in her wake. When the first guest arrives, I assume that I'm off the clock and join Beau at the table.

"I'm already exhausted." I slump into the empty seat next to Beau, the soft murmur of the slowly growing crowd hiding my criticism.

Beau pauses in the act of stuffing his face with samosa. "No one's even here yet."

I give him a dirty look and lean in to take a giant bite out of the delicious fried dough he's eating. I moan when the life-giving sustenance hits my tongue and mount a large-scale theft from his plate to rival Lord Elgin's campaign on the Parthenon.

He gives no resistance to my plan, pushing the plate closer to me.

Good man.

"Has my wife already sold all the items on your online sales?" Gavin asks.

Priya's laughing with a group of buyers who just walked in and I think that might be a distinct possibility.

"She's very good at her job." I'm loyal behind her back even though I'm the first to sass her to her face.

"I know." An affectionate look is on his face as he looks over at Priya.

Beau slides his drink over and I take it with zero guilt. It's an open bar anyway.

"Hi, beta." A voice comes from over my shoulder and then my face is surrounded by the glittering sequins of a bright pink sari as Chachi hugs me from behind. The weight attempts to crush me and I'm impressed, as always, by how strong she must be for all the times she wears the heavily beaded, beautiful garments.

To say nothing of how much her suitcase weighs when she gets back from her India trips. With shopping being the most important event on her itinerary, followed by a distant second of visiting family.

"Hi, Chachi." My voice is still muffled in the hug.

"Have you eaten?" she asks.

"Yup." I hold up the pilfered plate, silent about its origins.

"Hi, Gavin. Did you eat?"

"On it, Mom." He holds up his own plate as evidence.

She nods before moving on to the third person at the table and the only one she doesn't know. "Hello. Are you a friend of Gavin's?"

"He's certainly nice." Beau looks at me, eyes crying for help in the face of the Indian Inquisition. In reality, he's probably just being considerate Beau, checking in what I want to tell everyone about our...whatever.

"He's here with me." I decide to go with honesty, even though both men look ready to back up whatever I want to say.

She turns those sharp eyes at me and my back snaps straight. Maybe I wasn't ready to tell her about this, or to deal with the fallout.

"Really?" One word. Six letters. But so much *tone*. Entire novels say less than Rani Gupta just did with that one word. I'm reminded that this is the woman who runs three charities and owns one company that she deigns to allow her husband to run.

But maybe I can only tell half of the story and she won't notice. I was mostly raised by this woman.

"This is our client, Beau Abbot. He's visiting New York and needs help buying art. Beau, this is Rani Gupta." There. She can't harass a client.

"Hmm. And what else?" She can, it turns out, harass a client when it means also harassing family. And again, all that with only a few words.

"And… I've been showing him around the city, because New Yorkers are a very kind, nurturing, helpful people."

Gavin chortles but I refuse to look at him, maintaining my innocent, kind, nurturing, helpful New York smile.

Comprehension dawns on her face, changing her entire demeanor from cold, hardened investigator to warm maternal figure, mentally planning a wedding. "Is this the man?" She points at him like he isn't sitting at this table.

I blame Priya for this. She should have never mentioned anything, like I was kind enough to do for her.

"This is *a* man." I frantically look around for inspiration, everywhere but at Beau, and get help from an unexpected corner.

"Mom, I think Poppa Gupta is trying to fight Poppa Carlyle." Gavin points away from Beau and Chachi's gaze follows his finger across the room.

"I don't see them. Or hear them." She dismisses her son-in-law.

She's about to turn back to Beau but Gavin interrupts again. "They're definitely over there. It looks heated."

"Oh, for crying out loud…" Chachi leaves the table to mitigate whatever disaster is happening across the room.

"Thank you," I breathe out in relief to Gavin, internally adding onto his Christmas present, doubling—no, tripling—it, for his help. "Are they really fighting?" I ask Gavin.

"They will be soon enough. Just because they're

merging doesn't mean they can give up their natural need to be in charge. If they are, she can handle them, and if they aren't, she can defuse the situation before you lose the deposit because of all the bloodstains," Gavin says.

"Can I get you something? A drink? My kidney maybe?" I better start on the repayment.

He shakes his head and smiles at me. "We're family. And now I've got to see what Priya's doing, or she'll accuse me of stealing clients."

"If you need a reference, I'll vouch for you." He's won my sword for life over his actions.

"I'm sure it'll be needed." He nods at Beau. "See you later. Find me if you need some intel on hanging around this family."

He leaves and I turn to the person I've been avoiding since Chachi got here. "So. That's my aunt," I say, unnecessarily.

"Is Chachi her nickname?"

"No, it's Hindi for your dad's younger brother's wife."

"That is very specific."

"Yeah. Everyone in the immediate family gets a very specific title. And then everyone else like family friends or more distant relations are called 'Auntie' and 'Uncle' more generally."

Beau nods, taking in the information. "I guess she's heard of me." He smiles.

I do not want to have this conversation. I wish that the dads would go for a good distracting fistfight right now. Their tempers have been simmering for weeks over the joint show; they must be ready to boil over.

But of course, they can't make my life easier at any time. They're so contrary they can't even be contrary when I want them to.

"Priya...is the worst." I begin and then immediately stall. For a lack of knowing what to say.

Beau looks at me and opens his mouth like he's going to follow up on my nonresponse. But then I'm saved, because before he can ask me anything, he sits up straight and pulls a vibrating phone from his pocket. "Oh, I should take this. I'm sorry; I'll be right back."

"Take your time." I watch him walk to find a quiet corner of the room, bringing the phone to his ear.

While Beau's gone, I decide I might as well have some drinks and snacks on hand when he gets back, since I've been stealing his all night. I stop on the way to the bar to talk to some clients, testing my memory to ask them about their lives. It's draining and after three of them, I need that drink myself.

I don't know how Priya does this for entire parties.

I take the booty back to the table, looking around to see where Beau is. I don't see him, but I do see Gavin and Priya. Anyone who knows her knows what she's doing: working the client in front of her with charm and grace and a tenacity that would rival a bulldog's. Gavin lets her shine while he basks in her energy, looking so proud, and not trying to outdo her.

For all the sass I give them, they are a great example of a healthy, functional relationship. But that still doesn't make the idea of a relationship any less scary, if the tightening in my chest is any indication.

I munch on some of the food I got for Beau. If he really wants some, I'm going to need him to be around. Otherwise, I can't control what happens.

I'm halfway through some Tandoori chicken when I feel a tap on my shoulder, choking a little on the chicken as it goes down the wrong pipe.

"Oh shit, Sonia. I'm sorry, I didn't mean to scare you." Beau grabs my glass on the table and pushes it toward me. I shake my head and keep coughing. That's whiskey…it won't help if I drink it. Beau runs to get me some water. Finally, the coughing subsides.

"I'm so sorry," Beau says again when he comes back, water in hand.

Two sorrys in a row. And I don't think this one is about me choking.

"I have to leave New York."

Chapter Eighteen

My heart pounds with the news. A wave of panic crashes over my body, until I'm drowning in the sensation, taking deeper breaths to get any air in my lungs.

"I… I thought you had till the end of the week? Is everything okay?" I force out. There's a slight shake in my voice I can't hide, no matter how much I try.

Which is absurd. Because I don't even want him in sickness and health, through richer or poorer. Through arguments about north and south.

I just want him for another week. I don't think that's too much to ask.

He rushes to reassure me. "Everyone's fine, but we have a problem with the mulch vendor."

I have no response to that, never having had a mulch problem before.

Beau takes the silence as an invitation to talk more about it. "If we don't get the right mulch with the perfect amount of nutrients at the exact right times, we'll have a late growth spurt or rodents or not enough weed protection. Peaches are fickle."

"Apparently. And you have to go in person to deal with the…mulch problem?"

"Yes. Daniel is at a fruit tree conference out of state

and Mom's business has its own busy period. Dad tried to talk to them, but he's busy with other work and I'm the one who built a relationship with this vendor. They're not answering his calls and Dad wants me to take care of this in person, fast, before we don't have a crop next year." He looks genuinely disappointed, which is a small bandage on a gaping wound.

But better than nothing, I suppose.

"Since I'm mostly done with my meetings anyway, I'm heading back and I'll do everything else remotely. Even buying art."

"Maybe you can come back later, to finish up?" I ask lightly and before I can think about it too closely. Because past me would have opinions about present me making future plans.

"Yeah. I'll be back at some point. I can't say when."

"The real world calls." I stand up, collecting myself and even attempting a small smile. "I'm glad you were able to see the best city at the best time of year. And hopefully you'll acknowledge that it is the best Christmas."

There. He hasn't destroyed me with the news. I'm still standing and still me, advocating for the best city in the world. Even if I was the sort to be in relationships, depth of feeling can't happen this quickly. I'm safe.

"It was a lot of fun. More fun than I've had in a really long time, even if it was in a city. Actually, a surprising amount of fun. And I think that was because of you." He slides his arms around me, pulling me closer to the upper body that he got bench-pressing peach trees he ripped from the ground with his bare hands, probably.

"I know this is a long shot, since you have a lot of work to do around the holidays. But I want to extend the invitation for you to come down my way with me and see a

Southern Christmas. And not only in thanks for showing me around, but because I want to spend more time
with you."

The yes is halfway up my throat before I realize it.
But traveling down the country, spending the holiday
with him, leaving work, *and* meeting his family? That's
a lot. More than I've ever done in the past with anyone
else. And too far from casual.

I'm frozen between wanting to grab the invitation
and guard it in my treasure room like a dragon and
wanting to put it in a bottle and throw it in the ocean to
get it away from me, sure that he'll leave at some point.
When I least expect it, when I'm most invested in him,
to cause the most damage.

And if it's already this hard at the thought of him
leaving, I can't imagine what another week would do.
Or another after that.

He sees my indecision and rushes to head off the awkward moment. "That's a lot to throw at you all at once.
No need to make a decision now. I'm going to book a
flight for later tomorrow, and if you want to come, I'll
book one for you. And whatever return flight you want."

"I—I—I—" am becoming incapable of forming sen-
tences out loud. Or maybe I just have no idea what I'm
going to say.

Beau interrupts my loop, which definitely wasn't
going anywhere anyway. "Really, no pressure for an
answer. And if you decide to come after I've left, give
me a call and I can book you a ticket then." He looks
regretfully at his phone again. "But I should get back to
the hotel to plan and pack."

"I have to stay. At this work party." I regret the decision as soon as I verbalize it. I could have had at least

one more night with Beau, but the fear won out. Fear that if I went I'd buy the damn ticket myself and be on a plane in twenty-four hours.

Getting in deeper with every second.

"I understand. It's a lot to ask." But he's got a slight frown tugging at his lips. Maybe he's just as sad as me that he has to leave.

He looks around and his eyes linger on Chachi, who's looking in the opposite direction. He drops a quick, and unsatisfying, kiss on my lips and then just as abruptly steps back from me. "Bye, Sonia."

"Bye," I whisper.

He turns and walks away, not looking back. I try to stop looking when he gets to the table next to ours. And then I tell myself it's just sad to keep watching when he gets to the front door. None of that works, but I try one more time to tell myself how pathetic it is to keep looking in his direction when he's not even in sight anymore.

That's not working, so I try a different approach. I tell myself it'll be a lot better for my emotional health to stop staring at the spot where he left like I can conjure him with the force of my mind, but that doesn't work at one minute, two minutes or five. Or ten.

Help comes from an unexpected corner. Chacha comes to sit next to me, breaking my gaze from the blank space. "Hi, Sonia."

"Hi, Chacha. It's a good party."

"Thanks to you and Priya." Chacha raises his glass at me. "I just spoke with Beau outside. He said he was leaving but he thanked us for the help decorating his office. He said you gave him one-on-one help, and he wouldn't have been able to decorate even one room without you."

Right. I didn't tell anyone I was doing this. My mind

is still scrambled by Beau leaving, but Chacha is expecting an answer, his eyebrow raised in inquiry.

"He was a reluctant buyer who didn't have much knowledge about art. So I helped him. And he bought pieces from us."

"But how much time did you spend on him? And you went to other dealers?"

"We got a commission from them."

"This isn't what we do. We run too many shows to devote that much time to one client."

"It's a gamble, but it will be worth it." Definitely for me, because I've had fun doing it. But I think for Loot too, from what the preliminary numbers are saying.

Chacha shakes his head. "We don't have the resources. Not when we're trying to break into other areas of art." He guilts me by reminding me he only just agreed to let Priya do what she wants. And I don't want to ruin that for her.

"Fine. I won't do it again."

"Good." Chacha pats my knee. "You won't have time for it anyway, with your new position."

The one that I'm trying to avoid. But Chacha leaves before I can respond, the second man to cause strife in my life in the past half hour and then abandon me at this table. I stare blankly at the table, not having the emotional capacity to deal with either man or their news right now.

After an indeterminate amount of time, Priya sits down next to me. My eyes fly to her face instinctively, breaking my staring contest with the tablecloth. The eyes staring back at me are open wide in question. When the eyes don't get a response, the mouth joins in.

"Are you okay? What happened? You look like Gavin

stole your client from under you. Wait, did he? Do you want me to take him out?"

The question gets a laugh from me. However small it is. Because no matter how much Priya loves Gavin, she would definitely give him an earful if she thought he was interfering in Loot. I don't know how their dynamic is going to change when the auction houses finally complete the merger, but I would put money on them still arguing over who brings in the biggest sales numbers.

And this is the healthiest relationship in my life. No wonder there's no hope for me.

"No. It's not Gavin. It's Beau." I gesture to the entrance, which is, more importantly, also an exit, sobering with the move. "And Chacha."

"What happened?" Priya kneels carefully in front of me to take my hands. I start to tear up as it hits me that he's gone, and I raise my head in an attempt to keep the tears inside my eyes. No one else needs to know that I'm affected, thank you very much.

Priya, showing that brutal efficiency that makes her the best in the business, stands and drags me through the curious crowd, dodging all questions, comments, and columns in our way. Before I know what's happening, I'm in a quiet office off to the side of the event space.

In record time, Priya has me in a chair with a glass of wine in one hand and a samosa in the other. "Now tell me what's happened?" she asks as she closes the door, muting the revelry and music from the party.

"He's gone. Which he was always going to do anyway. So I don't even know why I care? It's just cut a few days out of the time we had together. And he asked me if I wanted to come with him but how would that even work?

Is it bring your own horse, or will one be provided? And can I opt out of horse-related activities?"

Priya lets me ramble it out, nodding along even though I know I'm getting more absurd with each point.

"You make many good, many horse-related points," she says. "But are you sure you want to turn down his offer?"

"I don't know," I wail, now glad that there's a loud party happening behind the door. A hiding in plain sight kind of thing. "And it's too late anyway."

"Well, it's never too late. Unless you wait twenty years. Then it may be too late. But I saw Beau at the beginning of this party, so I think we're in the window. It just depends on what you want. He lives far from your home, so that's something to consider. But you seem really cut up with him gone." She shakes her head. "You have to do what feels right for you."

"I don't know what that is."

I can't unlearn how it felt to watch my parents' plane fly away from me again and again. And then after airports stopped letting visitors go all the way to the gates, I only got to watch them walk away slowly, and then stand in a long, anticlimactic security line. Watch them creepily from the distance as they took their shoes off.

Why would I sign up to let someone else do that to me? But the heavy stone in my stomach contradicts me, making me think that it's already happened. That I already care for Beau. And I just had to watch him walk away from me. Despite not being at an airport, all the same emotions came rushing to the forefront.

"And Chacha offered me a new department. But that's just more people who can disappoint me and who I can disappoint. I don't want the responsibility."

"Oof. Poor timing."

"And he told me I couldn't do the interior decorating I was doing with Beau."

"What interior decorating thing? Is this something you want to do?" Priya shifts to work at lightning speed.

"It doesn't matter. There aren't enough resources."

"Now hold up on that—"

"I need to leave." I stand up, interrupting. I don't want to talk about work now.

Priya follows suit. "Alright. I'll just tell Mom we're leaving, and we can go to your place or mine. Or an ice cream shop, or a pizza place. Or both. We can even go to the less good cheesecake place you like best. Whatever you want."

I'm already shaking my head at her. "Stay. You love this and someone has to keep an eye on Gavin." I raise my eyebrows, trying to give her a meaningful look. With the tears it probably looks sad, but I tried.

"I'm not leaving you alone right now." The only thing that could stop her from being obsessed with work is her deep loyalty to the family she loves.

I give Priya a hug to distract from her from doing her amazing cousin duty. "I was thinking of checking in on the show at the office while no one's there. See if I can think of anything else to say during the sale to make a bidding frenzy."

Priya crosses her arms and looks at me…*incredulously*.

"Okay, that look is offensive. I am dedicated to my job." Good. Anger and affront I can deal with.

"And you're very good at it. But you're not go-to-the-office-at-nine-p.m.-on-a-weekend dedicated to it. That's a Priya move." She points to herself.

"I could be that dedicated." I'm defensive, but I know

she's right. If this hadn't happened with Beau, I would not be going to work in the evening.

"If you believe that, I'm not going to contradict you because I am a great cousin."

Priya calls me a car and waits with me in our side room until it gets here. I give her another hug, because she is a pretty great cousin even if I refuse to acknowledge it out loud.

It'll just make her arrogant. *More* arrogant.

The driver isn't chatty, but he does have Christmas music on. In a new experience, I get choked up to "All I Want for Christmas Is You." And "Rudolph the Red-Nosed Reindeer," damn it. All now associated with Christmas adventures with Beau. And any thought of Beau makes me want to retreat into a blanket fort.

When I get to the office, I flash my badge to the nighttime security guard, hoping he can't see my puffy eyes, and push the button for the elevator.

While it comes, I desperately try to get Beau's face out of my mind. Instead, I see him on all the "dates" we went on. And with each event getting too used to seeing him at the end of my day.

Who gets that used to another human in such a short amount of time? Did he put a spell on me? This can't be normal.

No, this entire situation is good for me. If he had left at the end of the week, I would have double the amount of days' worth of sad about him leaving. I can barely handle this. But could it even get worse?

I open the notes app on my phone so I don't have to go to my desk to get actual paper, and go directly to the empty exhibition space. It's eerie to wander through the same halls that are usually bustling with activity, like wandering through an abandoned post-apocalyptic museum space. Lights on sensors turn on when I walk by, but the rest of the space is shrouded in darkness.

That's fine, my mood right now would rather sit in the dark than have the lights shining on me, spotlighting my unhappiness. Plus, I don't think my mascara is doing me any favors, running down my face, like if Niagara Falls got dyed black and then dried up.

In the exhibition space, I aimlessly wander the lots. I make a couple of observations that Priya should know about, but then I run into the spot where I first overheard Beau being a jerk about art. I smile at the memory, but I can feel the smile is a lot dimmer than it's been this past week.

I stop in front of the Fragonard couple again. It seems like ages ago when I looked at them last, so confident that I would never want what they had.

Damn it, I do want a little of that now.

Not forever, of course. But why can't I have a little more time with Beau? Just through the end of the holiday season. It already hurts right now. And it hasn't gotten any better yet.

So why not enjoy a little more? What could be the worst thing that could happen?

Chapter Nineteen

I'm going home with Beau.

And it gives me time to get away from work, from a promotion I don't want and getting told I'm not going to add interior decorating to my job duties.

Revelations made, I toss a cheeky salute to the clandestine figures in the painting, already feeling lighter in the stomach vicinity. Then I get out my phone and see the time. I need to get moving. It would be a giant buzzkill if I've had the biggest epiphany of my life and Beau is asleep, phone on silent. And then I have to sit on it until he wakes up.

I'm doing it. I'm going country. I text Priya to put the decision out there in the world so I can't take it back. Well, I can, but Priya will be a butt about it if I do.

Yay! Don't get hay in unmentionable places. It's probably itchy. Typical Priya. I'll have your work covered for the next however long you need.

I'm not sure I deserve this amazing (and sometimes annoying) cousin, but I've got her and I'm keeping her.

Business taken care of, I start the walk to the Plaza. I compose and throw away a few speeches for Beau, then decide it'll be better if it's spontaneous.

Then I remember what happened when I went to an

improv class with a colleague for her birthday. It involved me getting nervous and tripping on the stage, busting open my nose surrounded by demented sociopaths who kept saying, "Yes. And?"

And? And someone needed to call me an ambulance. I was bleeding!

I start brainstorming again.

I enter the Plaza, so busy practicing the speech to myself that I don't see where I'm going. That's my excuse. When I crash right into a loitering concierge, I have no idea what his excuse is.

The man grunts as my phone and hand make contact with his midsection.

"Oh, sorry." I take a step to the side to get to the elevators. The man steps in front of me, blocking my path.

"Is there something I can help with?" he asks.

"No. I'm good." I try to step around him again, this time in the opposite direction.

The man moves with me again. "Are you staying here?"

"No. I'm meeting a friend." I'm trying to have a romantic moment here, dude. What's your damage?

I try to remember I've probably got terrifying traces of mascara on my face, along with red eyes despite how much I tried to clean up on the walk, and I'm racing through the lobby without watching where I'm going, late at night. So I may not be presenting my best foot forward right now. But he's ruining my moment.

This is not how TV told me this would go. Even if my romantic declaration is only a temporary romantic declaration, I still deserve to make it with all due haste. And with none of this obstruction.

"Only hotel guests can go up the elevators."

I take one more step to the opposite side, my shadow

getting quicker to block me as he realizes I'm not giving up. "I'm meeting a hotel guest. He invited me." I turned him down at first, sure. But this fool doesn't know that. And I don't particularly want to tell him. But it does make me wonder how bad my face looks. I tried to wipe at it with my jacket sleeve, but I didn't bother stopping to see what I looked like in a mirror between my realization and now. There was no time.

Maybe I should have taken the time.

"I can't let you up there."

"Excuse me? Do you have the secret to turning lead into gold up there? I was invited." I'm getting a little mad now. And a lot frustrated.

"Hotel guests only." My shadow decides if I can get away with repeating myself, so can he.

"Fine. I'll just call him and then you can tell your guest that he's not allowed to have guests." I dial Beau's number and hope his phone's not on silent or he's not asleep.

Just before the call goes to voice mail, the ringing stops and the line goes silent. Then, "Baby Girl?"

Thank god he doesn't keep his phone on silent like me and that he answered after my earlier rejection. But his voice is so rough, I think I did just wake him up. That roughness does things to me, sounding like the same low tone he uses in bed (and in elevators). But I tell my bits to stuff it; we're on a mission before they can get any attention.

"Hi, Old MacDonald."

"What's up?" There's hope in his voice, which sounds stronger with each sentence.

"Oh. You know. Just wanted to get your opinion on whether it's okay to wear a denim jacket with jeans and a denim shirt."

He rumbles a laugh, and I contemplate kicking the man in the shin for stopping me from seeing the laugh I earned.

"It's always okay to wear a Canadian tuxedo, especially if all that denim is skintight."

The laugh from my joke fades when I hear the hunger in his voice. I swallow. "I'm here." No more delaying.

Some sheets rustle in the background and I think Beau's sitting up. I have his attention. "At the hotel, here?"

"Yes."

"Well, come on up. Do you remember the room number?" The bed springs squeak as he gets out of the bed.

"I'm trying. But there's a man down here who's protecting your virtue or maybe all the hay you put in your safe and he won't let me up." Maybe I have one more joke in me.

"I'm coming down. Don't leave," he says sternly.

"Leave? I'm trying to get up there." I'm talking to silence, and when I look at the screen, I see a picture of the Rockefeller Christmas tree staring back at me.

I cross my arms and toss a superior look at the man cutting into the limited time I've got left with Beau. As soon as I hang up, the man tries to steer me to the door. I evade him and Beau comes down as we pantomime a bullfight. Where I'm the bull and without all the horrific animal abuse.

I stop when I see him, relieved that he's here before the overly eager hotel employee could call the cops and this got significantly less funny. And then on the heels of the relief, happiness grows inside me, sweeping away all the sadness I was feeling since he left earlier. An hour ago, I thought I'd never see him again and I was surprised by how much that affected me. But here he is, shirtless under a half-zipped jacket on top of sweatpants.

He comes directly to me, ignoring the concierge doing a *Benny Hill* skit in the lobby. He wraps his hands around each side of my neck and his thumbs stroke my cheek, making me forget how hard it was to get to him, and what my face must look like. He begins to lower his mouth when we get interrupted by my most recent mortal enemy.

This concierge can now join Heather Wilson from fourth grade on my list of horrible people whose misfortune would make me smile. Heather got on the list for making fun of me by asking "What's that?" and pointing to my newly formed boobs. Boobs that came before everyone else's and were a sideshow until everyone else started developing, significantly later.

Enjoy the terrible company, random man. I turn and give him a glare, so he knows exactly how I feel about him.

The throat clearing makes Beau also lift his head and turn it to the hotel employee. "What's the problem here?" I'm glad his cold voice isn't directed at me.

"Only hotel guests can use the elevators." The man is a lot less confident now that Beau's here.

"Well, I'm here now." He flashes his key card in front of the man and turns me to the elevators. "And she's coming up with me."

Beau drags me past the now apologizing employee. I'm taking a lot of petty glee that he's standing there sputtering while I go upstairs.

Confirming that elevators *do something* for the man, his hands wander up and down my back, caressing over my curves fast. Desperately. A physical indicator that maybe he was just as upset by the idea that we wouldn't be seeing each other anymore.

It's a nice ego boost.

"You're coming home with me?" Beau asks, wandering arms pulling me in close so he can whisper.

"Yes."

"What made you change your mind?"

I pause, worried that if I say the words out loud, they'll make me sound desperate.

Sure, I am. But he doesn't need to *know* that.

"When's the flight?" I hold my breath while I wait to see if he's going to press the issue or let me have as long as I need to lie to him and myself that everything is still casual. Besides the mounting evidence to the contrary.

His eyes narrow slightly, the only sign that he knows what I'm doing. "Not till the afternoon."

I let out the breath I was holding when I realize he's going to be a gentleman about it.

"So, we have time." I extend my neck up to offer my lips for a kiss.

"Plenty of time." Beau keeps steady eye contact while he makes the promise. I must be reading too much into it, but I think he's talking about more than just the holidays. But he can't be, since we all know this is ending.

I close the remaining distance for a kiss, ignoring my reaction to what Beau might be offering.

Maybe elevators do something for me, too.

I wake up before Beau does, snuggling deeper into him to hide from the day and reality. Beau, not wanting to cooperate in Mission: Avoidance, stirs and drops a kiss on the top of my head, then immediately shifts to give me another one on my lips.

"Mornin', Baby Girl."

"Morning, Old MacDonald."

He quirks his lips. "You ready for the farm?" His voice is still rough from sleep and his eyes are fighting to stay awake. I wish he'd give in and we could go back to enjoying a quiet cuddle.

"No." Straight to the point. I'm not that good an actress, even if I wanted to lie.

Beau barks out a laugh, eyes wide open now. He gives me a squeeze with the arms already around me. "I'm here to protect you."

"From what? Rogue cow poo? Roosters being loud at unholy hours? *Bugs*?"

"From whatever it is that makes your face look like that whenever I mention the farm. And we don't have cows, but we do have some horses."

"Rogue horse poo, then. Get ready to put your jacket down whenever I might step on it."

"I don't have that many jackets. I'll just warn you if I see it."

Well, surprisingly ungentlemanly when it comes to excrement. I sniff. "Guess we've found the upper limits of chivalry." I grab my phone to look at the time. "I better go back to my place and pack for this adventure." I can't help the involuntary wince as I describe the upcoming trip as an adventure.

Beau ignores the wince, bringing back the Southern gentleman, and gets out of bed to dress. I stretch while I watch those hay-bale-lifting muscles shift and flex to accomplish the task.

"I thought you wanted to get your stuff?" Beau asks as he (subtly, and therefore politely) leers at me, topless since the covers fell down when I sat up.

"All right." I throw the covers off and the leering gets a lot less subtle. I throw a challenging look over my shoulder as I put my clothes from last night back on, but he doesn't take the bait.

Damn manners.

At the airport, I push my suitcase through the check-in area, wondering if anything in the wheeled suitcase is appropriate. I have no idea what one wears to a func- tioning farm, but I brought a bunch of denim and some flannel button-down shirts, which should cover me. I also have no idea how serious he is about the animal ex- crement, so I packed my oldest pair of boots.

Just in case.

The travel is smooth and pleasant. When I travel for work, mostly it's just me. It's nice to have someone who can watch my stuff when I go to the bathroom or get a snack and who lets me use his carry-on allowance to get more luggage on for free. Even my stone-cold heart can admit having a person around can be good in these situations.

And the constant touches and pets aren't bad at all.

Waiting to check in, waiting in the security line, wait- ing to board, midflight, post-flight waiting while every- one stands up to rush the tiny aisle, doing it again for the connecting flight and post-flight waiting for our suit- cases at baggage claim. Wherever we are, he reaches for my hand or puts his arm around me. Wanting to be con- nected to me in small ways while we go about the busi- ness of traveling.

I thought I would be annoyed by the constant contact after being used to doing things on my own, but I'm not. It feels…natural. Comforting. Nice. Arousing. All at once.

Bags found (an activity that may have taken longer because Beau was busy nuzzling my neck, drawing my attention away from the luggage carousel), we walk toward the exit.

"Are there rocking chairs in this airport?" I crane my head behind us as we walk, disbelieving there are literal rocking chairs overlooking the tarmac. Kind of adorable and a good first impression from a place I don't know much about aside from popular culture.

"Yeah. Everyone loves a rocking chair."

I can't argue with that. My eyes scan the rest of the small space. I don't think I've ever been in an airport this small—it's only two gates. And a big difference from the loud bustle of JFK Airport, and even that of our connecting airport.

"Check it out. Someone's family loves embarrassing their person. I like their Christmas spirit." I point to a large group standing to one side of the door.

There are four adults and two kids and all of them are decked out in Christmas apparel, each person holding a handmade sign. The kids are wearing complete elf costumes, busily stomping their feet to make the bells jingle. The adults are letting it happen, eyes scanning for their aforementioned person.

"About that…" The odd tone of his voice makes me look up at him.

"What's up?" I ask when he doesn't continue.

Before he can answer, the Christmas enthusiasts over by the door find who they want and start screaming in welcome.

My eyes go to the distraction. "Wow. I think they found their long-lost prodigal child. Rough to be them."

Beau says something, but the words are lost when the family walks toward us, still making a ruckus.

They stop in front of us, and I smile at them, not wanting to agitate the enthusiastic people. I look behind me to see who they could be coming for. Then a woman in a Christmas sweater walks right up to Beau and gives him a hug.

Oh shit.

Beau turns to me in the embrace. "Sonia, meet my family."

Chapter Twenty

Are there any other three words he could have said that would send this much fear coursing through me? Sure, it's embarrassing that I talked light smack about his family, but I'm *really* not prepared to meet them even if I hadn't made the off-color comments. I'm an onion, with layers of anxiety right now.

I thought the worst thing I would have to deal with was chickens wanting revenge for all the chicken nuggies I've eaten over the years without remorse or maybe a sexy (but sticky) peach fight. I didn't think his family would even be here.

Which is ridiculous, since he's talked about how he works at a *family* business. Apparently when your parents are always on another continent, you don't consider that other people's family members are just around them all the time, doing mundane things like all of them picking him up from the airport.

And by the look on Beau's face, he *likes* it.

"Sonia, this is my mom, Eve, and my dad, Reed. My little sister, Annabelle, and her husband, Tucker. My niece, Harper, and nephew, Harry. Everyone, this is Sonia. She's visiting the South for a bit."

"Hi, everyone, whose names I definitely didn't get."

Might as well admit it now; less embarrassing for when I forget it all later.

"Welcome to South Carolina." His mother moves toward me like a Great White Shark. Okay, she looks perfectly nice and non-sharklike on her approach, but I am inherently wary about meeting the family, ready to paint her as a dangerous predator.

I extend my hand for a shake, but she's faster than me, and I'm enveloped in a sea of red sweater fabric. I get a bit of gingerbread man beard, or maybe a bit of his hat, in my mouth before she pulls away.

"Thank you," I mumble to her, getting ready for the greetings from the rest of the family. Forewarned is forearmed, and I'm ready for the rest of these huggers. Prepared, I don't ingest any more Christmas sweater fragments when they all move in for hugs, but I am too slow to avoid the half-eaten candy cane that Harry shoves in my mouth.

My eyes lock with Beau's as I slide the sticky candy out of my mouth and force out a thank-you to the expectant child in front of me. The gross child in front of me. But still, potential for disease aside, sharing is something I should probably encourage in the young one with an acknowledgement of his sacrifice. Beau, my champion, my knight, my Southern gentleman…laughs at me.

And makes no move to help me.

I stand there with the treat in my hand as Beau's family inundates him with greetings and questions. His dad is trying to talk about mulch-gate and his mom is asking how the Plaza was. His sister is asking what he got her, and his brother-in-law is saying something about a deer blind.

Does he have blind deer? Should someone call a vet?

The kids, on the other hand, are focusing their tiny but potent gazes at me like I'm an intriguing friend. Or an evil adversary. Who knows with small humans? They're so mysterious.

I wave at them with the candy cane in my hand, and their eyes go straight to the treasure. I look at the adults but they're all busy and I have no idea if these kids can plan a siege on me for the booty, so I slowly extend my recent gift. The little boy one takes the treat back from me, and then a fight promptly breaks out between both of them.

I look back at the adults, sure they'll do something now, but they ignore the battle unfolding in front of them. I take a few steps toward Beau and avert my gaze from the kids so I can claim lack of knowledge later.

Not my circus, not my monkeys.

After Beau has fielded a few questions from the adults, he catches me looking at him. He looks at my hand for the candy, and I jerk my head to the kids. Or in the direction where I last saw them, since I've been avoiding looking at them.

"Come on. I need to feed my guest." He puts his arm around me and walks toward the door.

I sigh in relief. I survived meeting his family, but I'm looking forward to some alone time with Beau. After we exit the airport, Beau leads us to a truck so large I look around for a ladder to get in. There's a little step next to the door, but it's kind of high up by itself.

"Apparently the giant trucks are not just a stereotype." I have no idea how to get in that without putting on a harness and climbing up the side.

"Yes. But I want to note we have an actual farm and need the vehicle to haul things. But don't worry; I've got you, Baby Girl," Beau says from behind me as he puts his hand on either side of my waist. He lifts me up into the road-boat.

Oh. Well, that's impressive.

I hope his parents can't tell how wiggly I get downstairs at the display of strength from their son.

"Holding up so far?" Beau whispers in my ear so his parents in the front seat can't hear.

"Hmm. Well, no one's said 'War of Northern Aggression' yet, so I think I'm okay. I guess." I joke, but there's a bit of fear under there as well. Hard not to with my less than pale complexion and where I am. Something I didn't really think about until now, being so concerned before with my relationship issues.

"And you won't hear it," Beau says, serious now. "Not from us. And no Confederate flags either, at least not from us. Or any of our friends. I can't promise anything beyond that, as much as I wish I could."

My eyes race to his with as much determination as Sherman coming for Atlanta. I know he can't control everyone who lives in his state, and that good and bad people live everywhere. I am reassured that no one in his immediate circle is going to say anything that makes me want to punch someone and cry. But still. "This is going to be…different."

Not that I can pretend all of New York state is racist- and Confederate-flag free. I know the warning about throwing stones from glass houses. But there do seem to be less of them at home. Or maybe they're quieter about it.

I have time to obsess over the new worry during the long drive. As the sun goes down, I really think about what I agreed to for the first time; to get in a plane and follow a mostly-stranger to his remote house, with his family.

This is the part in the horror movie where ominous banjo music should start playing.

When we get to the house, we get out and unload the luggage. The home is a two-story building with a white wood panel exterior. There are large windows that must let in a lot of light and a double story wraparound veranda, complete with rocking chairs and a built-in porch swing on the first floor. There are Christmas decorations, but all the lights are off because of the late hour and I can't properly judge their festivity.

There's nothing else around it. It's dark, so I can't be sure, but I don't see any other lights around us.

Beau unlocks the door, and his family follow us in. He has nice furniture pieces; lots of dark wood and worn leather to make everything lived in and inviting; not just for show. The walls are covered in pictures, both in color and black-and-white, but from the other indicators in the latter photos, not as an artistic choice and more because that was the only technology available at the time. Christmas decorations fill the house: garlands, statues, ornaments, and lights on every available surface.

Now this is my kind of impeccably decorated place.

I can't wait to explore more. Fine. More like snoop. I can't wait to *snoop*. Which I'll start right after his family leaves. I'm distracted from my plans when I hear heavy panting and the sound of nails on wood before I see the giant puppy sprinting to the front door.

"Who is this adorableness?" I ask as a giant mastiff comes barreling toward me. The giant comes up to my stomach on all fours and I would put down money that he's taller than me standing.

"This is Bubba."

Giant Bubba pushes his head into my stomach, I assume because he wants pets. I start scratching behind the ear and he leans into it, giant tongue hanging out. I guess that is what he wanted.

"We'll get some Zaxby's for you guys while you get settled in. You probably haven't had that before?" Eve asks.

"I haven't. But you don't need to go through all the trouble." They're coming back? Noooo…that's okay, guys. I can make us toast. Or a daal if there're enough ingredients. And then we can eat it with the toast.

"It's no trouble and this is the perfect introduction to the South." Eve tugs Reed out of the room and snags the keys on the way out. Then she stops in her tracks, the large man in a matching sweater almost running her over from behind. He deftly weaves out of the way at the last minute, telling me he's used to Eve's sudden changes in movement.

"Wait, are you a vegetarian? We can get something else if you are. If you're vegan, we can make you something at home, because there's probably nothing around here we can pick up that you can eat."

"Thank you for asking. But I do eat meat. Probably too much, if I'm honest."

"Great. Well, we don't care either way, but I haven't had Zaxby's in a while."

We watch them walk out of the room.

"I feel bad making them go out and come back here. They must want to get home. We can make something here." And I want to be alone with Beau, for reasons. Sexy reasons.

Beau tugs me into the kitchen. It's another nicely decorated room, with white tile backsplash and rustic gray wood making up the cabinets and island. He opens the vintage fridge and pulls out a pitcher of something brown and then gets two glasses out.

"It's actually no problem, since…they live here." Beau studiously ignores my gaze, taking longer than any other human has ever done to pour two glasses of whatever that is. Iced tea maybe?

"Excuse me? They live here? Like where I'm standing now here? This very house here? The house you invited me to? For a sleepover—with your parents?"

"Yes, to all of the above. But I wouldn't call it a sleepover *with* my parents…"

Great. He loves home and family so much he never left home. Besides not really knowing what that feels like, it's another sign that this can't go anywhere. I doubt he would move out for me if he hasn't moved yet. "I thought I was the Indian. Aren't I the one who's supposed to live with my parents forever?"

He points to the right side of the house. "My office is right there. The peach trees and the farm offices are all out there." He indicates outside, the details of which I can't see because of the dark. "It's convenient to live where I work; there's no commute. Daniel lives on the farm too, in another house just like this one, with his family." Beau gets it out in a rush. "And I like being close to family."

I think I've hit a nerve.

"You live your life. In your childhood home, if that's what you want." I hold up my arms in surrender. "Do you still have your childhood bedroom?"

"Technically," he mumbles. "But when I remodeled the room, I got rid of the Dale Earnhardt light switch cover and fan that has baseball bats as fan blades and a baseball as a light."

"I missed a Dale Earnhardt light switch cover?"

Beau leans in and lowers his voice. "Do you even know who that is?"

"Yes. With the driving." I pantomime turning a wheel. "Vroom vroom."

Beau inclines his head. "Yeah, the man with the driving. Mom still has it stored somewhere if you really want to see it."

"I think I'll probably survive either way."

"Want to have your first Southern experience?" Beau asks suddenly, changing the subject.

I look scandalized; is he propositioning me? "Your parents are coming back any second."

Beau rolls his eyes. "Not that. Later though, if you want. My room is on the opposite side of the house of theirs."

Kinky Southern gentleman.

"Come on." He grabs our drinks and herds me out of the front door. He motions for me to sit on one of the rockers next to a plastic Frosty the Snowman and then hands me the glass when I sit down.

I take a sip while he sits down next to me. "Oh. This sugar water you gave me is delicious." I take another large sip, possibly developing diabetes in the process. Worth it.

"It's sweet tea."

I guess that's why the sugar water is brown. "Emphasis on the sweet." More sips. "What's the Southern experience?" I eye Beau's still full glass. I've got designs on it if he doesn't get to drinking.

Beau extends his hands to the dark open space in front of him, settling deeper into the chair that he rocks back and forth. "This is it. Sitting on the porch on a rocking chair with sweet tea, watching the night."

I give myself some rocks in the chair. Well, this part is pleasant. "But what is there to look at?"

"Nature."

"It's dark," I whisper.

"It's peaceful."

"There's nothing to actually look at. Maybe if there was a TV here? Or we could move these drinks and chairs inside, by the TV." Inside is always better than outside.

Deep sigh from the owner of the full glass next to me. "Just give it a try. For me."

"Okay." It won't make me like doing this, but at least the beverage selection is top-notch. I down mine and take his cup from him.

He lets me, but not without comment. "Are you sure you can handle this much sweet tea on your first go?" He warns me like I'm a teenager experiencing alcohol for the first time.

"I think I can handle some sugar," I say with authority even though I know it's a lie. I'm going to be up for hours after all this sugar.

Beau reaches out and grabs the hand not drinking my new favorite drink and we rock in silence. Bubba comes out and rests his giant head in my lap. That's nice, too. Even if he is eyeing the drink in my hand and licking his giant chops. And drooling on my pants legs. But he's so cute doing it I can't get that mad.

My mind wanders from getting murdered in the sticks, to how Priya's doing, to if I'm missing any work drama, to if I remembered to water my plants before I left, to if I remembered to record Hallmark Christmas movies before I left, then lands on making sure I got everyone's presents ready.

Then I get bored.

I resort to examining the ends of my hair to see if I need a haircut. Yes, I could use one.

I sneak peeks at Beau, but he looks so peaceful doing nothing. I don't disturb him with any chatter, since he had such a good attitude when I dragged him to New York Christmas events. Instead I start thinking about all the things I need to do at work. And continue petting the dog.

My right foot starts jiggling and Beau puts his hand on top of it to calm it down.

I sigh. It's exhausting doing nothing. How do people do this? And why did I leave my phone in the house? I miss it so much. It's so shiny and always there for me and holds all the entertainment in the world. And sassy tweets.

His parents save me (and no one is more surprised than me that I'm happy to see them) by driving up to the house and parking in the driveway.

Eve gets out of the passenger seat, waving a bag of food at us on the porch. "Get ready for this magic."

Chapter Twenty-One

Back in the dining room, Reed sets a black takeout box in front of me. I take a big breath in, the warm box smelling like fried wonderfulness. Wonderfulness that I want in my belly, after a long day of traveling.

Eve puts a cup in front of me and I take a sip without asking any questions, smiling as my loyalty is rewarded with more sugar. Three glasses into this Southern sweet tea experience and I can already feel the addiction forming.

Why do I never get this? It must be on menus but I always order something else.

"If you can tear yourself away from the sweet tea, the chicken's pretty good as well."

Busted by Beau. Defiantly, I take another sip while looking Beau dead in the eyes. Point made, I open the box to see golden fried chicken strips, a thick piece of toast, fries, and some pink sauce.

I dig in and give the South this without reservation, trying not to moan in front of his people. This is delicious.

Bubba, sensing the newest person might be the weakest, sits next to me and rests his giant head on my lap again. This must be a thing with him, resting his head because it's too tiring to hold the weight up himself.

He's adorable, but I have no idea if he's allowed people food so he's out of luck. But then I see his face again and slip him some of the chicken without the breading. He's just so cute.

"This didn't exist when I first came to the South, but I did get fed another version of fried chicken and sweet tea." Eve smiles as she takes a bite of the chicken, looking like she's remembering another meal. One that must have ended well.

"Beau said you were from New York. Where did you move from?" I ask.

"From your neck of the woods... Manhattan. This was supposed to be a short visit. That hasn't really ended yet." The look she sends her partner is intimate, speaking to a long history together.

"A carpetbagger! Where did you live? I'm in SoHo."

"I was your neighbor in the Village."

"Hey, nice to meet you eight hundred miles and a few years from home! What brought you down here?"

"This one." She points a chicken finger at Reed like she was born doing it, despite what she just told me. "Met him on a girls' trip to Charleston the same weekend he was in the city for some fruit conference."

"And then he dragged you to the farm, hollerin' and carryin' on," Beau interrupts.

"He's lucky his job was less mobile than mine. And trust me; I looked into the logistics of moving an entire farm to Manhattan."

"Ha! She chased after me for my peaches." Reed tries to set the record straight, and without laughing, amazingly. Because he has to be making a pun. Right?

"Please stop now," Beau whimpers. See, his mind went there.

I laugh at the parental embarrassment happening in front of me. I'm a little jealous though, deep down inside. When I'm around my parents, it's so formal. A side effect of only seeing them once a year. I have a more comfortable, joking relationship with Chachi and Chacha.

And older Indian parents, at least the ones I know, don't joke about each other's...peaches. At least not in front of the children. The biggest affectionate quirk they have is calling each other "dear" while arguing. Unlike Priya and Gavin. Chachi's head practically exploded the first time she saw Priya kiss Gavin—and it was just a peck.

This is interesting.

"Well, I'm glad Beau brought you home. Because you seem lovely, but also we need more city defenders around here." Eve turns her attention back to me.

"Oh. Thank you," I say reflexively. But what does that mean? Does she think me and Beau are a thing? I mean, clearly, we're a bit of a thing; I'm here. But we're not a *thing* thing. And now I need to stop thinking the word *thing*. I've thought it so many times, it's stopped being a real word to me.

"Mom, you're scaring our guest." Gentleman Beau rushes to my rescue.

"She's from New York. In the last week she's probably seen a New Yorker assault a tourist who walked too slowly on the sidewalk, someone cutting their toenails on the subway, and Santa on Santa fornication during SantaCon. She can handle the sticks."

Ah, SantaCon. It was fun the first time. Then the drunk, sweaty Santas trying to aggressively hit on us got old.

"I can handle all that. But the silence and stillness of the country might defeat me." I couldn't even last a half hour waiting for the food in that rocker.

Seriously, so bored.

"I made them install the fastest and most reliable Wi-Fi so at least we can always stream to break up the silence," Eve says.

Oh, thank god there's good Wi-Fi. I wanted to ask Beau more about the internet situation, but I couldn't figure out a way to not make it sound like I was insulting his home again.

Meal done, Beau excuses us and tugs me away from the dining room, getting our luggage on the way. I dart looks back and forth between him and his parents, waiting for them to tell us we can't sleep in the same room. Regardless of how old we are.

But white parents, man. They let us wander off, clearly going to the same room, caught up in their own conversation. Even though we can fornicate in there with no chaperone.

This would not have flown in either Gupta household of my youth. When I was a teenager, definitely not, but also not now. Not without a ring on a certain finger, at the very least.

We walk down a hall without parental wrath stopping us in our tracks, and then up some stairs. Beau opens the door at the end of the hall for me and I walk in.

Bubba, realizing his people are separating, chooses us and meanders up the stairs too, his large frame sauntering into the room before Beau can close the door.

I look around while I wait for the parental smiting. His room is disappointingly adult, just like he said it would be. A huge bed dominates it, with the rest of the available space taken up by a simple dresser. The wall is a cool blue color, with zero posters identifying his potentially embarrassing childhood interests. Two open doors lead to the bathroom and the walk-in closet.

"Do you mind if he stays in here? He's used to sleeping with me." Beau looks adorably unwilling to kick the dog out.

"He's more than fine. I'm less sure if *I'm* allowed to be in here." I'm still waiting for one of the parents to burst in, call me a Jezebel and physically throw me out of the house.

"I'm a grown man." Beau's got laughter in his eyes. "But if you want another room, I can take you to a guest room. I want you to be comfortable."

"This is fine." As long as I'm not going to have to wear a Scarlet Letter at any point. I take my suitcase to the closet to show him I'm committed to the room choice. "How far are your parents again?"

"Other side of the house. Plenty far enough."

"That is *not* far enough." I emphatically disagree, my head shaking vigorously so he knows I mean business. About there being no business. The business of *no* business. "In the same house will never be far enough. Unless you live in Biltmore. You know, the biggest house in America over in Asheville? Built by some Vanderbilts." I clarify in case he's not up on his American historic houses.

Beau gets some clothes out of the dresser and then starts taking his clothes off. Which is a perfectly logical next step in getting ready for bed. But it feels so wrong in his parents' house.

I tear through my suitcase to find my own nightclothes and dash into the bathroom to change, closing the door once I'm in.

"Really? I've already seen it all," he yells far too loudly after me.

I get dressed in what has to be a personal record and open the door again. "Keep your voice down. It's different when your parents are right out there. It's weird enough thinking about what they think we're doing in here."

Beau's face scrunches up. "Sleeping, I hope."

I'm already shaking my head. "Not chancing it." I commandeer some pillows and set them up in the middle of the bed.

Beau, not helping, doesn't even offer moral support. He leans against his dresser, arms crossed like a giant, judgemental redwood. He gets in bed with a sigh when I'm done, Bubba jumping up behind him and claiming the foot of the bed. "I'm gonna miss falling asleep with you tucked in close," he says, over the wall.

I can only see his eyes and hair over the pillows, but it's enough to tempt me. Because I'm already missing him too. Desperately.

But. "I'm not as experienced as you are doing *things* with your parents around," I say with all the outrage of a virginal Victorian miss, not even going to chance saying the word *sex*.

Beau falls onto his back, staring at the ceiling and its boring, non-baseball-themed fan. "Please don't put it like that."

"Stay on your side and it won't be an issue." I break my own rules to lean over and land a quick kiss on his cheek, back on my side before his hands reach me.

It's going to be a long, lonely night.

* * *

Walls don't work.

I mean, it shouldn't be a surprise since people have spent millennia going under, over, and around them, and yeah, this one is made of pillows, so it's already got some structural deficiencies. But still. Here I am. Half on top of Beau with the pillows I carefully stacked last night scattered on the ground or at the foot of the bed. Bubba got in on the shuffle, cuddling against my other side.

Thank god he's upgraded the bed into a king-size one.

I sigh, not bothering to move from my position even though I'm being cooked between the twin furnaces of Beau and Bubba. It's too late to move now for virtue's sake, and I really enjoy this sandwich. Temperature notwithstanding.

The sigh wakes up Beau, who groggily picks his head up and takes in the tableau. "Who beat the wall?"

"Both of us?" That's not verified, but it would be nice if I wasn't the only one who was affected by the close proximity.

He pulls me in closer and I let him, ending up on his chest. "Now I get to show you the best Christmas," Beau says.

"Oh no. We've already had the best Christmas. But we can still have a very nice Christmas." I pat him on the chest.

"You can't make up your mind before I show you my events."

"Yes, I can. When you've had filet mignon, you don't need to have a fast-food burger to know the filet's better. But that burger can still be enjoyable. It's just not going to be objectively better."

He rolls out from under me, ignoring my flawless metaphor. Doesn't he know that he's the best part of a Southern Christmas? If so, why is he moving further away?

"Wait until you see what I've got planned for you first." Beau rubs his hands together.

Is it to get a hotel so we can have sex? Because that'd be a great plan.

I begrudgingly get out of bed and get ready. I cross fingers, toes, legs, arms, and any other miscellaneous body parts that his family has things to do and I get some more alone time with Beau.

When we get downstairs, there's a delicious breakfast spread set up for us. Eggs, pancakes, grits, bacon, biscuits and gravy, and an entire pitcher of sweet tea. Well, the day's already looking better, even if my luck didn't hold that much and we aren't alone. Beau's mom and dad are already at the table, halfway through their plates while we make our own.

"You going out to the mulch supplier today? I've got to head to the hiring fair for the upcoming season, so I'm glad you could come back," Reed says to Beau.

Oh yeah, the mulch. I had sort of forgotten why we were here instead of ordering room service from The Plaza right now.

Beau nods. "Yeah. Hopefully I'll be able to get it out of the way and then I can show Sonia how much better a South Carolina Christmas is than a New York Christmas."

Eve chokes on her eggs, needing a large gulp of her sweet tea before she can talk freely again. "I wouldn't take that bet."

"Hey!" Identical yells of indignation come from Reed

and Beau, with matching incredulous looks. Proving they're related.

"A Southern Christmas has charm, but it still doesn't compare." Eve draws her line in the sand, telling the men in her life exactly how she feels about her old life.

Father and son look at each other like everything they know should be called into question with this new bit of information from Mom/wife.

"Oh, stop looking like I kicked your dog. I love you both and my life here. That doesn't mean I can't like other places too. If I had put my foot down and taken you to New York more often, you would know that too."

Beau shakes himself from the stupor the new information gave him and turns back to me. "Do you want to come with me to the mulch vendor?"

Yes. But before I can say that very small, very quick word, Eve interrupts.

"You don't have to do that; you can stay here and help me start decorating our trees while Beau's gone."

Chapter Twenty-Two

How do I get out of this without being rude to my casual hookup turned slightly more serious hookup's mom? *Dear Abby* would have a lot to say about this. If I had the time to write to a newspaper and then wait for them to pick my letter and publish a response.

"I don't want to bother you. I can just keep bothering him until he gets done with work." There. I think Abby would appreciate the quick thinking.

"It's not a bother. I don't want you to be bored at the mulch shop. Plus, you seem like the kind of gal who enjoys a good Christmas decorating party. And I don't know if you caught it, but there are *multiple* trees to decorate."

Damn, I can't argue with that.

Eve takes the resulting silence as agreement. "Excellent. Reed dug out the decorations yesterday, so we can start whenever you're ready."

I give in, because there's no other option that doesn't involve me running away screaming in a dramatic manner or being a jerk to this nice woman. "That sounds great. I'll just check in with work to see if I need to do anything, if that's all right?"

"Sounds good. I've got some of my own work to get

done, if you want to join me in the office? It's got some
desks so you don't have to break your back working on
a laptop in a bed."

"Perfect." I smile, hoping it's not a grimace.

Back in Beau's room after breakfast, I drag out getting
ready. Not that his mom doesn't seem cool. But what if
she asks questions about us? What do I say?

The truth would be: I don't trust your son, but don't
feel that's a reflection on your parenting; I don't trust
anyone to stick around besides Priya and to a lesser extent Ajay, and that's only because I've known them since
I was an impressionable child. Instead, I would like to
get frisky with your son until I get him out of my system
and we can part, never to see each other again. Meeting you was an accident and I consistently find myself
wanting to run away into the sunset to avoid this very
conversation.

I don't think she'd appreciate that.

"You don't have to hang out with Mom if you don't
want to." Beau stands by the door, watching me check my
purse for the third time to make sure I have my charger.

I look up at him, the man who has the nerve to look
great while I'm an internal mess of nerves over how to
interact with his mom.

He's done with the suits now that he's back on the
farm, and he's got on faded jeans and a plaid button-down
shirt. Everything fits him like he bought it before he got
all those muscles, and now they're stretching the fabric
past the bounds of what it signed up for. At the same time,
the shirt is worn, making it look soft. The combination
makes me want to stroke it. Stroke him.

This is what I was picturing him wearing the entire

time we were together in New York. The image in my mind of the relaxed farmer: comfortable, sexy, functional clothes, but with less dirt than I imagined. No complaints on that last part.

I dressed for the occasion by throwing a plaid shirt over some leggings.

"No, it's cool. I'll just hang out with the mother of the man I did X-rated things to and I'm sure it'll be fine."

"It'll be great." He doesn't react to my characterization of the situation.

I give him a dirty look. I should have made him spend more time with Priya. One-on-one time. Then he wouldn't be quite so sanguine about leaving me alone with relatives.

Not aware of the torture I'm planning for him, Beau walks me to the office jauntily, dropping a kiss on my lips before I can avoid it. Not that I don't like his kisses, but now I can't exactly claim we're just friends to his mother. If she somehow didn't realize we slept in the same room last night.

He also leaves me alone before he has to deal with the repercussions of the kiss. I turn around and face his mother, who thankfully is looking at her computer like true city folk, minding her own business. Good to know you can take the girl out of the city, but you can't take the city out of the girl.

Assured she's not watching me, I look around the office. The large room is built for function, with three desks, one in front of three of the walls, and a table in the middle surrounded by chairs.

Two of the desks are covered with stacks of papers and older computers, and what I think is farming equipment. Work boots, dusty shirts and more farm equipment are all thrown in haphazard piles under and around those desks.

Eve is sitting at the third desk, one that's drastically different from the others in the room. Hers is the biggest, and it's dominated by a large, shiny new computer. Her space has mason jars, lace, vases of flowers, and pastel-colored books and binders piled around her.

"Feel free to grab a seat wherever. The center table might be the cleanest space available," Eve says without looking up from whatever she's typing. This I feel comfortable with. It's just like having a conversation with Priya: her talking to me while half her brain is busy on work.

I set up my iPad, open my email and get started. Eve doesn't try to start up a conversation to grill me about my relationship with her son, so I relax enough to get some work done. Or I can after the first half hour. Initially, I flinched every time she moved or sighed, sure that was the moment she was going to grill me, but I relaxed a little more each time she didn't ask me any questions.

I'm able to find some more pieces that Beau would like and send them his way. Even though Chacha said I can't do the interior decorating service, I'm not leaving Beau's project incomplete. I said I would help him and I'm seeing it through.

Bubba wanders into the room, lying down next to me and resting his huge head on my foot. He makes a very comforting coworker. Once I get past the fact that my foot is asleep. I proofread some exhibition blurbs while sending off some emails asking for updates on current projects from the team.

Priya, after getting some of my emails, now knows that I'm free and by a reliable Wi-Fi connection. And the interrogation begins.

How is it going? Do you need rescuing? Are you a horsewoman now?

Great. No. No. I hope the short answer will dissuade any further conversation, but Priya's much nosier ever since she got married.

How would I know if you need rescuing? You could have Stockholm syndrome. Even if getting it in a day is a bit much, even for you, drama llama. Either way, give me details on the visit!

FINE. He lives with his parents.

?? I thought we were the Indians. What else?

We just got here. There's nothing to tell except for it's kind of hot down here for winter and I had some fried food and liquid sugar. And he made me sit outside.

Ew. But that does sound accurate. From the TV.

I don't answer, knowing Priya and I can go on like this for a while if one of us doesn't stop. And since it's me getting the probing questions this time, I'll take that step and cut it off.

A few hours of uninterrupted work time later, I finish everything that I need to do for the day. A light day since I am on vacation. Well, a Gupta vacation. Then I start scrolling social media, not wanting to interrupt Eve since we're in a comfortable silence.

"I'm ready whenever you are," Eve says a half hour later, standing up from her desk to stretch.

"I'm done with the important stuff."

"Excellent. Let's go decorate."

Eve picks up one box of decorations and tells me which one she wants me to carry. Even after we take our boxes, there's still a small tower of boxes labeled "Christmas," which gets my very fervent approval at their enthusiasm for the holiday.

She leads me out the front door and to the front yard of the house. This is the first time I've seen the place in daylight, and I can see the rows and rows of currently bare peach trees that were hidden in the darkness last night. I thought the light would make the land less creepy, but there's hundreds, maybe thousands of long, bony branches like skeleton fingers reaching up and out from the ground, hoping to ensnare…well, probably a young female virgin. Demons and vampires and witches in non-romance books (and the men who write them) are usually super concerned with a woman's lack of sexual experience.

And we're as remote as I thought last night, since I still can't see any evidence of neighbors.

But then I turn around and see the house is decorated like a Christmas wonderland, brightly colored lights strung on the façade, and plastic figurines of standard Christmas fare—Santa, reindeer, penguins, and presents. Even a little plastic palm tree with Christmas decorations on its palm fronds. All the decorations I couldn't really make out last night.

Less horror movie.

"It's our tradition to decorate the oldest peach tree in the orchard. The one that great-great grandpoppas Abbot and Jackson planted to start the business." Eve points to the tree closest to the house in the yard, on its own and not in a neat row. It's eight feet tall and completely bare of any leaves, just like the others. But the fact that it's set aside makes it the creepiest of the horror movie trees. Like it's their king.

"We decorate a tree inside as well, but we always start with this one." Eve sets down the box of decorations and I follow her lead. Four ladders are already set up around the tree and we get to work hanging lights and ornaments. Hopefully this tree will look less terrifying now. But it could just turn out like a zombie with a red-and-green bow on his head.

"What do you do?" Eve asks casually, throwing me the end of a string of lights.

Ah, here we go. She's shown admirable restraint, but now she wants to know about the woman her son brought home. I get it, but that doesn't stop the anxiety rising in my chest. And being on a ladder whilst getting the interrogation doesn't help anything.

"I work at an auction house. It's a family business as well, actually. I help put on our exhibition shows and sales. Get pieces, write about and price them, display them, advertise our shows and then host auctions."

"That's exciting. And glamorous."

"It has its moments." There are days I'm jetting off to London or New Delhi to stay at a mansion and inspect a collection of art, but most times it's carpal tunnel and eyestrain in front of my computer. "How about you?" Please, let's not talk about me.

"I do event planning. Weddings, engagement parties,

graduations, birthdays, divorces, holidays, whatever anyone wants to celebrate. We have an old barn on the farm we've converted where I can do events, but I can also plan for any other venue or home."

"That must be better drama than a reality TV show." My tone is complimentary, since watching reality TV is a large part of my free time.

Eve laughs. "Oh, a kindred spirit. And yes." She peeks around the branches so I can see her gleeful smile. "It's filled with drama that I enjoy unless and until it prevents me from getting an event ready."

Now that we've moved on from talking about me, I ask her about the city to keep that train heading away from my life. We chat about some of her favorite places when she lived there and what's changed since her time. Beau's mom is funny and nice, not at all like the passive-aggressive investigator who takes an immediate dislike to the woman coming to steal her son like I thought she would be.

And not that I'm trying to steal her son, either.

An hour after we started, the sound of a truck pulling up to the front of the house interrupts our conversation. I track its movement until it stops in front of the tree and Beau gets out of it, his long legs having no problem finding the ground.

"Hi. How's the mulch-mergency?" I yell from my ladder, reaching for an ornament in my bag that's used to hold picked peaches during the harvest season.

"I don't think you're giving mulch the gravity it deserves."

"I concede that point."

"Well, it's getting better. They gave me some and we're working on finding some more. They gave me a discount for next year to keep our business, but we'll see if they find the rest of the mulch for us this year. I also went to a few more vendors and was able to get a little more. Amazing what begging in person can do."

"Get a bag of ornaments and a ladder and make your-self useful," Eve orders from her spot on the other side of the tree.

Beau obliges and soon he's next to me, decorating a real tree. To give him credit where it's due, I wouldn't get to do this in New York.

We're half-done when another truck drives up to the house. Beau's sister and her family get out, waving to us.

"Yay, you're not done with the decorating." Annabelle gets her own bag and ladder while Tucker sets the kids up in the corner with some toys and Bubba to babysit.

We're all working together, and I relax. This family togetherness time isn't as bad as I thought it would be.

Until Annabelle asks, "Are you guys dating?"

Chapter Twenty-Three

I knew it was going *too* well.

I should have expected that someone would ask, but I got so comfortable when his mom didn't press and let my guard down and now I'm freaking out on a ladder, too high off the ground. From a question more terrifying than these horror-movie trees. When my heart calms down, and I hang a few ornaments to stall, I turn the question over to Beau.

"Yeah, Beau. What's up with that?" Not my proudest moment, courage wise. But I've come to terms with that.

"I think Anna-Banana should stay out of other people's relationships or I start telling her husband about that Christmas she got drunk on hot chocolate with peppermint schnapps and danced with the tree and yelled at Mom for 'getting frisky with her man,' because Mom put the star on top of the tree."

I laugh on my ladder. And cause the ladder to shake in a way that has me clutching whatever I can reach, which is a tiny tree branch. The spirit of Santa, which is probably a real thing, keeps me upright *and* keeps all the branches on the tree.

"Moooomm. Beauregard Dean is being a butt," Annabelle whines.

"First of all, both of you are being butts, and second, you are not representing the South, and more importantly my parenting, very well right now in front of our guest." Eve doesn't even stop hanging ornaments in response to the sibling battle. This must be a regular occurrence.

"I'm just trying to help," Annabelle says.

"Tell me more about this schnapps situation," Tucker says to his wife.

"It's nothing." She glares at her brother.

"You ought not yell at your family," Tucker says, laughing at his wife.

"Shove it, Tuck," Annabelle snaps at the man.

Beau winks at me, awkward question avoided.

"Beauregard?" I drag out all the syllables of the new name. And there's so many of them. Syllables that roll around in my mouth, causing more lip action than when he actually kisses me. It's quite the name.

"It's still just Beau," he says mildly.

"But he loves to be called Beauregard. Especially Beauregard Dean," Annabelle says.

"Just as much as she loves Anna-Banana," Beau says.

"Should I tell Sonia about your first weekend in college?"

"Shove it, sis."

I laugh again at the looks exchanged between sister and brother. They're just like Priya, Ajay, and me. Eve still isn't paying attention to her bickering children, hanging ornaments in her happy Christmas place.

My mom never got comfortable with the way we all bickered growing up. She looked out of place whenever we started and she was visiting, not knowing how to react to us. She mostly told us it wasn't seemly for the heirs of Loot to be arguing, which made Chachi laugh and say we were learning conflict resolution the hard way, but we were learning. As we got older, the arguing got more affectionate, just like with Beau and Annabelle. Mom still didn't approve, but she kept her disapproval to disappointed looks from across the room.

I think it was better when she was scolding me over the cool indifference.

Back in the present, we finish the tree outside and move the decorating party inside. I take one last look at the decorated tree, with lights turned on, and the sunset in the background over the rows of peach trees. This would make a good painting, with the beautiful colors and the creepy tree neutralized by the decorations. Not just a zombie with a bow on then. I take a quick photo with my phone. Maybe I'll paint it when I'm back in the city, since I won't be doing any creative interior decorating anymore.

Inside, Eve starts the fireplace, even though it is in no way cold enough to need it. I respect the dedication to the theme, even though I'm going to start sweating soon. She brings some eggnog and decorated sugar cookies from the kitchen to sustain us through the demanding work. Further respect for the woman who has Christmas cookies on hand during the holiday season.

The familiar smells of the pine tree, eggnog, cookies and the sound of the crackling fire smooth any remaining nerves I had about being around Beau's family, and I get comfortable with the flow of this group of people who know each other so well. There's a lot of affectionate teasing and laughter. A family completely relaxed with each other.

I can't help but compare them again with my own

parents and our relationship. Another pang hits my chest when I realize how much I've lost because they moved away.

Bubba, who must be a superior dog able to sense my feelings and that I need comfort, lies down in front of the part of the tree I'm decorating and rests his head on his paws. Or he's pouting because no one is giving him any cookies. Either way, I have to reach out to my full extension to reach the branches over him, so his support and/or protest is noted.

"I hope you're not decorated out," Eve says.

I scoff. I've never been decorated out. My apartment gets a refresh too often because it's the only space I can play with, and I regularly search Zillow for houses I can decorate in my head. It's why it hurts that I finally applied my passion to work and now Chacha says I can't do it anymore. "I willingly decorated twenty-five trees as part of last year's Christmas sale at work. So I'm in my element."

"You have Christmas-themed problems." Beau hands me the end of the string of lights.

"It's called Christmas spirit, Scrooge MacButt." I take the string and then see Beau's niece and nephew playing with some ornaments next to me. "Am I allowed to say utt-bay around here?" I whisper out of the corner of my mouth.

"Probably not. But they hear worse when their mother gets sauced watching *Real Housewives*, and when their Paw-Paw, also sauced, watches baseball."

"As long as no one sues me for ruining impressionable minds, I'm good." We're still whispering, lost in our own world doing one of my favorite activities during my favorite time of year. And he's rising fast in the ranks to be my favorite person.

The thought makes me hurry to finish the strand of lights we're working on so I can physically step away from him. As if a little physical distance will let me enjoy spending time with him but stop me from getting too involved with the man. When I hear it in my head, it sounds…like that's not how things work. But I can hope.

But maybe I should put another box of Christmas ornaments between us. Just in case it *does* work like that.

The little ones don't help me feel more comfortable, since they won't stop looking at me. I don't know how they knew we were talking about them, but they're looking at me expectantly. I don't know what to do around children, not having been around many since I was one. But I remember how much they liked it when I gave back that candy cane, so I hold out two cookies for them. They take them and mercifully stop looking at me.

I guess I should have asked if they were allowed, but it worked and no one's yelling at me that I overstepped, so I'm going to call that a success.

"These are all the amazing ornaments the kids have made for me over the years," Eve says as we unpack each one from the box I used to put more space between me and Beau, pausing to look at each of them lovingly, probably remembering the story that goes with them.

"The *embarrassing* ornaments that we'd rather not look at ever again, because we were young and shouldn't be forever haunted by the clay-molding ability of our youth," Annabelle says.

I laugh and bump into Beau as I move to hang another ornament. The same heat that he inspired in me in New York hasn't lessened since we've moved states. I have plenty of data points by now to prove it's not going anywhere: him brushing my back with his chest as he slides by to reach an empty spot on the tree, his hand touching my arm to stop me tripping over the coffee table as I step back to admire my work, his breath on my head as he reaches over me to hang an ornament on a branch above me.

This is the most erotic tree decorating I've ever been involved in, despite my efforts to stay away from him in front of his family.

"What's this?" I clear my throat and pick up the next ornament in the box, jerking it behind me when Beau rushes to grab it from me like a football player snatching a ball from the air in the last minute of the Super Bowl.

"Is this baby Beau? He's so cute. What is he wearing?" I bump my hip out to keep him away while I take a closer look at the picture.

A miniature boy stands in the cutest little suit, standing by a little girl in a lacy white dress and a bouquet of flowers.

"Are you at a wedding?" I look closer to see if there's anyone else in the picture.

"Oh, he's at a wedding all right—his own," his sister says from the other side of the tree.

"You got child married? Where am I again?" I look around to make sure I don't hear those banjos.

"He did *not* get real married." The other Yankee in the room rushes to reassure me. "I had just explained what marriage was and he said it sounded fun and decided he was going to marry one of the girls in the class."

"She's very cute." Being jealous of a child isn't a great look, yet here we are.

"Beau cried when Mom told him they weren't really married, and decided he was going to get married as soon as he could, so he could build a house next to Mom and

Dad and start his own family on the farm," Annabelle happily says, probably still sour about that peppermint schnapps/Christmas tree reveal.

I look at him in fear and awkwardness and a little bit of disappointment. I don't want to get married, and this guy has been planning his wedding and planning where to put down roots (or where to continue them, in this case) since he was a kid.

The disappointment gets stronger when I realize I shouldn't have come here. Now I met his lovely family and they've probably fitted me for a wedding dress in their minds, and I'm going to disappoint them and the man who can make me come by looking at me hard.

"Look, Mom told me I would get to hang out with my best friend for the rest of my life and we would have a party with a really big cake and all the presents I wanted. I tried to marry Daniel first, but our teacher said we couldn't," Beau says.

"Well, that's rude." And bigoted.

"He was later fired for drinking on the job," Eve whispers. It's nice when bad things happen to bad people.

"Have you still got that wedding planning book?" I swallow the disappointment down deeper. I'm going to leave soon, so I can just schedule a time to feel all the disappointment then.

"My biggest plans were that I wanted a chocolate cake and I hoped Barney would be the entertainment."

"Well, purple would be a sweet color scheme." I turn to the tree so I don't have to think about what I'm doing here with the man who wants a commitment.

But I can't stop myself from following up, even though I do wait for everyone else to get distracted by their own tasks. "Do you still want to live here? On the farm?"

"Of course. I had a great childhood here. It's all I know, except for when I was an hour away for college. Besides vacations, why would I want to leave here?"

"To experience new things?"

"That's what those vacations are for. But home is comfortable, and I like comfortable."

Well, then. Even if I did want to keep Beau around for longer than the holiday (which I don't), he's not going to be in New York. And I can't move here; my life in is New York.

By the end of the day, we finish the tree, most of the cookies, and all of the rum.

"Sonia, do you want to put the star on the tree?" Eve asks.

I look around to see if anyone is mad that she offered it to me. "I couldn't take that job from someone else."

"No one here is as obsessed with Christmas as you, Baby Girl. You can do it." Beau hands me the star.

"If no one cares." I look at Annabelle to make sure she's not glaring at me with the white-hot glare of a thousand burning Christmas lights. She's chasing after her kids, who're probably hopped up on the sugar that I gave them. Oops.

I climb on the back of their leather sectional so I can reach the top of the tree and add the finishing touch. Beau guides me back down, settling me next to him with a casual hand to my waist.

Reed comes home shortly after I put up the star, with some steaks that he grills. The rest of us prepare the sides and salad, as well as the dessert (more Christmas cookies that I volunteer to decorate before anyone else can claim them).

We have a nice dinner, every hour with the warm family making me more comfortable, despite my best intentions to remain aloof. Eve shares some more embarrassing stories of both of her children as the dinner entertainment, because she's the best. Bubba and the kids know I'm the weak link, because all three set up shop around me at the dinner table, the rugrats getting actual seats and Bubba slobbering on my knee.

I smile at the children and they smile back, so I think we're becoming friends. If children can make friends with adults instead of just long-conning them for candy. Not to be forgotten, Bubba sighs so deep he makes my napkin float back to me, so I slip him some steak after belatedly finding out that he is allowed the occasional people food.

Beau and Annabelle volunteer (aka are told by their mom) to do dishes, and I sip some more eggnog.

"Now that the choring is out of the way." Annabelle races back into the living room after the dishes are done. "Let's go to MacGregor's tonight!"

Chapter Twenty-Four

"What is MacGregor's?" I ask in the silence.

Beau sits down, showing us all how willing he is to go out tonight. And then goes and confirms it with his words. "A bar. But why go out when we can get drunk with our mom?"

"Fine, you drink with Mom and my children, and I'll drink with your big city girlfriend."

Whoa, Nelly. And look how country I am already using horse terms in my head? "We haven't really defined anything, as such."

"Ow, your girlfriend doesn't even claim you. You definitely need to get MacGregor's drunk."

Before Beau can offer any more reasons he can't come, Annabelle is kissing her kids on the head and telling them to be good for Grandma and Paw-paw. Tucker follows her lead.

"Bye, Bubbykins. Have a good night and get lots of sleep." I take his head in my hands, looking him in the eyes as I say the words, and then kiss his furry head, not wanting him to feel left out with the kids getting all the love.

"What's the dress code for MacGregor's? I have cocktail dresses, nice blouses and skinny jeans, heels, wedges...

just let me know and I can change into whatever." In my mind, I run through the clothes I dumped in my giant suitcases.

"Oh, darlin', that's the cutest thing you've said all night," Annabelle says.

I purse my lips in confusion, tilting my head. Her words are all nice and the tone is kind of nice as well, I think, but somehow, I don't think that sentence was complimentary.

"Did she just insult me?" I whisper to Beau out of the corner of my mouth.

"Yes. I think she avoided 'Bless your heart' because by now even you thick Yankees know that's an insult," he whispers back. Louder, he says, "What you have on now is fine. It's a very low-key bar."

"It doesn't put on airs like a fancy city bar," Annabelle says.

Why do people think they're so nice down here? She's smiling, but I'm getting mocked.

"I'll put on a low heel. Maybe some booties." I'm not going to abandon all my standards. Eve throws me an approving nod.

I come back downstairs to a cutthroat game of rock, paper, scissors among Beau, Tucker, and Annabelle. I wonder if the bar plan is forgotten and this is what we're doing now, but Eve tells me they're deciding who's driving tonight.

Tucker loses and grunts his disappointment. But his eyes follow his wife's dancing form around the room and he has a small smile on his face, not that mad at his impending sobriety.

I need more single friends. This level of sacrifice, consideration, and affection is making me itch under the collar. Or under my regular plaid button-down, because apparently in the South it's always extra-casual Friday.

We pile into another truck because I think it's illegal to have a sedan here. Annabelle takes control of the radio, putting on a country station and singing along with the songs. I don't know any of them, but the first one is a man singing about checking me for ticks.

Wait, is that a danger I have to worry about? What do I do if I find a tick? Where's the closest hospital? Upon hearing more of the song, though, apparently this singer's just trying to flirt.

That was terrifying.

"Keep in mind this isn't The Plaza," Beau warns me.

"I'm not a snob." I can hang, damn it.

"You're the one who tried to get dressed up for Mac-Gregor's." Making it sound like a cardinal sin.

"I just asked so I would be prepared." And they all answered. No one held the backsass, but it's fine, next time I'll ask for it on the side. "It's rude to over- and under-dress for an occasion. I'm being polite, Beauregard Dean."

"Ah. I was wonderin' how long it would take to make that a thing."

"It is a great name. A loooong name."

"It's a family name."

"So defensive, Beauregard Dean." I shake my head in disappointment.

Beau opens his mouth, probably to defend his name's honor some more, but Tucker parks the truck outside of a building with a neon sign telling me we're at Mac-Gregor's. There are a few other buildings next to it, but they're all closed at this time of night. Beau helps me down from the truck and walks me into the building behind his sister.

Okay. I can see why they were giving me crap now for the cocktail dress comment.

The first thing I notice is the décor: a haphazard mix of roosters, tigers, and bulldogs (I think that's a sports thing, or I have questions), wood, neon signs creating an atmospheric glow over everything, and chairs held together by duct tape and a prayer, I think.

I gingerly sit down on one of the bar stools at the bar, waiting for the bartender to come over.

"What can I get you?" the bartender asks when she gets to us.

"I'll have a whiskey ginger."

Everyone else orders as well and Beau throws down a twenty and turns around.

"Wait." I grab Beau's sleeve. "You have to finish paying." Is the farm having some financial trouble?

"Oh, Baby Girl." He shakes his head, pityingly. "I did pay."

I look at the money, not understanding that. "Okay. But what about the tip?" He didn't strike me as a bad tipper. I open my purse to find some cash to put down.

Beau puts his hand on my arm to stop me. "The tip is there."

I look from the money to Beau's face, and then back to the money. That can't be right. I look above the bar and see a board with prices on it and do a double take when I read them.

"What is this wondrous magic? I will have five more drinks, please," I yell after the bartender.

"How about we drink these first, Baby Girl?" Beau steers me to the table his sister already took over.

"The drinks are so reasonably priced; we have to drink more. This will never happen to me again."

"It could if you come back here." Beau throws it out too casually, like he's not suggesting the terrifying possibility of a future together.

And I'm not drunk enough for that conversation. Maybe after three more dirt-cheap drinks I can start to think about approaching the topic.

"No wonder you're staying at The Plaza when you visit New York," I mumble, not letting the prices go. "You've been saving all this money drinking down here."

"Wait till you see the housing prices," Beau says.

"Shut. Your. Mouth. Please." There are things I don't need to see in life, especially when my own mortgage payment is due soon.

More songs that I don't recognize come on, with Annabelle dancing along. But she's a mother, so she's an expert at multitasking. "Is your family going to miss you so close to Christmas?" she asks me.

"Probably a bit. I'm the most obsessed with Christmas, so I'm sure my cousins, aunt, and uncle might miss some of the events I drag them to. But most likely they'll be glad to get a break this year."

"What about your parents?"

"Don't be so nosy." Beau tries to intervene on my behalf.

"It's fine. We're not really that close since they live in India, so they won't notice that I'm here. They usually visit in the summer."

The first time they decided to not come around Christmas I was disappointed, but I didn't ask them to change it. I already knew it wouldn't have made a difference, like it didn't make a difference when I was young and cried for them to stay longer during their visits.

"That's messed up," Annabelle says.

Now her husband intervenes on my behalf, tossing an arm around his wife's shoulders and pulling her in for a kiss. "She has no filter. Sorry."

"It's fine. It is messed up."

I'm usually okay with it. Chachi and Chacha treat me like another kid, and the cousins treat me like a sibling. I do have a loving family. I don't know what I'm missing until I hang out with other people's families, and they start asking about mine. It's hitting me extra hard spending time with the happy and loving and functional Abbots. Because no matter how wonderful Chachi and Chacha are, that doesn't change the fact that my own parents left me.

Annabelle changes the subject by dragging me on the dance floor and teaching me some of these intricate moves. There's so much to remember, and these cheap drinks are not helping my mental ability any.

Which is why my guard is down (more like distracted), when Annabelle decides she wants a drunken heart-to-heart.

"He won't move."

"What?" I yell at her. Partly because the music is loud and partly because she didn't introduce this topic. And partly because I'm trying to do a kick ball change.

"Look, you seem nice and you get along with Beau well. But I've known my brother my whole life, and he loves home. He won't move. So unless you and your city stilettos want to move here, I don't think this is going to end well."

"Oh." That stops my dancing.

"I'm not trying to be mean. I just don't want you guys to get hurt."

The pang in my heart region says she did succeed in affecting me, whatever her intention was. "Don't worry, it's not like that. We know it's casual."

"If you say so."

"I do say so." Now whether or not I fully believe it myself is another story.

"Shhh. You're gonna wake up your parents," I whisper as we sneak into the house after Tucker dropped us off at the end of the night.

"We have really good walls here. You don't have to sneak in like we're in high school," he whispers, bumping into a side table and proving he enjoyed the thrifty alcohol prices as much as I did.

"Shhhh!" I whisper-yell at him.

I did end up getting a lot of drinks. And in solidarity, so did Annabelle. Her warning forgotten with the alcohol, we found out we both loved reality television, bonding over the most memorable storylines we could remember. And Annabelle taught me even more line dances. Why they want to make dancing so complicated they have to count during it is beyond me; just move your bodies to whatever feels right.

All in all, it was a good night.

I bump into the next table in our path and now I've got drunk Beau shushing me. I crumple into laughter, Beau joining me on the floor in front of the stairs. So close.

"Beau. We can't let them know we're out past curfew."

"Baby Girl. I'm an adult. I don't have a curfew. We're being quiet out of good manners because there's people asleep in the house." More whisper-yelling that becomes more yelling than whispering the longer we're talking.

We stumble up the stairs and into Beau's room, falling into the bed in relief that we made it without getting caught.

Super secret spy school, here I come. I will have the margarita instead of the martini, and blended, not shaken, please.

While I'm putting in my future drinks order, Beau caresses his hands up my arm, and I moan out loud before throwing my hands over my mouth.

"We can't!"

"But I miss you." He nibbles on my neck and I melt into the sensation.

"I'm right here."

"More specifically, I miss this." He runs his hand up my leg and finds my clit through my leggings like he's a heat-seeking missile.

And it's getting very hot down there.

"Then we should have gotten a hotel room like I originally suggested." I arch my back and lean into his hand, slowly grinding against it to get him where I want him.

"You never suggested that."

"I thought it."

"Very good idea. Do you want to call Tucker and find a hotel that he can drive us to?"

"No." But I can't stop thinking about his parents and it's not helping this particular situation. "I have an idea! To the bat cave!"

Chapter Twenty-Five

"Okay." He gets up and blindly follows me even though he must have no idea what I mean. I take him back down the labyrinth of obstacles known as his house.

"Make sure you have your keys."

"O…kay." He sounds less sure this time. But he does get them out of his pockets.

"Just trust me. We won't do anything illegal." I reconsider. "It may be a gray area; I'm not completely up on the law down here."

I open the door to the garage and take the keys from his hand. Unlocking the door to his truck, I climb into the back seat. Or, for honesty's sake, should point out I valiantly *try* to climb in, but alcohol and it's high up, so after a few failed attempts I feel big hands on my butt pushing me. This is different than the gentlemanly arm at the waist, but better.

Definitely better. The heat pooling in my lower stomach agrees heartily.

"What now?" Beau asks as he climbs in behind me. The light in the truck fades after he closes the door behind him, leaving us in the dark.

"Ta-da! Bat cave hotel. How do you like it?" I show him the inside of his own truck.

"And you'll have sex in this?"

"For sure."

"Then I love it." He reaches around my neck to pull me closer. Firmly away from his parents, I give in, moving closer and enthusiastically kissing him back for the first time since we got here.

I climb on top of him and hit my head on the ceiling. I break away from the kiss to curse and rub my head.

"Are you okay?" he asks.

"Yes. It's fine." The alcohol is doing some work to distract from the pain. "Keep going."

I catch his lips again, shoving my hands under his shirt. He unbuttons my shirt and tears it off, punching the back of the driver's seat in his haste. The move traps my shirt and arms behind my back and I laugh at the way this is going. But the will is strong, even if the flesh is failing us just a little, and we carry on.

Beau sees the humor in the present scenario as well and chuckles, but he focuses on wrestling the rest of my shirt off. He unclasps my bra and shoves the cups down, replacing the cups with his mouth.

"Oh, shit," I moan.

"What, did I hit something?" His hands start running up and down my body to find any sign of injury, his voice growly from the whiskey and passion.

"No. I just realized we have to get these skintight leggings off in this tiny space."

He spanks my ass. From his position it doesn't have much strength, but I still feel the effects of it.

"Woman, are you doubting me?" he growls.

"I don't know. Are you gonna spank me again?" I shouldn't be surprised by now at the hints of caveman I see from Beau when we fuck, but they always make me happy. Like a surprise that I forget about every time since he's such a laid-back Dr. Jekyll during the day and then the lights go off and I get to fuck a sexy Mr. Hyde.

He does spank me again and then twists with me on his lap so my back is on the seat, seat belt buckle digging into my back, with Beau on top of me. My legs are wrapped around his waist, and I have no idea where his are in the tiny space.

He peels off my underwear and leggings, only grunting occasionally as he jerks my legs around in the small space to make the task easier, my laughter probably not helping so much. He gets them off and I lean up so I can tear the bra off the rest of the way. It lands somewhere in the front of the truck.

Fully naked, I rub against a fully clothed Beau. Getting wetter, I almost come from feeling my bare skin rub against the fabric of his clothes in the cramped confines of the truck, from how scandalous it all is. But then I remember how much better it feels when he's naked.

In that vein, my fingers scramble to undo the buttons on his shirt. I get that off with little drama or comedy, but when I get to his pants, I look up at him, lost. There's no way I can get these off in the space allotted to me.

Beau realizes the issue and shimmies, with whispered curses, until he disrobes himself. At the last second, he grabs his pants and fishes out a condom, which he puts on without me having to ask. There's the gentleman again, never too far away.

Beau slides his now naked body onto mine, his taut muscles making mine contract when they brush me. My body reacts like this touch is a surprise, just like the first time, but also anticipates the feelings like a favorite treat. It's very confusing for me, the reaction he elicits.

Beau does some more maneuvering and I feel the tip of his penis enter me. He shallowly thrusts a few times and then he stops and starts cursing, a common occurrence in this particular sex location.

"What?"

"I can't get further."

I can't help laughing at the situation we're in. Naked and so close to heaven but with one more obstacle in the way.

Beau thrusts in with my movement, and groans. "Woman, are you laughing at me while I'm inside you?"

"Barely inside me," I say before I can stop myself. Then immediately regret it. Men don't usually like it when you mock them mid-coitus.

Before I can apologize, his eyes narrow, and he growls at me. "Gauntlet. Thrown."

"Oh, shit." But I'm not worried; I'm excited.

He grabs me by the hips and pulls me further under him. I barely feel the seat belt dragging across my back because of the sensations he's causing at my front. After another few readjustments on his end, he pushes in deep.

Oh, god yes.

He reaches down to play with my clit, and I get wetter, pulling him in deeper. Once he's all the way in, he starts thrusting in earnest, and I take over rubbing my clit. I turn my face into the seat when I come, making sure the car muffles my moan. Beau keeps thrusting a few more times and then he comes too.

He collapses on top of me and then shifts next to me when I squeak. But since we're not in a king size bed, or even a twin-size bed, he falls off the seat and lands on the floorboard on his side.

I laugh again. Nothing went right, but we both came, and it was a lot of fun. I couldn't ask for more.

Beau moans and grabs his lower back where it hit the central console. He doesn't look as amused at the events of the night. I roll over to my side, hand tucked under my head, naked, skin sticking to the seat, while I watch him try to stretch in the cramped space.

"No post-coital snuggling?" I ask, still whispering.

"Sure. Just as soon as I get some IcyHot and we get back to the very comfortable bed."

"Reasonable request, Old MacDonald." I grab his shirt and wrap it around me like a robe. There's no way I'm getting back into those leggings right now. I'm sticky with sweat, and the back of the truck, although larger than any other I've been in, hasn't gotten any bigger in the last thirty seconds.

I get out and put my underwear back on, which gives Beau some more room to get in his pants. After collecting the rest of the clothes, he leads me out of the garage. I gasp when we get into the house but try to keep it down.

"What?" he asks, stopping to see what could have caused that reaction in me.

"Your neck is actually red. Like you have a red neck." I point to the expanse of neck now visible since I'm wearing his shirt. "But how did it get red in the wintertime?"

"The sun is dangerous even if it's not summer. And it was a sunny day." Now his face is getting red too. "You know what, c'mere."

Before I know what he's doing, he bends low and then stands, with me dangling off his right shoulder after the move.

I laugh, then immediately think of his parents and

try to stifle the sound. Instead I enjoy the new view of Beau's butt, which continues walking up the stairs.

"Wheeee... I'm a sexy sack of potatoes," I whisper to him, impressed all over again at whatever farm task gave him this strength.

"The sexiest," he agrees, swatting at my butt as he goes up the stairs.

Back in the safety of the bedroom, Beau tosses me on his bed. I decide to keep his shirt, and crawl under the covers while watching Beau put on some pajama pants before he gets in bed too. I fall asleep curled into his side, his arm wrapped around me tight.

With zero thoughts about a pillow wall this time.

I wake up to someone telling mammas not to let their babies grow up to be cowboys. I wonder if this is the strangest sleep talking I've heard, but a turn of my head shows Beau's still asleep with his mouth closed.

His phone, on the other hand, is awake and so very loud. And really insistent that cowboying is not a solid career choice for young people.

I shove at Beau, wanting him to tell the phone I get the point and I promise never to condone the cowboy lifestyle for any potential progeny. The phone stops by itself, which is good because Beau didn't respond to my prodding, and I settle back into Beau's warmth. But then the phone starts again and I shove at Beau harder.

Some of us were up very late and our bodies do not process alcohol as easily as they did a few years ago.

Beau rolls over and gets the phone, finally answering the call.

"Hello?" His voice is still rough from sleep and alcohol, and he rolls back over to pull me where I was before the rude person called.

"I'll ask her."

After a pause. Then some exasperation. "No, not right now. When she wakes up."

Another pause. A longer pause. The person on the other end of the phone sure can talk. Beau interrupts whatever they're saying, "I'll call you back, Anna-Banana. After I talk to her. After we wake up whenever we want, because she's on vacation."

Call ended, he puts the phone back on his bedside table.

I try to go back to sleep, but curiosity won't let me. "What's up? It sounds serious."

"Nah, it's just Annabelle. She wants to know if you and I want to do something with her and Tucker today."

I yawn. "Oh, sure. I should check email for a second but then I'll be free for the day. What does she have planned?"

"She said it's up to you. But she suggested that you get in some 'red shit' while you're here."

"Red? Like the proletariat controlling the means of production red?"

"What? No. Like redneck."

"Oh, that makes more sense."

"She suggested taking you hunting."

"Oh, hell no," I say flatly, visions of Bambi floating across my brain.

"I thought that would be the response."

"I mean, I don't want to do a murder."

A pregnant pause. "You do eat meat though."

"I didn't say eating meat was murder. I said hunting would be. In that it's killing with malice aforethought." The literal definition of murder. "It's legal murder and I get it, but still. I don't want to do it. Not my idea of fun."

"But. What? What's eating meat then? Isn't it murder too?" Poor confused Old MacDonald.

"At worst? Accessory after the fact. I'm okay with accessory after the fact. I can live with that. Totally different crime. *Lesser* crime."

"No hunting. Got it."

I think he'd agree to anything to be out of this conversation.

"Don't you have to work? Don't feel like you have to entertain me."

"I want to." Beau rubs my back, dropping a kiss on my head even though I just called his sister a legal murderer. "And the mulch guy is working on the issue. They just needed to see me in person and now they're finding all sorts of mulch that they said wasn't there. I'll go to the store later this week to look disappointed some more."

But his presence isn't helping me keep things as light or casual as I want them to be. So it would be great if this giant mulch emergency that dragged him out of New York and out of the no-thinking-about-the-future bubble we were in could be a little more urgent than a two-day fix.

Damn, inconvenient mulch.

His arm tightens around me and he moves to lean over me. "I know exactly where we should take you." He looks happy at whatever solution he came up with, which is only slightly worrying.

"What's the plan?"

"How do you feel about NASCAR?"

Chapter Twenty-Six

After Beau's mysterious question about NASCAR, which he refuses to explain at all, he pulls me back to his side and says we can sleep in, because we're going to an evening event.

When we finally get up, Beau makes breakfast. The cinnamon monkey bread is delicious and very messy. Then we both have some laptop time, getting some work done on holiday. I even show him more pieces that I think will do great in his new offices, and he bids on them right there. I can also show him some pictures I'm being sent as pieces are delivered to his office space. It's slowly coming together.

And then I send the info to Priya, so she knows this interior design division can be good from a financial standpoint. I guess I'm not done with that idea.

I get this in response:

How is the trip? Is it Zeus and anyone but his wife or is it more Medieval Abelard and Heloise? If she wasn't talking about me, I would be impressed with the on-point references.

...those images are equally terrifying.

But you haven't answered the question!

Somewhere between wild bull orgy and flirty letters from monastery to nunnery.

That doesn't give me any details.

It's more the frescoes that show one couple in Pompeii in the brothel. It is NOT the reliefs on the Khajuraho Temple. Those were some frisky sculptures.

Lame. Get on it, single girl.

Marrieds are terrifying. She wasn't this sexually adventurous when she was single, but now she's all about it. Or all about wanting to hear other people getting it in adventurous ways.

I look over to Beau on his desk, chewing the side of his lip as he answers some emails. I'm seeing the allure of getting it on in adventurous ways with this man.

After enough time working that we don't have to feel too guilty about vacationing, Beau loads me in the truck.

The truck I have very fond memories of.

He asked his parents if they wanted to come, but they declined, saying they were busy. He called his sister next, who said they were bringing the kids so they would drive alone. Annabelle works with Eve as an event planner, making it easy to take time off, and Tucker had already put in for PTO from his job to be home with the kids on their winter break.

"Can you tell me where we're going now?" I plug the AUX cable into my phone to take over the sound.

"On a little road trip to Speedway in Lights at the Bristol Dragway in Tennessee." He gets on the freeway.

"What do those words mean?"

"It's a racetrack and around the holidays they decorate the track with a bunch of Christmas light displays. And you get to drive on the actual track to see the lights. At a reasonable speed," he says before I can tell him there's no way I'm racing around at a wild speed.

I'm also happy I don't have to watch actual NAS-CAR. I can't watch cars going in a circle for hours. He's not that cute.

But I'm lucky I don't have to test my strength to stand up to him if it was an actual NASCAR race. Because I'm not super confident I would be able to resist and then I would be drinking beers I don't like and watching the cars go round and round. And round.

"That does sound like fun," I concede. "How far is it?"

"Four hours." Beau puts on cruise control, settling in for the long ride.

"Four hours?!" That's more than a little road trip.

"Four hours. So I can show you why a Southern Christmas beats a Yankee Christmas. And since it's far I've booked a hotel for the night." He taps me on the knee.

"Oh." Then I think about it some more. "Ohhh." As fun as boning in a truck is, a bed would be better. Hell, even a floor would be better than the back of a truck.

"Yeah. I thought you would be okay with that part."

"Shit got a lot more Yankee this and Yankee that since you got back down here."

"It's our way," he answers placidly.

Okay, then. "So what do we do for the next four hours?"

Eat a lot of junk food, the answer turns out.

Beau stops at a Cracker Barrel, where we load up on biscuits, muffins, chocolate, and chips. And an assortment of beverages I haven't heard of. Which is impressive in today's world of giant conglomerates stocking stores coast to coast.

We line up at the cash register to make our purchases and a woman behind us looks over our shoulders. "Ooh, I want to be going with you and all those snacks."

I turn around, surprised at the new conversation.

"Ha-ha." I look at her, laughing awkwardly, and then turn back around to face the cashier.

"Where are you guys headed?" the woman behind us asks.

Who is she, the CIA? "Road trip," I answer succinctly, not giving this stranger my future location. My Chachi didn't raise no fool when it comes to stranger dangers.

"We're heading on up to Bristol for Speedway in Lights," Beau says. Someone didn't watch the stranger danger videos. I'll pull them up on my phone when we get back into the car.

"That's so much fun! We've been every year since we've had kids and last year was the best since my daughter was home from college and she brought a boyfriend! I think he had a lot of fun since it was his first time doing something like that. He's from Boston, so it was nice to show him some Southern cooking." The woman rambles and rambles on.

"It's good to expose those less fortunate." Beau nods like the woman trying to tell him her life story at the Cracker Barrel counter is perfectly normal behavior.

"I hope we made a good impression on him. I'm ready to be a mee-maw. Well, after she's done with college."

"Sure, sure," I say into this strange conversation. Is

a requirement for being a mee-maw oversharing with strangers? Because if so, she's already there.

The cashier, becoming my favorite person in the entirety of the South, rings up our purchases and takes the money without giving us her life story. And she does it quickly, so we can get out of here. She gets an extra generous tip in the tip jar.

"You have a great holiday, ma'am," Beau says as he picks up the packages.

"Y'all too." Chatty Cathy waves us off.

When we get back in the truck, I can't hold it in anymore. "What was that all about?"

"What?" Beau starts the vehicle and backs out of the parking spot.

"Do you know her? Is she a long-lost aunt? A distant cousin?"

"What?"

"The woman in the line. Who told you everything about her daughter's dating life? A lot of sharing happening."

"She was just being friendly," Beau says. I don't know if he's distracted by driving or if he genuinely doesn't think this is weird. But I most certainly do think it's weird. "We talk to the people we see out in the world down here. It's called being polite."

I curl my lip in distaste. "It sounds terrible."

"There's so many people in New York. Don't you ever talk to each other?"

"Not when we're clearly busy with other tasks. We respect other people's time too much to bother them with supplemental chatter." I shake my head at Beau's outlook on life. Again.

Despite his incorrect opinions, I still really like this

man in front of me. Enough to follow him to the wild unknown for my favorite holiday. An action that is very unlike me. Before I can obsess about that too much, the scent of the baked goods in my lap lulls me into forgetting all the confusion. Or at least pushing it aside.

The power of carbs.

Beau is singing along to some Shania Twain while I take another bite of biscuit. Outside the truck window, the scenery changes from trees abandoned by their leaves to trees who gained some light snow when we get into the Blue Ridge Mountains.

"This is really pretty." I haven't seen a building in way too long, which makes me a little restless, but the snow makes a damn pretty picture hugging the trees like I was wrapped around Beau last night.

We spend the trip alternating between singing obnoxiously to music from the early 2000s until I suggest we play a sober Never Have I Ever.

"Never have I ever broken a bone." I start off innocently, not wanting to scare him right out the gate.

"Oof. That would make me drink, if that's what we were doing. I broke my arm climbing a tree. Well, falling off one. Then I fractured my wrist playing baseball. My turn now. Never have I ever gone skinny-dipping."

"Oh yeah, I'm drinking to that." I take a sip of the Cheerwine.

"Was it coed?" Beau sounds so shocked.

"Yes, it was."

Now Beau is silent.

"Never have I ever sexted." Since he already introduced nakedness into the conversation.

"Not one naughty picture or sassy text?" Beau asks. "I would have to drink there."

"Men, mostly, have ruined it for themselves with all this revenge porn! I'm not sending a temporary, casual partner that ammo if we break up badly. No thanks."

"All right, fair. Never have I ever been sent to the principal's office."

"No drinks to that." But if he thinks he can make this PG again, he's wrong. "Never have I ever had sex in public."

"Would drink to that. There's not a lot of options when your parents work from the house. Never have I ever been single for more than six months since I started high school."

The words make me choke on the soda I'm drinking. I knew he wanted marriage and the white picket fence but by god, that is terrifying.

"First of all, I would drink to that. I would drink an entire handle of alcohol at that. Second, why? How?"

Beau shrugs and avoids my eyes. Sure, he's driving, so it's also prudent, but I think he's using that as an excuse. "I like relationships. My parents are happy together, and I want the same thing. Someone to do fun Christmas activities with and just hang around the house with. A partner."

"But none of them have worked out yet. Hasn't that been a lot of pain to go through?"

"Yes, there's been a lot of heartbreak. But I know what's possible, and the pain is worth it. And if we broke up, it probably wasn't right anyway, so better to know that before we made a serious commitment."

"Why the dry spell right now?"

"I've been getting the battery business set up. First traveling to Atlanta and then spending all the time on the business plan. It's important to make something of my own in the family and contribute to the business. So it's made me a bit more distracted than I usually would be and my last girlfriend didn't appreciate it. Then there was no time to date anyone new after she broke up with me. And it's hard to find someone in a small town."

Aha! The city wins that one; there's so many people to date there. But I don't rub it in, because I'm still shocked.

"When was your last relationship?"

"Maybe high school." I did give relationships a try once upon a time, but then he went cross-country for college, which was exactly the right choice for him, but it felt like I was being left yet again.

"Why not since?"

"Guess it's just not good timing. I've always been busy with school and then work. Travel for work made it especially hard, and the effort never seemed worth it."

"That's a shame, because you are great company."

"Well, obviously. Are you going to move to New York to be with the battery business full-time?" I shove the pastry in my mouth too late to stop the question from coming out.

"I don't think I'll ever need to. I can make trips there and they can come here when needed."

"Wouldn't it be easier to just move there? Or commit a larger amount of time there? For a fledgling business and all that." The pastry bite does not stop me from pressing, even though he's confirmed my suspicions.

Beau hesitates, the most uncomfortable I've seen him in our acquaintance. Even more so than when I caught him bad-mouthing my art. "I wasn't planning to move. I always expected I'd spend my whole life here. My parents made a great childhood for me, and a large part of it was growing up in our small town. But I will be visiting to keep an eye on things."

"So you will be in the city?"

"On and off."

Fantastic. But in sarcasm tone. That's going to make life harder, constantly wondering if he's around the corner, ordering street meat and hating on art that I love. Constantly being reminded that I'm too wary to commit, but I have good reason because the person that I lo—like actually does leave regularly for his home in the South.

Because I don't love him. It would be way too early to love anyone other than a puppy, for whom the phrase "love at first sight" was invented.

The long drive ends just when I'm about to burst from all the Cheerwine I've drank on this trip. I got pretty excited at first when I thought Beau was handing me some adult juice in a can and then got sad when I realized it was just cherry Coke. Then happy again when I realized it was pretty good cherry Coke.

Wine or not, I drank a bunch and now I'm on a sugar high and I have to pee.

"We're gonna meet Annabelle and the family for some snacks and then we'll drive through the lights," Beau says.

"Sure." As long as there's a bathroom somewhere near there.

Beau pulls into a spot next to another truck. Well, that describes a lot of vehicles in the parking lot. Specifically, he parks next to a gray truck with people related to him in it, and I start the long treacherous climb down from my seat.

"Hi, everyone," I shout out as I fall three stories. Or however high up this truck is.

"Hey!" I get four responses back, even from the mini humans.

"How was the drive?" Annabelle asks.

"Good. Lots of food and liquids. So I'll be right back."

She sees that I'm looking around and gets the hint. She turns me around gently, giving me a light push toward the bathrooms now in front of me.

Needs met, I walk back to the trucks, slowing to take in the scene waiting for me. Beau's down on one knee to talk to Harper, who's showing him her fire engine with an earnest energy. Harry, not wanting to lose any of his uncle's attention, extends his completed coloring book page toward Beau.

Beau, showing a diplomacy that probably serves him well juggling multiple investors, employees, and potential clients for his new business, gives each of them equal attention. He fawns over each of them enough that they're not jealous of each other, sending adoring looks up at him.

It makes the little-used organ in my chest increase its pace. At least, it's regularly used for the proper function of distributing blood throughout my body, but not so much for the emotional baggage we put on that organ.

Because he's adorable.

And it's still scary that I'm having this much of a reaction to seeing him, and not just for sex. That kind smile and his absurd desire to open every door for me keep dragging me back. Because how can a package like that lead to any pain?

But it will. It always does.

"Sonia's back, you hooligans. Now we can go," Beau says.

They look at me, abandoning their beloved uncle for

the allure of a shiny new person. Fickle humans. See, more proof that people aren't meant for loyalty.

"Let's do this thing."

"Y'all come with us." Harper drops her prized possession of a few minutes ago and races to grab my hand.

I automatically bend over to grasp the little hand, hoping I don't crush it. It's too tiny. Maybe I can hold her hand once we grow those bones a little more. Harry, not wanting to be left out, abandons his uncle as well. That's a lot of rejections in a row.

Harry runs toward me, even tinier hand extended, and I bend down my last upright side to make it easy on the little human.

I look up at Beau from my hunched position. He's taken the opportunity to stand upright, and my back twinges in jealousy. He sends a teasing smile my way and I know he can see how awkward I am right now.

"Show me how to do this light thing, please." I know how much I like knowing things other people don't, so maybe the little humans will like teaching me.

They happily take the bait, walking me past the back seats of their parents' vehicle, to the truck bed. Beau, in on the secret procedure I'm seeing for the first time, opens the tailgate to show me a cozy setup.

I laugh as I take in the inflatable mattress covered in more blankets than I've ever seen in one place, with toys thrown around the space. They strung little fairy lights along the back of the truck, with a battery-operated, light-up Frosty and Rudolph set up to keep the occupants company.

"When did you guys have time to get this set up?" I ask.

"Beau took you on the scenic route," Tucker says.

I laugh as I help Harry in while Beau helps Harper. He tosses some chocolate bars in after them and winks as the children greedily snatch the goods and tear into them.

He helps me in next, lifting me with as much effort as he used to lift Harper (in my mind at least, and I won't hear any different).

Once I get settled, Harry snuggles in close to me. I think this is because I gave him that candy cane back when we met. Easiest sacrifice ever since it was sticky and half-eaten.

Beau gets in after me and stretches out in the space, his hand stroking my shoulder and a small portion of my upper back where it rests.

"What are the highlights here?" I ask as the parents get in the front to drive us around.

"Santa's race day camper!" That's Harper.

"The Christmas castle!" From Harry.

"The flashing arches you drive through! Just like Mario Kart!" Beau now.

Wow those are some enthusiastic responses. The kids I can understand, but Beau has a lot of enthusiasm for this. Maybe a smidge too much?

Then I remember that I have a standing appointment to make a gingerbread house every year. Nah, this is an appropriate level of enthusiasm for anything Christmas related.

"Don't give me that look, Baby Girl. I watched you push aside innocent children to make a LEGO key chain at Rockefeller Center, so don't throw stones over this way." That threat would have so much more weight if Beau wasn't redoing one of Harper's braids for her, his large hands gentle with the small girl's hair and a shiny bow sitting in his lap.

Already reading my mind like a married couple who've seen each other every day for the past twenty-seven years. This is fine. This is all fine. Not too deep at all.

"You play with LEGOs?" Harry asks, interested now.

"I know my way around a LEGO set." Especially all the Christmas LEGO sets I bring out each holiday season, a collection that grows by a few every year.

Tucker starts the vehicle and I lean against the tailgate as the kids move to clutch the sides, watching the lights pass by. I do love a good theme, and the way they integrate Santa and racing is cute. Even if I'm only personally obsessed with one of those things.

There's Santa driving a race car, one kicking up his feet next to a camper (Harper was right; it's the best one), and Frosty being a pit boss for the reindeer, refueling with carrots and giving their horseshoes a polish.

My stomach hurts from laughing so hard at the kids' shenanigans. They have no filter when they're talking about the lights, dragging us side to side in the back to see the best views, and they're hilarious.

And they can surprise me.

"Are you and Uncle Beau married?" Harry asks out of the blue.

Chapter Twenty-Seven

The kid gets a direct hit, like the most effective assassin who lulls you into a false sense of security and then slides the blade into the base of your neck when they're hugging you. Just like Beau's sister did when we were enjoying ourselves decorating the tree. On ladders way too high in the air for serious questions.

Which is why I almost choke on the water I'm drinking.

"Um." Kids are curious so this should not have been that much of a surprise. I'm getting soft. "No." I try to think of what would soften that harsh denial, but words are escaping me.

Because of the blade sticking out of the base of my neck. It's distracting.

"But you're adults. And you're always together." Harry brings up excellent points.

I look at Beau but the man has forgotten all of his words. Or refuses to use any of them in a badly timed vow of silence.

"They don't need to be married to be together. We watch TV together and we're not married." Older sister Harper drops some logic on her baby brother. She's going to be all right.

Probably president someday.

"Yes, what she said." I hope that'll be the end of it.

"But we're family. Are they family?" Harry asks, persistently.

"No." I'm back to one-word denials.

"Then what are you?"

Damn. I thought Southern mothers were a force to be reckoned with, but they have nothing on Southern children.

"We're friends." Beau finally decides to dig up some of that Southern gentleman. After I've floundered for his amusement, of course.

"But you kissed her. Do you kiss friends?" Harry asks.

How many knives does this little assassin have? I thought his bag was full of half-eaten candy canes and toys. I clamp my mouth shut. I'm not going to explain friends with benefits to this precious pre-fuckboy angel baby face.

"You can kiss anyone, Harry, as long as they agree to it. And kisses can mean different things depending on the type of kiss they are and who they're for." Beau plants a loud, exaggerated kiss on Harper's and Harry's heads, to their happy, high-pitched giggles.

I hold my breath, waiting for the next attack of the overly curious child assassin. But it doesn't come. Not because we handled this so well. More because an uneaten candy bar caught his eye and before he could poke more holes in our logic, he's shoving sugar in his mouth. Or aiming for his mouth and getting it on his cheeks. That's probably best so he doesn't get as much of a sugar rush this close to bedtime.

Either way, saved for the however long the candy lasts.

But despite my worry, the rest of the night is surprisingly pleasant. Not having spent much time with kids, I was worried the night was going to be filled with unhappy crying and maybe some throwing up. But we have a lot in common. We all love candy and Christmas and bright lights.

They have such big personalities for their little bodies. Harper, being the oldest, bosses her little brother around with all the confidence of a future leader. She even conned her brother out of some of his hot chocolate.

So a corrupt future leader, to be fair.

And she never misses an opportunity to tell her brother why he's wrong. I think she's my hero. Smart, corrupt, future leader that she is.

Harry, on the other hand, is so good-natured. I haven't decided if he's being nice to his sister by giving in to her, or if he's that oblivious and easy-going. Either way he doesn't stop smiling.

Since I never thought I'd get married, I definitely never thought about having kids. Maybe committing to a puppy one day if I get a little lonely, a thought I've had more often since my best friend found the love of her life. Because a puppy can't leave me; I need to feed it.

But I could see how people want to do this. For the entertainment value alone really, these kids rank up there with reality TV.

Like when Harper whispered to her brother that every time someone farted, part of their insides flew out of their butt, and if they did it enough all their insides would be gone, and then Harry spent the rest of the drive trying to keep a fart in until Beau figured out what happened and set the record straight.

I laughed so hard my stomach hurt when Harry let out a loud, smelly toot, the look on his face a combination of bliss and satisfaction. And then I made eye contact with Beau, who was trying to keep it in, and started laughing all over again.

Fart humor really is ageless.

But it's easy to say that on a good day like today, when we're all having a good time at a family outing. I'd probably think differently if I had to deal with the hard work: bad days and body fluid emergencies and crying with no easily discernible cause. Maybe I should ask Priya if she's thinking about having kids. I'd get all the benefits of spending fun time with the rugrats without doing any full-time commitment.

Even though I bet she won't unless I tell her it will be good for business and help her make more sales.

After we drive around the track twice and eat so much popcorn and hot chocolate that I bet I'm going to hear about a shortage on the news tomorrow, it's time to leave. The kids are out. Beau and I have to carry them back into the truck after the last loop around the track, neither kid waking up through the move. I miss being that heavy a sleeper.

We say good-night to Annabelle and Tucker, who are heading to a hotel for the night as well. I climb back into Beau's truck, where all my stuff like my glittery metal water bottle, lip balm and hand sanitizer have made themselves at home in their new location: Beau's center console. They look comfortable there.

"Did you have fun?" Beau asks, driving us to the hotel.

"It was a lot of fun. Still can't compare to a New York Christmas though." Before he gets too big for his britches.

"I've got time, Baby Girl." He grabs my hand and kisses it, then doesn't let go as he sets our hands on the center console.

I wait for the familiar surge of panic at the thought of

the future and Beau, even if it's only about later this week. But it doesn't come. My stomach is calm and I think I'm even *excited* about what other adventures the man has planned for me.

It must be something in the air. I'm not used to this much fresh air; it's really doing things to my head.

"We'll see." It's the best that I can manage at this particular time, affected as I am with the fresh-air sickness.

Twenty minutes later, Beau pulls up to a large brick building, complete with its own veranda and rocking chairs. He handles check-in and takes our bags in hand, directing me to the elevators. He leads us to the room and then drops the luggage off just inside the door.

"We've got another amazing Christmas activity scheduled for tomorrow, so we should probably rest up."

I look at the inviting, fluffy white sheets and grab his hand. "Then you better be quick."

Without discussing it further, we each start ripping off our own clothes, not ready to take the time to slowly undress each other or savor the parts that we uncover.

Undressed and condom on, we clash in the middle of the bed, Beau getting me under him in record time while kissing me. I feel his hand on my clit, sliding through the slight wetness he finds there and making it increase. We both display a bit of urgency in our actions, whether it's so we can rest up for the next day of Christmasing, or whether it's because our time is limited, or maybe because we haven't had a bed for this in a while, I don't know.

All I can do is enjoy where we are now.

A short time later, he pushes into me inch by inch, the frenzy not making him any less careful with me, a gentleman in every circumstance. A short time after that he starts to thrust, and then I'm coming. Not very long after that, he comes, collapsing next to me.

He kisses the top of my head, chest heaving, and I'm glad we didn't bother turning any of the lights on when we came in. Because it is beyond me to try to get up, even to save the environment.

We stay on top of the covers, getting under them beyond us too. Despite how physically satisfied I am, I feel a prickle of unease with the recent development of settling into time with Beau without more…well, unease.

I wake up snuggled in warmth surrounding me on all sides. I expected the warmth under me and to my side, but the warmth on top of me does make me wonder. I lift my head up to see what's causing it and see I'm wrapped in the comforter I fell asleep on.

"Mornin'," Beau says from next to me, also under the sheets.

"Good morning." I snuggle back into the warmth, pressing a kiss on his chest to thank him for getting us under the covers.

"You're gonna love the surprise today." Beau sounds uncharacteristically smug and I peek up at him. His eyes stay closed, but his lips are twisted into a "I've won" smile.

"Where are we going?" Now I'm curious. He hasn't ever been this confident in our informal competition. The one with no judges, no criteria, and no prize. And yet, the one we're both very invested in.

"This one's going to be a complete surprise. And you're going to love it." He opens his eyes and looks down at me with so much pride for whatever he has planned, I don't press to spoil the surprise.

An hour and a half and two Cheerwines later, Beau pulls over on the side of the road.

"Are you ready for this?"

I look around, seeing the field of naked trees around us. And no civilization. What can be out here? But whatever it is, I resolve to pretend to like anything he planned for me, because he's been so lovely and looks so hopeful. If it's camping, it's going to be hard though.

"Being cannibalized on the side of the road?" I can't resist a joke.

"Your mind is a scary place."

"My mind. Every woman's mind. Whatever." I shrug.

His face falls. "I don't reckon I can keep being this excited after that bit of reality."

"I live with it, and I want my non-cannibalism-related surprise." I slap him lightly and repeatedly on the arm. I came to the wilderness with no internet. And potential cannibals, damn it.

Beau gets a bit of his enthusiasm back, but not back to where he was before I brought up danger. "Look up there, at the top of the hill." He turns me gently to face the top of that aforementioned hill. "I'm taking you to Biltmore, Baby Girl."

My face lights up in genuine excitement as I see the outline of the house roof in the distance. I gasp and jump around him a little. "No way! You're really taking me to Biltmore??"

Chapter Twenty-Eight

Biltmore is the vacation home built by a rich Vanderbilt in 1889. It looks like a French château on the outside, and on the inside has the spirit of the richest rich people going on a Grand Tour around Europe and buying up all the art.

It's beautiful. And I can't wait to see it.

"You did good, Old MacDonald." I let him have a few moments of revelry before I drop the axe. "Not to be pedantic, but old George Vanderbilt *was* from New York. Staten Island to be exact."

"And he brought his Yankee ass down here to God's country to build his obnoxiously big house."

"One of his *many* houses."

"His *biggest* house."

I put my hands on my hips. "Did you read the pamphlet after you made this decision?"

Beau ducks his head down, à la guilty puppy. "Maybe. But it's still true."

"It's the biggest because there's so much land down here."

"Do you still want to go to this house?"

I fling my hands up. "Yes. The South is great and George

loved it for its natural beauty and hospitable people and artery-clogging delicious food."

"Very little effort." He shakes his head in disappointment. "But we're already here so I'm going to take you and rub it in that this is all in the South."

"And I will meekly accept all your taunts." Until we come back down the hill that Biltmore is on. Well, until we get back to somewhere I can catch a ride if he kicks me out of the truck because of the level of sass happening.

"Until we get done with the tour," he says.

Shit, he knows me already.

I decide silence is the better part of valor, late though the decision may be. Instead, I give him a kiss. This is a fantastic date to take an auctioneer on.

We drive up the hill, past the acres and acres of land the house surrounds itself with to ensure maximum privacy. Thick patches of trees with some wintery green tower over each side of the road, daring us to keep going. But I know what treasures are at the end of those trees, so I'm going to keep going, if it's all the same to the guardians.

We park in the lot and walk the rest of the way up. Then we turn a corner and I catch my breath.

Because this is combining all my favorite things. A large, decorated Christmas tree dominates the manicured lawn. In the background is a graceful French château. Large buses drive up the long drive to deposit their charges right in front of the edifice, their own sounds of wonder audible the closer we get to the entrance.

It's also a lot colder here in North Carolina than it has been in South Carolina. Which means I'll need to find a heat source. Oh no. Whatever shall I do?

Snuggle up to Beau and enjoy all my dreams coming

true all at once. Even if it could still be a little better, I suppose. If we were in New York. But I won't say that since this date is still so nice as it is.

"I'm very impressed by this Carolina right now." I give him a compliment wrapped in a dig, because while he might get all the points for being thoughtful and perfect, I don't do flowers and fancy words. Too close to a relationship.

Beau takes umbrage, as expected. "We are by far the better Carolina. We have better beaches, almost no snow and have you tried our peaches?" Beau throws an arm around me, but he's shivering more than me. Poor lamb would not enjoy a long New York winter.

"No. But I hear Georgia is the state of the peaches." We make the walk up the drive, past the decorated trees and their unlit lights.

"We make more, and tastier, peaches." Beau gets as close to a huff as I've seen him.

"But doesn't California make more peaches than both of those states? Combined?"

"We don't say that name in these parts," he grumbles.

Beau is saved from the intense peach interrogation by us getting to the entrance of the big house. An employee with a reddened nose hands us audio guides.

I lift the bulky phone-looking device to my ear and start the tour to soak up some history as I step into the door, immediately feeling the warmth from the space. We walk into the conservatory, lights streaming in from the glass ceiling, illuminating the garlands and poinsettias set up in the grand space. It's even decorated for Christmas inside!

I get my phone out in my other hand, ready to document this impeccably decorated home.

Beau tugs at my elbow, interrupting said soaking of history. He gets the stink eye for that. "Ma'am, do you need the trunks brought in from the carriage?" He deepens his accent to heretofore unheard depths.

My eyes relax from their tight glare, and my nose rises in the universal language of high society. "Fortesburry, of course you bring the bags in. Do you think these hands have done manual labor?" I lift my hands, palms up and still holding the electrical equipment, and re-adjust imaginary long gloves. My voice has gotten more nasally and a lot more condescending.

Just like the Vanderbilts of old, I imagine. Or their friends.

"I don't reckon they have, ma'am. Right away, ma'am." He tips an imaginary hat at me.

And so it continues, in every room.

In the dining room, as I snap a photo:

"Are there an okay number of fireplaces in this room?" Beau asks.

And down my audio guide goes. "No, of course not. Three is for peasants. I demand one more befitting my station. And another Christmas tree." I walk past a giant decorated Christmas tree. "And while we're at it, the fourth deer head from the right is looking at me strangely. Handle it."

"I'll get my rifle."

"See to it."

By the outside veranda, the audio guide doesn't even make it to the ear this time, and I start our game: "Fortesburry, make the trees have leaves again. They look so depressing like that."

In the library: "Ma'am, now don't go getting all out

of sorts, but there's some shirtless people kissing above you."

I look up and tsk him. "It's trompe l'oeil, Fortesburry. Take a class on architectural history before you occupy the same space as me."

In George's master bedroom: "Would ma'am like the turndown service?" Beau asks.

"Well, Fortesburry, I don't know. What does your turndown service entail?"

Beau slides an arm around me and pulls me into his side. "Anything you damn well want," he growls in my ear, his accent deep but not the fake deep he was just doing. And then, in the same bedroom where George Vanderbilt put the moves on Edith Stuyvesant Dresser, he puts the moves on me.

When Beau's tongue touches my lips, that's my last coherent thought for a while. Until the nosy busybody behind me clears her throat like we aren't in a rich man's bedroom that has probably seen worse than a tame kiss. We break apart, begrudgingly.

In the kitchen after fleeing from being caught in flagrante delicto in the bedroom: "Fortesburry, I smell gingerbread. Acquire some for me."

Beau stands behind the giant gingerbread house, with the gingerbread smell pumping through the room, and he pantomimes breaking a piece off. And then he runs when he catches the attention of an employee.

By the time the tour spits us out by the restaurant and gift shop, I realize I haven't listened to any of the audio guide I was excited about, but I still had a lot of fun. Even more fun than I usually have at historic sites. And I usually have a lot of fun at historic sites.

That was all because of the man next to me. The Fortesburry to my Vanderbilt.

But I buy the guidebook so I can still read all the history I missed later. And pick up presents for Priya and Ajay.

Beau revives Fortesburry when we're in the gift shop, offering to whittle me every object I touch. I don't know how he's going to whittle me a shirt, but I don't want to wear it. Not even for that really good dick.

"Hungry after putting us peasants in our place?" Beau asks after I pay for my goods, despite Beau trying to hand over his card at the last minute. But I know his ways now and beat him to the cashier. I also grabbed his and refused to give it back until the transaction was over.

"Always hungry. But I don't think I was very successful putting you in any sort of place."

"I think you'd be surprised if you knew the effect you had on me, Baby Girl."

I stand there and open and close my mouth a few times, not sure how to react to that. Because he's having an effect on me too, despite how much I keep reminding myself to stay strong.

Beau, being the nice man who's too charming for my own good, gets me moving again without making me respond to his emotional statement. "Let's get you some pimento cheese in the old stables." He turns me in the direction of the food.

The old stables, as it turns out, is quite the fancy restaurant now that they've kicked out the equine residents and turned their stalls into plush booths. The décor and the delicious pimento cheese dip go a long way to making up for the fact that Beau is making me wish I wanted more, making me wish that I could have a relationship like a normal person.

"I'll give you this, Old MacDonald: all this food makes the South a real contender in the Christmas competition." I lean back in the booth, stomach bursting with the food I've consumed in the past hour. I send up thanks to whoever invented leggings, and then brave souls who first used them as real pants. Heroes.

"Really?" he asks incredulously. "Not when I drove you on a racetrack with Christmas lights? Or when we decorated a real peach tree? This house?" He flails his arms out in the direction of the museum we just came from.

I pick up my drink and take a sip, not wanting to crush the golden retriever sitting in front of me. "It gets cold out here, doesn't it?" I add a theatrical shiver so he knows I'm serious and not just trying to change the subject. It is colder here than in South Carolina, but it's still not New York cold.

"Freezing." His flat gaze pins me to the booth and I sink into it a little to avoid the probing eyes.

Oh damn. I always thought it was cheesy in the rom-com when one love interest is looking at a sunset or a particularly nice painting, and says, "Beautiful," but the other love interest is looking at the first person and not the scene, and says, "Yeah, beautiful."

I wish I could have a little of that "Beautiful" sentiment now, because Beau saying freezing and looking into my soul when I'm talking about the weather is way harsh.

It's getting dark outside, so I try another atmosphere-related segue. "We should head back now, huh? So it's not too dark on the drive back."

Beau does that thing where he gives in to what I'm saying, but I still don't feel like I win. "Sure. Let's head out." Stomach full of pimento cheese and arms laden with souvenirs, we head to the parking lot.

"Beau, the lights are on now." I slap his arm in excitement. Okay, now the Christmas moment is perfect.

But I spoke too soon.

Chapter Twenty-Nine

Because when we're walking to the tree to get a Christmas selfie, I feel a cold wet pinch on my cheek.

I gasp. "Beau. Did you organize this?" A few snowflakes follow their friend, a light dusting on my upturned face. The perfect amount for a Christmas moment but not hard enough to be an inconvenience.

He's shaking his head at me, smiling at my enthusiasm. "I really wish I could take credit for this and that you could live life thinking I'm powerful enough to control the weather, but this is just winter in Asheville."

"You should have taken the credit when you had the chance."

"Honesty is important."

"Honesty makes you a chump who I don't think controls the weather."

Beau, using a now familiar move against me, shakes his head at me again and doesn't say anything.

Pictures taken, we survive the trek to the car with minimal whining from the native New Yorker and a lot of sad sighs and shivering from the Southerner. Once we get to the parking lot, I stand on my side of the truck waiting for Beau to unlock the door.

"Oh crap," Beau says from the other side of the truck.

"What happened? What's wrong?"

I walk to the front of the truck and peer over the hood. And still can't see anything. This is a very large vehicle.

"It's going to be an icy drive out of here." Beau unlocks the doors and gets an ice scraper. He scrapes the ice that I didn't notice off the windshield as I get in and make myself comfortable for the road trip back.

I open my door and yell out the side, "Keys?"

Beau tosses them to me and I turn on the engine and turn up the heat, working like a team so that Beau can be nice and toasty when he gets back from improving our visibility in the cold. And for me. A nice situation when doing the right thing also means I get to be comfortable.

The best kind of altruism.

I have to remember I said I was turning the heat on for him when he opens the door and a burst of cold air races in before he can get in and close it again. I squelch the uncharitable thoughts about him as I shiver from the cold he lets in.

"It might take us a little longer to get home tonight," Beau says.

"I don't have anywhere else to be." Plus I'll probably get more Zaxby's out of this.

I'm practically Southern already.

True to his word, it takes us five times longer to get down the estate mountain than it did to get up. If I was suspicious, I would say that Beau really did make this weather happen so we could take our time down this gorgeous mountain with its half-frozen rivers and beautifully manicured trees as the sun goes down. To further his evil plot to get me to appreciate nature over the magnificence of an efficiently planned-out city.

Joke's on him, because I can always visit and enjoy this

area, but it will never beat skyscrapers and the heaven of two a.m. pizza in the city.

Once we get off the mountain and out the gates of the estate, the roads get better, and we can drive the speed limit again. I guess I don't have a reason to suggest another night away from his parents. Not a credible one besides wanting to have sex with Beau.

At least we do get some Zaxby's. Maybe they need a franchise owner in New York, and I won't have to say goodbye to them when I leave. I could have them cater every auction I lead, making my clients the happiest in New York.

We get back to Beau's house at ten p.m. and I hope his parents are asleep. They're nice enough but their relationship with their children makes me resent what I missed out on with my parents. Then the resentment turns to sadness in a way I haven't been forced to confront in a long time.

Why couldn't my parents have told the business to screw itself and stayed with me? Why didn't they just tell me I was coming to India, despite whatever "opportunities" I'd be missing? Looking back, it seems like there were so many options they could have gone with that kept them in my life.

The anger toward my parents may be a recent revival, but it's a welcome distraction from mooning over Beau, I guess.

Luck, having gleefully abandoned me at the start of this trip by making his parents live here, extends the olive branch over my way by making the house dark when we drive up. We unload the truck and make our way into the quiet house.

I feel very James Bond (and sober this time) as we sneak

across the dark first floor to the stairs, but then the sound
of puppy fingernails on a hardwood floor breaks up the
peace. Bubba's folds flap as he runs down the stairs, making as much noise as possible.

I watch, melting into a puddle at that big lovable
face coming to welcome me home, er, to Beau's home.
Even knowing there's no way his parents will stay asleep
through that. Bubba puts on the brakes before he gets
to us and then proceeds to slide the rest of the way into
our luggage.

"Hi, Bubba." Beau bends (not that far because the dog
is a giant) and pets the dog. Bubba, being a smart cookie,
turns so Beau can scratch his butt. And rubs his face
on my hand, letting me know he wants ear scratches.

"I think he missed you," Beau whispers from his position near the dog's butt.

"He's a dog. I'm confident he greets everyone like
this." But I scratch him because I'm not totally without
a heart.

"Hey, guys, how was your trip?" Eve asks as she comes
down the stairs in her PJs, yawning.

"Fun. Took Sonia to Biltmore on the way back," Beau
says.

"Ooh, that's one of my favorite places in the US."

"It was wonderful. We didn't mean to wake you," I say,
still whispering in case Reed is asleep.

Eve waves away my apology. "Bubba's the real culprit.
He was sleeping with us and he used your father to launch
out of bed when he heard the front door open."

Beau winces in sympathy. "How's Dad?"

Eve pauses, meaningfully. "He'll be fine. Maybe by the
morning. I'm getting him some ice, so that should help."
She looks up the stairs, not looking super confident in

the diagnosis. "Anyway, I'm glad I caught you, because I wanted to talk to you about the parade."

Interest well piqued. "There's gonna be a parade?"

"A Christmas parade." Beau knows how much I'd like that detail.

"That culminates with a live nativity." Eve helps her son's case.

"With people?"

"And goats, and horses, and maybe a camel if they can swing the camel insurance. Beau's Mee-maw will be there."

"A camel? And a Mee-maw?" I'm all in on this parade now.

"If they can afford the camel insurance." Beau's face shows fear at the thought of how disappointed I'll be if there aren't camels. And he's right. "Well, Mee-maw will be there regardless of the insurance situation."

"Rehearsal is tomorrow at eleven." Eve gets us back on track. "Sonia, we'll try to get you on a camel."

Eve just became my favorite Abbot. Sorry, Beau. Try harder, maybe.

"About this camel—" I say.

Beau tugs me up the stairs. "I might have to deal with the mulch vendor but I'll see if I can put him off."

Eve sighs. "Fine, if mulch is more important to you than your mother's business, that's fine. Just give me the scraps of your attention."

Beau rolls his eyes but doesn't take the bait. "Love you, Mom. See you in the morning."

"That was some A+ mom guilt. I'm not sure what the parade has to do with her business, but I love her overall energy."

"Her company plans and puts it on. For the advertising. Not sure why she needs to advertise since she's the only event planning company in town, but she still takes it seriously."

"Ah. That makes sense then."

"You don't have to be in it if you don't want to." Beau opens his door and lets me go into his room first. I realize he's been opening doors for me the entire time we're here, and I haven't even noticed. The South is having a bad effect on me. When I get back to New York, I might legitimately not remember how to open doors.

That'll be embarrassing.

I dump my bags on the floor and collapse into bed, not worrying about reconstructing the wall. I would just climb/ roll over it sometime in the night. Instead, I halfheartedly wiggle out of my clothes. I should have done this before my body hit the soft mattress, because all my motivation fled when I landed. It's been a long few days. Fun, but activity filled.

While I'm struggling, Beau strips down to his boxers before he gets on the bed, flaunting his excellent decision-making skills.

Showing he's a gentleman, he takes my leggings and shirt off before collapsing in bed. We're still in his parents' house, so I lean over the bed to snag his T-shirt to prevent any accidental groping that could turn into purposeful groping and then purposeful forking.

"I am an adult," Beau whispers in my ear as he cuddles me from behind.

"This isn't even about a respect thing. I just think it'd be awkward if they hear anything."

"Fair." He still falls asleep holding a boob, a move I'm not mad at.

Maybe we can sneak out to the truck again soon.

* * *

Reed is making breakfast while Eve is doing some work on her iPad and sipping coffee when we get downstairs after a leisurely, snuggly morning. Beau and I sit on the island next to her after making our own plates of food.

Beau, getting his workaholic nature from his mother, grabs his own iPad to check email. I get out my phone, since all the cool kids are doing it.

"Damn it," Beau mumbles.

"Language," his father yells from the stove, not turning around to deliver the reprimand.

"He's a damn adult and there's nothing wrong with his damn language," Beau's very New York mother says.

Beau, clearly used to this exchange from his childhood, ignores it. "I do have to deal with the mulch people today. I'm going to be late to the rehearsal."

"No, you're not going to be late to my rehearsal," Eve says.

"I have to if we want mulch this season." Beau turns to me. "You can come with me, it should be quick, or you can leave with Mom if you want to see the setup."

Oh no. It's too early in the day for Beau to be giving me terrifying ultimatums. I'll just pout into my eggs and sausage instead of deciding right away. We all finish eating and I help Beau with cleanup. More as a procrastination technique than an innate goodness or manners.

Back in the room, Beau asks me again what I want to do.

"Mulch sounds more boring the more you say it. So I'm choosing your mom over you. But I'm bringing my iPad to get some work done at the rehearsal."

Beau shrugs. "When you regret it, remember I gave you the choice."

Chapter Thirty

Beau is right; I regret this.

I tried to find a quiet corner of the barn where Eve is staging, hoping to do my own work while still looking like I'm helping Eve. I've done it plenty of times with Priya, and if I can convince her I'm helping while doing something else, I should be able to convince anyone.

I do get through enough of my email to not feel guilty for abandoning Priya before the Christmas auction, but then I make my first mistake.

I look up.

Eve catches my eye like a wild predator used to taking down large game. She stalks toward me, confident movements spelling my doom. And then, using a sweet tea voice so sugary I assume she picked it up here because no New Yorker is that nice, she asks if I could help with "just a little decorating."

My second mistake is believing her when she says it'll only be "just a little decorating." Which is how I end up with a mound of dusty blankets in my arms, piled so high I can't see over them. But I can smell them, and I can't stop sneezing from the dust they're pumping into my nostrils. Eve pulls me along, assigning blankets to goats, donkeys, and horses as we go. And ignoring my sneezing fits.

Then I'm standing in for a wise man at one point, so she makes me try on robes to see how the scene will look. They smell worse than the blankets, somehow.

And then she has me paint a manger.

I still haven't seen a camel yet.

After we're done with that, I see my chance to escape. "I should get back to work."

"Work is so important." Her acquired accent is getting deeper now. Does this whole family weaponize this damn accent? "But the camel is coming and it would be so helpful if you could work with him—you were interested in him at breakfast. And we just have a few more tasks until we're ready for camel time."

"Um." I look longingly at my iPad in the corner. "Sure."

Then I start painting mason jars.

"You're a new face." A voice breaks into my concentration while I arrange a small bouquet of flowers into the mason jars I was just painting.

"Hello." I look up into the hazel eyes of an older woman. Christmas tree eyes. A relation of Beau's?

"I haven't seen you here before." She's not angry, but she clearly wants more information from the stranger. She tilts her head to consider me.

"Just visiting." I'm not from the South; she'll have to try harder than that to get information out of me. But if she needs some good conversation, I've met a chatty broad up somewhere in North Carolina.

She scoffs. "No one visits this small town."

Very self-aware, this one. "I'm visiting a friend here."

"Oh." She sits down next to me and starts working with her own bouquet. I'll take her help with my task. "Who's that?"

"Beau Abbot." I give in. It's not like I'm here on a secret mission and I'm content with the fact that I made her work for the information.

Her face changes from a mild curiosity to a sharp interest, and I get nervous. Maybe I should start asking some questions of my own. "Do you know Beau?" Or does everyone here have those eyes?

She laughs at me. "You could say that."

Before I can follow up with the one woman in the South who chooses to hold her answers close to the chest, Eve comes over.

"Hey, Momma Abbot." She kisses the woman on her upturned cheek and turns to me. "Sonia, this is Beau's Mee-maw, Patsy. That means his grandma, to us Northern folk." I nod in appreciation for the confirmation of the definition I had assumed from context.

"Another Yankee? Why can't we keep you carpetbaggers away?" Mee-maw Patsy affectionately swats her daughter-in-law on the side, no real animosity in her tone.

"We're just here to steal all your men with our Northern succubus powers. And drink all your sweet tea." She extends her hand out to me and I reflexively return the high-five.

Where was I when the North was handing out succubus powers? I feel cheated.

"As long as she's not here to hurt Beau or take him to the North. I went to New York in 1985, and the crowds were too much."

Ugh. This whole trip has been the opposite of casual, no-feelings, fun vacation at every turn. Can't they tell I'm not ready for any of this? That I don't *want* this?

"It's not like that. We're casual." I'm proud of myself for getting the answer out amongst all my turmoil. I don't even beat myself up for not defending New York. She'll understand.

Well, maybe not. She's not the most forgiving city.

"Hmm. Tell me about yourself," Patsy says.

I look at Eve, worried about that tone, but she gives me a thumbs-up and then flees.

"Well, I work at an auction house…"

"The mulch is mine," Beau says when he strides into the barn, a bag of what I assume is mulch slung over his shoulder.

As excited as I am for him that he solved the great mulch fiasco, and how happy I am that the mulch is making his muscles flex and bulge with its weight, I currently can't really appreciate any of that because I have both arms clutching a camel's reins as he tries to pull me around the barn and I try to keep him in his designated corner.

Beau throws the mulch in a corner and walks over to me. "Were you able to get any work done?"

"About thirty minutes' worth."

"I'm impressed you got that much done."

"Help me with this camel," I beg, my pride forgotten now that I'm getting dragged around the barn like a dachshund getting walked by a bodybuilder.

"You were excited about him. You know they're stubborn." Beau pets the animal like they're old friends. The camel stops for Beau, of course.

"I respect that they don't feel the need to cater to the humans that take care of them." I can respect the camel and still curse him, right? Because that's where I am.

"Just tell him how much you respect him."

I give him the stink eye. A stink eye perfected by mimicking the look Ramses the camel gave me when I told him he had to stay in his corner and wait for his handler to get back from a lunch break. Beau's lucky I didn't include the spit that Ramses pointed in my general direction.

Beau takes the reins and I heave a sigh of relief. It's short-lived when I see how well-behaved Ramses is for Beau.

It's very rude, is all. I gave him so much respect.

"The mulch holiday debacle is sorted, then?" I ask him, enjoying petting Ramses now that he's a well-behaved camel. Even if it's not for me.

"All taken care of. I threatened to buy my mulch from a seller up North and then I threatened lawyers and I don't know or care which threat worked, but they 'found' us some more and some of the crew are getting that mulch around the trees as we speak."

"Congrats on your mulch." I wonder if Hallmark makes a card for this situation. I think not, but maybe they sell specialist farm-themed cards in agrarian regions.

"Want to go get some barbecue to celebrate tonight?"

"Sure. If I make it through this rehearsal without getting crushed to my death by this camel deciding I'm a comfortable spot to sit." The words are harsh but I keep petting him gently.

The trainer finishes up his break, making the chances of me being crushed by a camel decrease by quite a bit.

Until Hurricane Eve comes back through. Just as Beau hands the reins back to the very well-rested trainer, she joins our little group, bringing chaos wherever she goes.

"Sonia, you wanted to get on the camel, right?"

Before I met him, maybe. "I don't have the most experience with riding, like no horses or donkeys or ponies even. Maybe it's not the best idea."

"It'll be all right," the trainer says. "Ramses doesn't go very fast and I'll be close by."

"During the parade, I'll be on the horse next to you as a wise man," Beau says.

Well, I am trying a lot of new things lately. "Yeah, all right. I'm game if Ramses is."

Eve claps her hands to celebrate, but I can tell her mind is already on the next task to complete. If she and Priya ever meet and collaborate on a sale, the world is screwed. Or just rich people who'll be separated from their money. But who cares about them? "Excellent. Let's get you fitted in a robe."

"Am I a wise man now?" I ask to her already retreating back.

"Let's get you comfortable on Ramses," the trainer says when it's clear Eve isn't going to answer.

"Okay, Ramses. You heard I respect you. Now get me through this with no embarrassment, and I'll give you…" I turn to the trainer. "Wait, what do camels eat?"

"We have oats for him."

I nod and turn back to the majestic spitter in front of me. "Oats. We have lots and lots of oats and they're all yours if we do this well.

"I'm Sonia, by the way." I extend my hand to the man I hope can control his animal.

"Carl." He shakes my hand and, probably knowing that I'm stalling, motions for me to get on Ramses.

I make one last-ditch effort to procrastinate by looking at Beau, but he's settled on some hay to watch the show.

"Does Ramses *like* people riding him?" I ask Carl the camel wrangler as I approach Ramses.

"Depends on the day."

I snap my head around to see if he's joking, but he's playing it straight so I can't tell. Instead, Carl says something to Ramses that makes him get down on the ground, which does feel like a good start to the adventure. I get into the camel saddle and the second my butt touches it, Ramses gets up. Slowly, thankfully, one limb languidly getting off the floor at a time.

"What do I do now?" I steadfastly don't look down at the ground. Because then I would realize how high up I am and I don't need that particular piece of information at this point in time.

"Just hang on." Carl leads me around the barn.

I start the ride clutching the saddle but loosen up as it goes on. Ramses is being a relatively well-behaved stubborn camel and I don't have to worry about him spitting at me from this angle.

"Look, Beau, I'm doing it! I'm pretty much a natural born rider, I think," I say as we pass Beau the first time.

"You look great. You too, Ramses."

"Maybe I should look into getting some sort of riding animal when I get back to New York," I say on my second time around.

"Think of all the cute riding clothes I could get! And accessories!" I say as I get around the third time.

But Beau isn't where I left him that third time. He's not anywhere around the bale of hay, actually. I look around, employing some of that natural curiosity us Guptas get. Which other people have the gall to call nosiness.

Unfortunately, stealth and ninja-like reflexes are not traits the Guptas are blessed with, and Ramses shifts his feet the more that I twist on top of him. But it's worth the momentary lack of balance when I spot Beau near the entrance to the barn. I contort myself even more, like I'm trying out for Cirque du Soleil, to get a better view of who he's talking to.

Because he's chatting with a very attractive, tiny brunette woman who's looking up at him like he just told her the secret to solving climate change. I bend down closer to Rameses's head. "Calm down, you worrywart, she might be his cousin."

My head still craned, I see her touch his upper arm and *linger* on her way down. I mean, I can still hope she's his cousin. Me and Beau, we're in a thing. I don't know what it is, and it's not a full-blown relationship, but it's a *thing*. And no one else need apply while the *thing* is ongoing.

The mysterious woman goes in for a hug that lasts much longer than it needs to, in my humble opinion.

"Ramses, I'm beginning to think she is not his relation," I whisper through clenched teeth.

Carl directs Ramses on (what seems like) a very sharp turn, and my eyes stay glued on the nefarious woman. Who hasn't let go of my…hasn't let go of *the* farmer.

Physics, teaming up with the mysterious villain to ruin my day, kicks in. I start to slide off the blanket on top of the saddle as Ramses gets further away from Beau, and don't realize it until my body tips past the point of no return and slides completely off the camel.

I fall down the length of Ramses as he kicks to get away from me, barely missing my head. My left arm isn't as lucky, and a sharp pain explodes in my wrist as it makes contact with the ground.

"Oh, shit." Pain radiates up my arm. Still having momentum from the fall, I keep rolling away from the fleeing Ramses, who's taking my fledgling riding career with him.

I end up in the fetal position, left arm clutched in close to my chest, breathing choppy as tears flow down my face. I focus on keeping my hand close as activity explodes around me, a rush of feet and calves coming into my view.

"Are you okay?" Eve sounds frantic above me, and I think the fashionable heels must be her. Who else would wear heels in a barn?

"She's in the fetal position hugging her arm, I don't think she's doing great right now," Beau snaps from somewhere above me as well. I see some boots and think those could be his, but a lot of people are wearing boots around here.

"Clear the way, I'm a doctor."

Oh, that's lovely. And I'd tell the nice voice that if I wasn't focusing so much on getting a full breath in. Until the owner of the voice bends down closer to get in my field of vision.

Great. My doctor is also my nemesis.

Chapter Thirty-One

Can't I have one tiny break? Would that be too much to ask for?

"I think I'm going to be fine." I find the strength in me to lie to my nemesis.

"Of course you are. Just lie back and let me have a little look at that arm. If it's all good, there's no problem. And if something is wrong, we'll get you patched up."

Why is she being so caring? Doesn't she know I just slept with the man she probably loves? Maybe she wants to get me to her medical offices and poison me in private. Ah. The nosiness of the Guptas is being followed by the drama of the Guptas.

"No, I think it's really okay." I sit up, holding out my left arm to prove everything is amazing.

Except even I can see my wrist is already starting to swell through my tear-filled eyes and I can't actually bend the normally bendy part. This is less than ideal.

She pokes at my inflamed wrist in a very cavalier manner, earning a pain-filled scowl directed her way.

"Yeah, let's get the X-ray to tell us that," Dr. Nemesis says.

"Come on, Sonia, get checked out for me. So I won't worry." Beau enters my vision next to the evil, sexy doctor.

"Sure, Beau." Ha! Take that, doctor lady, he wants me to get medical treatment.

Agreement secured, Beau slides his arms under my knees and back and lifts me up. I start to tell him it's just my arm that hurts and not my legs, but he looks so happy I'll let him carry on carrying me. And I'm not mad that I get to be held by Beau in front of my nemesis.

Beau takes me out to his truck without breaking a sweat and gently deposits me into the front seat. The pain has calmed down a little, but it still aches and sends sharp pain up my arm if I even think about moving it or look at it too hard.

"Are we going far?" I ask when Beau gets in the car.

"No, we're just around the corner," Dr. Nemesis says with her calm, soothing voice as she gets in the back seat of the truck. Haven't I suffered enough?

Dr. Woman-I-Refuse-To-Name-Because-I-Don't-Know-Her-Name is right. A painful fifteen minutes later, where Beau finds every pothole and pile of dirt that he can, we're at a medical office run out of a cute, potentially historic house.

Smooth, paved roads (mostly)...another point for the city. I'll tell Beau about it later.

But I think he knows because he looks harried as he apologizes for the bumpy ride. He helps me out of the seat while Dr. Nemesis opens the door for us.

"You don't have to open a clinic for me, I can go to whatever the local emergency room is, or maybe an urgent care." Not because I care about putting the hot doctor out, but because I don't want to be indebted to her.

"This is closer. And what kind of person would I be if I let you suffer when I could do something about it?"

Just my luck, she's Dr. Florence Nightingale.

She also gives me some anonymous pills that I take without too much question, because the pain has gotten worse again after the truck ride.

Sometime later, I think about what a good decision maker I am, because those pills were amazing, and not poison. Not only do I feel better about my wrist, but I also feel much kinder to this lovely woman.

These pills are magic.

Dr. Lovely goes to get the X-ray machine set up and leaves me in the exam room with Beau.

"She seems nice." The drugs help me mean it, forgetting my earlier jealousy.

"Amanda? Yeah, she's great. Best doctor in the whole county." Beau's distracted by looking at my wrist.

"So great. How do you all know each other?"

"Went to school together up till college."

Hmm, that's grand. How do I ask him if they've known each other, biblically?

Dr. Amanda comes back in before I find a subtle way to ask. "The X-ray machine's all ready, Sonia, if you want to come with me?"

"Sure." I'll go anywhere with the pretty, smart lady with the magic medicine. Apparently, I would be exceptionally easy to kidnap.

She leads me down the hall, and with no more pain in my wrist that I can feel right now, my brain is freed up to think of a way to pump her for information.

"Here we go, let's get this lead vest on. I have on good authority they're the height of fashion in Paris right now."

She's funny too? And pretty and smart and accomplished. I love this for her.

She takes the X-ray efficiently. "I'll just get the images." She excuses herself after dropping me off in the exam room.

"How's your arm?" Beau asks.

I look down at it, forgetting for a bit that it was injured. "Swollen. But I can't feel it right now."

"See, being friends with a doctor means you get the best meds."

"Did you get the best meds when you dated her?" That's the smoothest I can come up with, considering how much I want the answer, and a better segue doesn't seem to be coming.

Beau gets awkward and starts straightening up some children's books on the table next to him. Wait a minute. Is something happening with them? Do they have an on-again-off-again thing that I got dragged into? Do they have sister wives down here?

"We dated a few times, but there wasn't a spark. It was like going out with my sister. We called it a day and went back to being really good friends. With no benefits. There were never any benefits," he clarifies before I can ask.

"Hmm." That wasn't quite the answer I was hoping for. But it could have been worse, I suppose. A lot worse. "When did that happen?"

"Right after I got back from college. For just a few weeks."

Whatever. He's allowed to have a life before he met me. And we're not permanent either. So he's allowed to have a life after me as well. The only time he's not allowed to have a life with perfect Dr. Amanda is when he's with me.

I guess the restriction is just for the next few days. That thought is about as depressing as me breaking this arm. Or whatever I've done with it.

Dr. Amanda walks into the room holding some X-rays.

"What's up, Doc?" I say to defuse the tension between Beau and me.

"You must be feeling better for that quality of repartee," she says, but smiles kindly at me.

"Will my insurance pay for the judgement, or is that out of pocket?"

"It's a free sample. That I'm giving you because you have a fracture." She segues into a diagnosis, like a true professional. "It's a small fracture on your left wrist, so we're going to get a cast on you and then you'll get healed right up. Easy."

Maybe easy for her to say. It would be *easier* for me if my bone was in its original state, and I could enjoy the rest of this trip without restrictions or pain.

"Can I have a pink cast at least?"

"We can do that." Dr. Obliging pats me on the non-injured shoulder.

"Can I have a sparkly pink cast?"

"I don't think we have glittery cast material, but I can always check for you."

"Thank you," I mutter after the woman.

Beau sits next to me on the exam bed on my non-injured side and slides an arm around my waist. "You're holding up really well."

Well, the pain medication is helping. "I'm deducting points from the South for this."

"You can't do that. The camel was imported. Most likely."

"Nonsense. A Northern camel would never do me like this." I hold up my arm and immediately regret…everything I've done today.

"I think he was a Northern camel. I heard him ask about where the closest slice was, so, you know."

"Will you be the first person to sign my cast?" I change the subject because he's just talking nonsense now.

"Of course. I'll draw your art-lovin' self a picture and everything."

I sniff. Well, that should be worth some of this pain at least.

Amanda comes back to the room and I feel a lot kinder toward her with Beau wrapped around me like Saran Wrap.

She does the (non-glittery, but still pink) cast with minimal pain and Beau drives us back to the family barn.

Eve descends on me the second I get out of the truck. "I'm so sorry. I never would have put you on the camel if I knew he was so wild. Is there anything I can get you? Sweet tea? Some more Zaxby's? Guilt jewelry?"

"It's not your fault. And it's not the camel's fault either." But I'm not going to explain that it was all because I was creeping on Beau with the then-unknown Dr. Perfect. However, if it makes her feel better… "I'll take some sweet tea though, if it's not too much trouble."

Eve looks relieved to have a task to accomplish and rushes off to get me the drink.

I settle down on the same bale of hay Beau was watching me from earlier and watch the chaos in front of me. Now exempt from doing any work, so there is that at least.

Beau sits down next to me, arm wrapped around me again. Eve brings the cold drink, and I sip. This I can get used to. Well, maybe a blanket on this hay would be more comfortable. Or maybe just a leather couch instead would be better. And it'd be best to be inside, away from Ramses, who is giving me accusatory looks, like he knows he's getting blamed for my mistake.

"What is this all about anyway?" I watch the activity in front of us.

"Mom didn't give you the history?"

"No. But she was very specific about the tasks I needed to do."

"Sounds like Mom. The company started the tradition of having a Christmas parade with a live nativity when they started. The grandpas wanted to give back to the community, so they started the parade, plus a dinner for everyone and presents for the kids at the end in the town square. With games, booths and small rides."

"That's nice."

"If I were a cynical Northerner, instead of a kind, wholesome Southerner, I would say they also did it as a massive advertising opportunity. Especially when they were mostly only selling in the immediate area. They also sold some of the peach preserves at a booth in the square."

"No. The grandpas would never." I defend the men I've never met.

"Look who decided to come down our way!" a voice yells through the din of the crowd.

Chapter Thirty-Two

"Hello?"

A Black man around Beau's age that I'm sure I've never met moves to stand in front of me. He has a bright smile as he extends a hand out to me. Why is he so happy if we haven't met?

"I'm Daniel. Part-owner of this farm and Beau's partner in the energy business. And Beau's told me so much about you. Sonia, right?"

"That's me. It's nice to meet you." I shake his hand, wondering what Beau's been saying.

"What's this? Did the South do this to you, or did you come this way from the mean city?" He gestures toward my cast, as if I could have misinterpreted what injury he was talking about.

"A camel mishap. But I was told the camel is from the North?"

"Ramses? Nah, he's from Georgia."

I send an I-told-you-so look over my shoulder and Beau finds the hay on the other side of him very interesting. I bet you do, buddy. I bet you do.

"This is an...interesting drawing." Daniel points to my cast.

"Beau made it for me." I genuinely smile over my shoulder at Beau, loving what's on my cast so much I give my left arm a little hug close to my body.

Beau made a pictorial representation of my trip to the South so far, complete with sweet tea, fried chicken, a truck (with a heart next to it), Bubba, a peach Christmas tree, a racetrack, Biltmore, and a camel. Except he's not the best artist in the world, so I only know what everything is because he told me what each one was as he was drawing them.

And I'm going to frame the cast when it comes off.

On second thought, I'll take a picture of it and get that framed. It's going to smell pungent after six weeks on my unwashed arm, especially after accidentally dropping bits of candy and crumbs in there.

"Oh, no. We should take him to one of those wine-painting nights and improve that skill." Daniel gets closer to the cast to take in the drawings.

"I love it." I try on loyalty to a man. An unused coat in my closet since most of my relationships stay casual. But it's got a good fit to it. Nice and cozy too for the winter months.

"What are you doing down here?" Daniel asks.

"There was a mulch emergency," I say, like that should explain everything. And since Daniel works on this farm too, it does.

"Did you save our peaches?"

"I was very supportive through the whole process. Which is the most important thing, I think we'll all agree."

"So, you did nothing."

"She was very instrumental in the support department." Loyalty comes a lot easier for Beau.

Eve comes and steals Daniel, but I throw my shroud of guilt over Beau, telling Eve he's so helpful to me and

I can't imagine coping without him, what with this fractured wrist.

"Nicely done." Beau slides an arm around me. "You've got Southern mom guilt down already."

"It's exactly the same as Indian mom guilt, but at a lower volume." Chachi doesn't believe in a distinction between inside voices and outside voices. Neither does Priya.

"Did the South break you already?" Mee-maw intrudes on my and Beau's quality time. "Are you that delicate, Yankee?"

"A camel threw me across the length of a barn and I landed on a rocky floor. I could have a concussion." Not that my head was hit, but it's the principle of the matter.

Mee-maw harrumphs at me. "I was there. None of that happened."

"Well, I did fall from a very tall height. And my wrist is fractured." I hold up the pink cast, in a blatant attempt at sympathy. I even throw in some wide eyes and a slight quiver to my lips.

"When did you get here, Mee-maw?" Beau hugs his grandmother, and then turns to me. "And you've already met Sonia?" He raises his eyebrow at me.

"She's called me a Yankee numerous times now and a carpetbagger once."

"You guys *are* close."

"And now that you're here, Beau, you can explain what you two are to each other," Mee-maw says. "Couldn't get anything out of this one earlier."

"Mee-maw, we're…" Beau looks at me, but I can't help him; I have no idea what we're doing anymore.

This isn't quite the casual situation it started out as. "…friends."

"Don't piss on my leg and tell me it's raining," Mee-maw warns him, looking meaningfully at his arm still around me.

"That's all you're getting at the moment."

She shakes her head. "Young people and their needlessly complicated attitude to dating." Disappointed in the youth, Mee-maw wanders off to find someone more interesting to harangue. I breathe out in relief.

We watch the activity going on in front of us, happy to be sitting on the hay like we're king and queen at a farm-themed prom. Beau takes any excuse to touch me, rubbing my arm, touching my knee or elbow to get my attention, or playing with the ends of my hair.

In the brief time we've known each other, my body has gone from giddy excitement whenever he touches me to a deeper contentment that my body doesn't just like but is coming to expect as its right. I know I'm going to be wrecked at the end of the trip. There's going to be no way to survive this with any sort of dignity or grace.

I genuinely thought I could keep this as casual as every other romantic interaction I've had, but I've never felt this intensity of feelings before. I don't know why I arrogantly thought I could handle the barrage of emotions coming at me now. Maybe it was because I didn't feel like I was really getting to know Beau in New York, even though I was sharing a lot about me.

I could see some of him: his hate of art, his kindness, his banter, his forearms. But I didn't know him fully until I saw him in his home.

That's when I saw the love he has for his family. I also

saw the peace in his eyes when he looks over the peach orchard and the way he dotes on his niece and nephew.

And now I have to deal with the way I felt when I saw him with Amanda. With someone who isn't messed up. Who probably wants family and forever and isn't irrationally panicked when she sees a Mr. and Mrs. matching champagne glass set.

But under the panic, I know that I care about Beau.

It's too much for me. I think about how it would feel to watch Beau walk away over and over again to go back to the South, like I have with my parents, and it makes my chest tighten. And I can't quit my job to do…what would I even do down here besides make eyes at Beau?

But I can't figure out a way to extricate myself from the situation. Which is a lie. Because I could just buy a plane ticket back and it would be no big deal. But when I opened the web browser to buy a ticket when I ducked into the bathroom an hour ago, I didn't get past typing in "New" into location. I haven't tried it since.

Because even bigger than the panic is the need to spend more time with Beau.

"Are you okay?" Beau asks.

"Me? Yeah, I'm fine." Having a mild existential crisis, but otherwise just peachy. Ugh, great. Now I'm making peach puns.

"You looked like you were thinkin' deep thoughts," Beau whispers in my ear.

"Just wondering if I could sneak Bubba in my suitcase when I leave." Close enough. I wasn't thinking about Bubba, but I was thinking about leaving.

Beau snorts. "You'd have better luck dressing him up in a coat and buying him his own ticket."

I use my remaining good hand to stroke my chin, considering. "Yes, yes. I see your point. I'll take it under advisement." Bubba would look adorable in clothes. Hey, I think that is cheering me up slightly.

By evening, everyone is run ragged. Not us, because Beau and I sat down the entire time being brought snacks from whoever Eve ordered around. But everyone else looks tired. *Especially* the aforementioned volunteers.

When Eve is giving her final instructions for the parade the next day, Beau tugs me away.

"Don't you need to hear this?" I whisper, thinking the wrist guilt wouldn't protect me if Eve catches me and Beau fleeing her rehearsal. She seems like her guilt stops where her business begins.

Beau rolls his eyes. "I've been in this parade since I was the baby Jesus. I was demoted to random kid in Jerusalem, then promoted to young adult in Jerusalem, then again to my current role of wise man with the frankincense. Which I've been doing for years. I could do this parade in my sleep."

"I suppose they replaced me on Ramses." I have mixed feelings about that…we had some good times before it all ended in catastrophic injury.

"Yeah. But I think you're going to be part of the floats with the old people and the youths."

"That sounds okay, actually."

"So let's go," Beau whispers, slinking away from the circle around his mother, tugging me along in the great escape. I smile despite my earlier thoughts, not able to resist the mischievous little boy smile.

"Wait." I go back behind enemy lines to save a bottle someone brought us, which is still a quarter full of sweet tea.

Beau shakes his head at me in disappointment when he sees what I risked the whole operation for. "You have a problem."

"No, *you* have a problem. You and whoever decided this much sugar should be in one drink," I whisper defiantly, taking a big sip with no regrets.

"We're still clear." Beau shuffles me back to the truck. "And I can get you some of the best barbecue in South Carolina."

"Wahoo!" This I am excited for. Barbecue is delicious and I hear the South does it really well. Even better than the North, I'll concede.

The excitement carries me all the way through the car ride, through parking the car, and walking into the restaurant, non-injured hand tucked into Beau's. It gets even higher when I take in all the sensations hitting me at once. First it's the heat, hitting me like it has actual mass. In the area where they smoke the meat, smoke billows up to make the front of the restaurant hazy, and then the smell of cooking meat washes over me.

The décor doesn't disappoint either. Neon beer signs cut through the smoke, casting interesting shadows on the well-loved wood that dominates every flat surface. Just like that bar we went to the first night.

I have good memories of that bar, and of what happened after it in Beau's truck.

The sound of sizzling meat brings me back to the present. This is going to be a good night. And it won't even involve sex because we're back at the family home.

We get in line to order and Beau hands me a menu. My

excitement falters a lot when I read the laminated paper. Pulled pork, pork loin, and ribs. "Is there a second part of the menu I'm not seeing?"

"Nope. This is it."

"But where's the brisket?"

"They don't have brisket."

"But how do they not have brisket?" I ask in a small voice. A disappointed one.

"We do a lot of pork-based barbecue here." Beau's own excitement for the date fades as he takes in my reaction.

"Oh." This is not winning the South any points here. "But isn't this barbecue?"

"You're not going to be a fan of the mustard-based sauce either, are you?"

I flinch. "Wait, what?"

"I think you might prefer Texas-style barbecue. We should go somewhere else." Beau starts to tug me back toward the door.

I waffle. I feel bad. Beau looked so excited to show me this place, so I put the brakes on. "I should give this a try." But even I can hear the lack of conviction in my own voice and I think he'll be able to catch on too.

"You sound like I just offered to serve you kale."

I can't stop the shudder that racks my shoulders. "No. Trying new things is good." I've been doing a lot of that lately: sweet tea, warm Christmases, spending more than a few nights with a man, meeting a man's family. A lot of new things. And they've all gone pretty well.

There's still the panic. But also enjoyment at the slew of new things. And even though I'm still unsure about commitment, I am trying to be more open.

"I don't think you're going to like this."

I move us up as the line goes forward. "I've adjusted my expectations accordingly." To this not being something that is going to blow me away. But I can still enjoy it. Maybe.

"Okay. But don't blame me when you hate it."

"Your preference is noted but in no way guaranteed."

The line moves quickly and soon I'm ordering not-brisket. I'm not off to a good start giving the pulled pork a fair chance, but at least I didn't say it out loud. We fill up our drinks (sweet tea for me, obviously) and find a table.

I take the time to connect to the Wi-Fi and update Priya on the state of affairs by taking a picture of my cast and sending it to her.

So...this happened :(

She must be having a slow night because she responds right away.

THE SOUTH IS INJURING YOU!?? COME HOME NOW. WE WILL IMPORT BEAU UP HERE.

I roll my eyes and ignore that. How's work going?

I'm at the stage where I rage quit and yet haven't managed to actually leave the office. Or stop doing any work. Gavin is passive aggressively printing pictures of me and hanging them around the house, like at the dinner table and on the couch, to "remind himself what I look like."

Drama King.

I know, right?

Glad that dunking on her husband distracted Priya, I put the phone back in my purse.

"If you hate this, I can eat yours and we can get you some fried chicken. No pressure." He says that, but the expectant look on his face suggests there is pressure, he does care, and he'll cry in the corner for an hour if I say mean things about his meat.

Oh, saucy pun. Ha… Barbecue sauce-y pun. I'm on a roll… A barbecue roll. I laugh, getting a look from Beau but ignoring it. It's too hard to explain that I crack myself up.

Beau sets a large tray in front of me, filled with haphazard piles of meat. There are three tiny containers on the side, one with beans, one with something vaguely green but also swimming in butter, and the last with mac and cheese. Some rolls are thrown on top of the food, and I immediately grab one, just in case the pork isn't great.

Beau goes ham (more puns!) with the barbecue sauce, spreading it over the piles like a first grader making a volcano model for his annual science project. Then he's done and looks at me. *Expectantly.*

"This is a lot of pressure. Maybe can you go away while I eat and then you can come back when I'm done?"

"I won't take it personally if you don't like it. I promise."

"Your mouth says that, but your wild eyes say that I'll be sleeping with the peaches if I don't love it."

Beau's brow furrows. "How would I make you sleep with the peaches?"

"Off me and bury me in the peach orchard. Duh."

"Well. Like the pork and there won't be any problems."

Fresh out of distractions, I pick up a fork and dig in.

Chapter Thirty-Three

I draw out the chewing for as long as I can without anything getting gross. Not because I'm unsure. I already decided pulled pork is better than I thought it would be. It's no brisket. But it's a solid meal.

But with each chew, Beau moves in a tiny bit closer, waiting for the verdict. It's adorable how much he wants me to like it. And adorable that my opinion is important to him.

I swallow. "This is…" I take a sip of sweet tea, drawing it out even more. I get a few more inches out of Beau and then I give in. "This is good. Still no brisket," I warn before he can get too carried away with being right. "But much more edible than I thought it would be."

"You really don't have to finish it if you don't want to." Beau helps himself to some ribs.

I take one too, since all the cool kids are doing it and the pulled pork wasn't bad. I get some sauce on my cast in all the excitement but wipe it off before Beau can see.

We polish off the tray, me enjoying the food more than I thought I would. At one point, Beau gets some sauce on his cheek, and instead of thinking he's a filthy slob, in my mind I volunteer to lick that sauce right off him.

Proof that Beau is escalating to be a big problem. Because that's objectively gross.

In my past relationships with men, whenever things headed toward serious, I would look for reasons to bail. And messy eater was on that list. As were snores too loud, spends too much, is too stingy, works out too much, works out too little, too into art, and not into art enough.

It was a veritable Goldilocks and the bears. If she was trying to date the bears.

But Beau gets a pass. And not just because these ribs are so messy that I also got sauce all over me, so it would be unfair to hold it against him. He gets a pass because there's something about him I can't, or don't want to, dismiss. Even as my brain tells me to pull away.

Meal accomplished, Beau leads me back to the car. Once we get to the house, Beau pulls me aside before we leave the garage.

"What's up?" I ask.

"I just wanted to get a kiss before we go in there and you get weird."

"It's perfectly natural to get weird with your parents right across the hall and frankly, it's weird that *you* don't care mo…"

Beau leans in for the kiss before I can finish the familiar argument. I enthusiastically participate, sinking into him, my body melting as he heats me from the inside out.

His arms tighten to accommodate the extra weight, both of our bodies automatically shifting to curl around each other like two tree trunks that are entwined around each other after decades growing next to each other.

Just as the kiss gets good, Beau stops it. The heat dries up in an instant, Beau taking it with him when he pulls away. I make a sound of disappointment.

"If you want to see some action in the back of this truck again, we can do it." Beau's hand is already reaching back to open his door again.

"Oh boy, I am not drunk enough for that." It was very enjoyable last time, but without the alcohol dulling my inhibitions, I can't stop thinking of all the things that could do wrong. Like his parents wondering why the garage door opened but then they didn't hear anyone come in the house.

We go back to Beau's bedroom, silently working around each other in the small space to get ready for bed. It's a little harder since I don't have full use of my left arm, but Beau hands me my next dose of medicine and then gets to work digging into my suitcase to get my nightclothes.

When it's apparent that I can't easily undress and redress with my cast and arm pain, Beau takes over before I can work up to a mini meltdown.

I don't usually like relying on anyone for anything, because then I'd be screwed after they left. But it'd be absurd to stomp my foot and declare that I can take care of myself. Because I can't right now, as the numerous attempts to take my shirt off and the growing frustration showed me.

I give him a chaste kiss on his cheek in thanks for his help and settle into bed. Chaste in that it isn't a French kiss swapping saliva with abandon, but the feelings that the innocent kiss makes in me are not all that chaste.

I fall asleep snuggling with Beau, his arm rubbing my back and my cast thrown over his broad chest. Surrounded by warmth from the inside out.

I wake up in excruciating pain, like a knife stabbing me in my left wrist. During the night, we shifted, and sleep me decided that it would be a good idea to sleep on my injured arm. My wrist does not appreciate the idea.

I look around the room to see where we put the medication last night. That doesn't give me any answers, so I have to get up and rifle through my things. Being the considerate sort, I try to make as little noise as possible.

Being a bit of the clumsy sort, I make a lot of noise.

"How's the arm feeling?" Beau asks from the bed as I knock into the bedside table and send my own water bottle crashing down, the metal hitting the wooden side of the bed before bouncing on the carpet a few times.

At least the bottle had its cap firmly on it.

"Sorry to wake you." I avoid the question, hoping that avoiding talking about my arm will stop the pain. It doesn't work, but maybe it just needs to be ignored a little harder.

"It's fine. Are you looking for the meds?" He takes in the state of his floor, now covered in items that were formerly in my suitcase. I thought I might have thrown the medicine in the suitcase last night and it got lost in there. But it wasn't there.

I nod, too disappointed to give more of a response than that.

"I put it here last night without thinking after I handed you one." Beau reaches over to the bedside table on his side to show me the goods. "I'm sorry I made it harder for you."

That would be the place I hadn't looked yet. Beau takes out a pill for me and I take it with the water I'm glad isn't spilled all over the floor. After Beau opens the bottle for me.

I get back in bed, waiting for the medicine to kick in. "What's the plan for today?"

"It's parade day, and it's going to be a long day. But you have a fractured wrist, so I think we can milk that to miss most of the chaos." He wraps his arms around me.

"You would use me in that manner?" I'm fake affronted, albeit weakly, which means the medicine must be kicking in. Finally.

"In a second." Beau affectionately kisses me on the nose. "But I would bring you all the sweet tea your beautiful Yankee heart could desire, so I don't think you'd mind."

"That's an acceptable trade-off."

I've been spending a lot of time with Beau over the past few weeks and I'm consistently surprised at the contrasts of the man. He can be stoic and sweet and the perfect gentlemen, but then in the louder moments, during sex mostly, he shows a different side. Still nice, but raunchier, earthier, and a little less polite.

And he has a real sassy side to him. Especially about art and the city. So many opinions.

I like the contrasts. They're intriguing. Like I could spend a serious amount of time exploring them.

But like almost every happy thought I've had since I met him, they lead to more somber thoughts focused on the fact that the relationship has an expiration date. An expiration date where we'll both go to our respective corners of the country, keeping to our own sides of the East Coast.

And even though I don't want to be apart from Beau, I also still don't want to put myself in a position where I can be hurt.

So I guess I have some contradictions myself to work through.

We lie in the bed for a while longer, me wrapped in

Beau and a very fluffy duvet. I get out my phone to keep in contact with New York and Beau gets out his own, probably on the lookout for a new mulch guy, or some other equally agrarian concerns.

"I like having you here," Beau whispers to me as I'm answering emails.

"In the South?"

"Yes. But also here, in bed. On our phones but still together." He punctuates the sentiment with a kiss to my head.

"I like being with you too." It is nice to do my own thing with someone next to me. It fills in a little of the gap that Priya left when she dared to get a life outside of me and work.

We're interrupted by a knock on his door. "Come on, kids. Reed said I had to leave you alone and I have. But it's getting late and I need my wise man and float rider," Eve yells. Then knocks again. In case we missed the urgency of her words, I suppose.

"We'll be down in a second," Beau yells back.

"Hurry, please." Eve makes a final plea to get us downstairs quickly.

"Do you need help?" Beau asks as I get out of the bed.

"I think I'll be able to manage?" The answer comes out as a question. I really don't like not being able to do things by myself, but my wrist is telling me it doesn't care about insignificant things like my wishes.

I still try, managing all the necessary morning bathroom tasks until I have to get dressed. That's when my wrist protests most strongly, by throbbing like all my blood rushed to this one location and is desperate to leave my stubborn skin that has the temerity to keep it imprisoned.

And I'm naked, because it was easier to get the clothes off—thanks, wrist—than it is to get new ones back on. I come back into the bedroom, head hung in defeat.

"I could use that help," I say in a small voice. I hand him the clothes in my good hand without looking at him.

Beau doesn't gloat as he dresses me with as much care as he undressed me the night before. I don't think he means it to be sexual, but any time his hands are on me, I think X-rated thoughts. It gets to the point where I move when he does to avoid extraneous brushing up against him. With my luck, however, my moves make me brush against him even harder.

From the looks he's sending me, I can't tell if he thinks I'm doing it on purpose *to* touch him, or if he knows I'm doing it to avoid the contact.

Ordeal by horny flesh finally over, I'm dressed.

"Before we head down, I want to give you something." Beau stops me by gently grabbing my non-injured hand.

"A Christmas present?" I feel the panic rise at the thought that someone got me a present and I didn't get them one. That is not the Christmas spirit. And it would be worse to be in an unequal present situation with Beau. "I didn't know we were doing presents. It's not even Christmas."

"It's not really a Christmas present. I just saw it when I was out taking care of mulch and thought of you. And I want you to have it now because you might want to use some of the things while you're here."

"So it's just an item given around Christmas time?" I ask carefully. That still sounds like a Christmas present, but it does give me time to get him a gift for the holiday. A real one. Shit, I didn't even think I'd be around for Christmas.

"Sure." He goes into his closet and gets a large wrapped item from it.

"A non-Christmas present wrapped in Christmas wrapping paper?" I point at the reindeers in cute Christmas sweaters on the paper.

"It was the only thing I could find at this particular time of the year." Now he sounds annoyed. "I can keep this." He pulls the present out of my reach.

I put my hands up like a hostage negotiator talking to a guy in a bank demanding all the money and a helicopter. "Whoa, there. Let's not do something we'll regret." I do love presents. Even surprise presents from people I'm not prepared to give presents back to. I reach for the gift and Beau hands it over without any more threats.

I shake the present and start my pre-opening ritual. It involves most of the senses (I draw the line at tasting wrapping paper). Beau looks tolerant when I look at the gift from all angles. It's in a long rectangular box that's deep. I shake it a little and hear some smaller items bumping into each other. It feels like a medium weight.

Beau looks less tolerant when I move on to smelling the present. "Mom is waiting…"

"Okay, okay, since this isn't a Christmas present, I guess I can forgo finishing the whole ritual." My tone lets him know how much of a sacrifice I'm making in the name of expediency.

"Much obliged." His tone lets me know he doesn't grasp, or care about, the full extent of my sacrifice.

I get down to business, ignoring the monster trying to rush my enjoyment.

Most people choose one of two methods on how to open presents. There are the impatient ones like Ajay, who tears into them like he's been out to sea for months and this is the first hot meal he's had that hasn't come out of a can. And then there are the meticulous people in the world who wouldn't dare destroy the beauty of the paper, like Priya, slowly sliding their fingers under the tape to carefully unwrap and folding the paper when they're done to save it for their elaborate organizational rituals, I assume, before they even get to the present.

Me, I'm an ambi-opener. Just depends on my mood.

And right now, I'm exceptionally curious as to what this gift is, so I take the Ajay route. I rip into the paper and leave the remnants at my feet like physical reminders of my conquest.

When I get to the gift, I stop my frenzy. Everything is in a plain white box, so I put it on the bed to investigate further. I open it, wary about what's inside, already thinking about what I'll need to get him. Because there's no way I'm going to let anyone out-Christmas me.

Shoot, maybe I do see Christmas as a competition. A hard fact to swallow since I recently judged Priya for doing the same.

But then I see what's inside and I stop thinking about winning Christmas. Because the box is full of a few canvases of different sizes, a leather sketchbook and pens, and a wide variety of paints: oil, water, and acrylic that I can see from my quick glance.

He remembered. He remembered when I said I liked to paint.

I run my hands over the paints, looking up at him in appreciation. "You remembered."

Beau looks uncomfortable with the adoration. "I thought maybe you might want to paint something while you were here, or work on interior design sketches, but noticed you didn't bring anything with you. So if you were feeling the creative bug on vacation, you could enjoy."

"Thank you. This is really considerate of you."

"There's one more thing in there." He reaches under the large white canvases and pulls out a maroon sweater.

"What is this?" I didn't really see Beau getting me clothes.

"It's an ugly Christmas sweater for the University of South Carolina. The gamecocks." He holds up the small sweater against his large frame, modeling it for me.

The piece of clothing has lines of patterns, with little gamecocks in Christmas hats alternating with Santas, Christmas trees, and candy canes in rows across the fabric. Even the gamecocks and Santas have on ugly sweaters.

And it's the perfect garment, not only because of the Christmas cheer, but because of its connection to Beau. I snatch it out of his hands and hug it against my chest.

"This. Is. More amazing than the art supplies." I start slow and get the rest out in a rush.

Now I'm bouncing like all the kids who got a Tickle Me Elmo the year that toy was impossible to find for Christmas.

"Actually, I lied. There's one more part of this present."

"More?"

"Well, sort of." He reaches back into the magic closet of gifts and takes out another sweater, the same design but in a larger size.

Matching ugly Christmas sweaters?? I don't even care that they're for some random school in the South I've never been to, this gift rocks.

"I was already getting myself this one because Mom

loves an ugly Christmas sweater party, but then I saw they had one in your size and I knew I had to get it."

"Can I wear this to the parade?" I want to wear it now and never take it off.

"If you can fit it over your cast, sure. Because you're not in the costumed part anymore and you got injured in her rehearsals, I reckon you could show up in a bathing suit and Mom wouldn't care."

I gasp. "I would never ruin her aesthetic like that. Unless the bathing suit had Christmas trees on it." I'm not a grinch.

I lean in to kiss the thoughtful man in front of me, but before I can reach those amazingly soft lips, his mom's voice interrupts us. Again.

This is why some of my people stopped living with our parents.

The rest of the day is organized chaos run by the taskmaster Eve Abbot. She wrangles animals, children, and buzzed adults with a ruthless efficiency, all with a smile and a "Thank you" in that sugar-tea sweet voice.

Maybe one does get more flies with honey than vinegar. Hmm. Maybe point South.

Since I'm going to be sitting on the Abbot Farms float (next to peaches decorated for Christmas) waving with Annabelle's children, there isn't much training or organizing for me. I'm free to watch the spectacle around me in relaxation.

Groups of people socialize around Eve's schedule. Every time someone new comes, they bring snacks, stopping the activity for however long it takes to greet the person and clear out their food stash.

Eve seems to have built this into her schedule, because

she only moves people along if they stay past when the snacks are gone. Or she may know there's no use in trying to move anyone along until food is no longer a factor.

Dr. Amanda (who stops getting mean nicknames since Beau didn't get *her* a matching Christmas sweater) checks in with me during the prep period.

"How's the arm?" She takes a seat next to me on the hay and watches the activity too.

"Still feels fractured."

"Yeah. It's probably going to take a while before that feeling goes away. But if it ever gets worse, have Beau call me and we can take another look to make sure everything's going well."

"Thank you." I feel a little bad for the uncharitable thoughts I had about her yesterday. And I know they were because of the way she was talking to Beau and knowing that she's probably everything he's looking for: ready for commitment and living in the South. Also smart and beautiful to boot.

I can't even blame her for the injury because I could have just waited like a normal human and met her after my ride, instead of trying to recreate gymnastic contortions I'm not qualified for on the back of a camel. Not that I'm qualified off the camel, either.

"This is a nice tradition you all have here." I offer the olive branch.

"It is. I heard you really liked Christmas so I'm glad you've been able to see some of our best traditions."

I haven't spoken to her about that, "How'd you hear about that now?"

"I think Eve told her assistant, who told her hairdresser, who told the librarian and she's my cousin, so I found out at family dinner."

"Wow. That is…"

"Scary?" Amanda finishes for me.

"Yeah."

"You get used to it. Sort of." She smiles at me.

"But how do you buy condoms or lube?" I ask before I can stop myself, recognizing when the words are out of my mouth that people probably don't like to talk about that here.

But Amanda is a doctor and she doesn't scare easy. "With fake mustaches and sunglasses, I imagine. Or just knowing someone who doesn't care and bought some." She shrugs. "Then Amazon really helped the situation. But people still might not be able to get access depending on the situation."

"That seems problematic."

"Trust me, as a girl growing up here and as a doctor here now, I know. We are kind of close to Aiken, so we can go there, but it's still a ways to go. I try to buy some condoms for the clinic and offer them to patients if they want, but it's been slow to pick up. And the stink I caused when I started talking to teens about sexual health in their appointments, that was not fun. Still isn't actually."

Yeah, she's not so bad after all. Even a good egg. Still totally wrong for Beau though.

I hope.

"Well, let me know if you guys take donations for condoms and I'll Amazon you the biggest package of them you've ever seen. Lube too."

"I never say no to large boxes of condoms and lube."

"An excellent policy to have."

We laugh together and I get my phone out so she can enter the clinic's address in my notes. I would have ordered the first box right there, but I have no reception in the sticks, so the youth of Aiken County are going to have to wait. Which I realize is not a strong suit for teenagers.

"How long are you staying for?" Amanda asks me when I take my phone back.

I whip my head at her to see if she's being genuinely curious or if she wants me to go away so she can have Beau all to herself. Or if she's looking for juicy gossip to tell everyone right after she leaves.

Her face is as open and friendly it was before, so I don't think she's trying to do any of those things.

"I don't know. Sometime during or right after the holidays I would imagine, but Beau had to leave New York in such a hurry, so we weren't concerned about locking down the return flight."

And I would appreciate if people and situations could stop reminding me that I'll be going home soon. I can do that enough myself.

"Then we'll just have to savor the time we have with you." She can't really be this nice. Can she?

We sit together for a little while longer, chatting, until Eve spots Amanda and drags her away. She waves at me with one hand while getting dragged around like a rag doll behind Eve with the other.

The rest of the day, curious people come sit down with me and grill me on who I am, why I'm here, if I'm carrying Beau's baby, and to give me banana pudding.

The woman who gave me the pudding was the one to ask me if I was pregnant, but after tasting the delicious gift from the gods that is banana pudding, she could have asked me how much I made and I wouldn't have cared. Shoot, ask me my weight and I'll tell her happily. As long as I get more of this ambrosia.

I should have been irritated at the constant onslaught

of strangers I have to socialize with, but they told me so much about their own lives, from their partner troubles, to wedding planning, to the drama happening to get the new stop sign in over on Main Street, I can't maintain the irritation.

I do love reality TV.

Eve finishes the final preparations and lets everyone escape to find their own way to the parade start site, with strict instructions to be ready in a half hour at the local high school.

Beau comes to get me when we're released, already dressed in his robe and fake white beard.

"Hey there, old man. You better leave before my strapping young gentleman caller comes and beats you up for looking at my ankle, see," I say in my best '40s voice. They were concerned about the seductive power of ankles back then, right?

"I could take him." Beau sits down next to me. "How was the Southern Inquisition?" he asks, letting me know that he's been watching me all day. Warm feelings flutter around in my chest, which is currently covered by Beau's larger sweater since mine didn't fit over my cast and he wanted me to be able to wear it tonight.

Even though he didn't rescue me from the Southern Inquisition. Wait a minute…

"So you knew what was happening, and you still let me walk into it without being forewarned and therefore not forearmed? And without being saved?"

"You looked like you could handle yourself, and certain Yankee types get mad when I try to help them. I didn't want to offend anyone."

"Ha! You thought it was funny and let me suffer."

Beau snorts. "They all came to me right after they left

you and said how disappointed they were that they didn't get enough information out of the stubborn Northerner. Except Jean, who said you agreed to have my baby if she kept making you banana pudding." Beau quirks his eyebrow, asking for confirmation on that piece of information.

I keep my mouth closed because I might have said it in an effort to get more pudding. I would have said anything to get more nanner puddin'.

"I don't recall." I fall back on the answer every lawyer probably wished their clients would use more often.

"I get it. It's the best banana pudding in South Carolina, but don't tell my aunt I said that."

"I would never." Because I don't think I'll be meeting his aunt.

We walk to Beau's truck and load up the extra decorations Eve needs (I supervise, being incapacitated and all). We arrive at the site just as Eve's deadline is up and get some maternal stink eye for that.

Harper and Harry see me first and run over to me. They heard about the cast, because everyone here knows everything about me and nothing is secret, and demand the right to sign it. I give in with no argument and they pull Sharpies out of Harper's backpack, fighting amongst each other over who gets to go first.

I end the fight by pointing out that Harper can draw on one side while Harry draws on the other, and it works before I have to call in real adults to handle the situation. I'm basically that guy who did the Camp David Accords.

Harper draws a puppy wishing me to get better soon under a rainbow, and Harry draws what I think is a dragon, or a cow with fiery farts; I still don't know and I'm not asking. Both are art, whatever they are. Official auction-eer opinion.

I tell them there's still some banana pudding in the red truck by the edge of the parking lot and they hug me before running off. This kid thing is easy; they just want sugar. We have so much in common.

The parade itself is a lot of fun. The kids alternate waving, throwing candy canes and giving me an im-promptu tour of the town, with all the important land-marks, such as where they get pizza after Little League, the ice cream place they go to celebrate good grades, and the toy store with the best selection.

Beau walks in front of us with the live nativity group, and we're followed by floats that the local businesses and schools all made. It's beautiful, but I did notice that most of the town is in the parade, so there aren't that many people watching us from the sides.

But everyone is having a great time.

After the short route, we end in the town square, the floats lined up so they can be admired throughout the night. The area is already set up by Eve's magical over-worked elves and it looks festive, the highest compliment I can give an event.

A small stage takes up the space in front of a giant tree and there's an empty dance floor lined with tables and chairs. The tables are decorated with tiny Christmas tree centerpieces including tinier Christmas ornaments, and on one side a buffet line is set up. On the edges of the square, Christmas booths offer goods of the edible and visually pleasing variety.

Every other inch of the square is filled with Christmas decorations that I wish I could stuff in my luggage and steal along with Bubba. The decorations look vintage, lovingly carved out of wood, and hand-painted with small imperfections that make everything look even better. Bright lights entwine around buildings, signs, and the decorations themselves.

Everything gets a light dusting of fake snow; in case I was missing a white Christmas (which I was).

The buffet line is already getting more crowded than any other space, so I tug Beau in that direction. I'm even getting used to all the curious glances and interrogations I get about who I am. I think I'm adapting.

As people finish up their meals (which did include a fresh banana pudding, bless nosy Jean), Eve gets up on the stage and turns on her microphone to get everyone's attention.

"Hello, everyone!" When the din dies down, she continues. "I want to thank y'all for another amazing year." She waits while everyone claps. "I couldn't have done it without all my team and all the volunteers—for all their time, the food and everything else you see here."

Volunteer is a strange choice of words for the conscription of goods and services that occurred, but it's the Christmas season and no one else seems to mind, so I let it go.

"Before we get Santa out here with the presents—" the kids kick up some noise at that announcement, not liking the delay "—I want to invite up the family I couldn't have done this without, Abbots and Jacksons, to thank them personally for the help they gave, whether they wanted to or not. And to make them help me one more time by lighting this tree."

Beau gets up and reaches for my hand, but I shake my head. This is a family moment and I'm just a fling. He drops a quick kiss on my lips, not willing to debate the issue right here, and jogs to join his parents and sister, as well as her family. Daniel and his family get on the stage too.

They stand together, picture perfect, as the cameras around me go off.

And I can't stop the panic that races through me this time.

Chapter Thirty-Four

I thought I had mostly dealt with my family issues. I didn't get jealous when I saw families around the city. I stopped telling mall Santas that all I wanted for Christmas was for my parents to move back to New York. I even stopped crying when they left after their annual visits. I was happy with casual, fun flings.

I was *fine*.

So I don't know what about this scene is getting to me right now. What about this family has been getting under my skin this whole visit.

But something about watching *this* family, who have been so welcoming to me, on *this* stage on *this* night, near Christmas, watching the casual love and affection that gets thrown around…is too much to take right now.

It's all the anxiety of the night at the Loot party when Beau asked me to come here, and every time my parents left, starting with the one where they told me they were moving back, and the damn job offer at Loot, all compounded, multiplied, added and all the other math functions to make numbers bigger, to make my heart pound out of my chest.

And the pain behind the anxiety is excruciating.

Because not only is this something I've desperately

wanted since that first Christmas without my parents, there's no way Beau would ever leave this. And why would he? His family is amazing. Their home is amazing, their business is amazing, and the way they love each other is amazing.

There's no way I can ask him to leave it and he would probably tell me no if I did. But I don't want to leave Priya and the rest of the Guptas, the only constants in my life, either. They're the only thing I can count on. I also don't want to leave the job that I mostly enjoy, or the city that's home.

But I can't stay and fall more in love with him.

Because I do love him.

I'm screwed. The resulting increase of my breathing makes that fact abundantly clear. And the way this loose, oversized sweater suddenly feels suffocating.

I can't do this. Stay here, give up everything for him, and then watch him find some other reason to leave me. Except then I'll be away from the limited family I do have and in pain.

No, there must be levels of love. I can still save some of myself if I put some space between Beau and me. Now. Yes, space. I've identified what I need to make myself all better and it will work.

Now Priya would make a plan. A plan can get you through anything. Step one: leave. Step two: buy a plane ticket. Step three: eat my way through the Door Dash app once I get home. Step four: work through the pain. Then there's Ajay's advice: drink all the alcohol, stop making plans and *act*. Maybe I can make that a step five. Or make it step three and a half.

I feel my heart calm down marginally at the thought of a plan. Is this why Priya is constantly making them?

I don't hear what else Eve says, but everyone claps and the lights on the tree turn on. I focus on breathing and keeping down the impulse to flee. I know the odds of me getting an Uber to the airport are slim, since I feel like everyone in the town is currently at this parade, but I still look down at my phone and open the app.

No service.

That sounds about right for these sticks. I keep up the deep breathing as the people on the stage make their way back to the tables.

"I need to go," I say to Beau as soon as he gets back to me.

Beau goes on the alert, looking around at what could have caused the panic in my voice. "What's wrong?"

I take the coward's way out; I can't get into the truth right now. "I have to get back to New York. Emergency with the show." I hold up my phone like I got a text from Priya telling me I need to come home.

Never mind I don't have service.

"Does Loot not have enough mulch?" Beau tries for a joke and I attempt a smile back, the best I can do. It feels more like a grimace and Beau's face gets concerned, so it's not passing.

"I'll take you back to the house and then to the airport. I think you'll be able to catch the last flight out." Beau looks at his watch and starts getting his stuff together. "Do you want to say bye to everyone?" Without waiting for a response, Beau heads for his family, who are still chatting by the stage.

Okay. I guess I'm saying bye then.

"Hi, everyone. Thank you so much for your hospitality, but I have to leave. Work emergency," I say weakly, the words coming out a little breathless as I try to keep my pounding heart from pounding through layers of rib cage and muscles and skin. I think it adds to the illusion of this fake emergency though, so it can only help.

"What?"

"Now?"

"That's a bummer."

"Is everything okay?"

Each member of the Abbot family (and whatever Annabelle decided to do with her last name) chimes in with questions and disappointment.

"It should be fine." And I should be too, I hope. If I recovered from my parents, surely I can recover from Beau, who I've only known for a few weeks. He didn't even give me life. "Just a work thing that needs me. And no one else can do it."

Please don't ask for details. In the emotional turmoil I'm in right now I would not be able to think of a convincing excuse off the top of my head.

"Is there anything we can do to help?" Reed asks. Damn it, these people are so nice and I need to get as far away from them as I can. Like open an office in LA far. Or New Zealand far.

"No, thank you. Beau said he would get me to the airport. I think I've got it from there."

"It was so great meeting you." Eve reaches for a hug. "I'm sorry the South broke you. It didn't even do that to me when I got here," she says into my hair.

"It's not the South's fault." I share a small smile with the woman before hugging the rest of the family.

"We'll miss you." Annabelle hugs me.

"I'll miss you too."

She holds on a little longer than me. I attempt to move

back but she doesn't let go. "Oh, okay. We're still hugging."

I finally get freed and follow Beau to not-his-truck.

"Dad let me borrow his truck so we don't have to walk all the way back to the staging place." Beau unlocks the doors and I climb in.

Once inside, my heart calms down even more. Until I realize that I now have to spend more time in a small space with Beau, with no buffer humans.

I take out my phone and open my email. Maybe he can think I'm a very busy human working on this emergency I invented. I stare at the unrefreshed email, because I still have no service. I guess I should be glad his eyes are on the road and he can't see the subterfuge I've worked, and failed, to create.

"What's the emergency?" he asks.

"Rogue vendors." If it was a good enough excuse for him, it's a good enough excuse for me. "If I don't get back, there won't be any food for the Christmas dinner we're hosting right before the auction. Or alcohol. And full, drunk buyers spend more money." I can hear the crack in my voice and hope he thinks I'm just really dedicated to the job, to the point I'm getting choked up over a lack of canapes.

"That sucks. You can't do it over the phone?"

Probably. Since the issue doesn't exist. "I organized them. And people are more willing to work with you in person." I mirror the same words he used on me when he had to leave New York.

"So much technology but the old-school ways still work the best."

"Yeah."

"I hope it's a quick fix for you."

"Yeah." I keep my answers short. Less evidence to give me away.

We get to the house, and I flee up the stairs, ignoring Bubba as he tries to greet me like he hasn't seen me in a month. Don't get attached, little guy; I'm leaving just like everyone does. I don't want to be the one to teach you this lesson, but I have to if no one else will.

Beau stays downstairs with the dog, giving me some privacy.

I throw things my things into my suitcase with my uninjured arm, not worrying about the expensive packing cubes I got to make my life easier. I get the packing done in record time, changing into leggings and a comfortable shirt with a lot of difficulty and pain to my fractured wrist.

Beau runs up the stairs to take my suitcase before I can come down. I let him have one last display of gentlemanly behavior without complaint before I leave. Also my wrist couldn't have taken the luggage down the stairs anyway.

"Are you sure you can get a flight?" Beau asks.

If I have to, I will spend the night in the airport. Or outside the airport if it closes. There must be a hotel nearby. Even around the smallest airport I've ever seen in my life.

"It'll be fine." But I do open my phone and search for flights. Might as well buy one now while I'm hooked up to the house's Wi-Fi. My phone tells me there's one last flight that I can just barely make and then I'll have a long layover in Atlanta, but eventually I'll be back in New York. I buy it immediately while Beau loads up my suitcase.

A short, silent drive later, during which I grunt responses so Beau can't tell from my voice I'm still panicked, we're at the airport.

"I hope everything goes well with work." Beau makes a last-ditch effort to get me in conversation as he gets my suitcase out.

"Thank you. I think it'll be fine. I just need to be there." Or anywhere that isn't here.

"Well. I'll be back in New York to check on the battery team soon. Maybe we can meet for dinner?"

Hopefully I'll be done with his office by his first visit. A lot of pieces are already delivered and he bought more while we were in South Carolina, so I need to find him just a few more and arrange everything. Tasks that I will work overtime and on weekends to finish so it's all done and I won't have reasons to take his calls when he's in town.

"Sure. Shoot me a text when you get to the city."

Now please leave me alone so I can cry alone at an airport gate, like a cliché. I've held it together at the thought of how embarrassing it would be to cry in front of him. But I'm not a machine; I can't keep up this façade of emotionally stable person much longer.

"Yeah. Maybe I can come up sooner than the work needs? Maybe come up for a long weekend?" Beau sounds hopeful at the question, but he doesn't know how this ends because no one's ever left him. I, however, do know. Enough for the both of us.

I look at my phone to avoid the wave of intense longing that crashes into me at the suggestion. I've never wanted anything more. But to what end? Just to watch each other leave for years before we decide it's not worth it? But by that time, I'll not only be in love with him like I am now,

I'll also get too used to having him around, even if only periodically. So I'll be in pain *and* have to learn how to be completely alone again.

I hold up the phone, showing the time. "I better go so I don't miss the flight. But I'll text you."

Spoiler alert: I will not be texting him.

"Of course. Let me help you in."

No. I already let him do his last gentlemanly act toward me. "I don't think you can leave your car here. And anyway, I'll be fine. I think I can handle this two-gate airport." I send him a quick kiss on the check and then a quick smile. The very last bit of perfidy I can manage for the night.

"But your wrist."

"I only have to roll everything the short distance to the gate. I'll be good."

"Well. I really liked spending time with you. New York. Here. Wherever. I really like—"

"I had a really good time with you." I don't want to hear what he has to say. It can only make things harder now.

He doesn't press. "Call me if you can't get on the flight or need anything."

"Thank you." But I'm already walking toward the building.

Inside I stop behind the automatic doors, giving myself one last look back. Beau's still standing by his truck, looking toward me. I cut my look short so I don't do something I'll regret, like run out of the building and throw myself at Beau, promising to quit my job, telling him I love him and that I'm moving here.

Because even though I think I do love him, I can't

give up my entire life when there are no guarantees in love. I can't take the risk.

So I turn back around and walk straight to the check-in counter.

Chapter Thirty-Five

I get to Atlanta with no problem, except a lot of tears and pitying/ annoyed looks, and then I have a long wait. Plenty of time to make the call that I've been dreading.

I wipe the tears from my eyes before I click on the contact, because she'll be able to use her efficient magic to know something's wrong. And since I never cry, she'll know it's something major.

I had originally decided to stop crying when I was in middle school and realized that no matter how much I cried, my parents wouldn't stay. It's kind of stuck since then. And I'm really not enjoying that it's made a reappearance now.

With each ring I breathe a little easier, thinking I can avoid this conversation for a while if she doesn't answer.

But then the line goes silent, and Priya says, "What's up, buttercup?"

Priya's familiar voice breaks through my composure and my tears start leaking again despite my best efforts to keep them in my eyes.

"I'm at the airport in Atlanta waiting for my return flight home." It's hard to get the words out, but she hears enough.

"What? What's going on? Did you knock the peachperson out and stuff him in a suitcase? Because kidnapping is illegal, but I'll harbor your criminal ass. And your victim's ass, too."

Priya is off her game. Normally she can tell what I'm feeling before I have to explain it to her. I knew marriage made people soft.

"No. I left. I…couldn't… I just couldn't," I whisper to her, burying my face in my free hand.

Priya stays uncharacteristically silent and then is unusually subdued when she finally does say something. "I'm sorry, Sonia. I wish I could slap your parents for you."

That gets a little laugh from me. "I don't think Chachi and Chacha would be too happy with you."

Priya scoffs. "We both know Mom lets me get away with murder ever since I insisted Dad take more vacations away from my offices." Probably so Chacha doesn't hear her call his offices *her* offices. "Come home, Sonia. We'll take care of you."

"Yeah. You will."

"We always do."

"Love you."

"Love you more."

I don't bother arguing with the queen of competition. Just because she would really like it.

"Do you need anything?"

"No, I'm set. I'll see you soon."

"Text me your flight info so I can pick you up at the airport."

"I will."

"Bye."

I turn my phone over on my lap, the tough task done.

I'm lucky to have Priya and family here for me. But if the last few days have taught me anything, it's that I'm still really, really mad at my parents. Not an anger that I think about daily, or one that drives me to tears or yelling anymore. But one that apparently dictates a lot of the decisions that I make.

I mean, I knew it affected me a little bit. The steady stream of casual dating did clue me in. But I thought I *wanted* to date casually because I wanted to save myself the annoyance of other people's nonsense.

I didn't know I was *incapable* of forming those attachments. But I know now.

Unfortunately, knowing is only half the battle.

The heaviness in my stomach preventing me from eating the twelve-dollar croissant sitting on my lap proves that I am not in control of these emotions.

Maybe I imagined that I wouldn't want a partner like Priya and Chachi and even my mom have. Or maybe I thought I would let my issues go once I met the "right person."

But here I am. In love with Beau and in pain because I'm worried about there being a bigger pain in the future if he asks me to give up my entire life and move to South Carolina, or the pain if he just decides he's over it and leaves me.

My parents have a lot to answer for. And I've never confronted them about it. Which isn't fair to me. Why should I have to carry this burden without having my say to the people causing it?

Because usually I didn't want to ruin the few times a year I do see them. But what's the point in that?

Nothing is getting dealt with.

And the timing will never get any more perfect than it is now. I still have time off work because I'm supposed to be with Beau, and I'm literally at an airport.

And I have *resolve*.

I need an airline help desk. Now.

Too many layovers and two days later, I'm still determined.
I'm also very smelly, very cold, and very tired. And still
very sad. But I washed my face somewhere over Eastern
Europe and haven't cried since, so at least my eyes aren't
puffy and red anymore.

The airport help desk had been more than happy to
help me when they found out that price was not an issue.
And Priya said a succinct "Finally" when I told her why
she wouldn't need to pick me up at the airport and how I
was out of breath because I was running to catch a flight
whose doors were almost closed.

But last-minute plane tickets mean middle seats. So
I also have pain in my neck.

I did get an unexpected stop in England, where I had
some English breakfast tea (although who knew what
mealtime it was, running through as many time zones
as I did) and some whiskey. Because it must have been
five o'clock in one of the time zones I passed.

And I diligently avoided the texts from Beau asking
me if I got back safe to New York.

Now that I've landed in New Delhi on a Monday
morning, I call my parents' assistant, and after she gets
over her surprise and promises not to tell my parents anything, she sends a car for me.

While I'm waiting for the transportation, I continue
to ignore the texts from Beau, which haven't magically
gone away as I passed through all those time zones.

The car arrives and the driver takes me through New
Delhi traffic during rush hour, weaving around rick-

shaws, cars, and pedestrians, none of whom have any respect for the nonexistent lanes in the road.

We pass an inflatable brown Santa, Christmas having reached all corners of the world now. It gives me a slight injection of holiday magic, if not cheer, before my big confrontation.

I enter the building and get through security with little effort. The perks of always keeping my badge in my wallet, even on vacation. And having standing access to all Loot buildings.

The guard leaves little to the imagination about how he feels about my general appearance and smell as he waves me through. Thanks, guy. I'm going through some things.

One elevator trip later, I walk to my parents' joint office. Which is as far as I get before I get scared and freeze, hand raised to knock on the door. Viti, my parents' assistant, catches me before they do, coming up behind me.

"Why do you smell of body odor and sadness?" Her accented voice washes over me, too similar to my mom's for comfort at this time.

Her voice shocks me out of my trance and I turn. "Because I decided on a last-minute trip to India without luggage or first-class seats."

"Okay, then." She settles in next to me to look at the door to the office suite. "Did you come this way to see our high-quality wood and craftsmanship, or are you going in?"

"I hadn't decided yet." Do we only hire people with sass? We need to reconsider this business policy.

"Well. It would be a waste of all your effort if you went back now."

I crinkle my nose in distaste. "And exhausting if I went back without at least a night to sleep in between."

"You make a good point. It really seems like there's only one thing left to do." Viti gives me a light shove with her shoulder against mine.

When I just look at her, frozen in fear and sadness, she takes matters in her own hands and knocks on the door. Because she's busy and she doesn't have time for my family crises.

That's fair.

"Come in," Mom says through the door.

"Good luck," Viti whispers as she opens the door and holds it to let me go through it first.

"Thanks." I walk in quickly before I can flee.

"Viti, do you have the sales figures for our last event?" Mom asks as I walk in, not looking up from her computer. Is this a family skill that I never got? I would like to have half as much drive as these workaholics. Ugh, but not their sad personal lives.

The office is just like I remember: the same we're-richer-than-you-so-trust-us-with-your-treasures vibe as the New York office, but with an Indian flavor. There are scalloped arches framing the windows, with glistening marble on the floor. Mom commissioned the mural behind the desk of Krishna and Radha dancing when she took over the offices.

I played under that mural the few times I visited the offices here. Mom wasn't happy when I started drawing rainbows around the peacock at Radha's feet, not impressed with my eight-year-old level of skill.

"I do. And another surprise as well," Viti says when she sees that I'm not making my presence known.

"What is—Sonia?" Mom stands up, a mix of confused

and polite happiness on her face. "What are you doing here? Is everything okay? What happened to your arm?"

"Yeah. Well, no. But mostly, yeah." I ignore the bit about my cast. I have other things to focus on.

An arched eyebrow rises. "Yes, but no, but yes? Is this the education we spent so much money on in the States?"

I sigh in frustration. "Everything's fine. I just wanted to talk to you."

Mom gets over some of the shock of seeing me here and comes around her giant historic desk. I get a belated hug, but a strong one. "It's always good seeing you. But it's a long way to come for chai. Viti, can you call up some chai from the kitchen?"

"Of course. I'll leave the numbers here." Viti slides a folder on Mom's desk and gets out of the office before she can get dragged further into the family drama about to unfold.

"Did you want to pop into the bathroom before chai? Where are your bags?" She looks around me, probably looking for my luggage. Because that's what people bring when they travel across the globe.

"It was kind of a last-minute trip."

"What's going on?" Mom leads me to the couches in her room, moving three decorative pillows out of the way before I have the gall to sit on them. I put my purse on the glass tabletop being held up by a golden elephant that must be a new addition.

Before I can answer, Dad bursts through the door. "Deepa, where are the figures from the last sale?"

"Arjun, Sonia's here," Mom says in lieu of telling him the folder is on her desk.

"Sonia? What are you doing here?" He gives me his

own hug, getting used to the idea much faster than Mom did, and then sits down on the chair opposite the couch.

This is good that they're both in the same place and at the same time. I don't know if I can do this once much less go through it once for each parent.

"I need to talk to both of you."

Chapter Thirty-Six

"So you've said." Mom throws her hands up. "But you still haven't told me what you want to talk about."

Deep breath in. Deep breath out. And repeat. And repeat. Mom and Dad's impatient looks tell me they would like me to practice the calming breathing after I tell them what's going on.

"I'm mad at you both that you left me in America when you came back to India," I say without any warning or warm-up.

Not that I know what I could have said to warm them up to that.

"We thought it would be best if you lived in the US. You would have more opportunities there," Mom says while Dad sputters.

"Okay. But you could have stayed in New York with us."

"The company needed us here," Dad says.

"Fine. Whatever." I get the exact same responses I got every time I asked in my childhood. "But you could have visited more. Or made me come here more. There's a lot of vacation days in a school year and we're all rich enough to get plane tickets."

They look at each other in silent communication, the

kind only possible when you've spent the last thirty-five years with the same person.

"And fine. You didn't do any of that when I was a kid. That was your choice. But I'm an adult now and I can do something if I don't like our relationship. Or at least try to do something to change our relationship."

Silence meets the speech I planned for twenty-two hours. Not exactly the reaction I wanted. My parents look at me, both at a loss on how to handle this parenting development.

"So. We should have more family visits in a year. And talk more on the phone. Or text. I can teach you about emojis. And GIFs." I keep talking because the silence is a little too much to handle.

But then there's more silence. To fill the silence, I contemplate reciting Charles De Gaulle's speech to the French to rally them to fight Nazis. The same speech I had to memorize for French class and never forgot. *La France a perdu une bataille! Mais la France n'a pas perdu la guerre!*

Actually, that's kind of applicable, Charles. I lost the battle of my childhood, but I can still win the war now that we're all adults.

Before I can get into the speech, Mom speaks.

"It was hard." Mom's voice is low and she's looking at the same mural that I painted over. I wonder if she remembers me playing there, or if she just likes the pretty painting.

I keep looking at her, hoping she elaborates.

"To leave you every time. To know we wouldn't be tucking you in at night or making sure you had a good breakfast. Or watching you learn and grow and laugh and cry. Especially making you feel better when you cried.

Being with you for a short amount of time reminded us of everything we were missing, so we limited the time we came. To make it easier for us. Not that it ever did."

"Then why didn't you just take me with you?"

"We felt you would have better opportunities if you were educated in America." Mom has an answer for everything.

"Then why didn't you stay?"

Mom stays silent at that one and starts to tear up.

Dad chimes in, slumping in his chair and looking more tired than I've ever seen the man. I guess it's easy to hold it together when you only see someone for a few weeks a year. "That's my fault. I love our home in India and I didn't want to move. We did because it made the most sense for the business. Then we had you, and it made more sense. But after a few bad experiences with strangers he had hired to run Loot years after we all left, Kabir asked us to take over the headquarters. But you were in the middle of the school year."

He takes off his glasses and rubs his own eyes. I would never say it was because he was crying, because the man has been made of stone every time I cried when they left, but his face is suspiciously wet now.

"We were going to move you after the school year, but when we came back to get you, you looked so content with Priya and Ajay, and all your other friends. You were so excited about Halloween even though it was summer… you were going as a pink ranger."

I remember that year. The cousins, some friends and I planned to have a group costume as the Power Rangers. It was a good Halloween. I don't know that it was worth losing my parents over.

But Dad's not done. "You seemed so settled and happy.

And like your mom said, it was a better opportunity for you to be educated in New York. Our job was to safeguard your, Priya's and Ajay's legacy here." Dad reaches for Mom's hand because she hasn't stopped crying. "It seemed so logical at that time."

Mom can barely get words out, but she chimes in. "And then it was too late. You didn't need us because we were never there for you. And every time we saw you, we were reminded that you didn't need us. You reached for Chachi every time you needed anything, because she was the one that was always there. Even when I was there." Mom tentatively reaches out to hug me and then strengthens her arms around me when I don't pull away.

It feels really good to be hugged by my mom, so I wrap my arms around her as well, not ready for this hug to end any time soon.

I inhale deeply and smell chai. I remember how addicted to chai Mom is…needing about six cups to get through the day.

"We're sorry," she sobs into my shoulder.

"We really are. More than you'll know." Dad joins the hug and I feel surrounded by my parental love for the first time in a long time.

We stay like that for a while, until the communal flow of tears slows to a trickle and we hear a knock on the door.

"It'll probably be the chai tray." Mom wipes her eyes and untangles herself from the hug. "Come in," she yells to the door.

An employee brings in the tray and sets it up in front of us. Three cups of chai sit on the table, with three warm samosas piled next to them.

My stomach growls at the reminder that the only thing

I've had in the past day is airplane food and that expensive croissant.

"Uh, Dad. You have to let go so I can eat." I didn't expect Dad to be the one who refused to let go. But Mom is having some post-crying snacks and I want some too.

"Right." Dad pushes away and hands me a mug of chai and then puts some chutney on a plate with a samosa for me.

After the emotional talk we went through, everyone wants a bit of a break. But because I'm not a patient person, I only give us a half a cup and a few bites of food before I jump back in.

"What's the plan for seeing each other more?" More than a few weeks out of the year at least.

They do that married couple thing again where they communicate with a look. "We have been discussing this. Not that you'll believe us now, but we have been thinking of retiring," Mom says.

"Semi-retiring," Dad says. There's my dad. "But we could spend half the year in America and half the year in India. We trust our team here now, especially Viti, and we can do a lot remotely now, with technology. Plus, we're getting too old to yell at a full room of rich people, demanding more money."

"We've been discussing it for a while, but we didn't want to force ourselves on you," Mom says in between sips of her mug.

"No. I think that would be really good."

"Well, wait until you have your father interrogating your boyfriend like you're eighteen because he missed doing that when you were actually eighteen," Mom says.

Sadness punches into the happy moment, when I

think about the closest to a boyfriend I've gotten since high school.

And how he won't be meeting my parents.

"What's wrong, beta? Is there a boyfriend problem?" Mom puts down her teacup.

"I could talk to the boy, if there's an issue?" Dad asks awkwardly. He's really trying.

But that conversation could be bad. Especially since this is all my fault.

I had very good reasons at the time. They seem a little silly now, when I'm talking to my parents and realizing I should have given Beau the same courtesy.

"No. Please don't. It's fine." That's a lie, but I can only handle one relationship crisis at a time.

Chapter Thirty-Seven

"Where are the gingerbread house centerpieces?" Priya yells in my direction with her iPad in hand.

"In the kitchen. The chefs are putting the final touches on them and they'll be on the tables well before people get here." I hold my arms (and my faded pink cast) out to calm my boss like she's an escaped lioness from the zoo I have to corral back into her habitat. And she's not having any of it.

I should have stayed in India longer if this is what I was going to come home to. I still have unused vacation time saved up.

I did get a good weeklong vacation with my parents before coming back, first going shopping so I'd have some clothes. They took time off work and we mostly stayed at home, getting to know who we were as a family. They even took me to a couple of auctions, parading me around as their highly successful auctioneer daughter from the American office.

It felt good.

They're even getting on a plane in a week to spend New Year's here and to look for a condo so they can have a home when they come for longer visits. Which means I get to show them my favorite New York holiday events.

I finally get to be one of the annoying families traipsing around New York, embarrassed by my mom wanting
pictures everywhere and mad at my dad for not letting
me have an extra dessert with lunch.

It's going to be grand.

But that does make me think of all the Christmas-ing
I did with Beau, and that dims the perfection of the last
week.

He texted a few times, asking how I was or sending
me a picture of how his Christmas is going. I kept my
responses short and focused on business whenever he
tried to veer to the personal.

His offices are done now, mostly finished by email
from India and finalized when I got home. Room after
room of imposing wood and comfortable, luxurious
leather, with statues of Greek and Roman gods overlooking his deals and bestowing their prestige and good
fortune his way. And enough paintings of harvesting and
food to make anyone think about what's for lunch, and
about Beau and Daniel's other successful company. I even
snuck a statue of the Roman goddess of victory, Nike,
into his research facility that was earmarked for his main
office. Hopefully it'll give him some luck in the R&D.

I've made sure the lights are set up, the walls are
painted, and everything is in its place, ready to run a business. The only thing left to do is send the final invoice.

With the job done and my chilly responses when he
tries to ask about how I'm doing or when he should visit, I
don't think he'll be sending many more texts in the future.

I started seeing a therapist, who wants to have my
parents in for a session when they come. She made me
cry, and we've only had one session. She says the crying

is a good thing, but I still hate it. I can admit to myself and only myself that it does feel better when I'm done. Go figure.

She also thinks I should text Beau back. She hasn't said it in so many words, but I can read between the lines.

She says that's projection, but what does she know?

It was hard coming back since I was getting along so well with my parents, but Priya needed me. I could tell she was getting stressed over the Christmas sale. I could hear it when she called me seven times a day and asked me where things were, so I decided to come back and do what I could to help her before she explodes with all the stress.

It's mostly just keeping her calm enough so she can do all the things I know she can already do.

Now we're here, the week of Christmas, and our joint auction starts in less than an hour.

"But did all the lots get here?" Priya asks, wringing her hands.

"Yes. I've gone through them all with an employee over at Carlyle's and every piece is accounted for," I say. "And before you can freak out about anything else: the room is decorated, the tables are mostly set, and the valet is set up and ready to take cars. The cooks are busy cooking, the maids are busy milking and we've put a partridge in a pear tree."

That last part's not hyperbole. We have a pear tree, and a partridge. Well, a fake one at any rate.

Priya sighs deeply and flips over the cover on her iPad. "Okay. I'm being ridiculous."

Gavin walks by at the exact perfect moment and does

an exaggerated double take. "Sorry, did my wife just admit to a character flaw?"

"No. I heard nothing," I say promptly. I would kill for this woman; I would definitely lie for her.

Gavin slides an arm around his wife from behind and kisses her hair. Priya jerks away. "You're going to mess my hair up."

Gavin rolls his eyes. "You look great. This is going to be great. Our families can get along. And I'm going to mess up that hair later anyway."

The heat between the two makes me look at my own iPad screen and think about Gavin's words. That's why Priya has been so intense. Extra intense, even. I thought it was because the sale was bigger than usual, or maybe because a joint sale is always harder since it involves more coordinating.

But she was worried because she wants her old and new families to get along. I should have seen it sooner, but I've been distracted for the past couple of weeks.

"I'm going to be so glad when I get my only moderately workaholic wife back." He gives her another light kiss on her hair, not messing up a strand of it, and moves on to do his last-minute preparations for the half of the auction that he's conducting.

"I didn't know you were worried about the families getting along." I nudge Priya when Gavin walks around the corner.

Priya looks down at her feet. "I think my first memory was Dad cursing the Carlyles. I don't want every holiday and every family dinner to be tense, awkward and terrible forever."

"Chacha loves you more than he loves competition.

And they have been arguing, but it hasn't been mean-spirited. Or as mean-spirited as they used to be." Honesty compels me to add the last part.

"As someone CC'ed on those email threads, I think it's incredibly generous of you to say it hasn't been mean-spirited."

"Maybe that's just how they communicate."

Priya looks up at me. "But if this show doesn't work, then they'll be back to hating each other again."

I hug her close. "It's going to be fine, but even if it isn't, all the parents love you. Even mine, and they already promised to run interference between the houses. They do not care about this rivalry." I casually work into the conversation that my parents are visiting. Every time I say they're coming, it gets more real.

"I'm glad they're going to be here for you. Finally." Priya sinks into the hug for a few seconds longer than usual, and then pulls away, looking calmer and more like the take-no-prisoners businesswoman that I know and love. "Everything is done or is in the process of getting done by highly paid professionals."

I nod along, glad she's feeling better.

"That means you can distract me by telling me the plan to get over Beau, because I don't like it when you're sad."

I sigh. "I'm working on it." It's not going well, but I'm trying. "But I just started fixing my relationship with my parents. It's too much to deal with Beau on top of it."

"Sure you can."

"But I don't want to." I've been moving, and it's helped immensely. Going to India, bonding with my parents, coming back to the chaos of this sale and finishing Beau's office. It's all helped me keep busy and helped me avoid thinking about whether I made a giant mistake leaving Beau.

And I think it was a giant mistake. One I may not recover from. One that I'm beginning to think will have as big an effect on me as my parents did. Except this time I have no one to blame but me, since I left.

But unlike my parents, I sincerely doubt he'll wait over twenty years for me to figure it out myself.

"You need to."

"You're getting cut out of my will."

"Oh no, what will I do without your collection of magnets from around the world?"

"Well, you'll find out because you aren't getting mine."

"Maybe I'll go to South Carolina and start my own collection." Parting shot thrown, Priya wanders off to harass someone who's not me.

Little does she know that I've got price alerts set for flights to South Carolina.

But what would I even say? "Sorry, I'm a coward and I'm still a little bit of a coward, but now I'm a coward in therapy trying to work on things and anyway would you like to be with me as I slowly get over my issues? Even though there's still a chance I'll fail and run again."

I mean. That might work.

I have to do something. Because even though I'm not sure how it happened, when I *specifically* didn't want it to, he's important to me. I think it was bit by bit, ounce by ounce, second by second. Like that lobster getting cooked in a slowly warming pot, and now I'm terrified and about to be dinner.

Okay, maybe not all of the metaphor tracks.

I see him everywhere. In every damn Christmas tree,

Christmas light, and Santa I see, I think of him. Of what he would think of every Christmas decoration I see, like the Santa getting milk drunk with the elves in that one Christmas display on Fifth Avenue.

I know I can't go on like this. I do need to do something about him. Maybe I can get away with a text? As I enter the bustle of the kitchen, I promise I'll think about it after the sale.

The auction goes just as perfectly as every event Priya organizes. There was some Dad drama at the beginning over who would get to make an announcement. But I ended up doing it and we kept the dads apart and away from the stage. Then everything went smoother.

I'm almost finished sorting out the stuff that needs to be done tonight when I see a familiar head of closely cut dirty-blond hair.

Beau! What's he doing here? Did he come to see me? What am I wearing? Oh, okay. Classy black dress.

I smooth down the sides of it as I walk toward him and then give my hair a last smooth over to hopefully tuck in any flyaways. I can't do anything about the pounding of my heart except hope that no one else can hear it.

I stop right behind the mountain of a man. A mountain I very much missed climbing.

"I thought you hated art." I touch him lightly on the elbow. My fingers shake a little in anticipation of seeing Beau again and I clasp them behind me to hide it.

The man, who is decidedly not Beauregard Dean Abbot, turns around and gives me a questioning look.

"Oh, sorry." I back away and hold my hands up. "I thought you were someone else."

"No problem. Merry Christmas." The kind stranger moves away from me quickly.

"You, too."

This can't go on.

Chapter Thirty-Eight

"Priya, I'm doing it!" I burst through the office we set up for the show, hoping she's still in here but not checking before I barged in and made my announcements.

"Doing what?" Chacha asks me from his seat. Priya stands next to him, holding a document for him to review.

"Oh. Hey, everyone. Um. The guy I was seeing…and I went to South Carolina…and then I fled like an invading horde was after me…and I'm going to need some more time off to go back to South Carolina."

I wait for the fallout.

"Again? You just came back." Chacha's brow furrows at the lost profits.

"Yes. I do technically still have the time."

"This is not responsible for a future manager."

"Right. About that." No time like the present to put into effect my new plan to commit to the things I want without fear. A warm-up for Beau. "I don't want that job. Thank you for offering it to me. But I want to do interior designing. And I understand if I can't do it at Loot, but it is what I want to do with my life." Great, I just put something else on my table. Like I didn't have enough, now I have to find a new job.

"What—"

"This is a good time to give you your Christmas present, a little early." Priya has a sparkle in her eyes. "This is a selfish present, but I've been going over your sales and commission figures with Beau while you were gone, and it's profitable to have you help clients like this. Also moves some pieces we haven't been able to in our auctions. So I want you to start the department and staff it. Maybe under mine at first. Just a few people to start, maybe just one assistant and you. But we can expand once we build up the service and the demand for it."

"This can't be profitable," Chacha interjects. Priya performs some swipes on her tablet and Chacha's eyes widen. "Oh. I approve of the new department."

Priya rolls her eyes, like he has any control over Priya's department anymore. "And I've been busy, but we'll talk later about how you could have brought this to me originally and I would have supported you. Because I'm never too busy for you. And your new business cards that I had made to tell you this news are already wrapped and under the tree for you to open."

"Thank you. This is the best present." I didn't realize how much I would enjoy interior decorating, so I couldn't fight for it before now. I still wouldn't know if Beau hadn't come into the offices, confused about everything art related. But leave it to Priya to investigate any potential avenue for profit.

Priya moves around the table and grabs my hands, looking me directly in the eyes. "Now, on to the next issue. Are you sure about this? He lives far and you don't do well without amenities."

"I know he lives in a less than ideal place, but I have to see if we can make it work. I would regret it otherwise."

"All right. Good luck then." Priya hugs me hard, longer than a usual hug. I don't want to lose seeing her daily any more than she wants to lose a cousin, but I need to see where this goes.

"What? No. You can't leave now. We have even more to do to get this department set up. And you just had a vacation. Go later," Chacha says.

"I need to go now."

"I just heard about a new department; we all need to have meetings to see how this will work so we can hit the ground running next year."

If the last month has taught me anything, it's that I can fight for the things I want. I did fight for my parents, and I can fight for Beau and for my future job.

"Sorry, Chacha. I have to go. But I'll be back soon." I rush back out of the room before he can say anything else. I would rather deal with his anger later than not go and regret it. And finding another job is always an option.

Even though I'm pretty confident Priya wouldn't let it get to that.

I still have to figure out how we'll deal with living in different states. But I'll worry about that later. We can figure it out, but first I need to know Beau loves me too. That there's still something there he wants to fight for, too.

As I leave the room, I run into Chachi, who looks like she was loitering outside the room.

"I have to run, Chachi." I try to head her off before she can say anything. If I told her about everything, the conversation would last into the next year. Which is coming up in a week, but still long for a conversation.

"I heard! I was trying to find Kabir and Priya so we could get home at a reasonable time, and I'm so glad I did." Listening at doors. This family. "You have to take a private jet, as a Christmas present from me." She gets out her phone, presumably to start making plans.

"I can't take a jet. That's excessive."

"A seller owes us a favor. We sold an unsellable piece for him and he's very grateful. Long story." Chachi waves my concerns away. "This is for love!" She dances out of the room like we're in a Bollywood movie, except she lost her backup dancers somewhere along the song. And there's no music playing.

But I do catch her singing "Dilwale Dulhania Le Jayenge" to herself. Great, my life is a movie and Chachi thinks I'm bravehearted and wants me to take my bride away, if the translation of the title can be believed.

"I never said I was in love," I yell after her. She probably shouldn't have been the first person to say I was in love. That should have been me. To the person I'm in love with. Or Priya. Because best friends know everything about each other and know it first.

I don't get a response. Nor did I expect one. But I've got a jet to catch, apparently, so I'll ignore it.

Now what does one wear to grovel?

Turns out, among other things, one of the perks of flying in a private jet is that you get to take up all the space and turn it into a private dressing room at forty thousand feet. The flight attendant, who has probably gotten some unique requests in her day, doesn't bat an eye when I ask her what I look best in.

She dresses me in the blue gingham dress, suggesting that "the farmer might be more receptive to an apology if you're dressed like you just got done milking a cow." I mean, it couldn't hurt.

She also gets a lot of backstory that she probably isn't

prepared for. But again, she's a professional and is attentive to my drama. She asks if I want to go over my grovel speech, but since I still haven't written it yet, I decline.

I figured it would come to me after I had the perfect outfit. Then over Virginia I look great, but it still doesn't come to me. I watch an episode of *Veep*, thinking all the great writing will stimulate my creativity.

That doesn't help, although it is enjoyable. So alcohol must be the answer. The first whiskey is not illuminating but does make me care less that I don't know what I'm going to say, and the second makes me yell, "Turn this plane around!" so I don't have to come up with the speech.

Everyone on the plane takes their orders from Chachi apparently, so we do not turn around. Which leaves me in a tiny regional airport, in a very cute gingham dress with a bow in the back, tipsy, and with no idea what to say to make this right with Beau.

The flight attendant, probably still on those orders, calls a car for me before I can change my mind and get back on the jet.

So helpful.

The car drops me off in front of Beau's house and drives away. Probably on similar orders as the jet to abandon me here until this is sorted. I stand in front of the door, giving myself a pep talk to knock. I remember how much I love Beau and how good his arms are going to feel if he forgives me.

But that's not what makes me knock. I finally realize that they probably heard the car and since they're in the middle of nowhere, they know it's for them. They're going to wonder if someone's being creepy around their property.

I knock and wait a few seconds for them to answer.

"Oh well, I tried. Maybe I'll try again in a few months," I say to the door, so the house knows I'm not a coward.

I turn around and hear the door open. Damn it. I turn back around to face whoever it is that answered the door. "Heeeey."

Reed is in his pajamas. His eyes are squinted like he's getting used to the light and also probably in confusion.

"Is Beau here?"

"Didn't you leave?"

"Just for a little work emergency. Like the mulch." While also being nothing like mulch.

"And do you know it's one in the morning?"

A fact I didn't realize till now. "I'm sorry. I didn't realize it would be this late after the flight…and car ride…"

"He was really broken up when you left."

"Um. Oh."

"You shouldn't do that again." Reed has censure in his voice.

"I'm going to try really hard not to." I don't really want to move down here, so that might still be a problem. Not that I *won't* move here. But I'm really hoping we land on any other option. A New York option. Hell, an LA option would be fine.

Reed grunts and steps aside to let me in.

I sag in relief and step inside. Being on the receiving end of this is not fun. But I did hurt Beau and I deserve this. I just hope Reed doesn't passive aggressively clean a gun in front of me, warning me off his precious son like some deranged toxic-masculinity type.

He doesn't *seem* the type.

"Fine, then. I'll get him. You can help yourself to some sweet tea in the kitchen."

That's a nice improvement over the admonishing. I walk to the kitchen and after pouring myself a glass of the good stuff, I sit on a stool by the island and wait.

I hear Bubba first, the sounds of his heavy paws echoing in the large home. Then I see the precious wrinkles rushing into the kitchen to shove his head in my lap. I hope his owner has this excited a reaction to seeing me after the way I left.

I scratch Bubba behind the ears and he slowly moves so his butt is in front of me. I take the hint and scratch the sides of his rear for him.

"Where's your brother?" I ask in the universal tone reserved for babies and puppies and annoying Priya when she's on deadlines.

"I'm right here." A gravelly, sleep-roughened voice reminds me that I'm interrupting everyone's night.

Beau is leaning against the door frame, hands in his pajama pant pockets. He looks just as good as I remember him, with his shirt stretching along those muscles forged by the farm right outside. Probably doing it on purpose, to give me a taste of what I'm missing.

It's cold, but I deserve it.

"Hi." I slowly straighten and Bubba knocks his head into my hand, wondering what could be more important than scratching his head.

Only the rest of my life, you adorable puppy. Still, he's tall enough that I can talk and scratch.

"Hi." Beau is talking to me, but he doesn't run to sweep me up in his arms. Again, deserved. But I'm still allowed to dream. "I didn't expect to see you in South Carolina so soon. Or at all."

"Yes. Well, the Christmas sale was tonight, and it went really well..."

Bubba can tell this conversation is going to be boring, so he abandons me to chew on a bone in the corner.

"That's good. I know you were worried about that."

Okay. Here goes. Deep breath. "And also when I left
here I sort of went to India instead of New York and
I confronted my parents because your parents are so
amazing. This trip made me want to work on my relationship with mine, and that went well. And I've started
therapy, because even though I knew my childhood affected me I thought I had it under control. But then I
panicked at the Christmas parade and ran away, so I realized that I might not be as okay as I thought and everyone can use a little help." I take another deep breath.
"And anyway, I was an asshole. To you. I apologize for
that. And for the aforementioned running."

Beau blinks slowly and takes his hands out of his
pockets. His mouth is open slightly like he's getting
ready to respond but doesn't quite know what to say.

Or which part to respond to first.

How do you think I feel? This is my life. But I did
have longer to process this, so I can't be impatient. Well,
I can and will be impatient on the inside, but I really
should let him take as long as he needs on the outside.

"You've been busy." Beau finally responds but stays
rooted in the spot like he's been cemented in place right
in the middle of the hallway.

He wants more. And he deserves more. I was hoping to avoid having to lay *all* my vulnerabilities on the
table, but Beau is still standing in the doorway to the
kitchen and I'm still planted by this kitchen island. Not
ideal geography.

I look down at the counter so I don't have to look at

him when I say the next part, the part that digs even deeper into me.

"You make me so happy. But I was scared, because I didn't know how to deal with the fact that our lives are in different places, and that means one of us has to give something up or I have to watch you walk away, or I'll be the one walking, again and again after short visits. And I didn't think I could do that after watching my parents leave all those times. But the alternative has been worse. So if you'll have me, I want to try. I can't promise that I won't get scared again, but I *really* want to try for you. *With* you."

Okay. I think that's it. I have nothing else I can share with him. It would be nice to see how he's reacting to the news, but that's hard since I refuse to look up from my glass of sweet tea.

I hear footsteps and hope it's not just Bubba moving around me. I breathe out a little in relief when I see Beau's pale feet come into my peripheral vision.

I never thought I would be so happy to see feet.

Beau sits down on the seat next to me and lets out a deep sigh. Is that an "I'm done with you" sigh? Or a "You kook, oh the shenanigans you'll take me on for the rest of our lives together" sigh?

Because I can't tell.

"Can you look at me?" he asks.

Does he want to see me when he delivers the final, devastating shot? He doesn't have a sadistic streak in him, does he? This is the worst. I'm never going to be in the wrong again if it means I'm going to have to grovel like this.

"Sonia?" Beau tries to get my attention again. I look in his direction because the way he says my name causes every butterfly in me to flutter all their wings, causing a mini hurricane in my stomach.

"Yes." I begrudgingly raise my head higher and look straight at his collarbone.

"My eyes are up here." Beau raises both pointer fingers to his impressive pecs and directs my eyes upwards.

"I look where I please." Belligerent in the middle of my grand gesture. This is going well. But I do look up to meet his hazel eyes, which look very green right now. Even more like a Christmas tree.

"I love you. Despite the fact that you may be physically incapable of enjoying nature, and I think you'll melt if you live too far from a Target. I love you," he says.

Well, damn it.

Chapter Thirty-Nine

That's what I forgot to say in my speech. I was so worried about telling him why I left, but I forgot the most important part.

"I love you too. Obviously." The last part is more for me than me because I still can't believe I forgot to tell him.

Beau smiles in relief. I guess he didn't think it was that obvious. He leans forward and slides his arms around me, pulling me from my own chair to stand between his legs.

"Then that's all that matters." Beau goes in for a kiss, but I pull my head back.

"That's not all that matters. Literally all the points I brought up about us living in two different states still stand. And I don't think you've developed a hankering to live in civilization in the last few minutes," I wail.

Beau blows past my use of the word *hankering*. Rude. I was trying to make him feel more at ease.

"You aren't the only one who did some thinking after you left."

Fled. But thanks for making it seem less cowardly than it was.

"I do love home, my family, and the farm. They're

all I've known in a good life, and I didn't want to leave that. Maybe I was afraid to leave that."

This isn't going great right off the bat. My shoulders slump and my stomach drops like I'm on a roller coaster and I just went over the big drop. This is why I hate roller coasters.

"But I've also acknowledged that I want to do a lot that I can't do here. These last few weeks have been frustrating. Because I missed you, but also because I've been getting calls from the team about work and I just want to be there with them. I want to be solving problems with them and working hands-on for the research part. Just attending meetings via Zoom has made me antsy."

I perk up, just like Bubba's ears when he hears the word *food*. But I don't say anything yet. There's still a chance I'm making all this up and he's really warming up to tell me I can pound dirt but I hear he's buying a townhouse on the Upper East Side.

He sighs. "I need to be in New York to get this battery project working. So I'm moving to the evil city whether or not you want to be with me."

"You're moving to New York?" I'm going to need to hear that a minimum of five times before it sets in.

"I'm moving," he confirms. "I was trying to tell you, maybe see if that was news you would be receptive to, but you didn't seem interested in my calls." Accusatory eyes stare me in the face.

I shuffle my feet. "The cell reception is really spotty in India."

"You tweeted daily."

"Hmm." That I did. Taken down by technology. "I was going through some stuff." I grab Beau's face, one hand on either side of his face. "But I love you. And I'm not going to do that again." I hope. "Maybe you can come to some of the therapy sessions with me later? If that's not too much for you."

"I love you too. And I would love to come with you." Beau leans down for a kiss.

When his lips touch mine, all the tension, the worry, the sadness, and the anger I've felt floods out of me, replaced by a larger dose of the same relief I felt when I talked to my parents.

And when his tongue touches mine, I don't just forget all the negative feelings I've had for the past week; I forget everything.

His hands clutch my dress behind me, at the bow, and my hands frantically try to find a way to more skin. I forget any argument I had against not doing the nasty in his parents' house.

But then Bubba reminds me why this isn't a great idea right now. He must have gotten bored or felt like we were having fun without him, because he shoves his giant head between us, searching for attention.

We break away with a laugh and Beau wipes at my cheeks.

"Wait, why am I crying now? I'm happy," I say in frustration.

"You've been crying? Poor Baby Girl." Beau pulls up the bottom of his shirt so I can use it as an impromptu hankie.

"Yeah. I've had a rough few weeks."

"Well, these might be happy tears."

"They come when I'm happy too? What is this nonsense?" Is it like breaking the seal; now that I've cried once I won't be able to stop?

I'm going to need to buy more of those tiny travel tissue packs.

Impatient Bubba reminds us that we haven't petted him in a few minutes now and he's not happy about it. I pet him, face dry for the time being. "Are you already packed, or do you need help? I have a jet right now."

"Wait, you have a jet?"

"On loan from a matrimonially inclined aunt and a grateful art collector."

Beau nods, like that statement is perfectly reasonable. "I might need a little more time to pack. I just told my parents. They need a little more time to adjust." He reaches for me and I cuddle into his hug.

"So, like by New Year's…"

Epilogue

One Year Later

This exhibition is going great. That might be the champagne talking, or it might be because I thought it was going to be a disaster and it's been...better than a disaster.

I'd call it a Christmas miracle, but with all the work that went into it, there was nothing divine about it.

This is our coming-out party. After a year of setting up the department, hiring an assistant and a designer, making connections with furniture and antique dealers, and taking on a few clients while we figured out our policies, we're having a formal introduction party.

Priya blocked off some exhibition space and let me divide it into rooms that the team and I decorated. Each in a different style and for a different purpose, to show what we can do for clients. I incorporated furniture, paintings, and sculptures that we had in storage, pieces that wouldn't fit in any upcoming shows' themes.

And I might have included some of my own paintings too.

After Beau moved to New York, and developed a very New York schedule, I saw him less than I would have thought for someone who lives with me, even with my new responsibilities. In boredom, I broke out the paints he got me for Christmas and started painting more.

I'm really enjoying the balance between my creative work and my creative hobby. They've fulfilled that restlessness I felt working in Priya's department.

The paintings themselves are inspired by me and Beau, combining a little city and a little country with a side of cheekiness, like my first piece after he moved here: *A Herd of Wild (Ford) Mustangs*, which was just a group of convertible Mustangs driving through the open plains, with the sun setting in the background.

Beau chuckled when he saw it.

And then there's my favorite. A piece inspired by the last thing I looked at before my life changed. The Fragonard with the couple kissing in the partly closed doorway, heads leaning toward each other for the kiss, but bodies apart, ready to flee if they're caught.

I updated the painting, recreating a lot of the elements but making the woman dressed to the nines for a fancy night out in the city and the man dressed in boots, jeans, and an open plaid shirt covered in dirt fresh from the farm.

But the one part of the painting that remains is the sense of danger. Like they are going to be discovered at any second, and they shouldn't be together. But they don't care, my country Romeo and my city Juliet; it's worth the risk to them.

I understand the Fragonard painting a lot more now than I did a year ago when I saw it. Because I get it now. I get why the couple would risk getting caught, risk whatever consequence faces them or the sadness that goes with an ended relationship, for the rush of that kiss. I still get afraid occasionally that it'll all be over, but more often, I feel that rush.

And it is worth it. Any potential consequences or pain. It's all worth it to experience the good moments with Beau.

And I remember that every time I walk into our house. Not just because I see Beau, but because this painting isn't for sale like everything else in the exhibition. It's usually hanging in our entryway, where it'll return after the show.

Beau is convinced the couple is us. (Maybe. With some generalizations.) He said that depictions of his abs were greatly exaggerated, but what does he know? He's not the artist in the family. He's perfectly happy doing science and math, figuring out the more efficient battery problem. They've gotten close a few times, but no success yet.

Beau himself has adapted surprisingly well to the city. Maybe it's because every time he gets a trapped look in his eyes, we take a trip to the countryside for a weekend.

But the looks have been coming less frequently as he adapts to his new geography and the amenities now available to him. Like the food here, all different types of cuisines that he can get at all hours. And he has tested out the hours, bringing home entire feasts after a late night at work that fills our home with delicious smells after I've already eaten dinner. I eat again anyway. Got to enjoy the perks of the beautiful, multicultural, late-night city we live in.

The other day, he even managed a subway ride without making eye contact with strangers. I was so proud.

And with planes, it's been easy to go back and forth

so we get to spend time at the orchard with Beau's family as well.

My muse walks toward me, in one of the suits he's been wearing more since he moved to New York. I kind of miss the farm wear. But I don't think I've opened a door in months, so it's still the same Beau.

That's not true; I occasionally open them for him just to watch his brain short-circuit.

"I knew this was going to be a success." Beau gives me a kiss on the head, taking in the crowded room. All the people walking around with food and drink, looking at my work.

I roll my eyes. Not even factoring in my skill or lack thereof, Priya didn't just get me the space and cater my exhibition. She also got all of her best spending clients to come take a look at my interior design and paintings.

I've never been more nervous for a show Loot was putting on. But I shouldn't have worried, because I have the best team in the whole company. I settled into being a boss easier than I thought I would. Maybe because I have a small team, or because I love the work so much, or maybe the therapy is working, but I'm not consumed with fear that I'll let them down.

"Everything looks amazing," Eve says as she and Mom come up to us, Mom giving me the seventh hug she's given me this evening. Another victim of the champagne, I suspect.

"Thank you. And I'm so glad you guys could come." Both sets of parents, and Annabelle's family, came to visit for the season. Harper and Harry are *loving* a New York Christmas, just as much as I do. I might have made the Christmas events extra special so they would want to come back next year. Meaning I bought them lots of presents and sugar everywhere we went.

They're staunch city folk now.

My parents are making an effort too. It's their third trip to New York this year as they've scaled back work in India. They've even been texting when they're home. They really listened.

I snuggle in closer to Beau, surrounded by our families. I'm happy that I took the chance to be vulnerable, with him and with my parents. There was a huge chance I was going to get pain from one or both of those decisions, but if I hadn't, then I wouldn't have been as happy as I am now. .

I kiss Beau's neck, inhaling his cinnamon scent.

Yup, this is definitely worth it.

* * * * *

Acknowledgements

A second book! When I was querying, I wasn't sure I would ever get to publish one book, and now you're holding my second! It's a surreal feeling, and there are so many people who have helped get me here.

Thank you to Mom and Dad, for your love and support. Mom, even though you read the first book when I expressly asked you not to. To Rod and Oliver, for being the best coworkers in this work-from-home job, providing me with all the snacks and watercooler distractions that I miss out on not having an office job. I love you all.

Thank you to my agent, Jana Hanson, for believing in and championing my work, and for the team at Carina for bringing it out into the world. Thank you to Stephanie Doig, Nancy Fischer, Ronan Sadler, Stephanie Tzogas and especially Deborah Nemeth, an amazing editor who knows exactly how to fix a manuscript without changing author voice.

Thank you to all my family and friends. You're amazing, I wouldn't be who I am without you.

Thank you to the authors and readers who have read and shared *Two Houses*, including (but not limited to) Farah, Margot, Ayushi, Julie, KD, Sil, Kim and Falon.

And a giant thank-you to all the readers! Thank you for taking a chance on me and my words.

About the Author

Suleena Bibra has read romance in one form or another since she could pick her own books. She occasionally branches out to other genres, but really, what's the point if there's no kissing? She also loves to laugh, which probably has to do with her dad putting Monty Python on whenever her mom wasn't looking.

Possessing a "madness to gaze at trifles," Suleena studied art history in college and loves to travel every opportunity she gets. A bit indecisive, she has worked as a museum intern, lawyer, workers' compensation adjuster, and private investigator. Author is best, though, so she can continue living out a bunch of other careers without changing out of her pajamas.

Suleena writes rom-coms heavy on banter, shenanigans, and aggressive whimsy. She spends the rest of her time annoying her stubborn, but adorable, bulldog (who also doubles as her particularly lazy writing assistant) with her love.

For more on Suleena and her books, her website is www.suleenabibra.com and she is @SuleenaBibra on Twitter and Instagram.

Mixing love and art might end up being an epic disaster or the beginning of a beautiful collaboration.

Read on for a sneak peek of book one in the Love at Auction series,
Two Houses *by Suleena Bibra.*

Chapter One

Gavin Carlyle is here. Because of course he is.

Tension snaps my back ramrod straight and my fists clench at the sight of him, my body getting ready for a fight.

I've got too much to do today, and I can't deal with my mortal enemy since preschool. It takes a lot of energy to hate the same person for so long, but my natural pettiness really helps.

Character faults aside, I don't need him here now, when I'm trying to devote all my energy to wooing this client at a Four Seasons power lunch. Gavin looks busy (and annoyingly sexy in his suit) at his own table, so hopefully he'll stay away.

Or maybe a very specific, very small sinkhole will open up under his chair and swallow him into the earth, quickly closing before anyone else's day can be disturbed.

I subtly shift my chair and hunch down so I can't see Gavin, and force myself to relax. I turn my attention back to Harrison Richmond. The white man in front of me exudes power and money from his expensive suit to his flashy watch to the shoes on his feet. Shiny, well-made accessories and not a hair out of place to let us all know we couldn't measure up.

"How's your daughter doing?" I ask. We've been at lunch for about forty-five minutes now, and even though I just want to ask him about his art pieces, I've got at least another fifteen minutes of small talk to go. I'm timing it.

But subtly.

So far, I've gushed over his company's new ad campaign and his wife's latest charity ball. Which legitimately was fun. And for a good cause.

"She's doing great. She's doing a study abroad in England right now, and I don't know if she's going to come back home when it's over."

I laugh. "I did four years of college in England, and I threatened the same thing. I did come back though."

Harrison toasts me. "Good news then."

"The hardest part was definitely leaving the art and architecture behind. But I'm lucky that I get to work with some amazing pieces here." At last! A transition to the business we're here for.

Harrison has family money from some robber baron ancestor who was big in railroads, and he took that money and made even more investing in renewable energy. After he set his company up, he turned his attention to increasing his family's art collection, buying and selling some of the most beautiful pieces I've ever seen. Gossip says he's looking to sell a large chunk of his collection, so he can make room for pieces more to his current tastes.

I want to be the auctioneer who sells that collection.

"Loot is a fantastic house, but Kabir hasn't had much

experience outside Indian art and antiquities." He brings up Loot's biggest weakness.

But I know it is too, and I'm ready. "Dad doesn't have that experience," I say, throwing Dad under the bus. He's as cutthroat as I am; he'll understand. "But I studied Art History at Cambridge, and I've been working on more and more diverse sales since I started at Loot six years ago. I hope you consider us if you want to auction any of your pieces. I've been coveting your collection since I was a kid, and I've imagined a hundred different ways I could present your works."

And with a collection on this level, we can show the market that Loot is a serious contender in all types of art, not just Indian art.

My shoulders relax a little as business is finally introduced. It's a delicate balance between not wanting to scare the millionaires by discussing crass commercial concerns and needing to get that sale. But it's where I'm comfortable.

"Since you were a kid? You're making me feel old."

"Never. You get younger every year, Dorian Gray. But I have been around this business for a while."

Harrison smiles. "All right, how would you sell my work? On the off chance I want to sell."

The familiar electricity rushes through my veins, all my preparation focused on this moment.

"In this particular case, I would try to keep as much of the collection as possible together. I want to sell the Richmond experience. You come from an old family, and there are plenty of buyers who want to capture that connection. If possible, we could do the sale at your home in Long Island. And it would be minimum fuss for you; we'd rent a tent for the sale and make sure no one wandered around your estate."

I get out my iPad, bringing up a picture of some past house sales I've done to show him how much grandeur we can put in a tent, pointing out specific pieces he owns that could be the highlights.

"You've done your research on my art." He sounds impressed, and I mentally pat myself on the back. First step complete.

"It's never work to look at your pieces—"

"Priya Gupta," says a voice behind me, causing every muscle in my body to clench in anticipation for a hit. Not a physical one, but we can't be near each other without throwing verbal punches back and forth.

"Gavin Carlyle, what a *pleasant* surprise," I say through clenched teeth, turning to look at him so Harrison can't see the smile that's more of a snarl. I really want to add that it's a surprise that he was able to drag himself out of bed before noon, but I can't do that in front of the client. Because then *I'm* the unprofessional one.

"And, Harrison, good to see you again, so soon after the last time." He extends his hand to shake Harrison's.

Let the games begin. Because if they recently met, Gavin's heard the rumors and he's trying to get Harrison's collection for *his* family's auction house, Carlyle's.

We grew up as children of competing auction houses, and so I've never been entirely comfortable around Gavin. I fell into the pattern of competing with him academically like our parents were competing in the art market. Made more difficult around the eighth grade, when I realized how distractingly, and therefore distressingly, attractive he was.

The grudge pushed me to spend extra time studying so I got better grades than him, made me make that voodoo doll, and, of course, made me check Facebook religiously when we were in college to make sure he didn't win a Nobel Prize or start a company when I was studying out of the country.

Before Harrison can respond, something catches his eye behind me. Whatever it is must be important, because he gets up, throwing his napkin on the table. "If you'll both excuse me for a second, I see someone I have to talk to about a missing contract signature."

Harrison walks across the room, leaving us alone at the table.

"You're trying for Harrison's collection? Your auction house doesn't even do non-Indian art." Gavin glides into the seat across me. Vintage Gavin—feeling entitled to any space he sees.

"Loot might not, but I do. Which you already knew."

Because there's no way Gavin doesn't know what the competition is doing. He's too smart for that. And while it's true Loot has specialized in Indian art since Mom and Dad opened the first US office in New York, after I started working there, I slowly introduced non-Indian art to our sales. Because a bigger market means more profit.

Gavin shrugs. "I may have heard a rumor or two."

I contemplate throwing my roll at his head, but getting banned from the Four Seasons restaurant will stop all the business lunches I do here so I restrain myself.

I clasp my hands together in my lap under the table just in case they get any rogue ideas about that roll. "Everyone must be talking about it to reach you on a yacht in Croatia. Or was it driving along the southern coast of France last week?"

Gavin's a jetsetter auctioneer who takes a little too much pleasure in the jetsetting aspect. He flaunts that part of the job all over social media. Gavin with a tan, blond hair blowing in the breeze on a yacht in the Mediterranean. Gavin filling out a tux better than anyone has a right to at a charity event in Rome. Gavin going hiking in Peru, meeting adorable llamas and looking good with dirt artfully smudged on his stupid, perfect face.

And yes, I do follow his social media, through an anonymous account of course. I need to keep an eye out on the competition. And if that means also keeping an eye on those pecs, it's just a sacrifice I'll have to live with.

"Some of us know how to enjoy this job, and all the perks that come with it."

"Some of us just take joy in *doing* the job."

Gavin recoils in horror, hand to his heart to sell the emotion. "And let the supermodels sip champagne by themselves? I'm not a monster."

"Why don't you go back to those parched, lonely supermodels?" I snarl, immediately changing my face at the last word when I catch Harrison coming back to the table in my peripheral vision.

I turn a professional smile to Harrison, as Gavin scrambles up from his seat. "I hope your business was successful."

"It will be." Harrison smiles, confidence and satisfaction radiating from him.

"Good." I turn to Gavin. "Well, we can't keep you from your lunch." *So go away.* I motion back to his table, and the stunning, chicly dressed woman waiting for him.

Probably one of the supermodels from the yacht.

"Always a pleasure." Gavin extends his hand, and I don't know how to refuse without looking ungracious. I take it in a brief handshake, and immediately let it go like it's covered in bird poo.

I ignore how firm his handshake is, the same way I always do on the few occasions that we've made physical contact over the years. Because it's just not fair that someone this annoying feels this good.

Without my permission, my eyes track his trip back to his table. He saunters away, taking his time moving in the crowd that shifts to accommodate him.

Everything he does is effortless, from that walk, to his adorable I-just-got-out-of-bed tousled blond hair, to his bright blue eyes and lips that are always quirked in a smile. Of course he's happy; he's the heir apparent to his parents' successful auction house. With all obstacles bribed, bulldozed or bartered out of his way by his parents.

In contrast, everything I do takes effort. Every show I want at Loot, I have to work to get, since my dad wants to give them all to Ajay, my younger twin. Every collector I go after I have to convince we're a legitimate auction house, even though we've been in the States for over thirty years, since before I was born.

I'm tired.

But I love watching a show come together, listening to the prices get higher and higher for a piece that I know is going to cause a bidding frenzy. Or walking into one of our exhibits before the auction, seeing the museum-quality way we display the art.

It's worth it.

With Gavin safely back at his table, I turn my attention to Harrison. I wake up my iPad and show him some more of my highlights. I'm proud when I scroll through them. My entire life in artfully staged exhibitions and happy buyers. "And if you want, I can do a mock catalog for the sale we would do for you."

Usually I would have done the catalog before meeting with a potential seller, but I didn't want to be too presumptuous, since Harrison hasn't actually told anyone he wants to sell yet.

He flips through my iPad photos himself, nodding along here and there. The waitress comes with our tea, and I add milk and sugar to distract myself from the anxiety of watching him judge my life's work.

"This is great work, as always," Harrison says.

I smile at him, hoping this is a prelude to him giving us his collection. This sale wouldn't just make the market take us seriously; it would make Dad take me seriously.

Harrison leans in closer, lowering his voice. "And I am selling off a large part of the old collection. Make the catalog and I'll decide who to go with."

I'll take it! "When do you want the catalog by?" My mind is already spinning, going through different ways I can present the collection.

"A week, if that's not too little time? Now that I've decided to sell, I want to move quickly."

"No problem at all." *High-maintenance man, you just took away my sleep for the next week.* "If you wouldn't mind sending a list of the items you're thinking about including in the sale, I can make a theme, exhibition layout and catalog for them."

"I'll email you a list."

"Perfect. I look forward to showing you the finished product."

"I look forward to seeing it. But I still have meetings with other auction houses."

"Of course. I wouldn't have it any other way."

And then it'll be that much sweeter when I beat Gavin Carlyle.

Don't miss Two Houses *by Suleena Bibra,*
available now wherever ebooks are sold.

www.CarinaPress.com